ONCE UPON A GRIFFIN

CARDE JEAN

This is a work of fiction. The characters, incidents and dialogues in this book are of the author's imagination and are not to be construed as real. Any resemblance to actual events or persons, living or dead, is completely coincidental.

Cover Art by Carde Jean

Revised May 2025

I dedicate this book to my husband Ray, my first reader and biggest fan. And to my daughter Crystal, who encouraged me to keep going and made me a better writer.

CHAPTER ONE

Guinevere Griffin stopped in front of the Jinxed Cat, one of the seedier strip clubs in The Bronx. The steady throb of bass vibrated her car. Guin lowered the front passenger window. The rank summertime aroma of the nearby Hudson flooded her interior. Two men, one tall and dark-haired, the other short and red-faced, loitered beneath a flickering streetlight.

"Josh?" Guin called.

"That's me." The tall one stepped into the street. His white shirt had come untucked, and his navy jacket had a rumpled appearance.

His balding companion, staggered into the side of her car. "You our Ryde girl?"

"Yes, sir. Hop in." Unlocking the back doors with one hand, she hit *record* on her dash-cam with the other. The two men settled into the back seat, and Guin turned on the overhead light, illuminating her passengers.

The Rav4 entered the heavy traffic and headed for Highway 87. "You're going to Brooklyn?"

"Yeah." The odor of alcohol permeated the Rav4. Josh leered

through the rearview mirror. "What's a pretty redhead like you doing driving around two good-looking guys on a hot Friday night?"

Here we go. "Just doing my job."

"Can I make an order?" He snatched her pizza-delivery hat from the passenger seat. "I'm in the mood for a pizza. A pizza you." He thrust his head between the front seats and tugged her hair. "C'mon sweetheart, give me your number. I don't bite, unless you want me to."

She yanked her braid free. "You know you're being recorded?"

"Great. We can show our grandkids how we met."

His companion snorted. "Good one, Josh."

"How's about a little nibble?" A heavy dose of beer-breath gusted against her neck. His lips brushed her shoulder.

"That's it." She braked and made a U-turn, then turned left on East 169th Street.

"This ain't Brooklyn," grumbled her future spouse.

Guin parked in front of the well-lit, 44th Precinct police station. "If you don't get out now, I'll lay on this horn and have you forcibly removed."

Josh and his companion took to the sidewalk. Josh leaned into the car. "Don't expect no five-star rating or a tip, bitch."

"No worries."

After their car-rocking door slam, she put it into drive and traveled a few blocks before parking. She scrolled through her Ryde app and cancelled the last trip.

"Drunks, jerks, and more drunks. Why do I put up with this?" She rested her forehead on the steering wheel. "Because rent's almost due, and business is terrible."

The phone buzzed before she could place it in the dash holder. She had a pick-up at Manhattan's Four Seasons.

"Nice. Hopefully good tippers this time, Becky." She patted the car's dash. "Might actually make rent early this month."

Guin stopped in the hotel's loading zone. The doorman opened the passenger side door. Illuminated by the hotel's brightly lit entryway, two men attired in coats and ties approached her car. A third, seeming out-of-place in faded jeans and a green plaid shirt, followed.

"Hi, I'm Guin. I'll be your Ryde provider," she told the sandy-haired man who slid in behind her.

He belted in and loosened his tie. "I'm Derek. I arranged for the ride."

She couldn't quite place his subtle accent.

The other two men squeezed into the backseat. Guin hit the record button and flicked on the dome light before pulling into traffic. "You're going to the Coconut Club?"

"Right. We have a ten o'clock reservation, and we're here to party!" Derek threw his hands in the air.

"Calm down little man," said Plaid Shirt. His accent was similar to Derek's, the timbre of his voice a deep rumble.

A pair of startling dark blue, almond-shaped eyes smiled through the mirror. Guin's heart skipped a beat. She drew in a sharp breath. "Who're your friends, Derek?"

"Boden—totally dressed for the evening is on the right side and in the middle is Jaxzon."

"Pleased to meet you. Sorry, it's a little tight back there."

Dark azure beamed through the mirror. "Not at all." Jaxzon's accent was more pronounced than Derek's, his words articulate and formal.

"There is more than enough room. Your car is quite comfortable."

Guin patted the dash. "She gets me where I gotta go. Where you guys from?"

"South Africa," said Derek. "We're here on business and head back tomorrow."

They'd only traveled half a mile when a warning light flickered on her dashboard a millisecond before a chime sounded.

"What's that?" Boden asked.

"My tire pressure is dropping."

The thump of the back passenger tire informed her that "dropping" might be an understatement. She nursed her limping car to the lighted area of a loading zone then parked beside a closed sewing machine repair shop.

"I'm sorry, guys. I have to change my tire."

Jaxzon leaned between the seats. "Can we help?"

"No, thank you. I don't want you to miss your reservation."

Boden exited and inspected the flat. Guin joined him and couldn't help but notice the way he stuck out from his companions. Aside from his differing attire, he had the chiseled looks of a Greek god.

Guin chuckled. *The god of poor wardrobe choices.*

He ran a hand through his wavy black hair and smirked when their eyes met, small dimples formed under a dark five o'clock shadow.

Jaxzon extracted his tall, slim body from the backseat and removed his coat. His jet-black hair contrasted with his creamy pale skin, reminding Guin of her favorite Kpop artist. "What do you need us to do?"

"How long will this take?" asked Derek.

"Maybe fifteen minutes if I hurry." Guin swung open the cargo door. "Seriously guys, you don't need to stay. The club isn't too far. If you walk, I think you can still make it."

She set the jack and tool bag on the curb then tugged at the spare tire cover.

Derek glanced around the dark street. "How do we get there?"

She stopped wrestling with the cover and pointed. "Go one block, turn left, then down about six blocks and it'll be on your right. You can't miss it, lots of people, tacky neon palm tree. Maybe ten minutes."

"Thanks, Guin." Derek and Boden left in the direction of the club.

Jaxzon removed the cover from the spare.

Guin tossed it into the back. "Thanks. But really, you don't have to help. This is a dirty job."

"I would never leave a lady in distress."

"Thanks." She grinned. "I guess chivalry's not dead after all. Would you hand me the tire iron? It's in the bag."

He held up the jack handle. "This?"

"Um, no. Haven't you ever changed a tire?"

He shook his head.

"Alrighty then." She took the bag. "This is the tire iron, or lug wrench."

Guin fit the tire iron over a lug nut, positioning the handle horizontally. Holding the side of her car, she balanced on the handle, bouncing her weight until it turned.

"What are you doing?" he asked, with a bemused smile.

"Loosening the lugs. This is the easiest way. You don't know much about cars, do you?"

"This is true. I understand the mechanics of the combustion engine, although I am afraid, I do not know much more."

She assembled the handle, positioned the jack under the car, then turned the handle. *How could anyone go through a lifetime of never having to change a tire?* Jaxzon appeared to be around her age, maybe a few years older.

He crouched beside her. "May I?"

"Have at it. You've seriously never had a flat tire?"

"No. Do you do this often?"

"Not really. When you drive as much as I do, you learn fast. Especially in this city." She touched his shoulder. "That's high enough." She squatted beside the tire, unscrewing the lug nuts. "Do you have a light?"

Jaxzon turned on his phone light shining it while she worked. Together they changed the tire and after tightening the last lug nut, Guin wiped her hands on a rag. "Hang on, don't touch your face again." She retrieved a packet of wet naps from her glove box and tore one open.

Their eyes met as she wiped a black smudge from Jaxzon's chin. A single dimple appeared in his cheek. Heat crept into her chest. She turned away, hiding the blush.

"For your hands," she said, handing him the towelette.

"Thank you."

"Thank *you.* It can be a little scary around here, changing a tire this late at night. I'm glad you were with me." She tucked the bag into its cubby over the wheel well.

Someone moved in the shadows between the two brick buildings.

She seized the tire iron and leapt in front of Jaxzon, holding the tool above her head.

"Hold up, no need for that." Hands raised, Boden strolled into the light.

"Jeez." She lowered the tool and clutched her chest. "You scared the hell out of me. I thought you went with Derek." She put the tire iron away, and they hopped into the car. "Why didn't you go with him?"

"I thought you might need more help."

"That doesn't explain why you—hey, is that him?"

Derek walked through the crowded street toward the car. Guin stopped, and he joined Boden in the back.

Jaxzon turned in his seat. "What happened?"

Derek's big brown eyes met Guin's through the mirror. "I was too late. The guy was so rude too, said he waited a whole five minutes then gave our table away."

"I'm so sorry. I feel awful." *Bad enough to have a customer help you change a tire, now this?* "I think can make this right. I have a couple of friends who work at a champagne bar nearby. Best in New York, they tell me. I could probably get you in. What do you think?"

Jaxzon smiled. "That would be wonderful."

A short drive later, Guin stopped under a swirling array of blue and golden lights depicting a galaxy turning in on itself. Beside it, in bright silver letters, the word, *Kosmix* bathed the crowded sidewalk below in a vibrant purple glow.

Guin texted her friend DeShawn, the club's doorman, hoping

he'd hear his phone over the booming music. A moment later her phone buzzed with his response, "send them in."

"You're in! Tell the guy at the door Guin sent you. His name's DeShawn."

Boden and Derek, headed for the entrance.

Jaxzon hesitated. "How can I thank you, Guin?"

"No need, it wasn't a problem."

He unfolded a hundred-dollar bill. "This is for you."

"No." She waved his hand away. "Thank you, but that's too much.

Besides, I'm paid through the app."

"Please take it."

"I appreciate it, but I couldn't. If you want to tip someone, give it to DeShawn. He could use it; he's gonna be a father soon."

Jaxzon pocketed the bill. "Maybe you could join us for a drink?"

She patted the steering wheel. "Gotta work."

He frowned and shut the door, then opened it and stuck his head inside. "Just one drink? Non-alcoholic, my treat?"

Their gazes locked. Guin's breath caught. A sudden fire burned through her. There was something in those deep blue eyes that drew her as if nothing else mattered. In that brief second, it was as if their souls collided. Then like perfume in a breeze, the moment was gone. She exhaled, shaken by the depth of her reaction.

"Thirty minutes? I want to thank you properly for calling in a favor

for us."

"What the heck. I'm dressed for it, right?" She indicated the plain jeans, green tank-top, and brown leather sandals. Not exactly club attire.

His gaze held hers. "I had not noticed."

Heat crept into her face. She smiled, cursing her light complexion. "I need to park my car."

"Let me take care of it." He beckoned to the valet before Guin could object.

The attendant opened her door. She snagged her handbag before joining Jaxzon on the sidewalk. They caught up to the other two men, and as the group passed the line of people, a wave of protests went up. DeShawn, an imposing figure, glared at the crowd. The complaining stopped, and he ushered Guin and company through the door.

Once inside, DeShawn embraced Guin, lifting her in a back-popping hug, her feet dangling a foot off the floor.

"Oof. Hi, DeShawn."

DeShawn stood over six and a half feet tall and was close to three hundred pounds of pure muscle. "Hey, girl. Haven't seen you since Nadine's wedding, in what, December?" He set her down. "How's my favorite queen?"

"Ha ha, cut the queen crap, DeShawn." Guin poked him in the chest. "Sorry I've been such a ghost, but school and work keep me busy. I want you to meet my newest friends, Derek, Boden, and Jaxzon."

"Any friend of Guin's, as they say." DeShawn shook each man's hand and winked at her. "Raney's working. Go say hi. I bet you ain't seen much of her lately, or I would've heard about it."

"Thanks, you're the best." She tugged his shirt collar and kissed his cheek.

He cupped his face in feigned shock. "I'll never wash this cheek again." His rumbling laugh faded as he lumbered back outside.

"Come on, I'll introduce you to Raney. She's crazy, so be warned."

She led the three men to an extravagant chrome bar, bedazzled with mirrors and spinning lights that flickered and flashed to the pounding bass pulsing from overhead speakers.

The petite, pink-haired bartender put on a show for the patrons, mixing cocktails and flipping bottles in time to the music. When she spotted Guin, she fell back, clutching her chest in exaggerated shock. She ducked under the bar and flew into Guin's arms, gave her a hug and curtsied, shouting over the racket, "Oh, Queen Guinevere, how may I serve thee?"

"Cut the queen crap, Raney," Guin yelled back. "I'm here on business. These guys are from out of town."

"You're in luck. We had a late cancellation; you're getting a private booth." She winked at the men. "Your first bottle's on me."

Jaxzon grinned. "That is very generous."

"Thanks, Raney. Just pop for me, please."

Raney went back under the bar with a promise to come by on her break.

A server ushered them up a flight of stairs. They passed several small tables and came to a sizable private space overlooking the dance floor. Derek excused himself and made a beeline for a group of women in another booth. Boden mumbled something about going to find a real drink, leaving Jaxzon with Guin. They took seats in the wide, cushioned chairs on either side of a low table.

Jaxzon gave Guin a crooked smile, a dimple appearing in his left cheek. "You have good friends, Guin. Or is it 'Your Majesty?'"

"Please, just Guin."

"So, what *is* the story there?"

"It all started as a joke about my name. You know, Queen Guinevere and King Arthur? Then I was elected prom queen in high school. They won't let me forget it."

He squinted. "What is prom?"

"It's a formal dance for seniors at the end of the school year. They elect a king and queen. I didn't realize they nominated me until the night of the dance. Raney's doing, as a prank, and by some strange twist, I won. Raney nearly split her skirt laughing. Now she, DeShawn, and a few other jesters refer to me as 'Queen.' An inside joke that's been rolling along for four long years."

"Your friends sound...unique."

Guin returned his smile. "You can say that again."

The server set three flutes, a glass of cola, and an ice bucket holding a bottle of champagne on the table.

Jaxzon filled his glass. Graceful and poised, his movements were as fluid as the champagne he poured. So different from any man she'd seen outside a fashion magazine. High cheekbones, immaculate

haircut, clean-shaven face, and those eyes; she couldn't stop staring. "What business brings you to New York?"

"It is boring, nothing worth mentioning." He took a sip from his glass, peering at her over the rim.

Raney bounced into the booth and plopped herself into an empty chair. "What're we chatting about? Never mind. How did you two meet? Is this your first date? Where are the others?"

Guin widened her eyes at her friend. "Jeez Raney, slow down."

"I only have fifteen minutes. I need as much info as I can get. I never see you out, and I'm excited you're with someone." She extended her hand to Jaxzon. "What was your name again?"

"Jaxzon." He shook her hand, an amused smile on his face. "Guin and I met tonight. You went to school together?"

"Yeah, and she's supposed to be my best friend. How the heck did you make her come out with you? She never dates anyone."

Guin palmed her forehead as her cheeks flamed. "We're not on a date," she said through clenched teeth. She peered under her fingers at Jaxzon and mouthed, "Sorry."

His smile broadened.

"Well, Jaxzon, if you ever need a fun date, it would be Miss Guinevere Griffin. She's smart, funny, and did she tell you that she used to take care of the sweetest old man—my grandfather—and volunteers at the homeless shelter? Heart of gold. Body of a goddess. She's the total package."

"Oh, come *on*." Guin dragged Raney from her seat. "Please excuse us, Jaxzon."

Raney linked her arm through hers and shouted over the music, "What's with Mr. Blue Eyes?"

"He's a client, and you're embarrassing me." As if this were new for Raney.

"Since when do you go clubbing with clients? Since when do you go clubbing at all? You're such a hermit."

They wove their way through the crowd and headed downstairs. "I'm hardly a hermit. They were in a tight spot, and I wanted to help."

"Ah, another charity case for Saint Guin."

"Jeez, Raney. First queen, now saint? I like helping people. They seemed like decent guys so, why not?" She shrugged.

"Not to mention, they're all hunks. C'mon, admit it—you got the hots for Blue Eyes, cuz he's sure got it bad for you."

"Why would you even think that? You've known him for two minutes."

Raney hip-checked Guin. "Because he's been eyeballing you with those gorgeous peepers since you got here."

"Why is every conversation with you about my love life, or lack thereof?"

Raney tugged Guin's arm and shouted in her ear. "Just looking out for you, Queen Guinevere. Otherwise, how you gonna to find your King Arthur?"

"That's getting old, Raney. Besides, these guys are going back home in the morning, so there's no use pursuing anything."

She steered Guin into line at the lady's room and smirked. "You still got tonight."

"Not my style, and you know it." Raney entered a stall while Guin leaned against the vanity. "I'm fine on my own. I just can't. Besides, pretty eyes aren't everything."

"They don't hurt. You should come by more often. I could fix you up."

"Raney..." Guin rolled her eyes.

"Dammit, Guin. Just cuz some guys are jerks, doesn't mean you have to give up on all of them."

"I'm not giving up. I simply haven't found anyone I trust."

"You have to actually meet people before you can trust them." Raney exited the stall and washed up.

Guin sighed. "Come on, not tonight."

Raney linked her arm through Guin's, and they made their way toward the bar. "I'm sorry but seeing you with someone gave me hope that you'd finally moved on. Before that stuff happened with your family, you had dreams, you had goals. You were going to travel the world, then you were going to save it. What happened to the old Guin?"

"I'm still here. I've just had a few setbacks." She shrugged. "Besides, I had lunch with one of the volunteers at the shelter."

"Oh?" Raney paused to face Guin. "An actual date?"

"Well... there were two other volunteers with us. But he asked me, and I went, and I mostly talked with him."

Raney tilted her head. "So? How was it?"

"He was nice, but not my type."

"What's your type again?"

She gave Raney the side-eye. "Maybe blue-eyed strangers from Africa."

"I knew it!" Raney bobbed her head and waved her arms in the air.

"But I'm not into one-night stands."

"Then don't have one. Enjoy yourself. You need to ease back into the dating scene, one nice guy at a time."

They arrived at the bar, and the two women hugged. "I love you, Your Majesty, and I'm glad to see you having a good time. You deserve the best, so if this guy turns out to be a creep, you let me know, and I'll have DeShawn toss him back to wherever he came from."

"Ha ha. Will do. Love you."

Raney went behind the bar, and Guin made her way through the throng of people.

CHAPTER TWO

A busty brunette in a slinky black mini dress sat in Guin's chair, drinking champagne.

"Guin." Jaxzon stood when she approached. "This is Hillary. Hillary, this is Guin, my date."

Guin blinked. *Date?*

The woman's gaze swept Guin's everyday clothes, unmade-up face, and loosely braided hair. Hillary's eyes narrowed.

An unexpected stab of jealousy hit Guin as she extended her hand. "Hillary."

"Aren't you the girl who drove me last week? You're the Ryde girl, right?" Hillary ignored the hand and faced Jaxzon. "*This* is your date?"

"I remember you." She didn't. "Where did I take you?"

"It was a pleasure to meet you, Jaxzon." Hillary tucked a card into Jaxzon's breast pocket. "You have my number. Call anytime."

Once Hillary was out of earshot, his breath whistled between his teeth. "Thank you. You saved me again."

The earlier flare of resentment toward Hillary left Guin bewildered. "I-I should be going."

"Must you?"

"I'm keeping you from your friends and your last night in the big city."

"Not at all. I am enjoying your company. They understand I do not enjoy this type of entertainment."

"Why'd you come?"

"Derek planned this excursion. I did not want to disappoint him. Boden was against the trip." He gestured to where Boden sat at the bar, a drink at his elbow, and a scowl on his face. "Derek can be quite persuasive when he sets his mind on something. I would be grateful if you stayed. I could pay you for your time."

She raised an eyebrow. "Excuse me?"

Color flared in his cheeks. "I-I did not mean it that way, I mean... I meant, I am keeping you from your work, and I would pay if you stayed." He bowed his head. "That did not come out as I intended."

She grinned. "I knew what you meant. I can stay a bit longer, and you don't have to pay me. I'm enjoying your company too."

He smiled. His eyes flashed.

Her heart stopped for a full beat. Tonight, was a big night for firsts. She never used her friends for favors, never blushed at a mere glance, and never wanted to punch another woman over a man. Mostly though, she'd never felt this strongly about someone she'd just met.

Hell, you've never felt like this about anyone.

She sipped her drink. They locked gazes over the rim of her glass, causing the heat to return to her cheeks. "Do you have any hobbies? Play any sports?"

A whimsical smile played on his lips. He set his glass on the table and leaned forward. "Back home I like races."

"Ooh, what kind of races? Horses, cars, cats?" The sparkle of his eyes mesmerized her.

Jaxzon chuckled. "Cars, although I am sure a cat race would be quite stimulating. I always wanted to race." He gazed at the dance floor. "Silly, right?"

"Not at all. I wanted to be a doctor. Everyone has dreams. What do you like about racing?"

His brow furrowed. His full lips drew into a line.

Are they as soft as they appear? What the heck, Guin?

"I guess it would be the danger. To go as fast as I can and feel the rush of not knowing if I might crash and die."

"Wow. Aren't we a little morbid?"

His enthusiasm came off in waves. "But the surge of adrenaline. It must be so exhilarating."

"Have you ever driven a race car?"

"No. I am forbidden." He sat back, the excitement draining from his face.

"Forbidden? Did you lose your license or something?"

"No. I-I mean... Maybe forbidden is not the right word. What I mean is I am not able to." He averted his gaze. "Bad eyesight."

Derek danced with a leggy blonde in a pink tube dress. Boden still grumped at the bar. Jaxzon took another sip of champagne. When his gaze met hers, sadness registered in his eyes before he looked away.

"I have an idea; do you want to get out of here?"

He tilted his head. "What do you mean?"

"I mean, do you want to leave. With me?"

"Where would we go?"

"You'll see. Should we tell your friends?"

"Only if you want them to come too."

"No."

Guin pulled Jaxzon from his seat. They took the stairs and crossed the crowded dance floor, dodging moving bodies, and avoiding being seen by Derek and Boden.

Waiting for her car, she texted her friend Mabel from the shelter, whose son worked at Luna Park.

Jaxzon peered over her shoulder. "Who are you texting?"

"A friend." Guin grinned, excited with her plan. "I think you're gonna like this."

“You are not going to tell me where we are going?”

“Nope, it’s a surprise.”

The valet brought her car and held her door for her.

“Okay.” Jaxzon tipped the valet and sat in the passenger seat. “How long will this take?”

She pulled into traffic. “Not very, depends on traffic.”

“Is there time to become better acquainted with my kidnapper?”

“Oh? Is that what I’m doing?” she asked, feigning shock.

He laughed, a low chuckle that made her smile.

Bright streetlights slanted across the Rav4 as it wove through traffic to the edge of the city.

He settled back in his seat. “So, between driving people around the city, taking care of sweet grandfathers, helping the homeless, and kidnapping hapless visitors, what do you do with the rest of your time?”

“That’s about it, my life summed up in one sentence. Except on slow Ryde nights, I drive delivery for a pizza place. I also deliver food to shut-ins twice a week, and I take a couple courses at the community college. I want to take more, but not a lot of time or money last semester.”

“When do you sleep?”

“What’s sleep?”

Jaxzon grinned. “What are you studying?”

“Nothing specific. I’m not really sure what I want to do yet, though I’m leaning toward social work. I like helping people. I want to make a difference, to be a part of something bigger than myself. So far, I’ve spent four years taking required courses and doing a lot of flip-flopping.”

“You are not going to be a doctor?”

“No. I gave up that dream a long time ago. Medical school is way too expensive. Shoot, I barely make the rent now. Besides, I’m not sure I’d do well with all the blood. What do you do, besides boring business in New York and watching races? Any hobbies?”

“No.” He peered through the window. “Do you live downtown?”

Guin laughed. "Do I look like I can afford to live in the city?"

"I like your laugh."

"I like yours too." From the corner of her eye, she caught his smile. "I live in The Bronx, not too far from the city." The lights of Brooklyn shined ahead. "This is the Brooklyn Bridge. Have you seen a lot of New

York?"

"Not much. Business brings me here, though I am unable to spend much time on sight-seeing or traveling." His phone buzzed. Jaxzon typed a text then pocketed it. "Sorry. That was Boden, wondering where we went."

Leaving the bridge, she steered on to the expressway. "Tell him I've kidnapped you, and he can await my call with ransom demands."

He chuckled. "That may not be the best idea. Boden tends to take things too seriously." His phone vibrated.

"Aren't you gonna get that?"

"No. He understands."

A cluster of bright lights appeared ahead. Jaxzon leaned forward, peering through the windshield. "Where are we?"

"I told you, it's a surprise." Guin parked and jumped out. "You'd better lose the tie and jacket."

Jaxzon removed his coat and tie, throwing them across the front seat before following Guin. A lighted sign announcing, *Coney Island Raceway,* shone above them.

He gaped at the sign. Guin took his hand and led him through the entrance.

A short, mustached man in a yellow beret exited a narrow brick building beside the racetrack. "Guin!"

"Tony! Thank you for staying open for us."

"Anything for Mama's favorite. Besides, the track's been closed for two nights due to maintenance. We open again tomorrow."

"This is my friend, Jaxzon. Jaxzon, this is Tony. I work with his mom at the shelter."

Tony tipped his hat and shook Jaxzon's hand. "It's nice to meet a friend of Guin's."

"Likewise."

"You have twenty minutes. I set up two karts at the starting line. Leave them when you're done. Enjoy." Tony waved and went into the building.

Guin led Jaxzon to the racetrack where two go-karts idled.

"We get to drive these?"

"Yep. Twenty minutes. You up for a race?" She climbed into a kart and strapped on the seatbelt.

A wide grin split his face. "I cannot believe this." He jumped in the other kart and belted himself in.

She beamed. "Ready?"

His smile widened.

"Set?"

"Go!" they called in unison.

She mashed her foot on the pedal. Their karts shot through the starting line, triggering the timer.

He turned too sharp on the first curve. She giggled as she flew by. Slowing, she waited for him, then stomped on it when he passed. He took the next turn too wide.

Her braid unraveled and auburn hair streamed behind her as she barreled past. "Come on, Speed Racer," she taunted over her shoulder. "Keep up!"

Jaxzon straightened his kart then chased after her. They raced for two laps with Guin in the lead, until she misjudged a curve and careened into the track's edge. The kart bounced off the safety tires and came to a jolting stop facing sideways. Steering the kart until it faced forward, she hit the accelerator, then let it off, causing the kart to jerk then come to an abrupt stop.

He made a U-turn.

She bowed her head, allowing her hair to fall across her face, she peeked from beneath the auburn curtain as he neared. With a snort of laughter, she hit the gas and took off, leaving him behind, facing the wrong direction.

"Hey!"

She held the lead for the rest of the race until she lost control on a turn. This time he didn't fall for her tricks, and as their time ran out, he finished first, both fists pumping the air. She finished a close second, parking her kart alongside his.

He jumped from his kart and helped Guin from hers, drawing her into a hug. "That was the most fun I have had in… I cannot remember the last time."

The brief embrace took her by surprise. Hiding her burning face behind a veil of hair, she hurried to her car. "Sorry it wasn't fast enough to actually risk your life."

Jaxzon followed her through the gate. "It was amazing. I have never done anything like it. Thank you."

"It was nothing. I'm just glad you had fun."

Jaxzon took her by the elbow and spun her to face him. "Truly Guin, you made this night special." He gripped her shoulders and bent to meet her eyes. "Why did you do this for me?"

"I-I wanted to make you happy." She became lost in the depths of his gaze. "Besides, I wanted a little fun too."

He tucked a stray strand of hair behind her right ear. His fingers grazed her cheek. His gaze softened, dropping to her lips. She tilted her chin and leaned forward. His eyes widened. He released her and headed around the car.

Flustered and confused, she dug into her handbag, found her keys, and hit the remote button. How could she have misread the moment so terribly?

An uncomfortable silence filled the car for several miles until he took a deep breath and faced her. "I need to tell you something."

"What?"

"About me. About my situation." His phone buzzed. He ignored it.

"I want you to understand why I cannot, why we cannot—I do not wish to deceive you. I want to tell you the truth."

Stopping for a red light she faced him. "Is it that bad? Are you a criminal?" She smiled, attempting to make light of her earlier embarrassment. "Are you in the Japanese mob? Yakuza? Some crime family from Africa? Wait, don't tell me, I probably don't want to know."

Jaxzon chuckled. "No, I am not a criminal. I...I must marry in a few months."

CHAPTER THREE

Despite the sensation of having been punched in the gut, Guin concentrated on driving. "You're getting married? You're engaged?"

Jaxzon ran his hand over the door frame and stared through his window. "Not yet. Can we go somewhere and talk? I want you to fully understand."

Confused yet curious, she parked by the Shore Road Promenade. "Let's walk."

The city shimmered, mirrored in the waves rippling against the far shore. "I'm listening," she prompted, as they strolled toward the lights of the Verrazano Bridge.

"I am a crown prince, and my father has ordered me to marry."

"What?" She halted and searched his face for a trace of humor. "You're pulling my leg, right?"

His brow creased. "I am not sure what you mean?"

"Never mind." She continued on the path snaking along the shore. "Go on."

"I cannot tell you everything, you would never believe me if I did." He ran his fingers through his short hair, standing it on end. "I am uncertain on how to proceed. My life is complicated."

The full moon hung low in the sky; its reflection wavered in the dark waters. Guin took a deep breath then regretted it. "Woo! Welcome to the Narrows." She wrinkled her nose. "Start at the beginning. That usually works."

"My father has announced his abdication. Our laws dictate a king or queen must be married or engaged prior to ascending the throne. My father decreed that a suitable wife be chosen for me in three months' time."

"Chosen for you?" She frowned. "Like an arranged marriage?"

"Not exactly. Members of a special Council represent each district in our kingdom. This Council, members of our nobility, and our king choose the future queen."

"Wow." She filled her lungs with the briny, diesel-filled air. "Sounds like something from an Anne Hathaway movie."

He stopped walking. "Guin, everything I tell you is true. My father has commanded that each high house of our realm choose a suitor to represent them. Through a series of social events, they are presented to our king, the Council, the nobility, and the citizens of our realm. In the end, the woman whom they deem most suitable will be chosen as the next queen. It has been this way for centuries."

"You know this sounds crazy, right? I mean, that's some next level..." She waved her hand, at a loss for words. "You're really willing to marry someone who's been picked for you? Like in some twisted reality show?"

"This is our law, and I am bound by it. Please believe me. I wish for you to understand why it would be wrong for me to..." A pained expression crossed his features. His eyes searched hers.

"I believe you, Jaxzon." Something about him tugged at her. She wanted to comfort him, to connect with him. But still stinging from his earlier rejection, she blinked and lowered her gaze. "You have to marry someone you might not be attracted to?"

"Correct. My parents barely knew each other when they married, though over time, they did grow to love one another."

"You have no say at all?"

"I have a vote, though I have no power over the final choice. Unless more than one prospect is chosen. If that were the case, I would be given a choice of the women recommended."

A cooling breeze carried with it a salty tang. Guin's hair fluttered around her face. "How does it work? What are the events, and how does one win? Arm wrestling? Boxing matches?" She brushed a strand of hair from her face and slid it behind her ear.

"Events are hosted by the various territories. We attend formal balls and charity events during which the women are presented to the Council for review. It is called *Vekdromic* in my language." His lips curled into a smile. "But no wrestling matches or boxing. There are no tasks given, no challenges. The judging is informal. The prospects are eventually narrowed to a select few. From what I understand, many are only presented as suitors due to my father's decree. Most will drop out after the first night and others will be advised to step down. I was obviously not around for the last one, so I am unfamiliar with the mechanics. The goal is to find a woman who will be beneficial for the realm."

She headed for a bench facing the water. "The whole idea sounds archaic and more than a little sexist."

He hurried after her. "It works both ways. A princess's spouse would be chosen the same way. It is what is best for my kingdom, and I must abide by their choice. I have known this was a possibility for many years. I had an older sister, Jalain. I was always to be a prince, second in line until she produced an heir. She and my mother died when I was sixteen, making me the crown prince."

The pain of losing her own parents surfaced, causing a deep ache for his loss. "I'm so sorry. That must have been awful for you."

"Thank you." He stared at his hands, the creases on his brow deepening. "Even after ten years, it is still hard to talk about. The tragedy was terrible for everyone, my father, our kingdom. My mother and sister were much loved. I miss them both every day."

Waves from a passing ferry lapped against the sea wall. Guin took Jaxzon's hand, giving his fingers a gentle squeeze.

He sighed. "I believed I had more time. If I had been engaged or married prior to my father making his announcement, I might have married for love."

"Your father won't change his mind?"

"No. I am afraid that is impossible. My fate was sealed when he made his decree."

"I wish there was something I could say or do to help you in some way."

"Thank you. It is enough for you to have listened and understand the truth."

She smiled what she hoped to be a reassuring smile. "I hope you can come to love whomever they choose for you. Who knows—it happened for your parents, right?"

"Anything is possible. There are many suitable noblewomen in the realm, and I have yet to meet them all."

How can he bear to live like this? With so little control over his life?

His phone had buzzed intermittently throughout their conversation. He read the message then pocketed the phone. "Boden. He is worried that something has happened to me."

She grinned. "Like a kidnapping?"

The sparkle returned to his eyes. "Yes, I suppose that may be a theory he would consider. He did not want to make this trip. Derek insisted we have one last holiday before the *Vekdromic* begins."

"Then let's get you back to your friends." She held out her hand. He took it, and they headed to the car.

After leaving him at the club, she couldn't shake her curiosity about him, his predicament, and how her heart leapt at his touch. She'd always blushed easily, but the burning heat when their eyes met was something new. Why did he affect her this way?

Three hours and several customers later, her phone chimed. The address for Kosmix and Derek's name appeared. She flew across town. The three men climbed in, taking their previous seats.

Guin peered in the mirror. Jaxzon smiled. Boden hummed tunelessly under his breath. A gentle snore came from Derek while the familiar scent of alcohol wafted through the vehicle.

She parked in front of the Four Seasons then hopped out, hurrying around to offer her assistance.

A tipsy Boden exited the car grinning. "You are a wonderful person."

"Thanks, Drunky McDrunkerson."

Boden clutched her arm and stumbled, laughing as she steadied him. "Queen Griffin."

"Yeah, that never gets old. Can you walk?"

"Yeah." He leaned against the car.

She helped Jaxzon from the car. He smiled and kissed her hand. "Thank you, my lady."

She ducked into the car. Derek slept. "Looks like we need a little help here."

Boden leaned in and punched Derek's arm. "Wake up."

He mumbled, "*Dien sai tumo*?"

Boden tugged his arm. "No dummy, we're still in New York. Get out."

Derek climbed unsteadily to his feet, a smile on his face, his brown eyes sparkling. He took Guin's hand. "*Din quo van u*."

She smiled. "Back atcha."

Boden and Derek meandered to the hotel's entrance.

Derek glanced back and waved. "Thanks, Guin. We had a great time."

Guin saluted. "I didn't take your friends for the falling-down-drunk types."

"Not a regular occurrence to be sure." Jaxzon took a bundle of folded bills from his pocket. "This is for you."

"No." She waved the bills away. "Tonight was my pleasure, and I'm paid through the app. You don't owe me anything."

"It is only fair. I kept you from your work earlier. I want you to take this." He took her hand, tucking the bundle against her palm, then folded her fingers around it. "You do not know how much your kindness meant tonight." He raised her hand to his lips and kissed the back. "My lady."

The warmth of his lips caused a shiver to run through her arm. "Thank you, Jaxzon. I-I hope you find happiness. I truly do." Giving his hand a tug, she drew him close and kissed his cheek, then hurried around the car, jumped in, and drove away.

A deep sadness that could only be described as heartbreak suffused her soul as Jaxzon's silhouette receded in her mirror.

CHAPTER FOUR

Guin left her last customer in North Jersey at six in the morning. The three-hour round-trip and bad tip left her in a funky mood. By the time she closed her apartment door, all she wanted was a good day's sleep.

Her roommate's alarm went off as Guin climbed into bed. Stacy hit the snooze then buried her face in her pillow, mumbling, "You smell like the Hudson."

Guin sniffed her hair. The faint odor of diesel fuel and garbage filled her nostrils. "Yeah, that's bad."

The shower's warm water rinsed the stench from her hair as her mind wandered. Jaxzon's blue eyes flashing in the dim light. Her heart skipping when he said, "My lady." Her pulse racing when his thumb caressed her fingers, his lips touching her hand.

She wiped the mirror and wrapped a towel around her hair. Rifling through her roommate's bottles, tubes, and makeup items cluttering the counter, she found her toothpaste.

What was it about him? I wish...

Her reflection caught her eye. "What do you wish, Guinevere? Stop already, he's gone."

She brushed her teeth then went to bed, where nervous energy and visions of azure eyes kept sleep at bay. After an hour of tossing and turning, she abandoned her bed and dressed for a run, hoping a few laps around the park would tire her overactive mind.

Heat waves danced across the sidewalk and the odor of hot asphalt burned her nostrils. She tugged down her Yankees ball-cap to block the sun's glare and jogged toward the neighborhood park. Keith Urban's *Kiss a Girl* played in her ears, sending Guin back to the moment she believed Jaxzon was going to kiss her, and at how foolish she'd felt when he'd turned away.

Stop it. He's on his way home. She tapped her earbud, continuing along the sidewalk with the intro to *Kryptonite* blasting in her ears.

The sight of Derek, halfway down the block, brought Guin to an abrupt halt. He wore the same brown suit and beige shirt from the night before, though he'd lost the tie and carried the jacket over his forearm. She frowned as he glanced at his phone then at the nearby brownstone.

Once the initial shock wore off, she continued to jog, pocketing her earbuds.

He grinned and waved. "I found you."

She jogged to a stop in front of him. "You've found me, but how?"

Slipping the phone into his pocket, he lowered his voice. "I looked you up on the internet, you're listed in the white pages. I have a proposition for you."

Guin took a step back then squinted. "Excuse me?"

He held his hands up, palms out. "I mean, I came back for you—you're perfect. Jaxzon liked you, so I came back—"

Raising a hand, she halted him mid-babble. "You're not making any sense."

Boys on bicycles careened down the sidewalk, forcing the two to jump apart when the group passed between them. The boys hooted in delight when she hollered, "Hey, I'm walking here!"

Derek squinted after the boys and wiped a trickle of sweat from his temple. "Can we go inside somewhere and talk?"

"Sure." She led him to a small coffee shop on the next block.

The neighborhood gossip, Georgina, sat inside, eating her breakfast. The hostess sat Guin and Derek one booth over. Georgina was infamous for her snooping and overactive imagination, and when their eyes met, Guin gave her a brief smile before scooting over, using Derek's body for a wall.

She lowered her voice. "What's up?"

"Do you believe in love at first sight?"

"Who'd you fall in love with, Derek?"

"Not me. Answer the question. Do you?"

Heat flooded her face as Jaxzon's smile popped into her head. "I guess it could happen."

Derek grinned.

"Who are we talking about?"

A gray-haired server with the name "Chloe" embroidered on her breast pocket set two waters in front of them then handed each a menu. "Anything to drink?"

Guin placed the menu on the edge of the table. "Good morning, Chloe. A small tomato juice, please?"

He gave Chloe the menus. "Water is fine."

The server left, mumbling about big spenders.

He leaned forward. "Jaxzon talked about you all night." His brown eyes widened. "Did you actually take him racing?"

"That doesn't mean he's in love."

Georgina took a bite of her toast, appearing oblivious to their conversation.

"Who's to say? You left quite an impression on him. It got me thinking and as soon as we got home, I came back to talk to you. Jaxzon said he told you about his, uh, situation?"

"Yeah, he's supposed to marry soon."

"Yes." Derek sat straight and lifted his chin. "I come from a noble house. The king ordered all noble houses to sponsor a suitor for the prince."

Waving her hand, Guin put a finger to her lips.

He cocked his head. "Are you okay?"

"I'm fine. But keep your voice down, please?"

"What I mean is, my sister should represent our house. She considers herself too old, so she entrusted me with finding a suitable candidate. But I messed up."

"What exactly are you saying?"

"Sponsoring a suitor is a great honor. It's an even greater honor if our suitor is chosen. So, with you, and with Jaxzon maybe...?" He cleared his throat and declared, "I want you to represent my house."

Georgina glanced up, one eyebrow raised.

Guin placed an elbow on the table and a hand against her forehead, shielding her eyes and hiding her flaming face. "Me? Seriously? I'm not quite the princess type."

"I'm serious." He peered under her palm. "I believe Jaxzon deserves someone in the running who he genuinely likes."

"Let me get this straight." She ticked off her fingers. "You want me to drop everything here. Go with a complete stranger. To a country I've never been to before. Where I don't understand the language. To marry a man, I barely know?" She waggled five fingers at him. "Is this what you're saying?"

He bit his lip. "When you put it that way, it does sound a little unusual."

"Unusual? Derek, that's an understatement."

"You wouldn't need to be married right away."

Georgina stopped eating. Guin knew she'd gone into full eavesdrop mode. "Please Derek, keep your voice down." All she needed was for Georgina to run off and tell the whole neighborhood about this craziness.

"Guin, you'll have the whole summer to become better acquainted."

"Let's say I buy into this. Why would you choose me? I'm a nobody. How would I make a suitable choice for your house?"

"I-I don't have any other options. I kind of put it off until it's too late. We're obligated to present someone to the court in three days." He gave her a strained, toothy grin. "You're sort of my last hope."

She sat back and crossed her arms. "Wow. Derek. Stop the sweet talk. You're embarrassing me."

His face fell. Color flooded his cheeks. "I didn't mean it like that."

"But Jaxzon told me he can't marry whoever he wants. How am I supposed to get the support of the Council or whatever? Why are we discussing this? Maybe I don't want to go off to Africa to try and win the hand of a prince."

Georgina's head snapped up. Guin pressed her fingertips against her temples. *Crap!*

Derek sighed and stared out the window.

A man's voice echoed through her head, "*Come on, sweetheart*" and "*Don't expect no five-star rating or a tip, bitch.*" Another voice, suspiciously like Raney's, asked her, "*Whatcha gotta lose?*" Guin liked Jaxzon. *Face it, you more than liked him, and it's not like you're living the good life at the moment.*

Raney's voice rankled: "*You never have fun... You never do anything for yourself... You're such a hermit.*"

Guin's own mental voice joined in: *School's out and you've got enough to cover your bills for the summer.* "If I do this, what happens if I'm not chosen?"

"I'll bring you back, I promise. Everything will be as before. I can make up for any lost revenue. Please, there's something special about you. I believe in you and Jaxzon. He's one of my closest friends. I want him to be happy."

"It's only for the summer, and if I want to come home sooner, I can. Right? I can't believe I'm even thinking of doing this."

Derek's brown puppy-eyes never left her face. "I'll bring you home whenever you ask."

She pictured Jaxzon again, his lips brushing her skin. The way his smile caused a skip in her heart. *And he's going to be a king?* She laughed.

"What?"

"If I do this, and I'm chosen, I'll actually *be* Queen Guinevere." The irony made her dizzy.

He smiled. "Well?"

"Oh man. I'll do it. Wait till Raney hears this."

He jumped in his seat. "Yes!"

People stared. The man behind Guin scowled. Georgina headed for the exit.

Guin shushed him. "Come on, let's go back to my place."

Chloe appeared with a large glass of tomato juice. Derek grinned and dropped a ten-dollar bill onto the table. "Stellar service, lightning fast." He gave Chloe a peace sign before linking his arm through Guin's.

~

Back at her apartment, Guin changed into jeans, her Yankees jersey, and tennis shoes. "What kind of clothes should I bring?" she called, searching her closet.

Derek answered from her living room. "Whatever you like. We'll buy everything you'll need when we arrive. Fashions are slightly different there."

She threw a few pairs of jeans and two sleeveless dresses into the suitcase then added a black skirt, a couple of nice blouses, and a pair of heels. *Not very ball ready, am I?* She shrugged then threw in a few bras and the entire contents of her underwear drawer.

Once packed, she jotted a note to her roommates, placed the money Jaxzon had given her in an envelope labeled *Rent*, then left both beside her keys on the kitchen table. She called the shelter and Sottocasa's Pizza, letting them know she wouldn't be available for the summer. Lastly, she shoved her passport into her handbag and put on her Yankees ball cap, then followed Derek to the street where he hailed a cab.

The taxi made its way to the airport through the light Saturday afternoon traffic. "Do the people in your country speak a different language?"

"Some people speak English, but you'll be okay. We have interpreters."

"Oh." She settled into her seat, then squinted at Derek. "Hey, didn't you tell me you went home today? How could you go all the way home and back in such a short time?"

He rubbed the back of his neck. "Did I? I meant Jaxzon and Boden went home. I stayed behind to find you."

"Oh. But how did they return home so fast? It takes at least seven hours just to fly to London."

He twisted in his seat to face her. "I'm sorry for being so incoherent earlier. I didn't sleep much last night, and I'm a bit hungover. Then I was excited to find you and desperate to make you understand."

Uncertain, she scrutinized his face. There were no signs of malice in his wide eyes. She sat back, deciding to wait until the airport before making a final decision on whether she wanted to continue or not.

The taxi exited the 278, and the driver glanced through the mirror. "Which terminal?"

"Three," Derek told him.

He glared at Derek through the mirror. "There is no terminal three. Either A, B, C..."

"Oh yeah, sorry, B." He gave Guin a weak smile.

Her uneasiness grew.

After paying the driver, Derek steered her through the crowded walkways to the parking structure. He studied his phone and entered the elevator alcove.

She stopped short. "Do we have to take the elevator? I know it sounds silly, but they make me ill. Cars? No problem. Airplane? Bring it on. But put me in a tiny moving sardine box? No way. Ever since I was a baby, they've made me sick."

"We can take the stairs."

They traveled deeper into the garage, and she became more uncertain. He came to a stop in an empty corner, far from parked cars or the nearest exit. He checked his phone again. Strange symbols filled the screen.

She glanced around. He stood between her and the nearest exit. "Are we looking for a car, or waiting for someone to pick us up?"

"No car. We only have about ten seconds before the next phase. No time to explain. You'll have to trust me."

"I don't know. This is getting too weird." Her heart raced. Panic wasn't far off.

Derek handed over her suitcase and an oval, metallic object. "Hold on to this."

A tiny red light blinked up at her. "What is it?"

"Trust me." He gripped her shoulders and pushed.

Guin stumbled backward.

CHAPTER FIVE

White-hot sparks like demonic fireflies burned behind Guin's closed eyes. A rushing filled her ears. Disembodied voices echoed nonsensically. The sensation of falling with nothing to hold onto caused her head to spin.

Tremors ran from the top of her head to the tips of her toes. A painful, viselike pressure built within her skull, but lessened when she removed her hands from her temples. An unbearable clattering sounded within her head.

She clenched her jaw. The sound ceased.

A voice echoed in her ears, speaking in an alien language. Light glared when she tried to open her eyes. The pain gradually receded from her body, though the tremors continued. The glare dulled. The form of a person standing nearby came into view, though the face remained unfocused.

"Guin, are you okay?" Derek bent over her, blocking the light overhead, his dark eyes peering into hers.

"You shoved me into a wall, Derek," she said through clenched teeth. She attempted to lift her head. Her stomach lurched. Derek's face swam from her vision. Guin let her head fall back. Her body trembled from the effort.

"I'm so sorry. I had no idea you'd be affected this way."

"What happened? Where are we?" Her jaw ached. Her teeth chattered uncontrollably.

A woman's face appeared beside Derek's.

He put his hand on Guin's shoulder. "They need to give you something to make you feel better. They want to know if you could be pregnant."

"What?" Keeping her jaw locked, she tilted her head to the side in an attempt to view her surroundings. The movement caused her head to spin. "Are we in a hospital?"

"We're at a Shift Station. Let them give you medication, and you'll understand. You had a bad Shift."

She blinked. "A bad what?" *Was he talking about work?* Her body shuddered.

"Please, Guin. This will make you better. They can't give you medication without your consent, and they need to know if you're pregnant."

His face floated in and out of her vision.

"Give me the shot. I'm not pregnant." There was a slight pressure on her wrist. The trembling stopped. Her vision cleared. The dizziness abated.

He helped her sit. Concern filled his wide eyes. "Better?"

Rubbing her sore jaw she glared around the room. The walls, the tiled floor, the padded bed she sat on, were solid white. "Where the hell are we, what the hell happened to me, and why the hell did you shove me into a wall?" Running her fingers over the back of her head, she checked for damage.

"I'm so sorry. We were out of time, and I was worried you'd change your mind if I tried to explain. Do you feel better?"

She crossed her arms. "I'm fine, but if you think I'm going with you now, you have another think coming."

"You've already gone with me. We're here. This is where I'm from." He went to the door. "*Dein vestint*."

Suspicion, anger, and confusion wrestled within her. "What are you saying?"

A tall, dark-eyed woman entered the room. Her clothing reminded Guin of something speed skaters wore—white, form-fitting, with sleeves ending at the wrists—only her hands and face remained uncovered. On her palm sat a tiny, golden device, the size and shape of a grain of rice, with a thin, hairlike filament attached to one end.

"What's this?"

"It's called a *loqu*, a translator. When you insert it, you will be able to understand our language," Derek said.

"Insert it where?"

"In your ear, of course." He removed an identical device from his own ear. "They don't hurt; everyone wears them. There are about a million languages and dialects here. This will translate them all."

Curious, Guin took the *loqu*, then glancing between Derek and the woman, she brushed her hair to one side and placed the device in her ear. When she released the filament, it slid over her tragus, anchoring itself beside her silver, star-shaped stud. She tugged the filament and the *loqu* released, then she let it slide back into her ear.

"Better?" the woman asked.

"I understood you. Or were you speaking English?"

"She's speaking our language."

Guin touched her ear. "These things are great."

The woman smiled. "My name is Tocha. Welcome to Arwon. I'll be back shortly." Tocha left.

Guin raised an eyebrow. "Arwon?"

"Arwon is the name of our planet."

"I don't think this thing is working properly." She removed the loqu. "Where are we again?"

"Arwon. My planet."

Tilting her head, she slid the loqu in. "Say that again. I thought you said we're on another planet."

"Guin, you heard me right. This is where I'm from."

She shook her head. "That's impossible. I'm sure I would remember traveling to another planet. We were in the parking garage, then you pushed me. Was I knocked out?" Searching the back of her head for a lump, she asked, "How long was I unconscious?"

"You weren't knocked out. Let me explain."

He sat beside her. She scooted away, crossed her arms, and shot him a dark look. "Yes, Derek. Please, explain."

"I didn't push you, I *guided* you. We Shifted. Do you remember the device and my saying I was waiting for the next phase?"

"I remember. But that sure felt like a push to me."

"The device is called a dislocater; it's used to open a portal which allows us to Shift between worlds. I was holding another, and we came through together. The Shifts come in phases, and they can materialize in different locations at different times. When we arrived at the airport, I used my telecon to trace one."

He pointed his phone's screen in her direction. The screen displayed a map with strange symbols. "LaGuardia has several, and there are thousands more throughout your world. You can only Shift by using the dislocater. I don't understand the mechanics; physics was never my strong point, but when you held the dislocater, I guided you through the portal, and we Shifted. Newcomers are required to come through this station to register. Everyone coming from Earth is required to go through decontamination."

"So, if I were to believe you—which I don't—you're telling me you're from a different planet, and Jaxzon is from a different planet? And you want me to join in some crazy competition, with a bunch of women from another planet, for the chance to marry a prince *from another planet*?" Guin's heart pounded. She clutched her churning gut, fighting to control the hysteria in her voice. "Is this what you're telling me?"

"If you put it that way, yes. But is this any different from going to another country for the same purpose?"

"Yes, Derek, it is! A lot different!" She ran her fingers through her hair. "How do I even know if we're the same species?"

His laugh turned into a cough when she narrowed her eyes. "We're the same species. We're simply from different worlds. You'd be surprised how many planets in this galaxy have people much like us." He grinned. "There are some differences. Some people have certain characteristics unique to their worlds. Humans originated from the same galaxy very far from this one. We even share some of the same basic languages and customs."

Guin searched his innocent eyes. *Was it possible?* She bit her lower lip and went to the door. A massive white desk sat in the center of the station with monitors lining the top. People wearing the same uniforms as Tocha worked, speaking in low voices. A woman whose face was a pale shade of turquoise looked up from her desk. Her golden eyes met Guin's, and she smiled.

Shock and wonder replaced Guin's anger at the possibility that Derek was telling the truth. "Is that woman blue?"

"Yes. She's from Bethion. Their skin is blue; otherwise, they're just like us."

"You're telling the truth, aren't you?"

"I'm telling the truth."

"But why didn't you simply tell me? Why did you have to scare the bejeezus out of me?"

"Would you have believed me?"

"Of cour—" She shook her head. "Probably not. But you could have at least given me a choice."

"I'm truly sorry. It's against our laws to tell people from other planets about this." He waved his hand. "If I had told you, and you hadn't come, I would be in big trouble."

"Will you be in trouble now?"

"I'll be fine. But you'll need to be prepared if you decide to stay. Do you want to continue?" Derek implored her with his eyes.

Not sure if she was dreaming this whole craziness, curiosity took over and Guin found herself wanting to know more. "Okay. What's next?"

He picked up the suitcase and gave Guin her handbag. "First, we need to get you ready for our atmosphere." He escorted her through a short hallway and poked his head in a room. "She's ready."

CHAPTER SIX

A solitary chair much like a dentist's, complete with headrest and a bright light, occupied the center of the room. Tocha pointed to the chair. "Have a seat."

Guin gulped. "What are we doing now?"

Tocha tapped on a screen embedded in the wall. "The computer will mix the elements needed to administer the proper inoculates for you to survive here. They'll assist your body in adapting to the atmosphere on this and neighboring planets."

"Neighboring planets?"

A door slid open beneath the screen, revealing a short beaker filled with an amber liquid. "The computer measures the precise dosage and dispenses the mixture."

Guin's eyes widened. Tocha's lips didn't match her words, like a foreign film with dubbed voices.

"I will place a bio-breathing device into your sinus cavity, which will filter impurities in our atmosphere. Yours is being programmed now."

Pointing to the beaker, Guin asked, "So, I drink that, shove a device up my nose, and I'm good to go?"

Tocha laughed. "Simply put, but...yes."

Taking the beaker she sniffed the liquid. There was no detectible odor. Her chest tightened. "H—how do I know this isn't some kind of trick?"

Derek squeezed her shoulder. "I promise, you're in no danger."

"Said the man who shoved me into a wall. Sorry, *guided.*" She swirled the liquid. "Bottom's up, I guess." Placing the beaker to her lips, Guin squeezed her eyes shut then tipped her head back, downing the mixture in one swallow. "I don't feel anything. Is it working?"

Tocha smiled. "You won't feel any different. We've had many Tellurians come through with no adverse effects."

"What's a Tellurian?"

"People from Earth," said Derek. "Some people call you 'Earthers,' which most Tellurians don't like."

"Why not call us 'humans' or 'Earthlings,' like in the movies?"

"We're all human, and most consider 'Earthling' an insult."

"Oh. Learn something new every day, right?"

His grin lit his face. "You're going to be learning a lot of new things here."

A buzz came from an overhead speaker, and a voice announced, "Your *terukin* programming is complete."

"I'll be a moment." Tocha left the room.

Guin sat forward, inspecting the chair for straps or locks. "*Terukin*?"

"To help you breathe." He pointed to his face. "Everyone has one. You won't even notice it."

She sat back in the chair. Her foot beat a rapid staccato against the footrest. Squeezing her knees together she took a deep breath. *What the hell am I doing? Am I this desperate for a date?* She giggled.

Derek inclined his head.

"Sorry, kinda freaking out here. It isn't every day I leave Earth." Guin still couldn't believe most of what was happening. *Am I seri-*

ously on another planet and going to travel to more? The realization terrified and excited her. "Maybe when we go outside."

"Maybe what, when we go outside?"

"I was thinking, maybe it'll be easier to believe everything when I can check out Arwon. Is it much different from Earth?"

"Yeah, we have two moons, and two suns, and the colors are different from Earth. There are some unusual animals too. I think you'll like it, and some other worlds can be a little wild."

Tocha returned carrying a tray. "Do I have your permission to proceed with the implant, or do you wish to go home?"

Derek shot Guin a peace sign. "Up to you. Now that you understand what's going on, what do you say?"

The implement Tocha held flashed in the light. Raney's voice accused Guin of never having fun or a sense of adventure. Why had she decided to come in the first place? Did it matter if she was on a different world? No matter how much the prospect blew her mind?

Did she want to go home now? And there was Jaxzon, his touch, his scent, the way he looked at her, and *OMG, I'm on another planet!* This intrigued her beyond anything else. *Talk about an adventure.* Her heart pulsated in her ears.

She swallowed. "I've come this far; I might as well go through with it. Bring on the nose job." She took a deep breath then gripping the chair's arms, laid her head back and closed her eyes. "I'm ready."

When her eyes stopped watering from the insertion of the apparatus, Guin hopped from the chair. Excitement replaced her earlier trepidation. "Are we finished here?"

"Are you prone to motion sickness?" Tocha asked.

"Not really. I mean, elevators make me sick. I get dizzy, and have panic attacks when I ride them."

"Your reaction to the Shift happens to people who experience motion sickness." Tocha held a pen-like device. "This is *trivol* and will alleviate the problem when you Shift again. Although I'm sorry, it won't help with the elevators. Do I have your permission to administer trivol?"

"Definitely. I never want to go through that again."

Tocha placed the gadget against Guin's wrist and depressed a button. Her wrist tingled.

"This should last about thirty Arwon days, so you'll need another dose within that time before Shifting again." She handed Guin a pair of glasses. "You'll also need these until you adapt to our suns. They've been programmed for you and will adjust as you become accustomed to the light variances."

"I feel like James Bond." Guin donned the glasses. "How do I look?"

Derek grinned. "Very stylish."

She put the glasses into her handbag. "Now what?"

"Now we go home. My home."

They descended two flights of stairs and entered an immense lobby filled with people coming and going. A woman hurried past. The folds of her bright purple skirt swished around her knees, and her frilly pink blouse obliterated the bottom portion of her face behind its ruffled neckline.

Derek smirked. "Ruffles are in this year."

"I see. Not sure that's my style. I'm not into frilly things."

"Then you're going to love the newest ballgowns." He guided her to the exit. "Put on your glasses."

"Ballgowns? Like enormous, puffy princess-type ballgowns?"

A dark, shining sidewalk separated the buildings from the street. Two suns hung low, yet bright in the fuchsia sky. Derek swept his arm. "Welcome to the city of Kurrel."

Sleek, wheel-less vehicles passed by on the glossy road. "Whoa, are those hover cars?"

"Cool, right? And yes, ballgowns, although you don't have to wear the puffy kind if you don't want. Too much fabric if you ask me—takes too long to take off."

"How would you know?"

His face flushed, and his pace quickened.

"Uh-huh, now I'm getting a glimpse of the real Derek."

A bright red vehicle parked at the curb. A wide door raised, and four men exited. The door closed, and the empty hover drifted away.

"Who's driving?" she asked.

"They're self-driving."

"I guess I'd be out of a job here." She stopped short. An ostrich-sized, purple-and-gold-feathered, birdlike creature appeared to be roosting in midair high above the buildings. "Are we in a dome?"

Derek followed her gaze. "Yes. That's a *bhanthu*. Nasty creatures, but they have beautiful feathers." He propelled her toward the tall, mirrored building next to the Shift Station. "All the major cities are built inside domes. Visitors who can't adapt to the atmosphere, even with a terukin—stay within the domes."

"Will I be okay outside?"

"Sure. Boden is half Tellurian—his mother's from Earth. She had no problems."

"Boden's mother is from Earth?" She smiled, recalling Jaxzon's handsome friend. "Are there a lot of Tellurians here?"

"I wouldn't say a lot. The laws forbid bringing anyone from Earth, except under certain conditions."

Guin stopped. "What do you mean, conditions?"

Derek rubbed the back of his neck. His gaze wandered from her face to the sidewalk, then to a passing vehicle before coming back to rest somewhere around her chin. "In the last of your century, during times of war on Earth, some Tellurians came here in case you blew yourselves into oblivion. I believe Boden's mother came during an Earth crisis."

"What is the condition under which you brought me?"

"Well..." He averted his eyes.

She gestured to the Shift Station. "What did you tell them?"

"I told them Jaxzon ordered me to bring you here."

Her heart skipped a beat. "Did he?"

"He doesn't know. But he's going to be happy you're here."

Guin groaned. "What happens if he isn't or someone finds out? Will you be in trouble? Will I be in trouble?"

"Everything will be fine, and he'll back me once he sees you."

"Will he?"

He took her arm. "Come on. This is the transportation hub. We have to get home before it gets too late, and it's a long ride."

Shaking her head, she allowed herself to be led into the silver building. Guin removed her glasses. "It's so quiet."

Despite the presence of hundreds of people, nothing louder than murmurs of conversation, or the clicking of heels and scuffs of footsteps sounded throughout the great hall. A sharp contrast to the shouted conversations and chaos of Grand Central.

Derek ushered her through a lighted archway and onto a moving walkway that sloped downward, transporting them into the bowels of the station, and ending in a depot. A chain of tall hovers lined the platform. Passengers disembarked through an exit at the back, while others boarded through the front.

Guin followed him to a sleek, metallic-green hover standing alone at the furthest end of the line. "This one's ours, watch your step."

Five rows of plush seats, two on either side, filled most of the cabin. A thick silver carpet covered the floor, and a mirrored door adorned the back wall. A panel at the front lit at his approach. He waved his wrist over a screen embedded in the panel. "I'm entering the destination into the tele-screen. Have a seat." He tapped the screen as symbols appeared.

She sank into the lush, green seat cushions. People continued to fill the hovers in front of theirs. "Why isn't anyone else getting on?"

He glanced back as the hatch shut. "Private." He tapped the screen one last time then took the seat across from hers and winked. "One of the perks of knowing me."

The hover slid to the left, and with a burst of acceleration, entered a narrow, lighted tunnel.

She grasped the chair arms. "Whoa."

He grinned. "You okay?"

"This is nothing like the Number Two back home." Guin relaxed her grip.

The hover jetted along, accelerating until the tunnel entrances on both sides became dark blurs.

"How fast do these go?" she asked.

"By Earth measurements, five hundred miles an hour or so."

"Wow. How far is your house?"

"Three thousand Earth miles. We should arrive in around six of your hours. The road is mostly underground, so you'll have to wait until morning for the real sights I'm afraid. I wish you could have seen the sunsset. They're amazing."

"Besides balls, what else am I looking forward to in this, um, contest?"

"I'm not sure, actually. The last one was before I was born."

Guin took her phone from her bag. "Can we check?" She hit the power button and waited for her home screen.

"Not on that, I'm afraid."

"Oh." Although the icons were there, the words *no service* appeared in the top corner of the screen. "I didn't think about that. Wait. No phones? No internet at all?"

"We do have something comparable." He showed her his phone. "We call these *telecons,* and the internet is called the *Circuit.*"

"Hello Niqi," he said into the telecon.

A woman's sultry voice purred, "Yes, my love, what is your pleasure?"

Guin raised an eyebrow.

He flushed. "Niqi, change to voice module three."

A metallic voice stated, "Voice changed, module three."

"Niqi, display *Vekdromic* events."

Hiding a grin, she moved across the aisle. The symbols on his phone made no sense to her. She frowned. "I didn't think of that either."

"The first event is the Grande Masque on Arwon. Other planets will host an event—balls, charity events, or something traditional to the host planet."

"Grande Masque? Like a costume party?"

"Right. The Masque is His Majesty's most anticipated annual ball. Each suitor will be presented during the event. You're going to be attending many formal balls and events over the next few months."

"Can you find out what they did last time?"

"Niqi, show related events for the last Vekdromic." He scrolled through pictures. "There was an eating contest, 'who could eat the most broiled cats in one sitting.'" He showed her a picture of cute, furry kittens.

Guin's eyes widened. "What?"

"Kidding. I do love a good cat video, don't you?" A video of a cat swatting a glass off a table played on his telecon.

She slapped his arm. "Derek! You almost gave me a heart attack. You have cats here?"

"Sure. We have lots of animals from Earth, and many that are completely different. Every planet has its own flora and fauna, like each of your continents."

Not discovering anything more concrete other than mentions of formal balls, charity events, and press interviews with the last Vekdromic's finalists, he ended his search. "That's odd. I would think there'd be more information about such a momentous occasion."

"Is there a picture of Jaxzon's mother?"

He enlarged the picture, then handed the telecon to Guin. A stunning young woman smiled from the screen. Her waist-length black hair framed her delicate features and brown, almond-shaped eyes. Except for their color, Jaxzon had her eyes.

"She was beautiful. What was her name?"

"Neyris."

"Neyris. What a lovely name." She handed the telecon back. "Thank you." She returned to her seat.

Derek settled in and was soon snoring.

What have you gotten yourself into, Guinevere? Do you truly believe Jaxzon could fall in love with you? Could you fall in love with him? Do you even want to be a queen? Is this a dream?

"Nobody could make this up," she said aloud. "You're either having a very *vivid* dream, you're certifiable, or this is very real."

She lifted his telecon from the seat beside him and clicked on various icons until she found a collection of photographs. Many depicted Derek posing with beautiful women or handsome men in various stages of undress. A few of the people were blue, and one was a light shade of orange, otherwise they appeared to be everyday people that she might know from home.

One picture was of Derek, Boden, and Jaxzon standing in front of a stone wall. Jaxzon's smile dazzled her, and even from a photograph, his eyes pierced hers.

Guin shut off the telecon. The lack of sleep and adrenaline rushes she'd experienced in the last twenty-four hours left her exhausted. The artificial light dimmed, and she drifted off.

CHAPTER SEVEN

The tunnel lights had vanished. Guin cupped her hands around her face to cut the glare and leaned them against the window. The glimmer of lights shone through distant trees. "Where are we?"

"Almost home, only a few more miles," Derek said.

The interior dimmed, and the outlines of buildings came into view. The hover decelerated as they approached a broad pair of ornate, wrought-iron gates. Bright lamps drowned the night, illuminating wide gates swinging inward to reveal a sweeping, tree-lined driveway. Resting at the top sat a grand manor with tall wooden doors nestled within a stone archway.

"We're home," Derek announced.

The hover's hatch opened, and she hesitated as a warm breeze blew in through the door. A flowery fragrance hung in the air.

He patted her shoulder. "You'll be okay."

She followed him from the hover and up the stone steps. The hover's hatch closed with a slight hiss, and the vehicle floated silently down the driveway.

The massive wooden door opened at his touch, revealing a grand entryway. A mosaic of tiles covered the hall's floors, and a staircase curved to the right. Numerous archways opened in several directions on both floors. The house had an ancient, castle-like décor.

"This is your house? How big is your family?"

"Only me and my sister now. Come on, I'll show you to your room." He led her up the carpeted stairs to the second-floor landing and down a dark hallway.

Silver sconces sprang to life at his approach and faded as she passed. "I thought houses here would be more modern and made of some strange futuristic material."

"Most are, but Delori likes this look."

"What do you mean?"

"It's a type of hologram. Quaint old castles and manors are in right now. Delori picked this design. I liked the old one—stainless steel and lots of glass."

Guin poked a finger against the wall. "It looks solid to me."

"It should. Delori demands only the best. I'm putting you on this side, so she doesn't come across you accidentally. She never comes to this wing."

"You didn't tell your sister about me?"

"Yeah, well, I figured she wouldn't say no if you were already here."

Her heart dropped. "Oh, Derek. I hope she won't be angry when she finds out."

"She'll be furious, but don't worry. I'll take care of everything."

At the end of the hallway, he opened a door. The light came on as they entered. An enormous four-poster bed stood against the far wall. A highly polished armoire sat opposite with a mirrored dressing table to the right. A floor-to-ceiling, curtain-less window filled the outside wall.

He placed her suitcase on the bed and opened a door to an adjoining bathroom. Bright lights, mirrored walls, and chrome fixtures gave the room a clean, modern look. The glass enclosed bathtub filled nearly half the room and sported four shower heads.

"Wow," she said in awe. "My whole apartment could fit in here."

"Leave your handbag and we'll eat. Are you hungry?"

"Famished."

They headed downstairs, and after crossing a cavernous dining room, they entered an extensive, fully equipped kitchen, replete with stainless steel appliances.

"Now this is what I call a kitchen," said Guin.

Derek glanced around. "It might be over the top for our immediate needs, although when Delori is away on business, I throw some epic parties. Come on, I'll cook for you."

Guin took a seat at the oversized butcher block in the center of the kitchen. He mixed familiar ingredients in a bowl. Familiar, except the eggs were red, the butter a light purple, and the milk had an orange tint. He lit the griddle, plopped a blob of butter on it, and scooped a spoonful of the burnt-orange mixture from the bowl. He did this six times, took a spatula from a ceramic jar and waited.

Amused and a little surprised, she asked, "Derek, are you making me pancakes?"

"This is about the only thing I can cook." He grinned. "Do you like pancakes?"

"My favorite. You got syrup?"

"There." He pointed to an enormous refrigerator. "Dishes are behind you, forks in that drawer."

The refrigerator contained cartons and bottles of food items labeled with strange symbols. She held up a bottle with brown liquid. "This one?"

"No, the pink one." He flipped the pancakes over, then slid them onto plates. He set one in front of Guin and pulled up a stool.

She took a tentative bite. The syrup had a spicy tang. "Delicious. Almost like home."

Between bites, he explained how Delori had run the estate since their mother died. "Delori was only twenty-one, and I was eleven. Our father passed before I was born."

Guin stopped eating. "I'm so sorry, Derek."

"Thanks. It's been rougher on Delori than me. She's had a lot to deal with—the estate, our county's citizens, her lazy, irresponsible, yet devilishly handsome brother. I'm a pretty big pain to her. She's lost a lot. Besides our parents, she lost her best friend—twice."

"What do you mean?"

"We were always close to the royal family. Queen Neyris and our mother grew up together, and we spent a lot of time with them. Princess Jalain and Delori were best friends. When Jalain became engaged, Delori refused to see her and grew depressed, throwing herself into business. She became a recluse and somewhat of a tyrant. She was so tough on our domestic staff that most quit, making it difficult to hire more once word got around.

"After Neyris's and Jalain's murders, Delori went into a deeper depression. She wouldn't talk to anyone for weeks. She seemed older, bitter, and easily annoyed. I was—I am—her least favorite person." He scratched the day's growth of stubble on his chin. "She gave me the task of finding someone to represent our house, knowing—I guess you could say I associate with a lot of single women. She thought I might find an acceptable suitor." Derek wore a sheepish grin. "But most the women I associate with...let's say they would not represent our house well."

She raised her eyebrows. "So, instead you asked me?"

"Well...yeah."

She frowned. "Jaxzon told me his mother and sister died, but he didn't say they'd been murdered. What happened?"

"Queen Neyris and Princess Jalain were on a diplomatic trip to Xaitera. They had taken the royal shuttle to shift supplies to Xaitera for a charity event. For some inexplicable reason, their pilot went insane or something. He changed course and flew into one of the planet's satellites. Everyone on board died, including Boden's father, the commander of the king's guard."

Her appetite lost, Guin set her fork on her plate. "Why would the pilot do such a thing?"

"No one knows." He pushed a piece of pancake around the plate, sopping up the last drops of syrup. "In his last transmission he told his wife and son he was sorry."

"Why did they take a shuttle?" She tilted her head. "Wouldn't it be easier to Shift to another planet?"

"You can't Shift large quantities of material from the planet. Some of the phases in space are huge and can accommodate a whole fleet of ships in one Shift."

She nodded. "That makes sense."

"I know you must have more questions, but we'd better get some sleep. Delori will be awake in a couple of hours, and I'm sure she'll want to talk to me when she does."

Guin gathered their dishes.

The lights went out with a wave of Derek's hand. "Don't bother, Willis will get them."

"Who's Willis?"

"The cleaning android."

"Really?" Guin scanned the darkened corners, hoping to catch a glimpse of Willis as she followed Derek from the kitchen.

She hugged him outside her bedroom door. "Thank you, Derek, for everything."

"Don't thank me yet. Delori might vaporize us both in the morning."

Beams from Arwon's double suns spilled through the high windows, creating shadowy purple pools in the corners of the entryway when Guin crept downstairs the following morning. She jabbed a finger against the doorway's dark molding, her fingertip disappeared. Since Derek's knock on her door that morning, she'd been poking her fingers through the hologram all morning, and it still amazed her.

A woman's enraged voice came through the dining hall door. "An *Earthling*? Why do you do these things? How can you be so obtuse?"

"I—"

"Don't give me excuses. You knew what this meant for our house. We will be the laughingstock if we present an Earthling to the Council. This could ruin us."

"Stop calling her that! You know nothing about her."

"Neither do you, you imbecile! You've known her for less than two days. You transported her here illegally, and now you expect *me* to present her to the Council. To the nobility? To the *king*? Why was I encumbered with an incompetent idiot for a brother?"

A hot flash of anger propelled Guin forward, and she stormed through the door.

Derek and Delori squared off across a wide, metallic-blue dining table. He gripped the back of a matching chair, his head bent.

Delori—an older female version of Derek—glared, manicured hands on the hips of a conservative gray skirt, chestnut hair swept back in a tight bun, and dark brown eyes flashing with rage.

She didn't break her gaze until Guin stepped between the two and offered her hand. "Hello, I'm Guinevere Griffin."

Folding her arms across her chest, Delori's gaze traveled from Guin's feet to her face, then slid to Derek. "Is this the best you could do? You've rejected better on a bad night."

Guin's jaw and hand both fell, repelled by the venom in the woman's words.

Derek slammed the chair into the table. His hands curled into fists. "You have no right to speak to her in that manner."

His sister appeared stunned as she stared at his livid face.

He unclenched his fists. "You're wrong. I may not know much about Guin, but I've spent enough time with her to know she's a good person. Give her a chance. She must be ready for the Grande Masque, and I can't do it alone. We need your help."

After staring daggers at her brother, Delori turned her glare on Guin, looking her up and down. Her mouth twitched. "If I agree to work with you, you will do everything I ask, no questions."

"I—"

"I said no questions, and I mean I don't want to hear anything from you except 'yes ma'am' or 'no ma'am.' Do you understand?"

He implored Guin with his eyes.

"Well?" asked Delori, recrossing her arms.

Mirroring Delori, Guin glared back. "No ma'am."

Derek inhaled sharply.

His sister's cheek twitched.

"I may be a lowly Earthling, but I am not your dog. I've taken a lot of crap from a lot of people, and I will not stand here and be abused by you, nor will I watch you abuse your brother. And I will never give away my right to question what anyone tells me to do."

Eyes darkening, Delori's lips pressed into a thin line.

Her brother quit breathing altogether.

"I will try, to the best of my abilities to do what you ask of me," Guin continued, "but I need you to respect me—at least to my face. If we are going to do this, for the honor of *your* house, we're going to do it together."

His gulp was the only sound as she and Delori stared icily at one another.

"No one talks to me in that manner." Her gaze slipped to her brother. "I might be able to work with her."

His mouth dropped open, then snapped shut under his sister's glare.

She gave Guin a curt nod. "Go eat and meet me in the solarium."

When Delori left the room, he took Guin's hands. "That. Was. Fabulous! I can't believe you challenged her. I can't believe you told her no. I thought her head was going to explode."

Poking her head through the doorway, Delori beckoned her brother. "Derek, may I speak to you for a moment?"

He froze and blinked at Guin, mouthing, "Be right back" before following his sister.

Guin headed to the kitchen.

Joining her as she rummaged through the refrigerator, Derek helped her find bread for toast and informed her that Delori was in the process of finding Guin a costume for the Masque. "This is the best time of the year." He rubbed his palms together. "Parties galore."

"You're not a very complicated guy, are you?"

He grinned. "About as deep as a puddle. I like to enjoy myself. What can I say?"

"Where's the solarium? Also, *what's* a solarium?"

"A fancy sunroom. Come on, I'll show you."

He led the way through the hall until they emerged into a domed, glass room. Unusual plants of every size, shape, and color filled pots throughout. A pink and yellow leafed plant hummed when she touched its lime-green flowers.

Sitting before a tele-screen in a gazebo at the center of the room, Delori cleared her throat. "What size do you wear?"

Guin made her way to the gazebo. "I'm a five back home."

"Size five, Earth. Convert. We're lucky they have anything left this close to the Masque." She swiveled the screen toward Guin. "Choose."

Two costumes filled the screen. A fairy-like, lavender dress with sparkly wings, and a flowing white toga with a gold braided belt and sandals. The woman in the picture wore a golden circlet in her hair and a white mask with gold trim.

Derek peered over Guin's shoulder. "The goddess, no question."

Delori's expression darkened. "I wasn't speaking to you. Guinevere, choose."

"I agree, the goddess."

"Fine. I'll make the order. You will be fitted tomorrow. While in town, we will have your hair done. Do you do your own makeup?"

"I don't wear any."

Delori scrutinized Guin's face. "I see. You'll need eyeliner, mascara, and a bit of lipstick. Today, we will go over the rules of etiquette required when meeting nobility. I don't suppose you've met royalty?"

"Only Jaxzon, and I didn't realize he was a prince at the time."

"You will be meeting King Jaezain, as well as other kings, queens, princes, princesses, noblemen and noblewomen from throughout the galaxy. You will also meet Council members, who are probably the most influential people in the realm. You will learn their basic customs. We can't have you insulting anyone and ruining our name. Speaking of names, how do you wish to be announced? You are an official member of our house, and though you have no title, you may be referred to as either 'Lady' or 'Miss.' Which do you prefer?"

The memory of Jaxzon's flashing eyes when he kissed her hand brought a smile. "Lady."

"You will be announced at each event as Lady Guinevere Griffin of House Vau'uan."

"That's your house name?"

Delori frowned at Derek. "You didn't tell her much, did you? Yes, Vau'uan is the name of our house. We certainly can't have you announced as being from Earth. The gossips will learn the truth soon enough. For now, say nothing of where you're from. The longer they take to figure things out, the better our chances of making a good impression and lessening the blow."

"Why is my being from Earth an issue? Boden's mother was from Earth. Did she have to hide her origins?"

"You are not Boden's mother. She was the wife of a prominent man and came here for a purpose, although lucky for you, that purpose went unfulfilled. Did my brother tell you why they brought people from Earth?"

"He mentioned something about wars?"

"Whenever your people appeared on the verge of blowing themselves into oblivion, our government would bring Earthl—Tellurians here for preservation and research."

Guin crossed her arms. "That's kind of gross. Why doesn't anyone on Earth know this?"

"Some have knowledge. You'd be surprised how many. Apparently, your world leaders don't believe your simple minds could take the shock of realizing you aren't alone in the universe."

"Who you calling simple?" *No wonder poor Derek is a bundle of nerves around this woman.*

"No time for this. We need you ready to meet the nobility of *this* world and learn as much about the politics of the dozens of planets in the realm. We also need to work on your wardrobe. You can't go around dressed in those rags."

"What's wrong with my dress?"

Derek put an arm around Guin's shoulder. "Ignore her. You look nice."

Late into the night, Delori went over each aspect of etiquette for greeting royals from every known realm in the galaxy. She went over the basics of the political climate for Arwon and other outlying planets. By the time Delori released her, Guin's head burst with useless knowledge. Around the second or third hour, it had become apparent manners were much the same everywhere, and that the politics here were as complicated and vast as the galaxy itself. Delori's instructions boiled down to remembering to curtsy and address the kings and queens by "Your Majesty," the princes and princesses by "Your Highness," and as for everyone else, Guin merely needed to remember their titles and try not to get involved too deeply in political discussions. Simple, but Delori went over every title and the politics for each planet in detail until Guin's eyes glazed over.

CHAPTER EIGHT

Jaxzon leaned on his wooden quarterstaff, waiting for Boden to join him in the gym for their daily sparring. But instead of his usual stretches, he allowed his mind to drift, daydreaming of Guin for the tenth time this morning.

Her eyes, her smile, and her ability to light up the cramped space of her car with both. When they first met, he had been practically speechless. When she saved their night after their missed reservation, he couldn't let her leave without learning more about her, and when they'd almost kissed... He admonished himself, still regretting that any chance for more had ended before it began.

The thrill of her touch, the scent of her hair when they'd embraced, the spark from her lips when she'd kissed his cheek. He brushed the spot with his fingertips and smiled as he recalled DeShawn's words—swearing he would never wash the spot again—Jaxzon could appreciate the sentiment.

He stumbled when his staff was knocked from under him.

"Wake up, Princey. I might have been an assassin," Boden chided.

Jaxzon threw the towel he had draped over his shoulder at

Boden, who batted it away, then climbed into the training ring. "You going to stand there or you going to join me?"

Following, Jaxzon faced off with his friend.

Boden spun his weapon in one hand, feinting left then sweeping right.

Slow to react, Jaxzon's feet were swept from under him. He crashed to the mat.

"That was easy," Boden said, hauling Jaxzon to his feet. "Where's your mind this morning?"

Shaking his head, Jaxzon rotated the staff in a lazy spin. Boden shrugged and attacked without warning, raising the weapon in a cross strike to Jaxzon's left, whose timing was off, allowing Boden to land a swift blow to his bicep. He brought his staff around, rapping Jaxzon's right wrist, causing him to drop his weapon.

Snatching his staff from the mat, Jaxzon shook his injured hand.

Boden scowled, his hazel eyes glinting. "Please tell me you aren't thinking of the Tellurian girl again."

Jaxzon rubbed his wrist, not sure if he was angry with his tone or how Boden read him so easily. "I slept badly."

"You hardly know her." The concern on Boden's face was laced with irritation. "Just get over her."

"I'm trying to." Flipping his staff in a shoulder spin, Jaxzon scanned the gym. "I can't get her off my mind. Does that sound crazy?"

In another ring, Cindy—Lieutenant Harvell—sparred with a training android.

"Yes." Boden aimed a forward poke at Jaxzon's ribs.

He knocked the staff downward. Boden countered with an up-strike. Jaxzon backed away, revolving his staff between them, knocking Boden's aside. He forced Jaxzon against the ropes where he shifted the spinning weapon to his side, preparing to go on the offensive. Taking advantage of the opening, Boden once again poked forward, catching Jaxzon in the ribs, eliciting a grunt of pain.

Boden grinned and backed away, twirling his staff in a forward spin. "It's not like you associate with many women."

"That's not—"

"Hold on, let me explain." Boden stopped his retreat. "Think about it. You've been surrounded by servants since birth, so when do you meet women?"

"I know—"

"You meet them at boring balls." Boden lunged forward, swinging his weapon in a down-strike. Jaxzon braced his feet and raised his staff in an overhead block, deflecting the blow. "And charity events." Boden said as his staff made contact.

Jaxzon countered with a forward thrust. Boden rotated his staff with his left hand and caught Jaxzon's with his right, jerking Jaxzon forward.

"Face it," Boden continued, holding Jaxzon's staff and tapping him none-too-gently on the shoulder with his own, punctuating each point. "The women you're surrounded by are a bunch of phony, backstabbing, plotting, conniving—" Apparently tiring of adjectives, he snarled, "bloodsuckers!" He thrust Jaxzon from him and stalked to the side of the ring.

Jaxzon had grown accustomed to Boden's characterizations of the noblewomen they encountered. He waited with sympathy while his friend drew a deep breath and calmed himself.

Boden looked Jaxzon in the eye. "No offense, but they only want to be with you because you're the prince. You finally encounter a woman who doesn't understand who, or what you are, so you're bound to read more into it than there is."

"She was different from any of the women I've met. She's so compassionate and kind."

"That's because the women you meet only want one thing from you. Your title."

They squared off, spinning their staffs in figure-eights.

Frowning at the possibility, Jaxzon swung at Boden's chest. "Are you saying because of a lack of comparison I fell for the first woman who didn't want something from me? Am I so easily deluded?"

Boden sidestepped and chuckled. "I wouldn't put it that way, but yes. I believe that to be the case." He jabbed forward then feinted right, Jaxzon's staff caught Boden's, driving it downward where it slammed into Jaxzon's shin, nearly knocking him off his feet.

He hopped on one foot, rubbing his injured leg.

His friend grinned. "I bet if I'd spent a couple hours with a kind, beautiful woman who took me racing, I'd probably fall for her too, and you know how I feel about women in general."

Jaxzon nodded. "I remember."

Boden felt women either snubbed him or used him, and after a terrible relationship with one in particular, he'd become suspicious and embittered toward them all. "She's a nice dream, Jaxzon, nothing more. That's all she can be."

"You're right." Jaxzon understood the meaning behind his friend's words.

He could never act upon his feelings for Guin and needed to concentrate on what mattered. He thrust further thoughts of her aside then lunged forward. His staff came down in a chopping motion at Boden's head, who dropped and rolled.

Within a split second, Jaxzon changed course and stabbed his staff into the mat, a hair's breadth from Boden's throat.

He froze. Jaxzon grinned then pulled him to his feet.

JAXZON SPENT the rest of his day in meetings. Unable to focus, he asked several times for questions to be repeated. During a lengthy consultation with the Vekdromic committee, the king ended the meeting, sending everyone except Jaxzon from the room.

His father took a seat opposite Jaxzon at the conference table. "What is it, son? What is occupying your mind?"

A wedding portrait of his parents, in which neither wore a smile, hung behind the king. The queen's eyes held a sadness that Jaxzon was now beginning to understand. "The same thing that has been occupying my mind for weeks, Father."

King Jaezain frowned. "Jaxzon, you must understand, if I had any other choice—"

"But you had a choice. You didn't have to step down; you could have stayed long enough for—"

"For what?" Jaezain's blue eyes flashed. "You are twenty-six years old and my sole heir. You have never shown interest in the noblewomen of our realm. Therefore, I am forced to make this decision for you. I cannot leave the kingdom without an heir."

"Our kingdom would not be left without an heir. Eventually I would have met someone, someone special, someone I might fall in love with, as normal people do."

"You are not a normal person. You are the crown prince of Druthenia. The Council will choose a suitable partner for you who is politically beneficial to our realm. One who will add strength in times of trouble and possibly solve the problems we currently face."

"A marriage won't solve any of our current problems, it will only make them less complicated." A clamp tightened on his chest. His father leaned toward strengthening the alliance with the King of Mikonia, a trusted ally, but whose son, Prince Kapre was a vapid womanizer, and his daughter, Princess Vertuma a devious shrew.

Jaezain studied him. "Kings don't live forever, Jaxzon. Their children ascend. If certain children come to power without checks and balances, our realm could be left in a precarious position. It is your duty to do what's right for your people. A king's duty to his people always comes before his personal desires. For centuries our predecessors married for the good of their citizenry, as did I, and so shall you. You are an honorable man, Jaxzon, and you'll do your duty."

Jaxzon flinched internally. His father counted on his being the dutiful son, the honorable Prince. His father's decision seemed so arbitrary. He was still young. He could rule another twenty years before handing Jaxzon the reign. Instead, he chose to force Jaxzon into a loveless marriage.

Jaezain's voice remained stern. "We've been over this. There is nothing either of us can do now. The Council has met. The presentations will be made at the Grande Masque. I am sorry, this is my final word, and I do not wish to speak of this again. You must do your duty."

"Yes, Sire."

After meeting with his father, Jaxzon wandered alone in the palace gardens. The fact that he would need to someday marry and produce an heir had seemed in the remote future. He'd always assumed he would have more time, and now he had none. In a few short months, he would have a wife and the responsibility of the thirty-three planets within their galaxy. Beneath the frowning statue of a long dead ancestor, he reflected on the women he'd become acquainted with and how they compared to Guin.

He wasn't foolish; women wanted to be with him because of his position. Though when Boden put a voice to this fact, he'd hit a nerve. Jaxzon had never met a woman who wasn't aware of his position. He couldn't recall a time when a woman hadn't treated him as the Prince, or worse, as a prize to be fought over and won. Didn't his father recall how emasculating being put on display could be? Jaxzon didn't agree with Boden's description of the noblewomen in the realm, although he couldn't imagine himself with any of the ones he'd met thus far.

But he could imagine himself with Guin. He closed his eyes, and she was there—her piercing green eyes, her sweet smile, and the warm touch of her hand. What sort of queen would she make? She had no diplomatic knowledge. She had no idea where he came from, and she isn't here. Boden was right, Jaxzon had been reacting to her kindness.

Marriage for an alliance would be best for his people. With the right woman he could do remarkable things for the kingdom. Their legacy could be greater than any that had come before and if the

Council and nobility choose wisely, his people might prosper in peace. There would be nothing he couldn't do.

He resolved to honor their choice, with whomever they chose to rule at his side, no matter his own misgivings. He headed to the palace, to his office, to his duty.

THE MORNING of the Masque found Jaxzon in his daily sparring session with Boden, who seemed in a particularly sour mood.

Dueling with low power *kiphos*, Jaxzon won every round, leaving Boden bruised and battered.

"Viyet!" He swore when the laser-blade caught him on his left shoulder for the third time. "Are you trying to take my arm off in the most painful way possible?" He grimaced and worked his shoulder.

Jaxzon grinned. "Where's your mind today? You should pay more attention."

The bright yellow blade disappeared as Boden switched off the device. He put the silver grip on a shelf and took his towel, slinging it over his bare shoulder. "At least your head is back where it should be."

"So, what's bothering thee, oh friend of mine?" Jaxzon draped his towel around his neck and held the ends.

"You know what's bothering me. I hate these affairs. I don't understand why you make me go. Do you relish my suffering?"

"Sometimes." Jaxzon laughed when his friend's scowl grew darker. "I count on you for distractions when I'm in a tight spot. You always know when to bail me out." His smile faded. "But seriously, I need my friend tonight. For moral support. Please?"

Boden sighed. "We're in for a long night, aren't we?"

"I'm afraid so."

Later, wearing one of his milder scowls, Boden sat across from Jaxzon as they ate their midday meal of broiled fish and sautéed vegetables.

"What's wrong? Tea cold?" asked Jaxzon.

The frown deepened, and Boden shook his head. He set his cup on the table and leaned forward. "Did you see what I have to wear?"

Jaxzon grinned.

Boden swore under his breath. "You're a cruel man. I hate this stuff, and yet you pick the stiffest, gaudiest, most awful outfit, and force me to wear it. For a prince, you can be a real nothus."

"You shouldn't say such things about my mother. Come on, the costume's not so bad. I'm wearing one and so is Derek. They're old military uniforms. What else would you wear to a masque?"

"I wouldn't wear anything to a masque, because I wouldn't go to a masque. And, if I'd been forced to go to one, I would wear my regular clothes, or one of those awful suits you make me wear to your other events."

"It's only one night, Boden. You get to wear a sword."

"Really? Hey, if I get to wear a sword, I'm in. That makes all the difference in the world."

Jaxzon chuckled and finished his meal, told Boden he had better see him at the Masque before going their separate ways.

CHAPTER NINE

Derek's usual morning knock woke Guin on the day of the Masque. "Wake up, sleepy girl. Today's the big day. We're picking up your costume." He carried a food-laden tray into Guin's room. "I brought you breakfast, but you can't eat it in bed. Get dressed and meet me downstairs."

"Are you coming with us?"

"Of course. I'm not leaving you alone with Delori. This way, if she's annoyed with me, she won't be too hard on you. Besides, I have to get my costume too. Jaxzon had it specially made."

"Ah. Thanks Derek." Guin dressed, munching toast and downing the glass of juice. The eggs and some greenish mushy stuff she left uneaten then met Derek in the manor's entryway.

He set the tray on a side table. "Put on your glasses."

A sleek black hover idled in the driveway. Guin's glasses adjusted to the light as the double suns rose over a purple vineyard in the distance. A heady gardenia-like fragrance filled the air.

The hover's window lowered, and Delori shot her arm out. She pointed at Guin and Derek, then at the hover.

"Our marching orders," he said under his breath.

The hover dipped and bounced as she and Derek took their seats. Plush, comfortable seats circled the vehicle's lush interior. Outside, the countryside glided past. Bluish tinted grass and orange-barked trees with bright violet leaves flew by. Besides the unusual colors, the landscape appeared to be typical rolling hillsides.

Guin marveled at the similarity to Earth until they passed what appeared to be a herd of short, furry, copper-colored, rhino-like creatures. "What are those?"

He followed her finger. "Toxiden. They're an ancient animal, been around for millions of years. They roam freely across our county."

"Enough zoology lessons for the day," Delori snapped, tearing Guin's attention from the scenery. "First, you're getting a new wardrobe. I've called ahead. Two of the finest clothing boutiques are standing by with their latest designs in your size. We will then obtain suitable footwear and attend your costume fitting. The Masque begins at dusk, and you must be there prior to the arrival of the king and prince. Once they enter, you and the other ladies will progress through a receiving line where you will be presented to Council members, nobility, and royalty."

She aimed a finger at Guin. "You will greet each by his or her title, meet their eyes and shake their hand. You wish to be their queen. You mustn't lose their respect before you gain it. Always remember to show strength and courage."

"Is that how I'll win your respect?"

"Who said you can?" Delori's dark eyes glinted in her stony face. "You have a long way to go toward earning my respect."

Guin held Delori's icy gaze.

Derek cleared his throat. "Sorry to break up the staring contest, but we're here."

Over the next several hours, Guin endured Delori's scathing criticism as she tried on dresses, slacks, skirts, blouses, shirts, and countless hats, earrings, belts, and accessories.

Guin protested to much of the clothing, telling Delori she didn't feel comfortable with her spending so much money. Delori would have none of it. She told Guin, "It would be scandalous for you to wear the same outfit to two different events. You will not dishonor the Vau'uan name through a bad sense of fashion."

Her stony glare halted Guin's laughter at such an absurd notion.

She tried on everything thrown at her and endured Delori's criticisms; Guin's eyes were too green for this outfit, her hair too dark for another. She was too thin, hips too wide, toes too long. The list went on, and she was left puzzled as to how her breasts could be both too large and too small in a single blouse.

She objected to the over-the-top, ruffly, puffy-sleeved monstrosities the attendant insisted were the latest fashion. To Guin's surprise Delori agreed, and they settled on more conservative styles with minimal ruffle and puff.

By the time they arrived for Guin's costume fitting, the hover overflowed with bags, boxes, and wrapped packages.

The costume shop appeared empty when they arrived. Most of the shelves and racks were barren. The proprietor, a short, stout woman, introduced herself as Petula and went to retrieve Guin's gown.

Her breath caught at the sight of her costume. The white fabric shimmered with a million tiny points of silver light, contrasting beautifully with the gold brocade bordering the neckline and hem. A golden twist of braided fabric wrapped around her waist and crossed at the back, then joined below her breasts. The upper part of the gown was in the fashion of a toga. A golden eagle's-head pin held the extra fabric on her left shoulder. Side-slits ran to her hips, while the right shoulder and upper chest were left bare. "Is this appropriate for the occasion?"

Derek let out a low whistle. "You're going to be the talk of the Masque. Every eye will be on you."

"Thank you, Derek."

"For once my brother is correct, and yes, this costume is quite suitable for the occasion. You are covered appropriately and what's left bare is acceptable." Delori arched an eyebrow at the attendant. "Shoes?"

Petula brought Guin a pair of golden high heels with laces criss-crossing from the ankles to the knees.

After the fitting, Guin changed into her jeans, and they left the costume shop with another pair of boxes to stuff into the hover. They climbed in and the hover glided down the street and around the corner to the hair salon.

The stylist, a Bethan named Themeron, was a lovely shade of aquamarine. He took Guin's hands and peered into her eyes. "This is a first. I've never seen anyone with this combination of hair and eye color. You're rarer than a *delporium*."

"What's a *delporium*?" Guin asked, still fascinated by the difference between the movements people's lips made and the words she heard.

He unwound her braid. "It's a mythological creature that doesn't exist. Sorry, bad joke."

"Oh, like a unicorn."

"What's a unicorn?"

"A horse with a horn in the middle of its forehead. They're supposed to be magical."

"What's a horse?"

Derek interrupted, "Guin, there aren't horses here, but there are unicorns."

Guin's eyes widened. "Seriously?"

He grinned. "Got ya." The two men burst into laughter.

"Are we done here?" cut in Delori. "We need you back at the manor and ready before it gets too late."

Themeron and Derek hid their smiles. The hairdresser went back to work, washing, drying, and styling Guin's hair.

"Finished." He spun her chair to face the mirror.

"Wow." Two French braids came together above her right shoulder. The unbraided ends flowed over her chest and back in dark auburn ringlets.

Delori handed him the golden circlet, which he fastened around her forehead. Using a comb, he plucked wisps of hair from her braids, framing her face in gentle curls.

"Perfect." He leaned back, admiring his work.

Derek grinned. "You'll be the most beautiful goddess in the universe."

Delori scrutinized the hairdo. "It'll do. Let's go."

Guin hugged Themeron. "You're fantastic. I want you to do my hair from now on."

"You come back anytime. We'll talk more about unicorns and delporiums."

GUIN FINISHED APPLYING lipstick when a tap came on her door. "Come in, Derek."

Derek entered wearing a green military uniform with silver, tasseled epaulets on the shoulders. Silver braiding crossed the white breast of his jacket and broad lampasses adorned the sides of his matching slacks. He wore a sword at his side and a worried expression on his face. "Please tell me you can dance." His gaze caught Guin's in the mirror. "Wow!"

"Thank you. You're pretty dashing yourself." She straightened his collar. "Now, what's this about dancing?"

"It *is* a ball after all, and there will be dancing. Delori asked me yesterday if you can dance. I forgot to ask, and if you can't, she's going to kill me."

"My father taught me to waltz and tango." Guin grinned. "And I can do a pretty mean worm."

He frowned. "I'm not sure I've heard of those, but I can teach you a couple of steps before we leave." He gripped her right hand and put the other on her waist. She laid hers on his shoulder. "This is a three count, one two three, one two three."

She squinted. "That sounds like a waltz."

"Oh. All right, let's try."

They waltzed around her bedroom, Guin following Derek's lead without fault.

"You have some skills." He lifted his left arm, guiding her into a graceful spin. "This is a common dance called an *ihli*."

"Any other moves I need to learn?"

"Maybe you should stick to what you know. When you're asked to dance, make sure they are playing an ihli before you accept. I'll teach you some others after tonight."

"Thanks, Derek."

His telecon buzzed. "Delori. Time to go."

A steel fist gripped Guin's stomach. "I'm gonna be sick."

"You've got this. You look amazing. Jaxzon already likes you, and you have Delori and me behind you. I won't leave your side, I promise."

Panic rose to the back of Guin's throat. *What am I doing here?* "I feel like an imposter. I know almost nothing about your world or your politics. How can I compete with women who have lived here their whole lives? What if they ask me what I think about the economy or how I would rule the galaxy?"

He put a hand over hers. "Tonight, isn't about politics. It's a social gathering, a get-to-know-you function. Didn't Delori go over how our government works at least once in the last three days?"

"Ad nauseam. But what if I forget, Derek? What if they ask me something she didn't go over?"

"Then smile your beautiful smile and change the subject."

She took a deep breath and pulled herself together. "You're a big help."

He grinned. "You ready?"

She mustered a smile, and with one last glance in the mirror she trailed him from the room.

Dressed in a light pink jacket and skirt, a frowning Delori waited in the front entryway, tapping her foot. In the hover, she lectured, "Journalists will be outside to broadcast the arrivals. They will be watching you closely because you're the unknown. If they ask you questions, simply smile and continue walking. Do not give interviews. *I'll* deal with them. Do you understand?"

"Yes, Delori, I understand. Smile and keep walking. Got it."

Delori's hard gaze lit on Derek. "Do you 'got it?'"

He grinned and imitated Guin's tone. "Yes, Delori. I understand. Smile and keep walking."

Delori sighed. "Please don't humiliate me tonight—either of you."

He winked at Guin.

They rode in silence until he pointed. "There. The palace."

Encapsulated in a dome, sat one of the largest buildings she'd ever seen.

Sprawling across her vision and practically disappearing in either direction, the palace appeared to be made from stone and wood, much like photographs of ancient Scottish castles. Battlements rose into the sky, there were parapets, a gatehouse...*and is there a drawbridge over a moat?* "Is the palace a hologram too?"

Derek shook his head. "No, that's the real deal. Gemston Palace is thousands of years old."

Their vehicle passed through the double doors of an airlock and fell in line behind a lengthy procession of sleek, black hovers. The road crossed the bridge and continued through a set of tall gates and curved into a horseshoe driveway, bending around the massive courtyard.

Men and women made their way to the entrance. Some women wore beautiful gowns of elegant design, others dressed in outlandish costumes with feathers and headdresses reminiscent of those worn by Las Vegas showgirls.

Their hover drew closer to the entryway, and Guin's butterflies morphed into killer bees, battering her insides. She drew a deep, steadying breath. When they were two hovers from the front, Derek tapped her shoulder and handed her the white and gold satin mask. *At least I have something to hide behind.*

Exiting the hover, Delori took the lead as Guin and Derek proceeded to the palace steps.

CHAPTER TEN

On either side of a roped-off walkway, cameras floated. Press members waved microphones at the arrivals. Reporters called to Derek, asking for Guin's name, requesting they turn every which way for a better shot. They threw questions at Delori and asked her if the Vau'uans were presenting Guin as a suitor. Delori chatted with the media while Derek escorted Guin to the top of the stairs and into Gemston.

Her heart rose in her throat as he escorted her through the oaken, iron-bound doors. Two magnificent, red-carpeted staircases curved to the left and right, leading into the heights of the massive hall. Dark green marble covered the floors, and two enormous chandeliers of sparkling crystal filled the ceiling above, spilling light among the mass of people below as they ascended a set of marble steps on the opposite end of the hall.

The scent of mingling perfumes, combined with a strong odor of cooking spices assaulted her nostrils, lending further queasiness to her already knotted abdomen.

Delori smoothed a brown curl from her forehead. "That went

well. I told them your name, and that you are representing our house. They're calling you the *Arcanum*."

"What's an Arcanum?"

"It means you're a secret, a mystery," said Derek.

"Yes, excellent publicity. The less they know, the more they talk. Give this to the herald." Delori handed him a card. "This has your names and how you are to be announced."

Guin and Derek fell in line and soon arrived at the top of the stairs leading into the ballroom below. She put a hand to her throat, her pulse hammered against her fingertips.

Thrown by twelve massive chandeliers, rainbow prisms of light danced amongst the hundreds of attendees gathered below. At the furthest end of the ballroom, an immense dance floor sprawled before a gallery holding a full orchestra. Along the outer wall, stained-glassed doors opened to a dimly lit courtyard.

He handed the card to the herald, who announced, "Lord Derek of House Vau'uan presents Lady Guinevere Griffin."

She and Derek became the center of attention when they descended into the ballroom. Guin's cheeks burned, making her grateful for the mask. Her stomach twisted, and her grip on him tightened as she fought to maintain her composure.

He squeezed her arm. "They're jealous because you're the most beautiful woman in the room."

"How can you tell? We're all wearing masks."

"Because I've dated most of them."

"Oh, Derek." She giggled and the knot in her midsection loosened.

Delori waited near a grouping of tables. "I talked with the coordinator. There are fifty-three suitors. You will be presented by order of title, and since you have none, you will be last."

"Fifty-three? I guess that makes me the wild card."

Delori and Derek appeared puzzled.

"The Joker?" Guin asked, receiving blank stares. "No? Never mind. Is last good or bad?"

"Neither, although you may have an extra moment with the prince," said Delori.

Guin's pulse quickened.

Costumed guests milled about, eating and drinking. Dozens of servers wove throughout, carrying trays of drinks and taking orders. Tables set for dining stood grouped nearby, and more, bearing food, lined the wall.

I feel like Cinderella. Have to remember not to lose a shoe. An abrupt snort of nervous laughter tore from her throat.

Delori raised an eyebrow. Derek grinned.

Guin said, "Sorry. This reminds me a fairy tale or some strange reality show."

He chuckled.

Delori breathed a long, exasperated sigh. "They will announce nobility and Council members shortly. Pay close attention. These are the people who will be in the receiving line. Try to remember where they're from and the correct way to address each."

The last few suiters announced to the room descended the stairs. A mask-less, petite woman with large brown eyes and full lips painted a bright red entered. What drew Guin's attention was not the woman's beauty, but the billowing, feathery headdress she wore. The monstrosity almost doubled her height.

The woman shuffled from one stair to the next, her mermaid-style skirt making a full stride impossible. The light salmon color of the costume contrasted beautifully with her dark brown skin. The woman stumbled on the last step and her headdress tilted to one side.

Guin gasped.

At the last moment, she caught her balance and joined an older woman at the bottom of the stairs. The two talked in hushed whispers, the younger, animatedly gesturing to her unsteady headgear.

"What is that costume? I noticed a few women wearing those."

Derek followed Guin's gaze. "Headdresses worn on Xaitera in the olden days. Though a bit absurd, they are a time-honored tradition."

In the dining hall Jaxzon greeted Council members and nobility, shaking hands and making small talk, astounded that the people gathered there would make one of the most important decisions of his life. *How many have entered into loveless marriages for the sake of politics?* Would they truly impose the same on him? Would these Council members cause him to suffer for their own political gain?

He made a point of recalling something personal about each person he spoke with. High Councilwoman Yuly Angstroth had recently become a grandmother for the first time and appeared thrilled when the prince remembered. Jaxzon congratulated Jenk Milton on his son's appointment to the high court of Mikonia. The man puffed with pride.

Prince Kapre of Mikonia, wearing a costume much like Jaxzon's, though in his planet's black and gold, intercepted him. He wore his shoulder-length blond hair slicked back and his usual smirk. He dipped his head. "Your Highness."

Jaxzon returned the nod. "Your Highness."

Kapre winked then lowered his voice. "I suppose you and I will be brothers-in-law soon. Keep an eye on that bhanthu." He slapped Jaxzon's shoulder and strode away.

He frowned after Kapre. *What does he know that I don't?*

The room emptied as Council members and nobility were heralded into the ballroom. Jaxzon would be last, after his father. He attempted to convince himself that tonight's Grande Masque would be the same as any other. Except, he'd be meeting his future bride and mother of his children. Wincing at the prospect, he forced the notion from his mind and waited at the top of the stairs.

Boden, dressed in his red uniform, arrived late as usual, and sidled up to the bar. He glared with his patented scowl. Jaxzon's lips twitched when Boden tugged at the uniform's stiff collar.

Derek had a beautiful woman at his side. *Predictable Derek.*

To the left, purple-and-gold bhanthu feathers shimmered.

Kapre's sister, Princess Vertuma stood straight-backed amidst a gaggle of curtsying women. Jaxzon tightened his jaw and clenched his fists. *This is definitely going to be a long night.*

"Pay attention," commanded Delori when the herald announced the first Council member, Darian Beltar, to the room. "The five high Council members wear silver kaftans with a black pattern. These wearing plain silver are lower members. Each has one vote though the high members carry considerable sway over the lower."

Guin lost track of who was who after the fifteenth person. Delori continued giving advice or tips on the greeting of each.

The herald announced, "His Majesty, King Nov'Xam Syndow of Mikonia." Then, "Crown Prince Kapre of Mikonia."

Delori leaned toward Guin. "King Nov'Xam's daughter, Princess Vertuma, is a suitor. She's the favorite. Mikonia has wanted an intermarriage with Arwon for decades."

"Vertuma is a snake," said Derek in a low voice. "Watch your back with her. I'll point her out when I see her."

Guin jumped at the sound of blaring trumpets.

"His Majesty, King Jaezain Alruwei, ruler of Druthenia."

Derek drew her into a curtsy as he bowed.

The king descended. Except for their height, Jaxzon bore no resemblance to his father. The king's dark brown hair had signs of silver at the temples. His square jaw, straight nose, and thin lips were more like Boden's. He took his place at the farthest end of the line of royalty, nobles, and Council members as they looped around the dance floor.

The herald declared, "His Royal Highness, Crown Prince Jaxzon Alruwei of Druthenia."

Wearing a tight smile and a purple and gold form-fitting uniform, Jaxzon passed by. The erratic beating of her heart filled her ears. Heat flooded her face.

He took his place beside his father at the receiving line's end, and with the prince in line, the procession commenced.

A tall woman came forward, and a line formed behind her. She wore a form fitting, gold-and-purple feathered gown, the neckline plunging to her navel. Feathers adorned a French knot holding her ash-blonde hair back from a heart-shaped face. She wore a matching feathered mask. Derek nudged Guin. "That's Princess Vertuma. Her brother, Prince Kapre, once pursued Princess Jalain. They would greatly benefit from a royal intermarriage between Mikonia and Druthenia."

"What's Druthenia? I thought King Jaezain is the ruler of Arwon."

"He is." Delori grimaced, apparently annoyed with herself for forgetting to tell Guin this factoid. "The realm of Druthenia encompasses many other planets within our system and beyond, and is the largest realm in the galaxy. Although we are peaceful with smaller kingdoms, there are tensions over certain territories and mineral rights. King Nov'Xam is a great ally, though he is under pressure from some to expand his realm's holdings. Vertuma is your biggest competition and your toughest opponent. Be careful with her. She is not known for playing fair."

An hour went by before Guin proceeded through the line behind the petite, headdress-bedecked woman, who by some miracle maintained her balance while moving from one person to the next. The other ladies flowed through the line, getting farther ahead of the headdress and Guin.

Most of the Council members gave Guin's hand a brief shake then headed in the direction of food. Some complimented her costume or asked where she was from. She avoided the question by stating the Vau'uans had sponsored her.

King Nov'Xam took Guin's hands in his. His receding gray hair pulled back from a prominent widow's peak. An impeccably groomed mustache and beard surrounded an affable smile. He raised bushy black eyebrows. "You look lovely, my dear. How are Delori and Derek?"

"Thank you, Your Majesty. They are both well."

Prince Kapre stood beside his father, his ice-blue stare crawling over Guin's body. He introduced himself. She dipped her head in greeting.

His gaze followed as she introduced herself to the queen of Anciex beside him.

Only King Jaezain separated her from Jaxzon. Guin's heart skittered and thumped in her chest as she addressed the king and introduced herself. The king's eyes, much like Jaxzon's, were kind and mesmerizing, though a shade lighter.

He took her hand and smiled. "If there were a contest for best costume, you would be the winner."

Guin bowed her head. "Thank you, Your Majesty."

Jaezain faced his son. "Jaxzon, remind me to have a best-dressed competition at next year's Grande Masque."

Jaxzon appeared focused on the woman in the headdress as she wobbled away. "Yes, Father."

King Jaezain sighed then escorted the queen of Anciex to the head table.

Guin took a deep breath then bowed. She lowered her voice, imitating Derek's accent. "Your Royal Highness, I'm here representing house Vau'uan."

"I'm sorry, I missed your name. Have we met before?"

Keeping her head bent, Guin asked, "Have you forgotten me so soon?"

Jaxzon leaned forward. She ducked her head. "My lady, you have me at a disadvantage. Are you one of Derek's lady friends?"

She laughed and met his eyes. "One of *Derek's* lady friends?"

He'd been squinting at her, a puzzled expression on his face. His eyes widened. "Guin?"

"Yes." Her heart tripped over itself, her face burned.

"How? Derek?" He gripped her hands. "When did you arrive? How did you get here? Wait, why are you here?"

"I'm here for you."

The surrounding room had grown quiet, and he glanced around. The heads of those in the immediate vicinity had swiveled in their direction.

His expression went blank. The excitement left his eyes. He released her hands with a curt nod. "I must be fair with each of the ladies. I will find you later, we will talk then." Without a backward glance, he joined the king at the head table.

Guin's heart plummeted. This wasn't the reaction she'd hoped for. She headed to where she'd last seen Derek, ignoring the lingering stares trailing her across the room, and fighting the panic rising like a tidal wave in her chest.

CHAPTER ELEVEN

Guin found Derek conversing with a woman in a glimmering butterfly costume. He excused himself and took Guin's arm. "What did you say? What did he say? Was he surprised?"

She dusted glitter from his epaulet. "Yes, he was most certainly surprised. He said he would find me later and we'd talk."

"Excellent!" He shot his fist into the air and rotated it like a cowboy swinging a lasso.

She frowned at the gesture. "I'm not sure how excellent it is. You led me to believe he'd be much happier to see me than he was. We may have made a huge mistake."

"We're in a crowded room full of women vying for his attention. Jaxzon isn't the type to break out cheering under these circumstances. I'm sure he's happy you're here."

"I hope you're right, Derek." She took a deep, steadying breath.

The feathered headdress bobbed unsteadily toward Guin. Its wearer broke through a small knot of people. Her unwieldy headwear lurched forward, carrying the woman with it. She stumbled. Trying to regain her balance she careened to the left. The crowd of people surged back as the monstrosity bore down on them. Overcorrecting once more, the woman staggered to the right, forcing the people on that side to scurry out of her way.

Guin winced when the ridiculous high heels wobbled and the woman tripped, sending her plunging headlong to the floor. She sprawled face down, the headdress pinning her to the floor.

Guin hurried forward as a petite older woman attempted to lift the flailing lady.

Some who witnessed the tumble stared in shock, others covered their mouths to hide their laughter. A few roared at the sight of the floundering women. A hook-like fastener for the headdress had become entangled in the back of the costume's top. When the older woman attempted to remove the headwear, the younger woman screamed in pain. An argument ensued, devolving into a slap fight.

Guin knelt to unhook the fastener. The headdress fell to one side. She helped the woman to her feet.

Brushing her flattened hair from her face and straightening her clothes, she seethed, her chest rising and falling, her teeth clenched. "Mother. Get. Away. From me." She acknowledged Guin with a dip of her head. "Thank you." She limped away, disappearing through one of the arched doorways behind the serving tables.

The mother attempted to lift the offending headgear. Derek and two other gentlemen helped her hoist it and, tottering under the weight, she followed her daughter from the room.

Guin turned to Derek, horrified. Laughter showed in his eyes.

"Don't you dare laugh at her. Who was she?"

"Lady Breandor Zestari of Xaitera and her mother, Dame Eltes Zestari." He chuckled under his breath.

"You're terrible. I feel awful. I have to check on her." Tracking the sound of voices through the hallway she came to the open door of a powder room.

Breandor sat perched upon a poufy, pea-green seat in front of a mirrored wall, pick-combing her tight, bleached-white curls back to their natural state.

Her mother glared at her. "It's our tradition. Everyone wears them to the Royal Masque."

Breandor's eyes met Guin's. She shot her mother a sharp glance then extended her hand to Guin. "I don't believe we've been properly introduced. I'm Breandor Zestari, and this is my mother, Eltes. Mother, this is Guinevere Griffin of house Vau'uan."

"You know my name?"

"I was there when you introduced yourself fifty times tonight."

"Of course. Pleased to meet you, but call me Guin. I'm sorry we had to meet that way." She cast a glance at the headdress lying across two seats. "Are you okay?"

Breandor pressed her lips together. Their gaze connected through the mirror. They burst into laughter.

"I'm so, so sorry." Guin struggled to suppress her laughter, but spying the headdress, she broke into fresh giggles.

Breandor collapsed onto the seat, holding her stomach.

"I don't understand what's gotten into you." Eltes crossed her arms, her foot tapping the tiled floor. "You think it's humorous to make a spectacle of yourself in front of the prince?"

Guin tried to maintain her composure and sank into a chair, clutching her aching sides.

Eltes glared at both women. "Since you no longer require my assistance, I'm going back to the ball."

After a few tries and failures, they were able to get themselves under control. Guin checked her makeup.

Breandor straightened her skirt. "That felt wonderful. I haven't laughed like that in a while."

"Me neither. I have a pain in my side." Guin held her rib cage. "Breandor, I'm so sorry for laughing, but the whole thing was so..."

"Absurd! And please, call me Bree. Only my parents call me Breandor. I sure wish I could have worn a costume like yours. Everyone is talking about you."

"They are?"

"Oh yes. Some are crazy jealous, and everyone is wondering

where you came from. We've never heard of you. How did you meet Prince Jaxzon?"

Guin's heart dropped as she recalled Jaxzon's response. Tears threatened. She plucked a tissue from the dispenser, making a show of fixing her makeup to avoid answering. Her grandmother's voice sounded in her head, "*True Griffin's don't cry*". She swallowed against the lump rising in her throat.

"Are you okay?" Bree leaned forward. "Did I say something wrong?"

Guin shook her head and took a shaky breath, forcing back the forbidden emotion. "Can you keep a secret?"

Bree leaned in closer. "Absolutely."

"I'm from Earth."

Bree drew back, a small gasp escaping her lips. "Really?"

"Yes. I came here a few days ago."

"Wow, and the Vau'uans sponsored you?"

"Yes, but please, don't tell anyone. I'm beginning to wonder if I've made a terrible mistake in coming. I'm not sure what I was thinking."

"I won't say anything to anyone, especially my mother. Telling her would be like writing it in the sky." Bree rolled her eyes. "Super gossipy."

"Thanks, Bree. I appreciate it." Guin blew her nose.

"A lot of the women are only here because of the king's decree. More than half will drop out after tonight. Everyone knows who the next queen's going to be."

"Vertuma?"

"She's the politically correct choice." Bree placed her hand over Guin's. "But since we're here, we can't let a party go to waste, and I could really use a drink." She offered her arm. "Shall we?"

Hiding her red-rimmed eyes behind her mask, Guin took Bree's arm. They rejoined the ball to find Delori barking at Derek.

He pointed. "She's right here, Delori. I didn't lose her."

Delori spun around. "Hello Breandor. I see you've met Guinevere. Is your mother here?"

"Hello, Delori. She's around somewhere. I'm sure she'll be happy to see you."

"I need to speak to Guin alone first, please." Delori took Guin aside. "You missed the prince's announcement. The royal Vekdromic has begun. Get out there and mingle with the nobles and Council members. Dance with the men, chat with the women and wives. Make a good impression, be charming if you can manage it."

Exasperated with Delori's demeaning tone, and not in the mood, Guin rubbed her thumb against the side of her nose and gave a loud sniff, using her best over-the-top Brooklynite accent. "Yeah, I can do dat. You want I should kiss some hands and shake some babies too?"

Delori's eyes widened. "What? No!"

Guin pressed her lips together. The events of the evening had left her lightheaded with a strange giddiness. She laughed at the sour expression on Delori's face. "I'm sorry. Delori, I can't help myself. When I get nervous, I make jokes."

Delori glared.

"I'll introduce her around." Bree winked at Delori.

Guin allowed Bree to lead her away. "Where are we going?"

"You need a drink." She waved a server over. "What'll you have?"

"Whiskey, neat."

Bree and the server frowned at her.

"Or, whatever you're having. I guess whiskey doesn't translate."

Bree ordered two *ruvins*.

"What's in a ruvin?"

"What's in a whiskey?"

Guin frowned. "Good point."

An ihli played. Jaxzon escorted Vertuma to the dance floor.

Other couples soon followed.

A light touch on her elbow had Guin turning to find Derek. "May I have this dance?"

He led her in an ihli. Jaxzon and Vertuma passed by. He smiled when his eye caught Guin's. When the song ended she headed back to where Bree waited, holding two glasses, but was intercepted by an older gentleman who asked Guin to dance.

She danced two ihlis with different partners before reaching Bree, who handed her a half-empty glass. "Sorry, watching people enjoy themselves is thirsty work. Don't worry, I have two more on order."

Guin sniffed the drink. The dark red liquid had a mild aroma she couldn't place. She took a tentative sip, then downed the rest in one thirsty gulp.

"Sweet," she said, appreciating the burn at the back of her throat and the smokey flavor on her tongue. "It tastes like a decent whiskey."

Bree gasped. "Where did you learn to drink like that? Ruvin is more of a sipping drink. You just knocked back what would have taken me a whole ihli to finish. I fully expect you to fall over at any moment."

"Oh? I don't feel anything." Except for a slight tingle in her toes as the liquid warmed her insides. "Why aren't you dancing?"

"I guess after my earlier performance, word got around." She glanced sideways at Guin. "They're probably afraid I'll fall flat on my face."

Guin suppressed a laugh. Derek was engaged in conversation with a small group of costumed women. She caught his eye and inclined her head toward Bree. He joined them and when the orchestra played a new song, he asked her for the honor.

CHAPTER TWELVE

Bree and Derek glided across the floor. Guin waited for her next ruvin. Someone touched her elbow. Prince Kapre took her hand. "May I have this dance?"

"No, thank you. I'm not familiar with the steps."

Ignoring her protests, Kapre set her empty glass on a nearby table, then led her to the floor. He put his arm firmly around her waist and guided her in an easy two step. "So, you're one of Derek's girls. May I ask where he found you?"

In an attempt to put daylight between them, Guin pushed against Kapre's shoulder. "Are you always this rude?"

"I apologize if I've offended you. Apparently, I'm under the wrong assumption."

"Apparently."

"Let's start over. What planet and province are you from?"

Guin pressed her palm against his chest until his arms straightened. "You can ask whatever you wish, but could you please let me breathe?"

"We're dancing, and dancing calls for close contact."

Jaxzon drifted by, a woman in a catsuit encircled in his arms. He flashed a smile. Guin's pulse galloped.

"How do you know Prince Jaxzon? You've never attended other royal functions. I would remember you." Kapre asked.

"We only recently met." She sighed and continued her futile efforts to put space between them. "I'm a friend of the Vau'uans. They were kind enough to sponsor me."

Kapre turned her in a circle as the song ended. "Until we meet again."

After extricating herself from his grip, she searched for Bree and another ruvin. Boden joined Bree and Derek at the bar. Guin smiled. Boden had been so amusing in New York, calling her 'Queen Griffin' and nearly falling when she'd pulled him from her car.

She sidled up beside him. "Hello, Boden."

"Hello." His brow wrinkled. "Have we met?"

"In New York, remember?" She lifted her mask then laughed as recognition crept over his features.

The light hazel in Boden's eyes darkened, their golden flecks turned green. "Griffin?" He grimaced then shifted his attention to Derek. "You brought Griffin here?"

"Good to see you too, Boden," she muttered.

"Why are you here?" He rounded on Derek. "Why is she here?"

Placing her hands on her hips Guin glared. "Are all the men from this part of the galaxy so rude? First, Jaxzon essentially snubs me, then I'm accosted by the eight-armed Octo-Prince from hell, now this?"

Boden scowled at Derek. "Does Jaxzon know she's here?"

"He does," Jaxzon answered, appearing from nowhere. "And he would like this dance. My lady?"

After a moment's hesitation, Guin took his arm. "Of course." Her heart raced as he ushered her to the floor.

He took her into his arms. "I'm sorry about my earlier behavior. I believe I was in a state of shock when I saw you."

"No, I'm sorry, I didn't mean to..."

Performing a tight turn, he pulled her to his chest. His lips brushed her ear. "I'm glad you're here." He spun her away before resuming a more traditional ihli stance.

Her heart pummeled her sternum. "Me too."

They danced their way to the back of the ballroom, circling the outer edge of the floor until he danced her through the open doors to the courtyard. They glided farther from the palace. The music grew distant.

He held her close, scanning her face with an intensity that took her breath away. "Are you real, or am I dreaming?"

"I think I'm the one dreaming."

A few couples strolled through the garden. "Follow me." Glancing around, he released her waist, tightened his grip on her hand and guided her further from the palace. He stopped in a moonlit area surrounded by tall pink hedges. Small benches lined the walkway.

Touching her mask he asked, "May I?" Guin smiled. He removed the mask, putting it into his jacket. He brushed a wisp of hair from her temple. His smile broadened as he peered into her upturned face.

Hushed voices penetrated the hedge. He sat on a bench, placing a finger to his lips as she sat beside him.

The voices faded. He grasped her hand. "When did you get here?"

"The day you left. Derek came back and persuaded me to come with him. He told them you'd sent for me, so they'd let me stay."

Jaxzon chuckled. "I'll have to find a way to repay Derek, unless I have him arrested first."

Guin took a deep breath to calm the thunderous beat of her heart.

Taking another glance around, his gaze returned to hers. "I swear I wanted to stay in New York. I wanted to find you. I'm not sure what I would have done. I hated watching you drive away. I couldn't stop thinking of you." His face brightened. "I can't believe you're here."

"I can't believe it either. I've never done anything like this. I wondered if I was crazy, coming all this way. Although now, being here with you..."

"I wish I'd brought you here myself. I wanted..." He drew closer, caressing her cheek. "This." His lips touched hers.

Time slowed. His hand released hers and encircled her waist. She melted in his arms, leaning into his body, abandoning herself to his lips, as soft as she'd imagined.

Jaxzon's fingers curled into the fabric of her gown, clenching into fists. His arms tightened around her waist. Guin ran her hands through his silky hair. Her lips parted. She tasted the heady flavor of wine lingering on his lips. She breathed in his scent, a musky masculinity that left her dizzy.

Voices drifted from nearby. He broke away, moving down the bench, putting a respectable distance between them. The voices receded. He drew an unsteady breath. "I wanted to do that the night we met."

She grazed his lips with hers. "Me too."

He smiled against her mouth. "I can't be running off with you during every ball."

"You can try."

"That's tempting." He glanced around again. "We can't stay here long." His fingers traced the curve of her jaw. "I don't know what the future holds." He rested his forehead against hers. "But I want you in mine."

His breath against her lips and his touch sent a hot flash of passion through her. "I want you in mine too. That's why I'm here." She tilted her head, touching her lips to his.

He held her close, deepening the kiss. Too soon, he drew away, heaving a sigh. "I shouldn't. I must abide by the law, and I have a duty to my people." He faced the palace.

"Do you want me to leave?"

"Want you to?" His azure eyes blazed into hers. "Never. Although maybe you should go, for your sake. If the decision were mine to make, I would beg you to stay. You must understand, I have no say whatsoever in who the Council chooses." He took her hand. "I don't want you hurt."

Guin squared her shoulders. "I'm stronger than I look. I can take care of myself. I came a long way to be here. If you genuinely believe I should go, I will."

"I truly do not wish you to leave, but you must understand what you're in for. The Council is very much a political machine."

A heaviness engulfed her heart. She swallowed against the lump forming in her throat. "Jaxzon, I knew what I was in for when I left New York. I understood the odds would be against me, and I might not measure up to these other women. I'm willing to take the risk, and if you ask me to stay, I will."

"I wanted you to stay the moment I laid eyes on you."

She leaned forward and kissed him.

Jaxzon returned the kiss. "We should get back before someone sends a search party."

Handing over her mask, he led her to the palace doors. She used her thumb to wipe a smudge of lipstick from his lower lip. Jaxzon took her in his arms. They danced through the doors as the song ended.

"My lady." His lips brushed her hand, his fingers lingering as they parted.

She sought Bree, Derek, and Delori.

Bree arched her brows. "Where did you two go?"

"That is between Lady Guinevere and Prince Jaxzon," said Delori.

Taking the glass from Bree, Guin asked, "Ruvin?"

"Yes."

She threw back the shot and took a deep breath. "Thanks." Guin tugged Derek's hand. "Dance with me."

She led a surprised Derek to the dance floor where she told him what happened.

"I knew it," Derek said. "You two are meant to be together."

"It seems so crazy. I've never felt this way about anyone before. I don't even know him, yet it's like a part of me needs to be with him. I know I sound corny, but I feel like we were meant for each other."

A grin spread across Derek's face. "Then we're going to make sure you two stay together."

The evening wore on. Guin danced with almost every man in attendance. When she took a break to rest her feet, King Nov'Xam approached her.

He bowed. "May I have the honor?"

She curtsied. "Of course, Your Majesty."

King Nov'Xam turned out to be the opposite of his son Kapre—courteous, kind, and full of small talk. He didn't pry after asking a few basic questions. When the song ended, he tilted his head. "You are a delight. I hope we are able to spend more time together during future events."

"Thank you. I look forward to seeing you again."

"You're being watched," Derek said when she rejoined him.

Vertuma, along with a group of women, stared at Guin.

She dipped her head to the ladies. "Why are they staring at me?" she asked through clenched teeth.

"I guess they're measuring the competition." He grinned and waved to the group.

Bree joined Derek and Guin. "The Bethan is Sarya Athtar. She and Vertuma are close. I'm surprised she's even here. She would never try to outdo Vertuma. The brunette in the cat suit is Nuala. The other two are Banya and Loli, two of Vertuma's minions."

Vertuma and Sarya broke away from the others, striding toward Guin.

Sarya was a lovely shade of cobalt. Her eyes gave the appearance of spun gold and contrasted dramatically with her skin tone. She had a full bottom lip and a small button nose and wore a silver fairy costume.

"Is this a new friend of yours?" Vertuma asked Derek.

"Princess Vertuma, may I present Lady Guinevere Griffin. Lady

Guin, this is Princess Vertuma Syndow of Mikonia and Lady Sarya Athtar of Bethion."

Guin dipped her head. "Your Highness, Lady Sarya."

"Griffin?" Vertuma's brow furrowed. Her lip curled as though encountering a foul odor. "Are you from a noble house?"

"A distant relative," he said. "Recently reunited."

"Oh? I've never had the time to become acquainted with the lower houses. How do you know the prince?"

"We've only recently met. Lord Vau'uan introduced us a few days ago." Guin craned her neck to meet Vertuma's ice-blue glare. The woman seemed at least ten inches taller than Guin's petite five-foot-three.

"I see." Vertuma raised an eyebrow. "Word is, you two are more than simply friends, and after only a few days?"

"What are you implying?"

"Me? Whatever do you mean?" Vertuma gave a dismissive flip of her hand. "People do talk. I'm sure there's nothing to the rumors."

"I'm sure." Guin kept her tone level. "Pleasure to meet you, Princess. Lord Vau'uan, you wanted this dance? Please excuse us, Your Highness."

Derek led her in a two-step. "Vertuma has a habit of slithering under people's skin. I'm glad you were able to keep your cool."

"I've had drunks in my backseat who were more insulting. I can handle her type. Kill them with kindness and don't let them bother you."

"She'd make a powerful enemy. Vertuma's not noted for her altruistic tendencies."

Guin frowned. She'd never had an enemy. This was a new sensation she might have to get used to.

Delori suggested they leave when Boden rejoined their group. He informed Delori of the next event and sent her a digital copy of the itinerary.

When he finished his business, he turned to Guin. "May I have this dance?"

"Me?"

He extended his hand.

Intrigued, Guin accepted.

"Why are you here?"

"For the same reason as the other women."

"He's my best friend, and you're messing with his head. Since he met you, he hasn't been himself. He was getting past it then you showed up."

She mirrored his scowl. "What are you getting at?"

"He has a duty to his people, Griffin. What happens when the Council picks someone else? What happens when he can't be with you? If he's this distracted now, what happens later when he gets more attached? If he leaves, we'll be without a king."

"Why would he leave? I would never ask him to leave."

"I don't like complications, and Jaxzon doesn't need one. He has enough on his mind. You don't understand anything about him or his people. If you leave now, he'll be able to get over you."

"*You* don't know anything about *me*." She shook her hand loose from his grip and spun away.

He pulled her back with the arm still around her waist. "Don't hurt him Griffin, and don't hurt his people."

Confused and shaken, she broke loose. She found Derek and Delori. "I'm ready to leave."

CHAPTER THIRTEEN

The orchestra packed and guests said their last goodbyes. Jaxzon searched the room for Guin and, not seeing her, turned to leave but found himself face-to-face with Vertuma and Kapre.

Her icy blue eyes glimmered. "I had a lovely evening, Your Highness."

Kapre winked. "We do look forward to you joining the family."

Jaxzon fought the urge to knock the smirk from the man's face. "Please, excuse me. I've had a long day and wish to retire." He spun on his heel, ignoring Kapre's grin and Vertuma's frown.

Later while lying in bed, he closed his eyes and Guin appeared, with her wide green eyes, the smattering of freckles across her nose, and that unruly cowlick slipping over her right eye.

He grimaced when the voice of reason intruded on his daydream. Guin had no knowledge of his world or people. He hated the politics, though he understood them. The Council—along with his father and the rest of the nobility—would never place an unknown Tellurian on the throne beside him. He should send her home, save them both heartache and pain, yet he couldn't bring himself to send her away. Not after he'd seen her, talked to her, held her.

He felt more alive with her than with anyone. She must have a great deal of courage to leave her home and come so far on the off chance of *what?* She said she came for him.

Jaxzon faced the window as the moons rose above the trees. What did she think of this strange planet?

Boden's voice joined the king's. The words *duty* and *honor* played on an endless track in Jaxzon's head. He closed his eyes, and the voices were replaced by the warm rush he'd felt when holding her in his arms, her sweet lips. His first true kiss, and as first kisses went, theirs had been perfect.

Smiling into the dim room he fell asleep, replaying the moment in his dreams.

"You're late," Boden called the next morning when Jaxzon jogged into the gym.

Jaxzon seized a fluorostaff before climbing into the ring where Boden waited. "Sorry. Rough night." He held the staff's handle behind his neck, stretching his arms along its length and bending forward, loosening his tense muscles.

They faced each other. Boden appeared as tired as Jaxzon felt. They hit the switches on their staffs. Orange light sprang from both ends of the handles. The scent of ozone filled the air. Jaxzon adjusted the weapon to its lowest power and, springing forward, swept Boden's legs out from under him.

He hit the mat, the air rushing from his lungs. Two soldiers in another ring, sparring with laser persuaders—short club-like weapons—laughed as he regained his feet.

Jaxzon rotated his staff and grinned. "Where's your mind this morning? Still in a bottle of ruvin?"

"Just trying to bolster your confidence." Boden lunged left then changed direction as Jaxzon darted to his right.

The staff caught him in the ribs with a crackle. Flipping the end upward, Boden landed a solid blow to Jaxzon's chin, knocking him back into the ropes.

He recovered and went low, catching Boden across the knee, then bringing his staff up, knocked the end into Boden's wrist, who let go of his weapon with one hand. Sparks flew as Jaxzon slashed his weapon across the length of Boden's, knocking the fluorostaff from his grip.

He shook his wrist and rubbed his knee before retrieving his staff. "You're on your game today." He inspected the red welt on his wrist. "Nothing you want to talk about?"

"No. You?"

Boden shook his head and took a defensive stance, spinning his fluorostaff. Jaxzon grinned, enjoying using Boden's obvious hangover against him. He had been no help the previous night when Vertuma imposed herself upon Jaxzon, obliging him to dance with her five times. His friend had been nowhere to be found. Most likely his revenge for having to wear the red uniform.

He aimed at Boden's hand, who blocked. The staffs crackled loudly in the quiet gym when they came together, sparking upon contact. Boden swung at Jaxzon's head. He ducked at the last second, and Boden's swing went wide.

Jaxzon went low and connected with his opponent's already sore knee, causing him to drop to his good one. Boden attempted to roll away. The blow landed on his left shoulder followed by another to the same knee. Boden grunted and stopped moving, surrendering as Jaxzon held the orange tip of the staff to his throat.

After Jaxzon hauled him to his feet, Boden limped to the edge of the ring and collected his towel from the corner post. He climbed from the ring, wiping sweat from his face and torso. He put his weapon away, then sat and raised his pant leg. His knee had begun to swell from the abuse.

Jaxzon joined him and inspected the forming welt. "Looks painful."

"What the *pherx* did I do to you?"

Jaxzon ran his thumb over a small imperfection on the handle of his staff, unsure if he wanted to discuss Guin with Boden. He knew the argument, and wasn't sure it was a fight he could win.

Boden sighed. "I understand why you're attracted to this woman, but it won't work. You need to send her home. She'll never be chosen. She's no one—she has no title, and she holds no land or power. What does she have to offer? She's nothing more than a pretty face and—"

Jaxzon's staff caught Boden across his knee.

He clutched his leg and threw his arm up to catch the silver handle, preventing another blow. "*Viyet*! What was that for?"

"Don't speak of her in that manner. She means more to me than a pretty face. You'll never comprehend how much more." He yanked the staff from Boden's grasp, switched it off and set it in the rack, too tempted to use the weapon on his friend's skull.

"Bad form, Jaxzon." Boden reexamined his knee as a new welt appeared. "I'm only stating the truth. I understand you feel something for her. It was obvious the night you two met. Now that she's here, I'm worried you'll do something irresponsible."

"You don't think very highly of me if you believe that. Don't project your mistakes on me." Even as the words left his mouth, he regretted them.

Boden's jaw stiffened. His eyes flashed. "Ancient history, Jaxzon, and this isn't about me. This is about you and your duty. Griffin offers nothing to your people, and you know it. *Viyet*! She probably knows it." He ran a hand through his hair. "Evidently, you're too immature to do what's right for her, right for yourself, or right for your people. At least I was able to rectify my mistake. If you let this go too far, how will you rectify yours?"

He dropped his pant leg. "I sympathize with you, but, as you've so eloquently pointed out, love can make a man do foolish things. I'm simply saying, don't do anything foolish."

Jaxzon rubbed the back of his neck. The fight drained from him. He couldn't bring himself to meet his friend's eyes.

"I'm going to shower. I'm done training. My body and brain can't take anymore today. Let's talk about this later." He tossed his towel into the autowash tube.

Shame washed over Jaxzon as Boden limped from the gym.

Later, Jaxzon swirled red eggs around his plate, his mind far away.

Boden took the seat across from him. "What are you going to do about the Griffin situation?"

Jaxzon lowered his head and sighed.

"Viy*et*, Jaxzon. She doesn't have a chance with the vipers she's up against. Why didn't you send her home?"

His appetite lost, Jaxzon held a forkful of eggs above his plate. "I intended to, but as soon as we touched...she's so determined. I didn't want to hurt her." The eggs slid off his fork. "I'm torn, Boden. There's something about her. I don't know."

"You understand what happens if you don't abide by the Council's choice? You would forfeit your throne and leave us without a king."

"I've sworn to marry whomever the Council chooses, and when the time comes, I will. But, in the meantime, why can't I hope for more? Most of the women I met last night were only there because of my father's decree. Most have already dropped out, and many others have no chance of swaying the Council. Guin understands what she's up against, and she's made the choice to stay. Who am I to tell her to leave?"

"Because it's cruel to her and unfair to the other women if you show her favor."

"Who says I'm favoring her? I only danced with her once the whole night and, thanks to you, I danced with Vertuma five times. You're supposed to help me out in those situations."

"I was busy adjusting my collar. It impaired my ability to drink."

Jaxzon grinned. "Let's wait and see what happens, okay? I'm only asking you to be nice. What did you say to her last night? She seemed upset."

"I asked her if she knew what she was in for."

"Uh-huh."

"Just remember, duty comes first."

"Yes, *Father.*" Jaxzon left his uneaten meal on the table, then headed to his morning meeting.

CHAPTER FOURTEEN

Despite the dull ache of a hangover, the vivid image of their first kiss danced behind Guin's closed eyes. Her smile changed to a frown as the sour memory of her interaction with Boden replaced the sweet one of Jaxzon.

"What's Boden trying to say?" she mumbled as she rolled out of bed and dressed. "If Jaxzon can't be with me, he'll abdicate? I would never allow him to. Boden had no right. He doesn't know me. Who does he think he is?"

Snagging her toothbrush, she continued the conversation with her reflection in the bathroom mirror. "So what if those other women have more knowledge of these worlds than you do?" She pointed her toothbrush at herself to emphasize each point. "You're smart, you're a fast learner, and you'd make a fantastic queen."

Her reflection stared back at her. *Would you?*

"Yes." She shoved the traitorous notion from her mind, rinsed, spit, and traded her toothbrush for her hairbrush.

"You will be the best queen this kingdom has ever seen," she said between brushstrokes. "You're compassionate, you're sensible, you're much nicer than Vertuma." The brush stopped mid-stroke and she frowned at herself. "What's the story with her anyway? What makes her the one to beat?"

Guin divided her hair into three parts and braided. "She's nothing to worry about. Besides Jaxzon likes *you*." Smiling at the girl in the mirror, she was already in a better mood.

A tapping sounded on the door. "Come in Derek."

Derek bounded into the room like an over exuberant Golden Retriever. "You ready for your next public event?"

"Ready as I'll ever be. What is it?"

"Delori's waiting in the dining hall, she'll tell you all about it."

They linked arms and headed downstairs to find Delori eating breakfast.

After snagging a piece of pink fruit and toast, Guin sat beside Derek.

"Now that you're finally awake, we need to go over the itinerary for the next event," said Delori. "We will be staying at the king's estate on Bethion."

"Themeron's world? Cool. What's the event?" Guin bit into the fruit. The flavor of cinnamon apples burst in her mouth. "Oh my god, this is good."

"A charity event," said Delori. "Two years ago, a pandemic ravaged the planet, taking mostly young adults and leaving millions of children without parents."

"How awful. I didn't think those kinds of things would be a problem here."

"What kinds of things?" asked Derek.

"Pandemics and orphans."

He shrugged. "Our worlds may be more advanced than yours, but bad things still happen."

"How does it work, and how do we help?" Guin took another bite of the fabulous fruit.

Delori showed Guin a picture of smiling blue-hued children. "The charity, Darva's Kids, has helped thousands of orphans find permanent homes. They arrange for the fostering and adopting of children on

Bethion. A galaxy-wide media event called A Day in the Park is hosted by the group annually. Children and prospective parents meet and become acquainted with each other. The event is also the charity's largest fundraiser. This year, you and the other women of the Vekdromic will be helping as volunteers. They'll explain more when we arrive."

"What an awesome cause. I would be honored to help."

"It's not a choice." Delori graced Guin with one of her icy stares. "I expect you to avail yourself of our library to learn the history of Bethion and this charity. You will not embarrass us."

She glared at Delori's retreating back and muttered, "That would be wonderful, if I could read your books."

Willis rolled in and removed Delori's plates from the table. Clutching the dishes in his metal fingers, his black and gray cylindrical body whirled around and zipped back to the kitchen.

Derek put his arm around Guin's shoulder. "I'll help. Most of our history is on audio."

"I didn't want to say anything in front of Delori, but what's up with Boden? He was a complete tool last night."

"A what? Never mind, I think I know. What did he do?"

"He said Jaxzon might leave the realm without a king because of me. He was so angry and bitter. Is he always a jerk, or is it just me?"

"Boden can be overly protective of Jaxzon. I believe he's felt responsible for Jaxzon since the assassinations. A lot of people blamed Boden's father for the deaths of Jaxzon's mother and sister."

"That seems unfair. I mean, Boden's father died too, right?"

"He did."

"Jaxzon wouldn't leave if I'm not chosen, would he?"

"Let's not find out. The only real competition is Vertuma and maybe a couple other nobles who would make smart political choices. Though none of them have half your charm."

"This isn't a fairy tale, Derek, although I think I'm going to let you convince me. You don't happen to have a fairy godmother in your pocket, do you?"

He patted his pockets. "Sorry, fresh out. Let's see if we can't work our own magic."

The following week, Bethion's rainbow-colored clouds sparkled and glittered through the hover's windows as Guin, Delori, and Derek rode to the park. The planet had a peculiar beauty. Dr. Seuss himself might have created this strange and wondrous world. Tufts of coppery leaves fluttered in the breeze on the ends of pink-barked branches sticking out at strange angles from the squat, wide trees. Red-tinted grass ran across the park, ending in a purple-sand-filled area.

The park had been cordoned off for the event, with uniformed guards manning the barriers. In a shaded pavilion, folding chairs faced a podium bristling with microphones. Cameras floated overhead.

A group of Bethan children loitered across the street watching the park fill with charity workers and attendees. Guin waved to a tall boy dressed in oversized brown overalls. He didn't wave back.

A bus-sized hover stopped at the curb. Young children disembarked, filling the seats. Upon the arrival of King Jaezain and Prince Jaxzon, those in attendance bowed. Jaxzon sat beside his father near the podium.

A Bethan woman wearing a pink shirt with the words DARVA'S KIDS emblazoned across the front in dark blue letters, approached the podium. "His Majesty, King Jaezain, and His Highness, Prince Jaxzon, have always supported our cause, and we thank them both for their presence today."

She waited for the applause to end. "I would like to thank the ladies of the royal Vekdromic for graciously volunteering to help this year."

She addressed the cameras. "If you'd like to help a child by opening your hearts and homes, please come meet with us. The circuit lines are open for those unable to travel or you may contact Darva's Kids directly."

When the announcements concluded, volunteers circulated, separating the children and women into groups.

A helper approached Guin. "Would you rather help with paperwork or entertain the children?"

"Bree and I would love to help with the children."

Bree's eyebrows shot up. "I would?"

"Yeah, it'll be fun."

They were being introduced to their group, when a girl named Myera tugged on Guin's blouse and pointed to the kids across the street. "There's my best friend, Makham. She's in my class at school."

"Nice! Does she live near you?"

"No, she doesn't live anywhere."

"What do you mean?"

"She lives in the tree place with her mother. Her father died like mine."

"The tree place?"

Myera frowned. "They make their houses in the trees. Lots of kids live there now. Can she come play with us?"

"I don't see why not. This is Kids' Day, and they're kids, right?"

Myera grinned and nodded.

Guin told Bree she'd be back and went to the edge of the park. Ducking under a barrier, she crossed the street and approached the group of children. She crouched to the girl's level. "My name is Guin. Are you Makham?"

Makham smiled. "Yes, Miss."

"My name is Guin. Pleased to meet you." She offered her hand. "Would you like to go to the park and play with Myera?" Guin gestured to the park behind her.

Makham shook Guin's hand. "Yes, please."

"Would you like to come with us?" Guin asked the other children.

"We're not allowed in the park today. They blocked it," said the boy Guin had waved to earlier. "Are you trying to get us in trouble?"

"Not at all. I'm part of the group there, and I'm inviting you. Do you want to join us?" She noted the children's clothing. Some were worn in the knees or grass-stained, and none fit properly.

He grinned. "Yes, please."

Makham took Guin's hand, and before they left the curb, another little girl caught the other.

When Guin bent to duck under the barrier, a green-uniformed security officer blocked her way.

"Is something wrong?" she asked.

"They aren't with us."

"What do you mean?"

"These aren't our kids."

"What does that have to do with anything? It was my understanding we are here today to inspire others to open their hearts and homes to children who aren't their children. Are you saying we can't open the playground for these children because they aren't ours?"

The man crossed his arms, still barring the way.

The standoff had not gone unnoticed. A few people wandered over, Jaxzon among them. "Is there a problem here?"

The officer bowed. "Yes, Your Highness. The park is closed today, yet the lady is trying to bring in kids from the neighborhood."

Jaxzon tousled the hair of the girl beside Guin and was rewarded with a gap-toothed grin. "I don't believe seven more children are going to bother anyone. Do you?"

The officer glanced at Guin, then back at Jaxzon. "No, Your Highness." He removed the barrier, allowing Guin and the children to pass.

She curtsied. "Thank you, Your Highness."

Jaxzon bowed, dazzling her with his smile. "A pleasure, my lady."

Beaming, Myera and Makham sat side by side.

Guin and Bree led the children in play that soon spilled into the playground. They glided on floating swings suspended in mid-air and slid down slides of glowing lights. They climbed a castle-shaped tower. Bree and the children collapsed in laughter as Guin flew across the park on a zip-line, yodeling her best Tarzan yell. They laid on their backs, pointing to shapes in the rainbow clouds. The children giggling in disbelief when Guin described a giraffe.

The king and prince, with press in tow, meandered through the park, stopping to observe the children at play. Myera stole the show, explaining to reporters how Guin brought her best friend to the park. She mentioned her friend lived in the tree place, piquing the reporters' passion for a human-interest story. They questioned Makham until Guin gently reminded them that these were children and suggested they supply their contact information. Makham's mother could call if she wanted to be interviewed.

When the time came for the children to leave, Guin and Bree were bumped, bruised, and covered in purple sand. Guin had lost a hair tie, and one braid had come undone, yet she and Bree smiled as they received hugs, waving goodbye to their new young friends.

Makham and Myera approached Guin. "We have something for you, Lady Guin," said Myera.

From behind her back, Makham produced a chain of green and burgundy flowers. Guin knelt. Makham placed the crown of flowers on Guin's disheveled hair.

"Thank you, Queen Guin," the girls said in unison through their giggles. They hugged her then each other before Myera followed the other children to the bus. After the vehicle had driven from sight, Guin found herself surrounded by reporters and under a barrage of questions. They talked over each other and jostled for a closer position for their microphones.

"Where are you from?" one journalist shouted above the rest, causing the others to quiet.

"Now that I have your attention," Guin quipped, rubbing her sweaty palms on her jeans. "Thank you for coming to support this worthy cause. I understand this program is dear to King Jaezain's and Prince Jaxzon's hearts, and Darva's Kids has become very important to me. I want to thank the volunteers for everything they do. They are truly incredible."

"What made you bring those kids from across the street?" a reporter called.

"What's your name?" she asked.

"Thalia Vul, *Bethion Weekly*."

"I brought them here because it was the right thing to do. This is their park, and they shouldn't be blocked from playing here, even for one day. This park might be the only place they can go to forget their problems. Each lost a parent to the illness, and their one remaining parent is barely able to make ends meet.

"This program is wonderful. Yet who's helping those other children? They simply wanted to play in the park. I mean, this is only a park, right?" She glanced at the security guard. "Why should we care if kids can't play here for one day? I came to help children, and if by bringing those children over helped them in some small way, or caused them a modicum of happiness, then my mission was accomplished."

Volunteers and prospective parents broke into applause. Jaxzon leaned against the now-abandoned podium, beaming.

"Lady Guin, Alzine Bluth, *Galaxy Watch*. How do you know the prince?"

"We've only recently met." Guin brushed a strand of hair from her eyes with a shaky hand. The attention of so many people, caused her to break into a cold sweat.

A dark-haired reporter waved. "Zulla Thul'o, *Arwon Crown*. Where did you two meet?"

"Prince Jaxzon was on a business trip, and we bumped into each other." Guin's face warmed at the lie. She'd never been a good liar and hated dodging the question.

"I believe Lady Guin has answered enough questions for now," Jaxzon said, coming to her rescue. "The other ladies are waiting to tell you about their day."

The reporters bowed then dispersed.

Guin curtsied. "Thank you, Your Highness."

He flashed a grin before joining his father in their hover.

Prince Charming.

Bree sidled up to Guin. "We need to talk. Can you ride back with me?"

"Talk about what?"

"Not here. I'll have Mother go back with Delori. They used to be friends, once upon a time."

"Sounds good to me."

She found Derek and told him the plan, then joined Bree in her hover. "What's up?" she asked when the door had lowered.

"What's going on with you and Prince Jaxzon?"

Guin told Bree how she came to be there.

"Wow."

"I've never like felt this, Bree. I'm drawn to him like a magnet, except a hundred times stronger than any magnet you can imagine. He's so kind and sweet."

"Do you believe he feels the same?"

"I hope so. I mean, I crossed a freaking galaxy for a chance to be with him. Crazy, right?"

"Completely crazy."

"Holy crap." Guin massaged her temples and closed her eyes. "I feel like I'm on some insane reality show, waiting for my rose."

"Sometimes I don't understand a thing you say." Bree put an arm around Guin's shoulders. "I only came here because my mother is under the delusion that I need to win myself a prince to make my life complete. I would have dropped out that first night with all the others if I hadn't met you. I have no interest in winning a prince, although I think I can help you win yours."

"How?"

"With advice. So far, you've been playing everything right. You're still the mystery girl, so you'll make all the headlines. You helped the sad little kids. You challenged authority and proved you're strong enough to stand up for yourself and what you believe in. And that speech! You really laid it on."

"I'm not playing at anything, Bree. This is who I am."

"Even better." Bree shrugged. "Let's be logical. The Council has a lot of influence over who is chosen as the next queen, but they *are* elected officials. They can be bought. With votes. They're politicians first and do what their constituents want. You could have the sagest political advice, and know how everything in the galaxy works, and still lose the Council's support. But, if you win the hearts of the everyday citizen, you win the votes of the Council. And for you to win the citizens, you must win the press. Whatever journalists put out, people buy. It's a sad truth, but the media can make or break you."

"It's the same where I come from, and I understand the logic, but it's so manipulative. Can't I simply be myself?"

"I'm not telling you to lie. I'll bet you just being you will be enough to win over the whole galaxy, let alone a few reporters. I saw you with those children, you genuinely cared. You stood in front of cameras with dirt on your face, your hair a mess, your underwear full of sand talking to billions of people."

"What?"

"You gave them an earful, and I believe you inspired people. They're going to remember you and they're going to want to know more about you. You have a kind heart, and people respond to kindness."

"Billions of people watched?" A pit opened in Guin's stomach.

Bree laughed. "Yes, billions, and I bet they're showing you on every circuit in the galaxy. There aren't a lot of women like you, so naturally they're going to run with the story. The Arcanum, the unknown, the lady who cares."

"The Arcanum." She sighed. "I don't like being evasive. I'm proud of where I come from. I'm from New York, for chrissakes. I feel like a traitor to my city. Hell, to my world."

"Then stop evading. Next time they ask where you're from, tell them."

"What if they ask why I didn't say anything before?"

"Tell them you're worried about prejudice. A lot of people think Tellurians are lower class."

"Yeah, that makes me feel better."

"Everybody cheers the underdog, Guin, and I'm sure everyone will absolutely love you."

Guin picked sand from under her nail. "What about Vertuma? Isn't she the front runner?"

"People enjoy watching the mighty fall as much as they like seeing the underdog win. She expects to be chosen, so she's cocky and overconfident. She won't even see you coming."

Their arrival at the estate ended the conversation.

Guin went to her room to shower and change, then to Delori's room to learn where they were going next. Boden was informing Delori and Derek of the itinerary for the next event and explaining the Shift schedule.

"Hey Griffin, you made the headlines today." said Boden.

"I did?"

Derek showed her his telecon.

Guin's eyes widened as her smudged face, disheveled clothes, and messy, flower-bedecked hair, appeared on the screen, framed in words she couldn't read. "Oh no, what does it say?"

"Mission accomplished!" he interpreted, grinning like a fool.

"They're calling you Lady Heart. They love you, Guin."

"They couldn't use a better picture?"

"They did." Boden's telecon displayed a picture of her leading the children across the street.

Her jeans and white sleeveless button-up were still clean, her hair shone in the sun, both braids intact. Another picture showed her standing behind the barrier, squaring off with the security guard. "They're comparing you to a mother hen turned bhanthu. Some are wondering if the whole thing was a setup."

"Do you think we set it up?" she asked, before realizing she didn't care what Boden thought.

"I know you didn't. To ensure security, few people knew where the event would take place. Even the king and Jaxzon weren't aware until they arrived."

"You told the press this?" asked Delori.

He shrugged. "I will if they ask, though I'm sure the palace communications director has the same information."

"We go to Xaitera tomorrow," Delori told Guin. "Their annual charity ball will be held in eight days. I'll go over their customs with you after the evening meal."

Two long hours of Delori's grueling instruction later, Guin was alone in her room and dressed for bed, when someone knocked on her door.

What does she want now? She opened the door. "Delori, I—"

Jaxzon stood in the hallway. "May I come in?" His lips curled into a playful smile. "Or would you like me to call Delori so you can finish your sentence?"

Guin moved aside. "What are you doing here?"

"Why are we whispering?"

"So no one hears us."

"These walls are thick. Who's going to hear?" he asked in a loud voice.

She giggled. "When did you get here? How did you know I was in this room?"

"This is my home. I know the people who work here, and I have ways of making them talk." He grinned. "I thought you'd be happier to see me."

"I'm extremely happy to see you." Heat came to her cheeks—she only wore her Yankees jersey and pajama shorts.

He raised an eyebrow.

"Ah hell with it." She closed the space in two short steps, gripped his lapels, and pulled him into a fiery kiss he eagerly returned. His fingers entangled in her hair as he crushed her against him.

She ran her tongue over his lower lip, eliciting a small gasp. He broke the kiss and held her tightly.

Guin wrapped her arms around him, resting her head against his chest. His heartbeat drummed in her ear.

His lips brushed the top of her head. "I'm sorry."

"What are you sorry for?"

"I didn't mean to rush anything."

"You're not rushing me. I kissed you."

"You did, didn't you?" Jaxzon grinned. "You were wonderful today. I couldn't stop thinking of you. I needed to see you again."

She caressed the contours of his face, his lips, the curve of his jaw, then ran her hand through his hair.

Jaxzon closed his eyes. "What are you doing to me?"

"I don't know. You're doing something to me too."

"Whatever it is, I like it." He removed a strand of her hair from her

eyes.

"Me too."

"I wish I could stay longer. Boden is probably searching for me. It wouldn't be appropriate if he found me here."

He bent and captured her lips again, this time in a tender kiss which ended too soon. Leaning his forehead against hers his eyes held hers. "You make me want to break the rules. How can I be fair to the others when I only want to be with you?" Sighing, he drew away. "Sleep well, my lady." With one last brief kiss, he was gone.

Guin climbed into bed, her whole being vibrating with giddy happiness. The moon rose and traversed halfway across her window before her heart calmed and she was able to fall asleep, a smile on her face.

CHAPTER FIFTEEN

Xaitera's capitol, Vepopyn, had three levels of brightly colored buildings wrapped in clouds of gold hanging above a raging red sea.

Guin clutched her stomach as the hover carrying her, Delori, and Derek shot upward through a tube to the highest level, where the Zestari estate lay amongst rolling hills. "Is this real or another hologram?"

"It's real," said Derek. "The Xaiterans built their cities in the clouds when their seas rose and covered the land. They brought soil and vegetation to the upper levels, where they propagate and harvest all the food they need to survive."

The Zestari's estate shone silver and white against the sky's forest green. High windows overlooked a curved driveway surrounded by multi-hued flowering shrubs. The most prevalent were deep burnt-orange-leafed trees, whose violet-blue bark and cinnamon-colored flowers gave off a peppery scent.

Bree ushered them through the mansion's mirrored front doors to the second floor, showing them to their rooms.

After freshening up, Guin made her way downstairs to a sitting room where Delori and Derek chatted with Estes and Bree's father, Sir Boyce, who rose from his seat to greet Guin. The man's short curly hair had begun to gray, yet he had a youthful demeanor.

Bree put an arm around Guin. "Father was a member of the royal guard and earned his knighthood after saving King Jaezain's life."

Sir Boyce waved her away. "Now don't go bragging on me. I'm simply an old man who did his duty many years ago."

"Right." She winked at Guin. "Wait until dinner. He'll fill you in on the details."

Sir Boyce laughed. Guin found him charming. His broad smile and booming voice reminded her of James Earl Jones. Now she understood where Bree inherited her sense of humor and easygoing attitude.

During her stay, Guin joined in Bree's favorite pastime—shopping.

Bree dragged Guin to the lower cities on daily excursions, and on one trip, they encountered Vertuma with Sarya, Nuala, Banya, and Loli. A gaggle of journalists accompanied the princess, reporting on her doings.

Vertuma sneered and hissed in a low voice, "I see you two managed to scrape the dirt off."

"It's a pleasure to see you too, Your Highness." Guin inclined her head to the others. "Ladies."

Vertuma's eyes darkened, although she smiled for the cameras. "Would you two care to join us? We were about to dine."

Bree looped her arm through Guin's. "Thank you. We'd be delighted."

The women left the news people at the door of a high-end restaurant. Short, cylindrical cleaning droids zipped around, clearing tables and sterilizing booths. Crisp lines of black tile and brushed nickel gave the restaurant a clean, modern appearance.

Vertuma sat across from Guin, forcing Sarya to move over one chair. The server took their drink requests as she handed them menus.

"Thank you. I'll have unsweetened tea please." Guin opened her menu, whispering to Bree, "I can't read this. Could you order for me?"

"Of course, what do you like?"

"Whatever you're getting is fine."

Vertuma peered over her menu. "You do realize it's impolite to whisper."

"Pardon me, I was asking Bree what she recommends. I meant no offense." Guin forced a smile. "Do you know where the washroom is?"

Bree pushed her chair from the table. "I'll show you."

"Me too," said Nuala, and followed them to the lady's room.

When Guin returned, her drink had been delivered, and the others were ordering their food. Vertuma and Sarya gave the server their requests and excused themselves.

Nuala took a sip of her drink and made a face. "This isn't sweetened. You gave me the wrong one."

"You must have mine." Guin passed her glass to Nuala, who took a taste and nodded.

Vertuma returned, smiling sweetly at Guin. "How do you like having your face spread across the galaxy? I bet your parents are proud."

"I'm not sure. I don't pay much attention to the news."

Vertuma raised an eyebrow. "You mean to tell me you don't read what they're saying about the Arcanum?"

"Not really." Guin took a sip of tea. "I've found more interesting topics to fill my time."

"What could be more interesting than what people think of you?" asked Sarya.

"Pretty much everything. I'm not defined by what others think."

The food arrived. Guin thanked the server when she set the salad on her placemat.

"You're welcome, my lady."

Vertuma wrinkled her nose. "Why do you do that?"

"Do what?"

"Thank the staff for doing their jobs. Isn't getting paid thanks enough?"

Guin leaned forward. "My parents raised me to be grateful when people do something for me, whether they're getting paid or not. I believe people deserve to be respected and appreciated, don't you?"

Vertuma mirrored Guin. "No, I don't."

The rest of the meal passed in uncomfortable silence.

"How was your meal?" a newsman asked when they exited the restaurant.

"Excellent, and we had a wonderful chat. We're all dear friends now. We've been enjoying our girl-time together."

A woman with a camera came forward. "Can we get a group photo?"

"Absolutely," Vertuma replied, a fake smile plastered across her face. "It would be our pleasure." She put her arm around Guin and posed.

"Guin, can you answer a few questions?"

"Of course. Alzine, right?"

"You have a good memory. How do you feel being known as *the Arcanum*?"

"I never meant to be a mystery to anyone. I'm not used to being the center of attention or talking to groups of people. This is all new to me."

A tall reporter with a red bow tie raised his hand. "You appeared confident at the park. You really told some people off."

Although her face burned, she held the man's gaze. "I wasn't trying to tell anyone off. Though I do become defensive when it comes to orphans and children in need."

"Why?" Alzine asked.

Guin bit her lip and glanced at Bree, who nodded. She took a deep breath. "At the age of two I was orphaned, and my adoptive parents died when I was sixteen. I haven't shared much about myself, and I apologize. I am a private person and the whole...being in the camera's eye isn't my style. I have also not mentioned where I come from, and I wish to rectify that now. I am proud of my home planet, and I'm ready to clear up any mystery. I'm from New York City. I'm from Earth."

Gasps came from a few reporters and the women behind her. A volley of rapid-fire questions followed.

"When did you arrive?"

"Is your family royalty?"

"Did you meet the prince there?"

"Are you related to the Vau'uans?"

"Does Prince Jaxzon know?"

Before Guin could answer, a sharp cry came from behind her. She spun around.

Nuala doubled over, her face contorted in pain. She cried out again then vomited. Everyone jumped back as chunks of partially digested salad splattered the sidewalk.

Nuala's eyes widened in horror. She clutched her stomach and sobbed.

Guin put an arm around the woman's shoulders and led her into the restaurant, asking a server for water on the way to the restroom. Bree hurried after. They offered tissues, water, and emotional support as Nuala continued to vomit herself into dry heaves.

"Bree, can you call for the hover? We need to get Nuala to a doctor," said Guin.

Nuala took a sip of water and blew her nose. "No, I'll be okay. It's stopped."

"You should be checked for food poisoning. I'd feel better if you did." Guin put a hand on Nuala's arm. "Please?"

"Okay."

She and the other two left in Bree's hover. After the hospital, they dropped Nuala at the royal estate and headed back to Bree's.

"That was amazing," said Bree.

"What are you talking about? The whole situation was horrible."

"I mean, you're amazing, the way you took control. How did you stay so cool?"

"Practice." Guin wrinkled her nose. "I've held back plenty of other girls' hair and seen more than my fair share of people getting sick. Usually in the back seat of my car."

"You were incredible. You impressed everyone. Everyone except Vertuma, that is. Did you see her face?"

"No, I was kinda preoccupied. What did I miss?" Guin massaged her temples. The planet's twenty-nine-hour days seemed to be taking their toll, and what might be jet lag caught up to her as a headache formed.

"She was fuming, and I'm sure the cameras caught everything."

Guin frowned. "Why was she mad?"

"Because you bested her again. First, you dropped that bomb, then you swooped in and heroically rescued her friend in her time of need."

"You're being overly dramatic, Bree. I didn't swoop and I'm definitely not heroic. I simply helped the poor woman. She was sick, embarrassed, and crying. Anyone would have done it."

"Wrong. Not anyone." Bree pointed at Guin. "*You* didn't hesitate. The rest of us just stood there. If it had been up to Vertuma, she would have gone to get her nails done and left Nuala to fend for herself."

"Be that as it may, I'm sure someone would have helped eventually."

"I bet you're going to be the talk of the circuit again. Especially after you told them where you're from."

"Was that the proper time?" Worried she'd made a mistake, Guin bit her lip. "I mean, I knew someone was going to ask, I figured I might as well beat them to it."

"The timing was perfect, and thanks to poor Nuala, you were able to dodge the uncomfortable questions. I'm so sorry you lost your parents. May I ask what happened?"

"Not much to say. Like I told the reporters, I was adopted at two, then my adoptive parents died in a car accident. I'm sorry, it's difficult to talk about."

Bree squeezed Guin's fingers. "I understand."

A grinning Derek and a visibly upset Delori met them in the estate's dining hall.

"You're a hit!" he said, slinging an arm around Guin's shoulder and giving her a hug.

Delori glared at her brother. "We had plans for the announcement. The glare snapped to Guin. "You should have waited. I've been fielding calls all day. What made you tell them now?"

"Guin was brilliant," said Bree. "And the timing was perfect."

Delori's steely gaze landed on Bree, who shrugged.

Derek queued a video and handed his telecon to Guin. Reporters shouted questions at Guin, then all hell broke loose. Nuala became sick. Guin hurried to her, then led her away. The camera followed her then panned to the other women. Their faces registered disgust. The camera caught Vertuma, red-faced and furious. She waved off the reporters, then she and Sarya climbed into a hover, disappearing around the corner.

A studio reporter came on to say Guin was more of a mystery now they knew where she was from. "Who is this Tellurian?" he asked. "When did she arrive? When did she meet Prince Jaxzon? Stay tuned to learn more about the Tellurian from New York."

"On another station, they are calling you the Lady of New York and saying you're a saving grace." Derek laughed.

Guin's head throbbed. "What does that even mean?"

He shrugged. "No idea. One tabloid is calling you Princess Vertuma's royal pain. I wish I could see her face when she reads that one."

"Derek don't be unkind. Those are terrible things to say about both of us. She's not my favorite person, but let's not be cruel."

"This is why you'll be chosen. You're always thinking of others, even people as bad as Vertuma."

"I need to lie down. Please call me when dinner's ready." Guin headed to her room.

CHAPTER SIXTEEN

A*m I cut out for this?* Guin laid in bed, staring at the ceiling. *If I become queen, will everything I do be scrutinized and judged?* A light knock pulled her from her thoughts. "Come in, Derek."

The door opened, and Jaxzon let himself in.

Guin bounded off the bed and into his arms, holding him in a tight embrace, breathing him in. "I missed you."

"I missed you, too."

"Kiss me."

Taking her hand, he kissed the back with a mischievous grin.

She laughed. "Is that all?"

Kissing the inside of her wrist and trailing kisses along her arm, he ended in the crook of her neck.

Shivers traveled the length of her spine.

He gripped her chin. His lips grazed hers, his warm breath caressing her mouth. She grasped the back of his neck. Her fingers twisted in his hair. Tugging him down, she deepened the kiss, tasting his lips when she ran her tongue between them.

His breath caught. His moan vibrated against her mouth. Tracing kisses from her jaw to her ear he recaptured her mouth, then wound his arms around her, drawing her closer. He released her lips and held her, laying his cheek against the top of her head. "I saw the news. I came as soon as I heard."

"Heard what?"

Holding her at arm's length he peered into her eyes. "About your parents. Why didn't you tell me?"

"It didn't come up, I guess."

"When I told you about my mother and sister might have been a good time to mention your parents."

"From what I recall, I was kinda focused on something else. I didn't want to add my pain to yours."

"I guess we haven't spent a lot of time getting to know one another."

"We spent more time together in New York." She cocked her head. "Wanna go back?"

Dimples appeared as he smiled. "I truly wish we could."

Guin caressed the angle of his jaw. "How long are you staying?"

"I invited myself to dinner. The Zestaris must think me terribly rude. I had Derek show me to your door. We told Boden I needed to go over some things with Derek."

She leaned her body into his. "Instead, you're going over some things with me?"

He brushed a strand of hair from her forehead then combed his fingers through its length. His hand followed the curve of her spine, causing another shiver. "I guess I am." He bent, and their lips met in a heated kiss.

A light tap sounded on the door. They broke apart, and Guin went to answer. "Boden's on his way. Bree's running interference," said Derek.

Jaxzon thanked him and hurriedly kissed Guin before leaving.

She groaned in frustration, throwing herself on the bed.

Moments later there was another gentle knock.

Bree rushed in, closing the door behind her. "I didn't want Boden to know you're in the room next to Derek's. He's being a real pest."

"Thanks for helping us enjoy a few minutes alone."

"You're going to be thanking me a lot more. I arranged for Prince Jaxzon and Boden to stay the night."

Guin threw her arms around Bree. "You're the best friend ever."

Bree laughed. "I'll try to distract Boden after dinner, let you two have some alone time in the garden, maybe?"

"Perfect. I don't think we should be alone in my room again." Guin gave Bree a sidelong glance. "I believe that would be very dangerous."

"What do you mean?"

"I mean, if Derek hadn't shown up... Bree, those eyes, his touch, his scent. What the hell is he wearing, Pheromones for Men?" Guin flopped face first on her bed and screamed into the bedding. "He's driving me crazy."

"I think I get it," Bree said, chuckling. "I guess if we want to protect our prince's virtue, we're going to have to find other places for you two to meet?"

"Definitely."

That evening, Guin and Jaxzon exchanged glances throughout dinner. She spent what she determined to be an appropriate amount of time in after-dinner conversation, then excused herself, saying she had a long day.

"I'll try to give you an hour," Bree said when she came to fetch Guin. "Father is telling Boden his war stories, and he can talk."

They hurried downstairs to a side exit. "He's down this path in the garden to the right. Good luck."

Shadows danced in the pale moonlight. The scent of night-blooming flowers filled the air around her, as she made her way along the dimly lit walkway.

"Guin."

She took the path toward his voice. He caught her in his arms, drawing her into the shadows. His mouth found hers. She wound her arms around him, her lips parting. A deep rumble resonated from Jaxzon when she passed her tongue between his lips.

She broke the kiss and buried her face in his chest. "Jaxzon?"

"Yes, my lady?" His breath tickled her ear.

"Could you just hold me forever?"

He placed his fingers under her chin and gazed into her eyes. "Whatever my lady wishes." He wrapped her in his arms.

Guin breathed in his scent until she became dizzy with it. "Do you think I'll win?"

Jaxzon sighed. "Let's walk."

They strolled through the winding garden, their fingers intertwined. The sky grew lighter. Guin came to an abrupt stop as a light, lavender moon rose through the trees before her. Behind them a pale yellow, quarter-moon hung low in the sky.

"Beautiful, aren't they?" He held her against his chest.

She folded her arms over his. "So beautiful."

The lavender moon rose above the trees, illuminating the garden with an ethereal glow.

"I want to learn everything about your worlds." She rested against him, reveling in his closeness. "Where was your mother from?"

"Uetov4, from a province called Thenei."

"What was she like?"

He led her to a stone bench carved with intricate flowers and vines. "My mother was kind and gentle, yet strong in her convictions. She never surrendered when she knew she was right." A wistful smile played on his lips. "She liked to indulge me. My father believed a little too much. Boden and I were always in trouble. Between his father and my mother, we got away with quite a lot. Orist, the commander of the king's guard, who was a junior officer at the time, is still sore with Boden and the pranks we pulled. Mother would always smooth things over. When she reprimanded me, if she did, I felt awful. Before she died, I don't believe I spent a day of my life without seeing her. She meant everything to me, and I miss her greatly."

"It sounds like she loved you very much."

"She loved her family. She loved her people almost as much, and they adored her. She genuinely cared for others and put their needs before her own." He paused. "You remind me of her."

She lowered her head to hide her burning cheeks.

He lifted her chin. His eyes blazed into hers. "Honestly Guin, I've never met anyone as kind and caring as she was. Until you. And to answer your question, I believe once the Council sees what I see, they will realize that you would make a remarkable queen. Queen Guinevere."

"Cut the queen crap, Jaxzon." She slid her hand behind his neck, drawing him forward in a tender kiss.

He drew back, his eyes sparkling. "Now you tell me about your family. Where did you grow up? Do you have siblings? Tell me everything."

"Everything? How much time do we have?" She took a deep breath. "I grew up in Manhattan, not far from where I picked you up, actually. My parents were attorneys. They adopted me when I was two. They learned Mother was pregnant around the same time my adoption went through. By my third birthday, I had two baby sisters. Joyce and Joann. I nicknamed them JoJo because I couldn't tell them apart. They had a lot of health issues at birth. We always worried over them."

"Where are they now?"

"They're with their grandmother. They've enrolled in law school, following in their parent's footsteps. I'm so proud of them."

"What did they think of your leaving for so long?"

"I didn't tell them." She traced a finger over their entwined hands. "We haven't talked much in the last few years. We keep in touch through mutual friends."

"Why don't you talk? Are they far away?"

"No, they live in Manhattan. Grandmother lives in the same building we did."

Jaxzon tilted his head. "What happened?"

"The day after my eighteenth birthday, Grandmother announced that as a legal adult I should be able to care for myself and asked me to leave. I wouldn't have minded so much, except I didn't want to leave my sisters. I adore those girls."

"I bet they adore you too." Jaxzon brushed the rogue strand of hair from her eyes. "Why did your grandmother ask you to leave?"

"My sisters stayed over at her house one night when they were seven. Joyce asked why I couldn't stay too. Grandmother told them I wasn't family." She shook her head. "I was ten at the time and had been unaware I was adopted. I was so afraid to tell my parents that I knew."

"Why were you afraid?"

"I didn't want to hurt Mother and Father's feelings. I was afraid they'd stop loving me. I mean, I was never unloved, but there were times when I felt like an outsider. My life wasn't so bad. We took ski trips to Europe and visited just about every amusement park on the east coast. I spent most of the time with my nanny, who was awesome. And there was always the love from my sisters. Now you know my life story."

"After all that how did you turn out so sweet?" He rested his forehead against hers. The blue depths of his eyes probed her soul.

Her heart stumbled in her chest. "Nanny Jean always said, 'Life is what you make of it, and everyone has a choice in who they wish to be.'"

His breath warmed her lips. "Wise woman, your nanny."

"Mm-hm." She covered his mouth with hers.

The sweet taste of his lips, the smoldering of his eyes, the thrill of his arms, and the heat of his body were too much. Something between a moan and a purr escaped her throat as she lost herself in the intensity of the moment.

"Guin?" Bree's voice came from nearby. "I'm sorry. Boden is getting restless. Believe it or not, Father's running out of stories."

"Thank you, Bree," Jaxzon called. "I'll be there in a moment."

Guin sighed.

He squeezed her hand. "I will see you tomorrow."

He bent, and they shared another sweet kiss. "Goodnight, my lady."

"Goodnight, my prince."

Jaxzon's dimples made an appearance. "I like the way you say that." He released her then went inside.

CHAPTER SEVENTEEN

An excited murmur went through the room as Lady Guinevere Griffin of New York entered the Xaitera Charity Ball. Derek grinned and escorted her through the doorway.

The Xaitera Palace, though smaller than Arwon's was as grand, with marble floors, oaken doors, and chandeliers throughout. An ornate fountain occupied the center of the dance floor. Each tier of shimmering water cascaded into the next, creating a symphony of liquid music.

Guin wore a cobalt, form-fitting gown with beaded designs and a plunging neckline, accessorized with a necklace of sparkling, sapphire gems and matching earrings. Her hair had been swept into an elegant, high chignon. He guided her to where Delori waited with Bree and her parents.

"What an entrance," said Bree. "They couldn't take their eyes off you."

The herald announced the king and prince. Men bowed, and ladies curtsied when the two royals entered. Guin's heart rate rocketed, and Jaxzon's smile widened when their eyes met. His gaze lingered on her as he followed his father to the front of the room.

Once the announcements regarding the charity concluded, the ball officially commenced. She beamed at him across the crowded room as the orchestra played. Vertuma stepped in front of Jaxzon. He offered his arm, accompanying her to the dance floor.

Guin spun away, colliding with Prince Kapre. Handsome as ever with his shoulder-length, blond hair slicked back, and his black tuxedo contrasting sharply with his sea-blue eyes.

His smile dripped charm. "What a happy accident. May I have this dance?"

She hesitated.

He offered his arm. "I don't bite."

Where have I heard that before? She put her hand on his arm, allowing herself to be escorted to the floor, wary of his grip on her waist.

His mouth twitched into a smirk. "How did you manage it?"

"Manage what?"

"Upstaging my sister, not once, but twice." He chuckled. "I'm impressed."

"What are you talking about?"

"First with the kids, then the business with Nuala. You know how to put on a show."

Guin's feet stopped moving. Her jaw clenched. "I don't put on shows, and I didn't upstage anyone. I was simply trying to help."

"Relax. I'm *simply* making conversation."

She didn't move.

He glanced around. Couples danced past. "Vertuma needed to be taken down a notch or two. She gets a little full of herself."

Look who's talking. Guin glared, stiffening against his pull.

He loosened his grip. "I'm sorry. I'm being terrible, aren't I?"

Her anger lessened, and she let him lead her across the floor. "You've been an ass since we met."

"Ouch. That hurts. Are you always so painfully honest?"

"You don't appear hurt, and I'm not sure about painfully, but I don't lie."

Kapre grinned. "Point taken."

The song came to an end, and she turned to leave. He brought her hand to his lips, bowing. "Thank you, my lady."

She pulled her hand away. "Your Highness."

A familiar young man intercepted Guin. "Lady Guinevere, would you honor me with a dance?" He escorted her to the floor. "I'm Calen Grint. We met at the Masque."

"Good to see you again. Please, call me Guin."

He gave her a half-smile. "What's Earth like?"

She laughed. "That's a loaded question. I'm not sure where to begin."

"I'm sorry," he said, chuckling. "My friends and I are fascinated with you. The way you handled the press was brilliant."

"You're sweet."

"Brilliant is the word my mother used, and she would know." He tossed an unruly strand of dark hair from his eyes with a flip of his head. "My mother is one of the more prominent Council members. You impressed her, and that's not easy."

"Oh?"

"Dame Heldivar Grint. She is proud of her title, so when you meet her, don't forget to use it."

Guin curtsied when the song ended. "Thank you, Calen."

He bowed. "The pleasure was mine, Guin."

Noblemen and Council members intercepted Guin every time she attempted to find Jaxzon.

Each asked her what Earth was like and were curious to know how she came to be there. She gave polite answers, while managing to successfully steer the conversation back to their interests. Most seemed eager to talk about themselves.

After dancing with one particularly curious Council member, she excused herself and hurried to the lady's room. Princess Vertuma sat perched on a pink pouf before a vanity, holding court with several women.

Vertuma's icy powder-blue eyes flashed in the mirror. One perfectly plucked brow shot up. "Lady Guin, I noticed you dancing with my brother. It appears he's taken a liking to you. Now that I think of it, several men seem quite smitten by you."

"Oh?" Guin checked her makeup in the mirror. "I believe they were simply being polite."

"So, you and Prince Jaxzon were simply being polite?"

"I'm not sure what you're inferring. Jaxzon has always been a perfect gentleman."

"Jaxzon?" Vertuma appeared surprised. "You call the prince by his first name?"

Crap. "Excuse my error. I'm not used to royal titles."

"Most *Earthlings* aren't."

Loli gasped, earning daggers from Vertuma. Loli lowered her eyes. Vertuma's attention flicked back to Guin. "At least none of the ones I've heard of. I don't travel in the same circles with the lower classes, so of course I have never met an Earthling before."

"I'm honored to be your first." Guin curtsied, departing as anger flared on Vertuma's face.

Guin found Bree and asked if the bar stocked ruvin. Bree directed her to a serving area where she ordered two. Guin told her of her run-ins with the Syndows.

"She called you an Earthling?"

"Twice. But the name doesn't offend me. I figure she's trying to shock a reaction outta me." She grinned. "Joke's on her."

Bree's nose wrinkled. "She's vile. What was she implying between you and Prince Jaxzon? I wonder if someone told her you two are spending time together."

"I have no idea, and I don't care. It's no one's business."

"Guin, you should care. You can be ruined by a scandal. You don't want nasty rumors to spread."

"We've been careful. Only our close friends know. Besides, we're only talking, getting better acquainted. Isn't that what this whole Vekdromic is about?"

"There are other people. There are house staff, and the palace has staff. Some of those kitchen workers are the biggest gossips in the universe. Be careful is all I'm saying."

The server brought their drinks as Jaxzon made his way toward them with an older woman who wore a green beaded dress. Her salt-and- pepper hair had been swept into a bouffant reminiscent of hair-styles from the fifties on Earth. Handing her glass to Bree, Guin went forward to meet them.

Jaxzon introduced the woman. "Lady Guinevere Griffin, this is High Council Member, Dame Heldivar Grint."

Guin shook Heldivar's hand. "So nice to meet you again, Dame Grint."

"You are a beautiful woman." Heldivar's steely gaze swept over Guin. "You remind me of my late daughter. She was beautiful and exceptionally kind."

"Thank you, Dame Grint. I'm sorry for your loss."

"I was telling His Highness that you have earned the attention of many within the high Council. We would like to become better acquainted with you, away from these events." Heldivar waved a dismissive hand at the surrounding room. "Shall I arrange something?"

"Of course. I'd be delighted." Guin met the woman's dark gray eyes. "It would be my pleasure to learn more of the people I may be working with in the future."

"Confident, yet not cocky." Heldivar gave a curt nod. "I will make the arrangements. Expect to hear from me soon."

Guin dipped her head. "Thank you, ma'am."

"Your Highness." Heldivar bowed to Jaxzon then scanned the room. "Now where is that boy?" She headed off in Calen's direction.

Jaxzon offered his arm. "Will you honor me with this dance, my lady?"

"My pleasure, my prince."

"You look stunning tonight," he told her under his breath. "I almost fell to my knees when I caught sight of you. Everyone is talking about your gown as much as they're talking about the one wearing it. You've made quite an impression."

Heat flooded her face. "I only want to impress one person."

His breath caressed her ear. "I love it when you blush."

Goose flesh prickled her arms. He spun her away, then drew her close. "I return to Arwon tomorrow." He spun her again. "But I'll see you at the next event." His eyes flashed. "You'll never guess what it is."

"You're probably right. But I'm thinking it must be something you're looking forward to."

"Very much so." His smile widened. "We're going to the annual Thilon Twenty."

"Still in the dark here."

"A race." Excitement lit his face. "*The* race. The best pilots on the circuit will be competing."

"Ah. I should have known. You're almost as happy as when you climbed into the go-kart."

"That was one of the best nights of my life, Guin. Although, it now ranks a close second to the night I saw you at the Masque."

"They both rank in the top two on my list as well."

"I'm going to miss you terribly. It's going to be torture not seeing you." He leaned in closer, his voice hushed. "Holding you like this, kissing your sweet lips." The last strains of the song played. Jaxzon held her close until the last note faded. He kissed her hand. "My lady."

"My prince."

Guin made her way back to Bree, whose face had gone ashen. "Are you okay?" Guin gripped her arm, which was slick with sweat.

Bree's eyes widened. Her pupils dilated. She shook her head and took a deep breath. Her body stiffened before she collapsed.

"Bree!" Guin caught her as she fell and lowered her friend's convulsing body to the floor. "I need help!"

"I'm a physician." A man dropped to his knees and placed his coat beneath Bree's head. "We need a medic here!"

Another cry for help came from across the room. A medical team arrived for Bree and slid a board beneath her. The hover board lifted. They guided her shivering form from the room. Another medical team arrived, and the room erupted.

King Jaezain called for silence. "Please, do not panic. I must ask everyone to leave in an orderly fashion. If anyone feels ill, inform Our guard immediately, and you will be taken to a medical facility."

Jaxzon found Guin amidst the chaos. "Do you feel okay? Are you ill?"

"No. I have to go with Bree. I think she's dying."

"We'll take my hover." He guided her across the room, past the throng of people making their way out.

Boden appeared, wearing a plaid shirt and jeans. They hurried through a corridor and into a garage. Guin and the men climbed into a sleek hover. The vehicle slid forward, entered an air tube then dropped two levels. They accelerated, flying through a dark tunnel.

Jaxzon searched Guin's face. "Are you sure you're not sick?"

"Yes, I'm fine. Why wouldn't I be?"

"Because it appears as though someone poisoned Bree and another woman," said Boden.

Flashing his friend a frown, Jaxzon said, "We know nothing yet. There's no need to frighten her."

Guin's stomach dropped. "You think they were poisoned?"

He squeezed her hand. "We aren't sure of anything."

They arrived at the hospital and were joined by two of the king's guard. A nurse showed them to a private room where Eltes and Boyce waited.

Sir Boyce took Guin's hand. "The other woman, Maldea, is going to be fine. The doctor said they are still running tests to determine the cause of the illness. He's gone to check on Bree."

Guin gripped his hand. “She’s going to be okay too. Bree’s the strongest woman I know.”

“Thank you, Lady Guin.”

The doctor informed the Zestaris that Bree was recovering. They followed him from the room. Guin sighed in relief and sank into a chair, covering her face. Jaxzon encircled her in his arms. She buried her face in his chest.

“She’s going to be fine.” He rubbed her back. “Everything is going to be fine.”

“I’m so sorry. I’m not usually a crier.”

His gentle voice murmured close to her ear. “Don’t be sorry. You’re worried for your friend.” He removed the handkerchief from his breast pocket. “I honestly never knew what these were for, until now.” He placed the silky, monogrammed cloth in her hand.

She wiped her eyes. “This is the first time I’ve ever had to use one. Thank you for staying with me.”

“I will always be here for you.” Brushing the strand of hair from her face he tucked it behind her ear.

Boden cleared his throat. “Don’t you think we should get back? I’m sure the king will be wanting you.”

Jaxzon beckoned his guard. “Lieutenant Harvell, please inform my father that we won’t be leaving until we learn why these women became ill.”

She bowed then left the room.

Boden inclined his head toward Guin. “Won’t it appear suspicious if you’re here with Griffin?”

“Not here and not now. I’m not leaving her alone at a time like this.”

Boden took a chair against the wall, scowling at nothing in particular and the room in general.

Jaxzon conferred with a nurse then offered Guin his hand. “Would you like to see Bree?”

Eltes and Boyce were at her bedside. Bree smiled weakly and gave Guin a feeble wave.

She rushed to her side and took her hand. "How do you feel?"

"Weak," Bree said. "A bit out of sorts. They gave me something. It made me sleepy."

"Get some sleep, silly. You need to rest now."

"I wanted to speak with you and Prince Jaxzon first. I need you both to hear this. I gave Guin's drink to Maldea. I believe whatever made us sick was in those drinks."

Guin and Jaxzon exchanged a look. He left the room.

Guin kissed Bree's forehead. "Get some rest. I'll come back in the morning."

Bree's eyes fluttered then closed.

"Why would someone poison Griffin?" Boden sat across from Jaxzon and Guin as their hover glided along the tunnel to the Zestari estate.

"I don't know." Jaxzon called ahead to tell Derek and Delori to pack, saying that he wanted Guin at the royal estate for her protection. "I want you with her wherever she goes from now on."

Guin shook her head. "That isn't necessary. I doubt anyone is trying to hurt me. This must have been an accident."

"Right," agreed Boden. "Besides, I need to keep an eye on you."

"This is a command. Until we know what's going on, you are to stay with her and make sure she's safe."

Boden went rigid. His jaw tightened. "Yes, Your Highness."

"I'm sorry, Boden." Jaxzon's voice softened. "You're the only one I can trust with Guin. I couldn't bear it if something happened to her."

Boden relaxed. "You know I would do anything for you. You didn't need to make it a command."

She crossed her arms, perturbed at being assigned a bodyguard. Especially Boden. "Don't I have a say in this? I don't like the idea of someone following me around day and night, glowering at me and calling me Griffin."

"I won't take no for an answer. The doctor said you may have died if you'd taken the drug. I must leave tomorrow, and Boden will keep you safe."

Boden and Guin exchanged glares.

Jaxzon lifted her hand to his lips. "I want you safe. Please?"

Her will melted. She rested her head on his shoulder. "Okay."

He wrapped his arm around her and kissed the top of her head. "Thank you."

Boden sighed.

CHAPTER EIGHTEEN

Boden followed her everywhere, staying hidden most of the time. But, being forced to share a hover with him wherever she went, wore on Guin's nerves. He scowled at everything and didn't speak except in monosyllables. He appeared to take pleasure that these things bothered her.

On their way to the Zestari estate, he sat across from Guin, frowning at the passing landscape.

She gasped, pointing through the window. "What's that?"

Following her finger he raised an eyebrow.

"Ha, made you look."

He went back to frowning out the window.

"Come on Bodey old man, talk to me, or at least put on some music."

Boden touched the tele-screen. Music filled the hover.

Guin gritted her teeth. "Thanks."

She spent the afternoon with Bree, who had recovered with no ill effects. They researched how they might create a charity for the children on Bethion, but had trouble finding support from local governments. There were hundreds of forms to fill out, jurisdictions were sketchy. When they made calls, they were sent from one department to another and left on hold.

By the time Guin left, they hadn't accomplished much. Bree volunteered to send each Council member a personal message every day until someone answered.

Before returning to Arwon, Guin helped persuade a reluctant Eltes to allow Bree to continue in the Vekdromic.

On the day of the Thilon Twenty, an attendant at the Shift Station took Guin aside for another trivol shot as a precaution before she and Boden Shifted from Arwon.

On Thilon, she and Bree met the remaining women of the Vekdromic. They rode together between domes in a limo-sized hover.

Mists parted, swirling behind them as they cut through the vapors rising from steam vents. Yellow and pink rock formations, stacked like stairs rising into the heavens, appeared through the smoke-filled air.

Gravity was different there. Guin's braid lifted from her shoulder, floating in the air beside her.

The moon's only road passed through a deep ravine whose sides rose thousands of feet into a bright, neon green sky, then emptied on to an expansive mesa, overlooking a miles-deep valley. The Grand Canyon was an insignificant hole in comparison.

The flatland spread before them as they drove through the double doors of a dome. A massive grandstand floated above the deep gorge.

The hover came to a stop. A small group of reporters gathered to greet them. A familiar woman called to Guin when she exited the vehicle.

Guin waved. "Good morning, Thalia."

Thalia grinned. "Good morning, Lady Guin. Would you answer a few questions?"

"Of cour—"

"I would like to invite the ladies to view the race from my private box," Vertuma announced.

"How very generous of you, Princess," gushed Sarya, leading the others in a round of applause.

"We don't have time for further questions." Vertuma smiled for the cameras. "We wouldn't want to miss the start. I'm sure you'll understand."

The press members bowed.

With a flourish Vertuma led the ladies to a set of stairs leading into the grandstand.

Boden shadowed the group. Uniformed guards patrolled nearby.

The princess showed the women to a luxurious box decorated with plush seating and low tables. A viewing screen covered one wall.

"I've ordered drinks for everyone." Vertuma regarded Guin with a sneer. "Sorry, no ruvin for you. Wouldn't want an accident."

Sarya giggled. A few titters came from the other ladies.

Guin crossed her arms. "What are you implying now, Vertuma?"

Vertuma's eyes narrowed. "It appears people become violently ill when you're around." A sly smile spread across her face. "It makes me wonder if our lives are in danger simply by being in the same room with you."

Guin clenched her jaw. A few women averted their eyes; others stared, openly accusing. "If you're referring to Maldea's and Bree's illnesses, I can assure you, I had nothing to do with it. But if I make you uncomfortable, I will be more than happy to leave and allow you to better enjoy your day." She curtsied to Vertuma. "Thank you for the invitation."

"I'm with Guin. And you should know, those were our drinks tampered with. Why would she try to hurt me, let alone herself?" Bree took Guin's arm. "You should all be ashamed of yourselves."

They left the box then headed downstairs. When they reached the lower-level Guin hugged her friend. "Thanks, Bree."

"I couldn't let her say those things about you. She knew what she was saying wasn't true. She's trying to rattle you and spread rumors because the people like you. Ooh," Bree clenched her fists, "I so wanted to slap her."

"I'm glad you didn't, but thanks for the sentiment. Where do we go now?"

"I don't know. Where were we supposed to sit?"

"No idea. Let's find Jaxzon. Boden, can you take us to Jaxzon?"

"No."

This is getting old. "Fine." She took Bree's arm. "We'll find him ourselves."

"Come on, Boden," Bree pleaded, digging her feet in against Guin's pull. "Vertuma kicked us out of her lair. Where else can we go?"

Guin steadily succeeded in dragging Bree in the direction of a set of stairs.

"All right." He passed them. "You're going the wrong way, and I don't feel like chasing you two around all day. Follow me."

"Wow, Bree, he must like you. Those were the most words he's said in days."

Boden grunted. He showed them to a stairwell hanging over the gorge. Guin held firmly to Bree's arm as he led them up a set of stairs with a view of the dizzying drop below. They came to a door flanked by Jaxzon's personal guards. One opened the door for them.

Jaxzon's smile lit his face. "My lady."

Guin beamed. "Mind if we crash?"

"Mind?" He took her hands. "I'm delighted. I would have asked you myself if I'd believed I could sneak you in. How did you manage to get away?"

"Let's just say we won't be missed and leave it there. Now when does this race of yours start?"

He ushered Guin to a floor-to-ceiling glass wall. A panoramic view of the starting line spread before them. Dozens of spaceships hovered miles above the ground. Each craft had a unique design.

Some were no bigger than a Volkswagen, others were larger than a city bus. They all appeared sleek and fast.

Jaxzon pointed to the hovering contestants. "Each participant builds their own craft. They start and end here. The course goes ten kihals through canyons and gorges. At one point they go underwater, which slows things considerably yet challenges the skills of the pilot and the durability of their craft. They are prohibited any type of computerized navigation devices or controls and rely solely on their own reflexes and ingenuity."

"How far is a kihal?"

"About one hundred Earth miles. This event is twenty kihals, hence the name, Thilon Twenty."

"That's incredible. They travel two thousand miles? How long is this race?"

"Ninety of your minutes, more or less, depending on the weather. Sometimes there's rain between here and the turnaround."

The racers' ships rose higher into the air.

"Why are they so noisy?" Guin shouted above the din.

"Combustion engines," Jaxzon said, his mouth close to her ear.

The vehicles below roared, cutting off his voice. The sound reverberated throughout the canyon, shaking the grandstand within its dome.

A series of lights flashed on a floating platform. Bright orange. Green. Blue. The racers streaked through the starting poles, tearing away as though shot from a gun, one second there, the next gone.

Boden and Bree backed away from the viewing window. Jaxzon guided Guin back several paces until the window flickered and changed, showing the ships from above as they barreled through the gorge. The canyon walls narrowed, and the racers jockeyed for position.

Jaxzon and Boden argued over the skills of the driver currently in first place.

"Who's winning?" asked Guin.

Bree shrugged. "The big, ugly green one, I think. Want a drink? Full bar."

"Definitely."

Taking a bottle of ruvin from behind the counter at the back of the room, Bree poured, garnishing the drinks with a pink cherry-like fruit. They sank into the plush cushions of the sofa while the race continued.

Boden and Jaxzon remained glued to the viewer arguing with the unseen announcer.

"Father and his friends used to do that during Super Bowl games." She shook her head in amusement. "I've lost him, haven't I?"

"I believe it's a male bonding thing."

"Hmmm, must be." Guin sipped her ruvin. "Do you ever wonder if Boden has a different colored plaid shirt for each day of the week?"

Bree giggled.

Two racers stalled in the water, one completely sinking. The pilot ejected. Rescuers in a hovering craft hauled her from the raging water.

Boden and Jaxzon derided the pilots for the poor designs of their vehicles.

"Shoddy workmanship," scoffed Jaxzon, shaking his head in disgust. "I don't understand how those two qualified for such a prestigious race."

They went on to discuss the advantages and disadvantages of intakes and propulsion systems. Bree and Guin cheered the little purple ship overtaking the ugly green one, earning a scowl from Boden, who picked the green one to win.

The viewer flickered, changing back to a live view. The floor vibrated when the contestants screamed back into the canyon, streaking toward the finish line. Boden and Jaxzon returned to the railing. She and Bree joined them, cheering the small purple craft.

The walls reverberated with the roar of engines as the leading racers finished. The purple ship edged past the others then swooped over the dome in victory.

Guin and Bree jumped up and down, clapping and cheering. Guin pointed at Boden. "In your face!"

The four nursed their drinks while discussing the race's outcome until Derek poked his head in. "There you two are. We've been searching everywhere. The hover is leaving. We need to go."

"Until I see you next, my lady." Jaxzon's lips brushed her hand.

Boden cleared his throat. Bree elbowed him in the ribs.

"I hope to see you soon, my prince." Guin kissed Jaxzon's cheek, then took Bree's arm, rushing ahead of Boden through the door.

Vertuma raised an eyebrow when Guin and Bree joined the rest of the women in the limousine. "Where did you two slink off to?"

Guin ignored her, though Bree seemed more than happy to answer.

"We enjoyed the race from the finest seats in the house. In the king's box with Prince Jaxzon."

Conversation in the vehicle stopped. Every eye turned in Bree's direction.

The princess's darkened. "The rumors must be true." She peered around. "It appears as though the Earthling has seduced our prince. I wonder what his people will think?"

Sarya giggled.

"You're vile," Bree snapped.

Guin put a hand on Bree's arm. "I wonder, Princess Vertuma, what his people would think about your spreading rumors and name-calling? Not very queen-like behavior."

Jaw working, Vertuma faced the window, saying nothing more.

The ride to the Shift Station was a quiet one.

Bree and Guin waited in the hallway awaiting their turns to Shift. Guin rested her back against the wall as Vertuma's security team filed past.

Bree squeezed Guin's arm. "You sure told her."

"I'm not proud of myself for calling her out. I just couldn't let her say those things about Jaxzon and me or allow her to accuse me of hurting anyone. She's trying to turn the other women against me and so far, she's doing a wonderful job. What happens if she talks to the press, and they believe her?"

"Reporters love you," Bree assured her. "They've seen for themselves you're the better person. I wouldn't worry too much about what Her Highness says. They know what she's like."

"I suppose."

The Vekdromic gathered at the palace in Arwon for the evening meal. Afterward drinks were served near the fountain in the courtyard.

Bree, Guin, Derek, and Delori spoke together, admiring the garden.

Jaxzon joined them, placing a hand at the small of Guin's back. "Did you enjoy the race?"

"It was great. I guess those go-karts were child's play in comparison." Guin laughed. "After today I'm almost embarrassed I took you there."

"I told you, that was one of the best nights of my life. You gave me an opportunity I would never have been allowed here."

"Someone's staring." Derek tilted his head in Vertuma's direction.

The princess approached, slipping between Guin and Jaxzon.

"Not talking about me, are we? That isn't very polite." Her gaze seared into Guin's. "Or queen-like."

"Not at all," said Jaxzon. "I was asking the ladies if they enjoyed their day."

"Considering they were with you I would think you knew."

"Did you enjoy yourself, Vertuma?" he asked in a tight voice.

"It was a race. Aren't they all the same?"

"I suppose they might be for some. I find them quite exhilarating myself." His telecon buzzed. He glanced at it. "Please excuse me, I must speak with my father before he retires. Ladies." He bowed to each before leaving.

Gazing after Jaxzon, Vertuma sighed, then gave Guin's group a critical look before striding away.

Guin excused herself and went to her room, too tired to care what Vertuma thought.

CHAPTER NINETEEN

"A spa day?" Two days had passed since the race. Guin was back at the Vau'uan's estate.

"A spa day," Delori confirmed. "*Vuluptas* is a small moon teeming with mineral hot springs. You are invited to Iamatiki, one of the galaxy's most renowned beauty treatment facilities. You will be treated to their exclusive services. Derek will take you first thing in the morning. Get a good night's sleep."

Steam and yellow mists swirled around their hover as Guin rode with Derek and Boden to Iamatiki. Devoid of vegetation, the moon had a sickly gray appearance. The pungent odor of sulfur permeated everything, including the sealed compartment of their hover. Sunlight shone dimly through the smoke-choked skies.

The scent of burnt matches seared Guin's throat. "How do people live here?"

Derek shrugged. "Domes."

When they arrived, the receptionist shooed Derek and Boden away, along with the other male guards and chaperones. An attendant showed the ten remaining women of the Vekdromic inside, separating them into pairs.

Guin was partnered with a tall, dark-haired Phernaian named Nel.

Exotic oils perfumed the air. Strong fingers worked knots from Guin's muscles. For the first time since leaving Earth, she fully relaxed as the aromatherapy took effect, soothing away her stress and anxiety.

She smiled at Nel, who lay on a nearby table, her chin resting on her forearm. "My full name is Guinevere. Is your name short for something?"

"Yes. But I don't think you'd be able to pronounce it."

"Try me. I'm pretty good with accents."

"Xchitltnelwuvegle."

Guin's eyes widened. "Whoa."

Nel laughed. "I told you. Phernaians are born with two larynxes. One controlled by each lung. Our language has words with complex sounds."

"I bet you have a stellar singing voice."

"Me? No. Although our best singers can really reach the highs and lows, some at the same time."

Facials came next. With mudpacks of the moon's many minerals stiffening on their faces. She and Nel couldn't talk until the treatment was over.

Next, an aide fitted them with gas masks. They entered a sauna sitting above a steam vent. They reclined on wooden seats in the center of the room. A portal in the floor opened beneath them. Intense heat and billows of steam belched from the depths of Vuluptas, enveloping them in a vaporous, orange cloud.

Giggling at their face gear, they managed a muffled conversation while sweat ran in rivulets down their bodies. Once the treatment was complete, the vent closed. Fresh air filled the room. A cooling mist sprayed from above.

An aide offered fresh towels then showed them to a large room containing a glass-walled enclosure. A tumbler full of an icy drink awaited each. "Please, have a seat, ladies. This is a hyperbaric chamber. A variety of gasses will be introduced at high pressure. The effect will help tighten the skin, nurture the organs, and purify the blood."

The door closed. The woman tapped on a pad beside the door, then knocked on the glass. "If you need anything, hit this button." She pointed to a small speaker inside the chamber.

A slight hissing came from a vent, announcing the first gas to enter the glass box.

Guin sniffed, testing the air. Whatever they pumped into the booth was odorless. She lifted her glass of silver liquid. "Cheers, to new friends and purified blood."

Nel clinked her glass with Guin's, and they each took a sip.

Wrapped in a large spa towel, Guin continued their earlier conversation, "Your younger brother sounds as mischievous as my sisters were." She stretched her jaw to clear her ears when the pressure in the booth changed.

"Yes, he can be a real handf —" Nel's glass slipped from her grasp, shattering on the floor. Her lips reddened, and her face followed suit. She lurched forward

Guin caught her, dropping her own drink, adding to the glass scattered at their feet.

Nel stopped breathing.

Guin slid her knees under Nel, holding her above the floor. She used her own towel to sweep the broken glass to the side. She eased Nel to the floor then hit the button on the speaker, yelling for help. She tried prying open the door, but it wouldn't budge.

Guin performed CPR, blowing lungsful of air into her mouth as Nel's chest rose and fell with each puff. Her eyes fluttered. She drew a single breath. After several seconds, Nel failed to take another. Guin resumed CPR.

Her lungs burned, and her head throbbed. She grew lightheaded when Boden burst into the room. He typed on the panel. A rush of air whooshed out when the chamber's door opened.

He lifted Nel and carried her outside, shouting for the attendants.

By the time the attendant arrived, Nel was breathing on her own and trying to talk. Boden set her on a chair, where she adjusted her towel, thanking him as the attendant knelt beside her.

Guin remained in the chamber, fighting dizziness and shock. Boden handed her a fresh towel, turning away as she wrapped it around herself with trembling fingers.

"Watch the glass." He helped her to her feet then guided her to a chair.

Medical personnel arrived and assessed Nel. One of the medics shone a light in Guin's eyes then checked her pulse. "Do you feel ill?"

She shook her head.

"It appears to be oxygen poisoning," the other medic attending Nel said. "But we need to take you to the hospital to be sure."

They strapped her to a hovering stretcher and guided it from the room.

"Can you show me the tanks feeding this chamber?" Boden asked the attendant.

"They're locked in a storage room. This room isn't programmed for pure oxygen, not with a Phernaian inside."

"Show me the tanks," Boden ordered then followed her from the room.

Still in shock, Guin dressed then waited in the lobby for the other women to finish their treatments. Bree found her and introduced her partner, a beautiful, bald woman named Uso.

"We're leaving," Boden said when he entered the lobby. He steered Guin toward the exit.

Bree waved to Uso. "Why the hurry?"

Guin took her hand. "I'll tell you later."

They passed through the lobby, collecting Derek as they went.

"Hey, what happened? Medics came and took someone away. Is everything okay?"

Boden ushered them into the hover. "No, Derek, nothing's okay."

The four loaded into the vehicle. Boden tapped an address on the panel. "We're going back to Arwon. Jaxzon wants you home. The king is calling for a formal inquiry into these accidents."

"Home?" Guin asked.

"The Vau'uan's estate. He wants me to continue as your security."

"Thank you, Boden. If you hadn't come in when you did, she might have died. I couldn't continue CPR much longer. You saved her life."

"You saved her life. If you hadn't kept carbon dioxide in her, she might have died. Phernaian's atmosphere is mostly carbon dioxide. There was pure oxygen being pumped into your chamber. You weren't affected, but it could have killed her."

Bree had been looking from one to the other. "Can someone please tell me what's going on?"

"Yeah," said Derek. "Who are we talking about?"

Guin explained.

"I checked the tanks and the program," said Boden. "Someone messed with the system. They somehow managed to turn off everything except the oxygen. It appears someone is trying to get to Griffin."

"How do you figure I was the target? I breathe oxygen. Why couldn't it have been an accident?"

Boden shook his head. "How do you explain Bree's incident? Sounds to me like someone wants you out of the running."

"How did you know we were in trouble?"

"My instructions were to keep an eye on you. I was verifying your location when I saw you on the floor. Good thing too, there were seventeen minutes left on the timer."

By the end of the day, they were back at the Vau'uan's manor.

Jaxzon arrived with a contingent of guards, and Delori offered the dining hall for a briefing.

The commander of the king's guard, Orist, questioned Boden and Guin. "Did either of you see anyone suspicious in or around the room?"

They both answered no.

Glaring at Boden, Orist's Arctic eyes glinted. "You should have done a more thorough inspection before going in."

"There wasn't time. He was helping Nel." Neither man paid Guin any attention but continued staring blackly at each other.

Orist ran a hand over his shaved scalp. "It was substandard work. You should always be aware of your surroundings. If this is the type of protection you give, you'll never be alone with the prince again."

Boden's scowl deepened.

Jaxzon raised his hands. "Enough! You need to work together. I don't believe in coincidence. There's something going on here, and we need to find out what it is before someone is seriously hurt."

Boden broke his glare from Orist. He faced Jaxzon. "What do you need from me?"

"I need you to stay with Guin. If she is the target, I want someone with her wherever she goes."

"What about the other women? Will they be given extra protection too?" asked Guin.

"Yes. The King's Guard will be doubled at every event, and a royal guard will be assigned to each of the remaining women." Jaxzon addressed Orist. "We don't want more injuries, accidental or otherwise."

~

THAT EVENING, Guin sat in the solarium with her head tilted back. Strange stars hung in the sky above.

"What do you see up there?" Jaxzon asked from the doorway.

"I was searching for a familiar constellation, then I realized there is no Big Dipper here."

"Big Dipper?"

"Never mind. Are you staying tonight?"

"No, I'm expected at the palace. I'm leaving Boden and two other guards to make sure you're safe."

"Thank you. I can't believe anyone would want to hurt us." Her voice caught, and her lip trembled.

Jaxzon spread his arms, and she flew into them, resting her head against his chest. His heartbeat thundered in her ear, soothing her frayed nerves. Warmth and contentment filled her. She closed her eyes and sighed, wishing to stay here forever.

He lifted her chin placing a tender kiss on her lips. She caressed his neck. Her fingers played in his hair.

Releasing her, he sighed. "I'm sorry, I must go. My father is waiting for me. Goodnight, my lady."

Her heart sank. "Goodnight, my prince."

The full moon rose. She stood in its glow, tracking the stars in the sky, until Orist entered.

"King Jaezain would like a word with you," he said in his gruff voice.

Her heart rose to her throat. "Of course. Where is he?"

"I'm here, my dear," King Jaezain said, coming through the door.

Two uniformed guards took their stations nearby.

"Your Majesty." She dropped into a low curtsy.

"Rise, rise. No need for formalities. I want an *informal* word with you."

With Orist following, they strolled together through the rows of plants and flowers, the full moon bathing them with a bluish luminescence. His blue eyes sparkled. *So much like Jaxzon's.*

He wore a dark green jacket over a lighter mint-green shirt, a teal ascot wound around his neck with the ends tucked into the top of his shirt. "Lady Guinevere, you've made quite an impression upon the citizens of my realm, and I must admit, I am equally impressed. More importantly, you seem to have captured the full attention of my son."

The heat rose in her cheeks. "We've only recently met, Your Majesty."

"Lady, I may be getting older, however I am no fool." He brushed his fingers over a fuzzy, pink flower shaped like a fat caterpillar. "You and my son have been spending considerable time together."

He raised a hand before Guin could protest. "I am a ruler. I know much of what goes on in my realm, and particularly what happens within my own home. Not that I mind." He gazed at the moon. "My son has never shown much interest in any of our noblewomen, so I am intrigued. As an outsider, and one not having knowledge of our customs and laws, why do you believe you could rule at my son's side?"

Taken aback by the question, Guin took a moment before answering. "Sire, your son means more to me than a title, or a palace, or the power one gains as Queen. I'm not here to win a prize. I'm here because I feel something for Jaxzon, the man, not the prince. Granted, I may not understand your customs or laws. Yet I do understand Jaxzon. He possesses great strength and courage, he's honest and has integrity, and the ability to put the people's interests above his own, plus so much more. Jaxzon will be a great ruler, although I believe we will be greater together."

"Why do you believe so?"

"Because a ruler must compromise. A ruler needs the ability to understand both sides of every situation. Jaxzon cares deeply for his people, yet he is not one of them. He's led a privileged life and may not always comprehend the plight of the common person. On my planet and in my country, the governments are out of touch with what's happening to many of their people. As an outsider, I might help give a voice to those who would otherwise go unheard."

She lowered her eyes. "Begging Your Majesty's pardon, I don't mean to say you, or your government don't care, or you ignore those in need."

"As with the Bethan children?"

"Yes, I mean no—"

"And you are trying to do something about this injustice, without asking for my government's assistance?"

"We attempted to gain support from Council members. But the red tape has slowed the process. I-I was not aware you knew of our efforts."

"As I have mentioned, I am aware of much that goes on within my realm, and when a young woman from Earth appears and exposes my shortcomings, I do indeed take notice."

She bit her lip.

"No need to worry." He patted her arm. "I am not angered. On the contrary, I am grateful to you for bringing this disgrace to my attention. Those children and their families—along with thousands of others—are now receiving the help they need."

"Thank you, Your Majesty. This means more to me than you know."

They came to a bench, Jaezain sat and indicated she sit beside him. He took her hand. "All thanks should be to you. Heads have rolled since your revelation, and more will follow if anything such as this happens in the future."

Guin tried not to appear horrified. "I hope you don't mean that heads have literally rolled?"

King Jaezain chuckled. "No, Lady, a metaphor. Although, some are seeking new jobs."

"I'm sorry, I didn't want to cause anyone trouble."

"Do not apologize. If they cared to keep their jobs, they would have done them properly. What you have said regarding leadership is true. Sometimes a ruler must make harsh decisions." He cocked his head, peering at her through one slit eye. "You are an anomaly, Miss Griffin. Not many young women possess the passion and drive you have shown. You are endowed with extraordinary compassion, and you have proven, you truly care for our people. I must confess, I had my men do a thorough background check on you, and I am pleasantly surprised. For someone so young, you have led a remarkably meaningful, and inspirational life thus far. Your work with the elderly and the underprivileged has shown you have a kindness that is rare among most your age."

"A background check?"

"I would be irresponsible if I did not obtain as much knowledge of a young woman who may likely become our next Queen. Wouldn't you agree?" He winked. "Now, I had better return to my home before I am missed. I believe my son may be waiting for me. Please do enjoy the rest of your night, Lady Guinevere."

"Thank you, Your Majesty, and thank you for helping those children."

"You're welcome my dear. But if you run into similar situations during your time here, please bring them to my direct attention. No more speeches to the press."

Guin lowered her head as the heat crept into her cheeks. "Yes, Your Majesty."

"Goodnight, my dear."

"Goodnight, Sire."

CHAPTER TWENTY

The following week, Delori went over with Guin, the plans for the next event—a charity fashion show. The remaining ten women would be modeling clothes by Valdid, one of the most prominent designers in the galaxy.

Prior to the main event, the ladies of the Vekdromic were slated to make a publicity visit to an elderly care facility.

"Isn't that a little exploitative?" asked Guin.

"No. The visit will help promote the charity. The fashion show raises money every year for research into ailments affecting the elderly. The residents have agreed to take part in the event."

On the day of the visit, cameras followed them as they were introduced to the elderly residents. The ladies were given a tour of the facility—a homy two-story building resembling an old farmhouse with high gables and an enclosed porch encircling the structure. As Guin ran her finger along the doorjamb, her fingertip disappeared into the molding.

A hologram.

The home contained a recreation room with a wall-sized tele-screen, a high-tech kitchen with stainless steel appliances, and spacious living quarters for the two dozen or so residents.

Traversing the halls, she passed a room where a man sat alone facing the window. He had the same sun-hardened features and wispy white hair as Raney's Grandpa Dana. Guin paused in the doorway before following the rest of the group to a spacious common room.

Dozens of residents made their way into the room, either on their own or with an aide to guide their hover chairs. The man wasn't among them. She approached an attendant to ask after him.

"Oh, you mean Tolvie. He's been in and out of a catatonic state for weeks. More *in* lately. His family recently stopped visiting, so he sits staring through the window most days.

The women helped in running a game much like Bingo—but played with strange symbols and a droid doing the calling—Guin slipped from the common room and made her way through the hall to Tolvie's room.

She knocked. "May I come in?"

He didn't move.

"Hello, Mr. Tolvie."

Family pictures covered the walls, with more filling a side table. The images became animated when she passed by. Tolvie appeared in most, sitting aboard a grand sailboat, his hair blowing in the wind, the boat rocking beneath him. The photographs depicted him at first as a robust young man who, with each changing image, grew older—his hair thinning, his face cracking and creasing from the sun, wind, and age. Children in progressive stages of growth waved from the frames, their sun-tanned faces smiling.

"My name is Guin. I'm pleased to meet you, sir. You have a beautiful family." She bent to his level. "Are you a sailing man?"

Tolvie stared straight ahead.

"I have a friend, a man about your age, who loves to sail too. I call him Grandpa Dana. He's my best friend's grandfather. He used to take us sailing during summer break. He sometimes doesn't talk either. You know what I would do on those occasions?" She paused, hoping he might ask. "I sing him one of his favorite sailing songs. Would you like me to sing for you? The words are pretty silly, so don't laugh. Here it goes, 'come on the Sloop John B., my grandfather and me'."

She sang all three verses to "The John B. Sails", as taught to her by Grandpa Dana the summer her parents died. Tolvie didn't stir, although, for one flick of a second a sparkle appeared in his eyes.

"I hope you liked the song, Mr. Tolvie. I would love to come back and talk, or even sing again if you wish? You might teach me your favorite ballad?" Though he showed no response, Guin continued to tell him stories of her and Raney's summertime adventures with Grandpa Dana. "I would love to go for a sail here someday. Maybe you could join me?"

Tolvie didn't blink.

"I have to get back before I'm missed. I enjoyed meeting you. Have a good day, sir." She patted his hand, then headed back to the common room.

The residents still played their game. The ladies from the Vekdromic helped staff prepare lunch. Guin set the tables in the dining hall as cameras clicked and flashed.

That evening at the Vau'uan's, Guin packed for the coming week. Derek knocked on her door and without waiting for an answer he and Delori entered.

"What's wrong?" Guin asked.

"Nothing's wrong." Derek grinned and flipped his telecon toward her. Video of Guin singing to Tolvie played. "When did you shoot this?"

"Where did this come from? Who recorded this?"

"Apparently a reporter followed you and videoed the whole thing." Delori smiled. "You can't buy publicity like this."

Tears of outrage filled Guin's eyes. "That was a private moment. I wasn't aware anyone was watching, much less recording. It's an invasion of privacy."

"No such thing," said Delori. "You signed waivers, as did the man's family. The reporters had permission to record whatever you did at the facility."

"It's wrong. They're exploiting this poor man, and I won't have any part of it."

Derek lowered his telecon, frowning. "They didn't show his face, and they muted his name. No one will recognize him. They were touched by your compassion. I almost cried."

"But this isn't right, Derek." Her anger mixed with sorrow. She swallowed against the lump forming in her throat. "They should have asked. I would never have allowed them to record." Fighting off tears, she wiped her sleeve across her face, remembering her grandmother's admonishment.

"Aw, Guin." Derek sat on the bed and put his arm around her. "Don't be upset. You didn't know. Besides, you had a beautiful moment, pure and honest. People really go for this stuff."

"I simply wish they'd asked first or told me afterward. Seeing yourself singing like a fool to someone who isn't even aware of you is a bit shocking."

"If they weren't in love with you before, they will be now," he said. "The video has been viewed more than thirty million times on this site alone."

There was a gentle tapping on the door. Delori opened it to find Bree standing in the hallway with a huge grin on her face.

"Did you see it?" She bounced into the room and sat beside Guin. "You are amazing. Some people might have suspected you were putting on some sort of act before, but after this, everyone will know you're genuine." She slung an arm around Guin.

Guin frowned.

Delori answered another knock. Jaxzon and Boden joined the party.

Jaxzon closed the door. "You've seen the news? They're calling you the Angel of Arwon."

"She's upset," said Delori. "She believes the reporter was wrong to record without her knowledge."

"He was. They took a private moment and made it public." He knelt on one knee, taking Guin's hands into his. "But you had a beautiful moment. You touched our hearts with your kindness and compassion. I am honored to know you, Guinevere Griffin."

Boden cleared his throat. Everyone looked at him. His face flushed. "What? My throat itches."

Derek opened the door. "Come on, let's give them some privacy."

"Keep it short, Griffin," Boden said as Derek forced him from the room.

Jaxzon's arms encircled her waist. Their lips met in a gentle kiss. She leaned her head against his chest, calmed by the soothing beat of his heart. "Jaxzon," she whispered.

He smoothed her hair. "Guin."

This is where she wished to remain forever, nothing could hurt her when she was in his arms.

Boden tapped on the door and poked his head in. "Orist is heading this way."

Jaxzon sighed. "I wish they would leave me alone for one night."

"If we had a whole night, I'm not sure I'd let you go," said Guin.

"Then I better leave while we still have the strength." He grinned, then kissed her. "Good night, my lady."

"Good night, my prince."

CHAPTER TWENTY-ONE

Guin's anger at the intrusion ebbed after Delori informed her that the video became the catalyst for a record inpouring of donations to the charity. The fashion show had been projected to be one of the biggest money makers in their history.

The following week Guin, Bree, and the other ladies traveled in two luxurious hovers to the venue hosting the show, Benstoke Towers, the finest hotel in Kurrel.

Free from the control of Vertuma, Guin found the women she rode with were friendlier, although she didn't trust them not to turn on her the moment Vertuma was around.

The voluptuous bald lady from Tendraq, Uso, sat across from Guin. "We saw the recording of you with the old man. You were very sweet to him."

Embarrassed, Guin said, "Thank you, Uso."

Uso's bright, honey brown eyes flashed. "I heard over nine hundred billion people have seen it. You're breaking records for the most viewed video in history."

Her head bobbing with excitement, Un'Un, the representative

from Uetov4 said, "I heard it's over a trillion views. You are a popular person on my planet, possibly more popular than me."

The heat in Guin's face deepened. "You're so sweet, although I doubt that's true."

Un'Un smiled. Her resemblance to Jaxzon's mother was uncanny. She had the same dark, almond-shaped eyes, button nose, and creamy complexion as most inhabitants of Uetov4 Guin had met.

Upon their arrival, a short, dark-haired woman wearing a beige suit trimmed in cream ruffles and holding a tele-screen in the crook of her arm ushered the Vekdromic group into the lobby.

"Good morning, ladies." She peered over the rims of reading glasses. "I am Ivai, the production coordinator. The show will be held in the banquet hall of the roof-top restaurant. Follow me."

She stopped at a bank of elevator doors and pressed the call button for the one-hundredth floor.

Horrified, Guin waved Derek over. "I can't ride in one of those things for a hundred floors."

He informed Ivai they would meet her upstairs, then asked Guin, "What do you want to do?"

"I don't know. We would take at least half an hour or more to climb all those stairs. Isn't there another way?"

Boden joined them. "Why aren't you going with the others?"

Derek gestured to the closing doors. "Guin can't handle elevators. How about the three of us ride up alone? We can stop and get off whenever you need. Otherwise, you could bow out gracefully. I can tell them you're ill."

She took a deep, calming breath. *You're a grown woman Guinevere Griffin. It's only an elevator. Millions of people use them every day. They are completely safe. You will be fine.* "I can do this. If I feel sick or dizzy, we can take the stairs for a few flights then try again. Message Bree and tell her we'll be late."

He typed a text. "No signal. It might be the building."

They boarded the first elevator. Boden waved off two men who attempted to board with them and depressed the "100" button. The doors slid shut. Guin closed her eyes taking deep, even breaths. At the first upward movement, her gut lurched. She lasted only seconds before her head spun and her stomach knotted.

She gripped Derek's arm. He hit the third-floor button. The door slid open. She stumbled out, collapsing against the far wall. Her breath came in uneven gasps. He put an arm around her and guided her through the stairway door with Boden in tow.

"I'm so sorry. I've always been like this. My parents lived in the penthouse suite. I climbed thirty-five flights twice a day for school."

Derek frowned. "Why didn't they move?"

Guin shrugged. By the ninth landing he asked if she was ready to try again. The elevator rose four floors before she shook her head. They took to the stairs.

Ivai spotted Guin when they exited the stairwell on the one-hundredth floor. "You're late." Taking Guin's arm she hurried her to a room where models were having their hair and makeup done. Sitting Guin in a chair she called a stylist over, explaining how she wanted Guin's hair.

"We have two outfits for you tonight. You go on first and you will be our grand finale, so you must be perfect." She told the stylist to be quick then recruited a makeup person for when he was done. "We start in forty-five. Get a move on, people," she called, and whisked out of the room.

The stylist pulled Guin's hair back into a French knot. The makeup artist applied a powder base, eyeliner, mascara, lip liner, and a light application of lipstick. Studying her work, she leaned left and right, then shrugged. "You're done."

Ivai appeared from nowhere. She swept Guin into another room filled with gowns and accessories. She thrust a garment bag into Guin's hands. "Take off everything and put this on."

"Everything?"

"Yes. This dress is form-fitting, and we can't have lines. Valdid will be here shortly to make adjustments."

Guin stripped and slipped into the gown. The dress fit as though it had been made for her.

She was having trouble with the fastening when a man dressed in white entered the room. He wore his silver-lined, white tie tucked into his jacket. His egg-shell fedora sported a white satin band. His bronze-tanned face lit up as he beheld her. "Perfect," he said, holding her arms out to her sides. "I couldn't have done better with an in-person fitting." His smile broadened, showing his straight, white teeth. His golden-brown eyes crinkled at the edges. "I am Valdid. I designed this gown with an angel in mind, and now I have the Angel of Arwon to wear it."

Guin fiddled with a fold in her skirt, flustered by his use of the media's newest nickname for her.

His thick, black ponytail swished with his movements. He circled, appraising the fit from every angle, then fastened the dress, smoothing the fabric over her curves.

Having a man straightening and smoothing her clothing was strange, but he was all business. After finishing his adjustments, he leaned back.

The gown's silver fabric shimmered with each movement. Bright metallic lace, woven in an intricate pattern, decorated the A-line skirt. The back of the gown dipped below her waist.

"It's gorgeous," she said. "Thank you for allowing me to model it."

His bushy eyebrows shot up. "You thank me for allowing you to wear this gown?" He laughed. "It is I who thanks you for being my creative inspiration! You are truly the angel for whom I design. My design shines because you shine. I put my heart into this dress, and you have stolen my heart. Now I am putting my heart back into the dress. Yes?"

The designer accessorized the dress with a sparkling silver choker and flowing, multi-stranded earrings, then helped her slide into a pair of six- inch silver stilettos.

"Exquisite!" Clapping twice he called for Ivai.

Guin followed Ivai to an area behind a set of curtains separating the models from the audience. Patrons filled rows of seats, sipping drinks and waiting for the show to begin. In the center of the stage, a life-sized hologram of a smiling Valdid rotated. A strange symbol hung above his head.

"Wait here," said Ivai. "Once the music begins, you start your walk. Kiera will give you your cue." She pointed to a young lady who waved.

Near the end of the line of models, Bree waited her turn, dressed in a ruffly, puffy gown. Her hair had been fluffed into natural, tight curls.

She rushed over to Guin. "You look fabulous."

"So do you. I love your hair this way." Guin showed Bree the back of her dress.

She squealed. "Guin, you're stunning. That gown doesn't hide anything. I love it!"

"I'm covered. It's just a little low in the back."

"A little?"

"What's the symbol over Valdid's head?"

Bree peered through the sheer curtain. "His signature. He puts one somewhere on every gown he creates."

"Okay ladies," Ivai said in a low voice. "We are about to begin. Everyone in their places. When you're finished, go straight to your dressing rooms and change. Don't dawdle."

The lights in the room faded, and the stage lights brightened as the charity's organizer took the stage thanking everyone for their generous donations. She explained what the charity was for and introduced other members of the organization.

A strange metallic banging—what Guin supposed was music—filled the room. Kiera pointed. The audience gasped then applauded as Guin strode onto the catwalk, trying to remember the videos of models Delori had shown her. She ignored the familiar rush of blood in her cheeks and stopped at the halfway point. The fabric glimmered and sparkled as she spun. The skirt flared. She strutted to the end then back again, leaving the stage when the next model made her entrance.

She wished Bree luck, then headed to the changing room.

Ivai's assistant, Amnil, intercepted Guin and handed her a garment bag before leaving her to change.

She unzipped the bag. Where a gown should have been, were instead strips of purple cloth with a bit of sheer fabric, dangling from the hanger. Searching the bottom of the bag she found nothing more. "Oh, no way. I can't wear this."

Opening the door, she poked her head out and waved Amnil over. "I think there's been a mistake. There is no gown."

His expression was one of horror. He pushed past her into the room. After peering inside the bag, his frown relaxed into a smile. "This *is* your gown. I can help you if you'd like?"

"No, I can manage." She squinted at the gown again. "Can you show me what goes where?"

He explained how small patches of cloth, attached to a sheer fabric, would cover her breasts. The sheer fabric hung from a golden chain clasped around her neck. A wide swath of sheer purple fabric wound around her lower body, barely covering what needed to be covered. Mere shreds of dark purple cloth held together in a flare of see-through fabric comprised the skirt. He removed a tiny matching thong from the bag.

She widened her eyes. "I can't wear this. There must be a mistake.

This is too revealing."

"You should see what the others are wearing."

"Seriously?"

"This is the latest in fashion. Everyone will want one after tonight. Believe me."

"If you say so."

Once she had it on, the gown covered more than the last bikini she'd worn. The fabric complimented her skin tone and the green in her eyes.

A tap sounded on the door. Valdid entered. He extended his arms. "Voila!"

She laughed at his use of the familiar word.

He made minute adjustments to the garment, then replaced her silver necklace and earrings with gold ones then helped her into a pair of purple-and-gold platform shoes.

The stylist transformed Guin's hair; stylish amber curls coiled, cascading over her shoulders and down her back.

Ivai nodded her approval then taking Guin's arm, ushered her backstage. "This time, after your last turn, Valdid will meet you at the center of the stage. You will stand with him."

Bree waited at the front of the line. Her gown of sheer pure white fabric left little to the imagination, but she pulled it off with poise and dignity. Her dark skin contrasted beautifully with the white fabric. Her two-tone hair had been swept back in a French twist. Her thick eyebrows had been darkened further, while her eyelids had highlights of rich red with pink shadowing. Her full lips had been painted blood-red.

Guin's lips formed an "o" at her friend's appearance.

Bree smiled then stared gape-mouthed back at Guin. When her turn came, Bree strolled with confidence to the end of the stage, where Jaxzon sat in the front row.

A blush threatened to encompass Guin's entire body. Heartbeats pulsed in her ears. Her stomach tightened into a knot. "Remember," she murmured, "look over his head. You can do this, pretend he's not there."

She took a deep, calming breath. The last model reached the middle of the runway, and Guin strode forward.

All sound became a buzz and the crowd blurred. At the center of the stage, she stopped, spun, then continued down the catwalk.

Jaxzon's jaw dropped. He followed her every move, his eyes glittering in the lights.

She made it to the end, leaned from left to right, then returned.

Applause filled the hall. Valdid met her center stage, and she faced the audience. He wrapped an arm around her waist then raised his hand, sweeping it in a downward motion, presenting her to the crowd.

The designer bowed to Jaxzon. "Your Highness, you honor me with your attendance tonight."

Jaxzon dipped his head in return.

"Thank you to our patrons for your generous donations. I am especially grateful to the ladies of the Vekdromic for displaying my creations so beautifully." Valdid nodded to Guin. "And to my muse, our Angel of Arwon, I wish I had a hundred of you to inspire me. Whenever you find yourself in need of a gown, please, do not forget Valdid."

CHAPTER TWENTY-TWO

After leaving the stage and changing into her flowery blouse and jeans, Guin found Bree then located Derek and Boden by the stairwell exit.

"Bree, we'll take the elevator. Boden and Guin are taking the stairs. We'll meet them in the lobby." Derek said.

Bree frowned. "Why?"

Derek took her hand. "I'll tell you on the way down."

"Wuss," Guin teased, poking his chest. "Too much exercise?"

"Yep."

"So, Griffin's afraid of elevators?" Boden asked, opening the stair door.

"I'm not afraid. They give me motion sickness." This was mostly true. The sickness made her feel helpless. Being out of control terrified her.

He smirked. "Whatever you say. You sure seemed scared earlier."

"What did I ever do to you? I had hoped we'd moved past this." She jogged ahead of him.

After five flights, he asked if she wanted to try the elevator. She shrugged. At the next landing they exited the stairwell.

Boden jabbed the down button. "You did good today, Griffin."

"Did you say something nice to me?"

"Don't let it go to your head, just making conversation."

She sighed.

"That's odd." He squinted at the darkened numbers. "All ten elevators are on the first fl—"

An alarm sounded. Flashing red lights protruded from the walls. Guests exited their rooms, heading for the stairs. Gripping Guin's arm he followed the stream of people into the stairwell. Some speculated as to what the emergency could be. Others searched for information on their telecons.

No messages were going through.

She and Boden slowed behind a woman carrying a baby while struggling to corral three young children. Hotel guests hustled past. One boy tripped. Guin clutched the back of his shirt, saving him from a fall.

The mother took the boy's hand. "Thank you."

"Would you like some help?"

"No, I—you're the angel! I-I would love your help."

Guin scooped up the girl, while Boden carried the twin boys. They descended another twenty-five floors before they let the children walk a few flights on their own. He took the baby, giving her mother a break.

Upon exiting the stairwell, uniformed officers met Guin's group. They ushered them through the dust-filled lobby. A dark film covered the floor and furniture. A fine, choking powder hung in the air. They were shown outside to a cordoned-off area and ordered to wait.

The young woman took the child from Boden. "I wonder what happened."

Emergency vehicles filled the street. Uniformed officers guarded the hotel entrance.

He tried his telecon again. "Still no signal. Follow me." They approached a woman weaving her way through the crowd. Boden proffered his wrist. "I'm with the king's service."

The woman ran a small credit card-like machine over his arm. A metal tab popped from a slit on top of the scanner. She handed the tab to Boden, then attempted to scan Guin. "You don't scan."

"She's not from here. She's visiting from Earth."

Her eyes widened. "Viyet! You're alive! They said you died!"

"What? Why would anyone say I died?"

"They said you were in the elevator."

"What elevator?" Guin and Boden asked together.

"The one that fell."

Panic rose in Guin's throat, nearly choking her. "Derek! Bree!"

"She's alive, Stel. Over here, she's alive." The woman waved at a uniformed man, who hurried toward them.

Boden headed toward the hotel.

Guin stumbled after him. Cold terror gripped her heart. "Jaxzon!"

"No." He shook his head. "He left earlier."

A guard barred their way. "No one leaves without being scanned."

Boden handed him the tab. "I'm in the king's service. Let me pass."

The man hesitated until the woman with the scanner verified Guin had been cleared.

They ran to the front of the building. Boden swore when his call didn't go through, then typed a message.

An amplified voice echoed from above. "Guests of Benstoke Towers, please follow the green cones to the rear of the hotel. Everyone else, please clear the area. Let emergency workers do their jobs."

Groaning when his message didn't send, Boden ducked under the barrier surrounding the entrance. An officer intercepted him, and they conversed.

"Clear the area please," the voice repeated.

An unnatural buzzing filled Guin's ears. Her breath came in short bursts, her chest constricted.

"Clear the area, please!" the voice boomed.

The building twisted and spun, becoming purple sky.

Catching her inches from the ground, Boden lifted her in his arms. "Guin, are you okay? Say something."

She took deep calming breaths. The buzzing faded. His face came into focus. Fear and concern showed in his eyes as he searched her face.

An officer asked if she needed medical attention.

"I'm fine. Just a little dizzy. Put me down. I need to find Jaxzon. I need to find Bree and Derek. I need to know they're okay." She twisted in Boden's arms.

He set her on her feet, keeping a steadying arm around her. "Was anyone in the elevator?"

The officer shrugged. "They're still searching the rubble."

Guin's head swam. She swayed, her knees buckling.

Boden tightened his grip. "Is there a list of people who came out?"

The man inclined his chin toward the woman with the scanner.

She found Derek and Bree's names. "The public have been ordered to leave. Your friends may have left the area."

A wave of relief washed over Guin. "Oh, thank god! What about Prince Jaxzon?"

"I would remember if I'd seen the prince."

"Please check," Guin pleaded.

"Are you saying the prince was in the building?"

"No." Boden shook his head. "He left before everyone. He was not in the elevator."

Guin's fear rose like a tidal wave, replacing the relief of learning Derek and Bree were safe.

Boden's telecon buzzed, and he jabbed the screen. "Jaxzon?" He glanced at Guin. "He's safe. Yes, she's here with me."

Guin's legs trembled. She grasped Boden's waist for support. His arm looped around her shoulders. He handed her the telecon.

"Jaxzon?" she said in a hoarse whisper.

"Guin, I was terrified I'd lost you. They said you'd died." His voice caught. He cleared his throat. "I'm bringing my hover for you and the others."

"Hurry." She handed the telecon to Boden.

He gave her shoulder a squeeze. "Let's go."

She kept an arm around him, and they went to meet Jaxzon. They found Derek and Bree after several of their texts popped through on Boden's telecon. He texted back and received directions to where they waited. Bree and Guin rushed together. She hugged her friends, relieved to find them safe.

A hover came to a stop beside them. Jaxzon jumped out and crushed her in his arms.

"Not here," Boden growled. "Get in."

Jaxzon helped Guin into the vehicle then he and the others piled in behind. The hover whipped around and sped off, leaving the city. Jaxzon's arms encircled her, and she clung to him, never wanting to let go. Those moments when she believed he might have been in the elevator had been the worst moments of her life. She held him tighter, burying her face in his chest. She heaved a broken sigh.

He smoothed her hair.

"Do we know what happened?" Boden asked.

"All anyone can do now is speculate," Jaxzon said. "One of the elevators somehow malfunctioned and fell several floors. They said the car may have fallen from the top floor, although they aren't sure."

"How could such a thing happen?" Boden demanded. "They're equipped with safety features making an accident impossible."

"They're investigating now. They're taking their time and being thorough."

"We're lucky Griffin is afraid of elevators." Boden nudged her foot with his. "It could have been us."

She nudged him back. "I'm not afraid. They make me sick."

"They don't know if anyone was in the elevator?" he asked.

"So far it appears as though everyone is accounted for." Jaxzon sighed. "They are still doing a headcount and won't be certain until they can get to the car. The shaft was badly damaged."

Bree peered around Guin at Jaxzon. "Do you believe this is another coincidence?"

"Could this have to do with the Vekdromic?" Derek asked.

"I believe so," Jaxzon answered. "There can't be this many coincidental accidents."

"At least we know Griffin isn't the target," said Boden.

"Why?" asked Bree.

"She wasn't in the elevator. I'd think that if she were the target, they would have made sure she was in the elevator before sabotaging it."

"So, who is the target?" Guin asked.

"Maybe someone is trying to hurt us all," Bree suggested. "It seemed like Guin could be the target at first. Maybe everything's completely random? Someone could be trying to minimize the competition."

Guin shivered. "Why hurt innocent people? Who would be so evil?"

No one answered. On the way to the Vau'uan estate they agreed Bree and Guin would stay there with Boden and additional security.

When they arrived, Jaxzon asked for a moment alone. He escorted Guin to the solarium then spun, clutching her in his arms. "I have never so terrified in my life. I don't know what I'd do if something happened to you."

"I thought it was you. I was so scared, I almost fainted. Remind me to thank Boden for catching me."

"He did? You fainted?"

"I had just walked a hundred flights of stairs carrying a small child most of the way. I didn't know if you and Bree and Derek were safe. I guess I was a bit overwhelmed." She smiled. "I'm fine now. I'm always fine when I'm in your arms. I wish I never had to leave them."

"I wish the same." He lifted her chin, touching her lips in a sweet, gentle kiss. He leaned his forehead against hers. Taking a deep ragged breath, he sighed. His grip tightened. "I've been thinking..."

"You've been thinking?"

"I've been thinking you're the one, Guin. The only one. I'm thinking when I'm with those other women I feel nothing. Not a spark. Not even a glimmer of what I feel for you. I'm thinking when I see you, when I touch you, when I hold you in my arms, I burn for you. I'm thinking I love you. I love you more than my own life. I'm thinking I've loved you from the moment we met. And I'm thinking I will love you until the day I die."

Guin's heart halted for a beat. In the depths of his eyes, she recognized the reflection of her soul. She loved him and there would never be anyone else. Pulling him down in a fervent kiss, she ran her hand over his neck and into his hair. His lips parted. She moaned as his tongue twisted against hers, his words echoing in her ears.

"I love you too," she whispered. "More than anything, more than life."

His lips covered hers. She sank into their warmth. The outside world disappeared. Her only world was Jaxzon, his body, his lips, his scent, his taste. She drank him in. The sensation was exquisite. She never wanted this moment to end.

Orist cleared his throat from the doorway. "Sorry for the interruption, Your Highness."

They broke apart. Jaxzon kept a tight grip on Guin's waist.

The Commander approached, his gaze darting between them. "I expected you would want to hear immediately. The elevator was empty."

"Thank you, Orist, that is very good news," Jaxzon said.

"We're checking security recordings in case someone tampered with the controls. We may take a few days to review the footage. I have my men going back a week to be sure," Orist said.

"Excellent. Boden will stay at the Vau'uan's with Guin. I want you to handpick two of your best to join him. Make sure one is female."

"Yes, Your Highness. Immediately." Orist gave a slight nod. "Is Your Highness going to the palace tonight?"

"Yes, I need to speak with my father. He's called an emergency Council meeting first thing in the morning. Please have the hover ready. I'll be there in a moment."

Orist bowed then left.

"I must go. My father wishes me back tonight. I want you with me. However, that wouldn't be proper. I'm sorry."

"I understand."

He kissed her forehead. "I will try to come by tomorrow, though I'm not sure of the time. I have meetings and other business I need to tend to."

"I'll miss you, but running a galaxy takes precedence over seeing me."

"Nothing is more important to me than you." He kissed her again.

"I love you, my lady."

"I love you, my prince."

CHAPTER TWENTY-THREE

Night terrors plagued Guin's sleep. A sense of foreboding filled her with dread. Jaxzon hadn't been able to return, though he sent messages through an irritated Boden.

Orist assigned two guards who took shifts outside her door, following wherever she went. Eedras, a stout, silent man, never met her eyes. He gave her the creeps, making her glad he had the night shift. Za'Had, a tall, light-blue Bethan, kept to herself, although unlike Eedras, she was friendly and smiled from her station at the end of the hall. Guin grew comfortable with her daily presence.

After another restless night, she lay in bed, her mind wandering through the twists and turns she'd been through since her arrival on Arwon.

A light rap on her door pulled her from her reverie. She yawned and stretched. "Come in, Derek."

Derek bounded into the room, plopped himself on her bed, and handed her an envelope. "From Heldivar Grint."

"Jeez Derek, are you ever *not* in a cheerful mood?" She eyed the letter. "What is this?"

"I don't know. Your name's on the envelope." He stretched out beside her with his hands behind his head. "Life is grand. What's not to be cheerful about? Now open your letter. I bet it's good news."

Inside, Guin found a thick, cream-colored card decorated with pink rose-like flowers. She flipped the card over. Cocking her head, she peered sideways at him. "I can't read this."

He took the card and cleared his throat. "Guinevere Griffin, you're out. Pack your bags and go back to Earth where you belong."

She crossed her arms and grinned. "Derek."

"You're invited to high tea at the Grint Manor in five days."

"Does it say who else is invited? Will Bree be there?"

"Doesn't say. We can call Bree and ask."

Delori made calls. She learned the guest list was confidential. Everyone assumed Vertuma would be there, though no one was sure. According to gossip, only four women had been invited. To Guin's disappointment, Bree was not one of them.

Derek called her and handed the telecon to Guin.

"What happened?" Guin asked.

"My mother received a letter from the Council, sending their regrets. I was asked to step aside. I guess now we know what happened to the others."

"I'm so sorry, Bree."

"Why? That's one less woman you have to worry about." Bree laughed.

"Well, from what Delori can find out, there are only four of us attending Dame Grint's tea."

"That's fabulous, Guin. I knew you could do it."

~

For tea, Guin dressed in a pin-striped, black-and-white, form-fitting dress trimmed with short ruffles around the collar and knee-length hem.

Boden, Eedras, and Za'Had accompanied her to the Grint Estate.

Upon their arrival, Boden had her wait in the vehicle with Za'Had while the two men secured the grounds.

A staff member escorted Guin through an archway and announced her. The five high Council members, dressed in their silver and black, and two of Jaxzon's remaining suitors, Un'Un and Uso, were in attendance.

Calen Grint greeted her. "Lady Guin, so wonderful to see you."

Dame Grint beamed. "Thank you for coming, my dear."

"Thank you for inviting me."

"Come, meet my guests." Heldivar linked her arm through Guin's and led her further into the room, introducing her to Jenk Milton.

She recognized the small, dark-haired Xaiteran from past events. According to Delori's research, he had not been opposed to the suggestion of an intermarriage between Mikonia and Druthenia but seemed open-minded on the subject.

He greeted Guin with a warm smile. "Delighted to see you again. You've met Lady Uso Buqan?"

"Yes. You look lovely today, Uso."

"Thank you."

Heldivar greeted Trinza Scarrek and Lady Un'Un Vodis. "Un'Un and Trinza's mothers were from the same planet. Their families are close."

Guin dipped her head. Trinza, a Bethan, was the youngest member of the high Council. Delori had informed Guin that politically, Trinza leaned toward unity throughout the galaxy and believed most monarchies were a thing of the past.

Next, Heldivar introduced Council member Yuly Angstroth.

Guin remembered Yuly from the first ball. She'd been the only high Council member who had been short in her greeting then left. Delori's research suggested she would likely vote for Vertuma.

Ulzon Domme stood at Guin and Heldivar's approach. Guin recognized him from the Masque and subsequent events. He'd always spoken kindly to her.

He took her hand between his. "You are a picture today."

"Thank you. I'm happy to see you again."

Delori had told Guin these five people held considerable sway over the lower Council members, and if she impressed them, she might gain several votes.

"Tea is served," Heldivar announced. "Please follow me."

A staff member heralded Vertuma's late arrival. Yuly rushed forward to embrace the princess. The two women exchanged air kisses then followed Heldivar to the garden.

A substantial oval table sat under an arbor of pink flowers. The aroma of steeping tea mingled with the scent of the freshly cut flowers adorning the table.

Calen held the chair for his mother then Guin before taking a seat beside Dame Grint.

"This is beautiful," Guin said, admiring the setting.

Heldivar smiled. "Thank you. I do love these flowers; they represent our house name."

"Do you have high tea on Earth?" Calen asked.

"Not that I know of in my country, although they do in another called England. I visited as a child and teatime was my favorite meal of the day. I loved the little cakes and tiny sandwiches."

"Are there any such traditions in your country?" Ulzon asked.

"I'm sure they do, but I'm not aware of anything this formal."

The conversations around Guin went from tea, to weather, to politics. Vertuma was quite vocal on the subject of resources in Mikonia's system, namely the mineral *ichor* and how it would be more readily obtained if the two realms united.

"Why would the joining of our realms make obtaining ichor any easier?" Ulzon asked.

"The owners of Talos have threatened to limit the supply to drive prices higher or even destroy the moon if we do not bend to their whims." Vertuma sneered. "My father allows the owners to raise their prices, and soon only the richest worlds will be able to afford ichor. He believes the Talosians deserve control over their property and are within their rights to negotiate whatever prices they wish."

"There are factions arising throughout the galaxy who oppose this type of monopoly," Yuly added. "There is a possibility the owners have accumulated enough wealth to raise an army capable of destroying Mikonia if they wished to become autonomous."

"They would effortlessly defeat our forces if we dared move against them on our own," conceded Vertuma. "But, with the unification of our two realms, we might force the Talosians to either lower their prices or face the wrath of our empire. We would have the power to seize the mines and share the technology with the whole galaxy at little cost."

"Little cost?" Ulzon asked. "War seems an enormous cost to me. Druthenia is inordinately generous with the sharing of our wealth and technology amongst less prosperous realms. Why would we welcome war?"

"With the realms united, we would not risk war," Vertuma countered. "The Talosians would not dare fight the galaxy as a whole."

"They must realize that as allies of Mikonia, Druthenia would rise if they dared declare war." Ulzon shook his head. "War makes no sense and would only end with the destruction of Talos."

"The Talosians are a greedy people," said Trinza. "They believe Druthenia wants only their ichor. After all, we've proven that we are willing to pay the exorbitant prices as they are now. The Talosian government suspects that we would allow Mikonia to be destroyed simply to keep the supply unchecked."

"Where do you get this information?" Heldivar demanded. "No such threats have come from Talos. This is speculation, bordering on slander."

"We have our sources," purred Vertuma. "After all, we are closer to the problem. I understand either way Druthenia reaps the benefits, no matter the outcome. Many within your realm oppose the idea of Mikonia being expendable. Voters would be outraged if a few, very wealthy individuals destroyed an entire world while their royalty and elected officials conveniently stood by doing nothing. Your own people voiced their opinions regarding an intermarriage alliance, and from the research I've seen, most would approve."

"Who are the owners of the mines, and why would they risk a war for profit?" asked Guin. "How would a marriage make a difference, if the two realms are already allies?"

Vertuma glared. "There are more recent developments which we are dealing with at a local level. An outsider would not comprehend the complexities involved."

"The names of the owners are confidential," said Ulzon. "Ichor is essential for every technology we depend upon. From our loqu and dislocaters to our medical and space travel needs. The Council has only recently been informed of these threats, and the information is being evaluated to determine their validity. A meeting is scheduled with the Talosian representatives, at which time these issues will be addressed."

"We do not discuss Council business with outsiders," Yuly Angstroth stated. "I do believe this is a social gathering and not a political debate?" She raised a questioning brow in Heldivar's direction.

"Yes, please. Let us change the subject to more pleasant matters." Heldivar smiled at Guin. "Do tell us what Earth is like."

"Do you want to know anything specific?"

Un'Un leaned forward. "Do you have a pet Pokémon?"

Guin laughed before realizing Un'Un was serious. Her explanation lightened the mood considerably.

After tea, guests milled around the garden, sipping sparkling wine and enjoying the day. Guin admired the statuary and crisp lines of the topiary surrounding an ornate fountain, when Vertuma appeared beside her.

"Do you genuinely believe you would be the appropriate choice for Queen?" Vertuma asked.

"I believe the right choice would be a person who will put the interests and welfare of their people before their own."

"But these aren't your people, are they?"

"All people are my people." Guin met the princess's icy gaze. "I don't differentiate between race, nationality, or planets. We're the same under our skin. Everyone has hopes and dreams. Each of us matters to someone, and everyone matters to me. Even you." Without waiting for another snide remark, she strode away, sensing Vertuma's glare boring into her back.

Guin explained the conversation to Boden on the way to the Vau'uan estate. "Why would Vertuma discuss such a volatile subject as ichor at a tea party?"

"To bring attention to herself. From what you've told me, it sounds like a veiled threat of some sort, although I'm sure there's more she didn't say. I'm not big on politics, but this thing with Vertuma and Kapre wanting to unite the realms has been getting a lot of airtime lately, and many are in favor. The people are afraid of losing their technology. Ichor is what makes everything tick, to use an Earth expression, and if you ask me, people have become too dependent on it."

"I get it. People on Earth have also become overly dependent on technology and social media in recent years. When I first came here, I went through withdrawals. What's the next event?"

"Dates."

"Dates? Like days or fruit?"

"Jaxzon is taking the last four suitors on dates."

"Okay," Guin said with a laugh. "We're definitely getting into some crazy reality show parallels. Is he going to bring us each a rose?"

"I don't think so. Is this something they do on Earth?"

She gave an abbreviated run-down on her understanding of certain television shows.

He frowned. "Earth has some pretty strange ideas of what passes for entertainment."

"Tell me about it. When's my date?"

"In four days. Jaxzon said he wanted to save the best for last. I'm assuming he meant you."

"Where is he taking me?"

"He didn't say. You and I are meeting him in Kurrel. He sent his private train, so we go in style. Afterward, you Shift with him to Uetov4 for their ball. Next there's a memorial on Tendraq, and then Mikonia for their annual ball. Then I guess you get a turn. You ready for a party at your place in New York?"

Her eyes widened. "What? Seriously?"

He grinned. "Got you."

"Oh, you're so dead!" She punched his arm. "I wondered how I was going to fit everyone into my tiny apartment, and I definitely don't have enough wine glasses."

Boden chuckled, his dimples showing under his dark scruff.

Guin laughed. "Who are you, and what did you do with Boden?"

CHAPTER TWENTY-FOUR

Together, Guin and Bree viewed the coverage of Jaxzon's date with Vertuma.

He acted the perfect gentleman, holding her chair and opening doors. After a quiet dinner, the prince and princess strolled through the city, journalists in tow. She leaned close saying something. When he leaned in, she kissed him.

The news commentator gasped.

He drew back, placing her arm on his, then continued to stroll.

"Poor Jaxzon," Guin said through her laughter.

"Why are you laughing? That snake kissed him."

"It was clearly one-sided. Besides, he loves me, and one kiss won't change that."

The prince and princess chatted with reporters. During their interview, Jaxzon brushed an imaginary hair from his forehead while winking into the camera.

A smile spread across Guin's face. "I love you too, Jaxzon."

Nothing dramatic happened during his dates with Un'Un and Uso, although after each, he managed to brush hair from his face, dazzling everyone with his smile and a wink.

Guin packed a bag for her train trip, leaving the rest of her luggage for Derek to take to Uetov4. That night, she and Boden, along with her guards, travelled the six hours to Kurrel in the king's private hovers.

Guin awoke upon their arrival. She showered and changed before joining Boden. They entered a small diner. The homey décor brought with it memories of her first-ever date when she was fifteen. She laughed.

He squinted at her through the glowing hologram menu hanging between them. "What?"

"We're on our first date."

Boden flushed. "This is hardly a date."

"Ah, come on, big guy." She poked his chest. "I'm pulling your leg. But I hope Jaxzon isn't the jealous type."

"Ha ha. You're quite the comedian." His elusive dimples made another rare appearance.

Pouring pink syrup on her pancakes Guin said, "Keep 'em laughing, I always say."

Za'Had passed by the window. Eedras lurked nearby.

"Don't those two ever eat?"

"Don't you know anything? They're robots."

"Seriously?" she asked, squinting at the guard through the window.

"You're so gullible."

She cocked her head. "Bodey with a sense of humor. Who woulda thunk it?"

"I'm a man of many talents, Griffin." He smiled at her over the rim of his teacup.

"Why do you do that?"

"Do what?"

"Call me Griffin. Ever since we met, you've called me by my last name."

"Habit, I guess."

"Habit?"

"From when I trained for the guard, maybe?" He set his cup down. "Does it bother you?"

"No, I'm used to it. When you called me Guin, I was kinda startled."

"When?"

"When I fainted." She touched his forearm. "Thank you for being there. I never told you how much that meant to me. I'm not sure what would've happened if you hadn't caught me."

"You would have face-planted on the sidewalk." He sat back, folding his arms. "Finish eating."

Grumpy Boden rears his ugly head.

They ate their breakfast and headed into the city to pass some time. He pointed out landmarks and explained how the dome structures worked. They came to a massive park in the center of the city much like Central Park. Guin felt a stab of homesickness. She tried to picture what her friends and family were doing.

They probably think I fell off the face of the earth. She laughed at the irony.

"Now what's so funny?"

"I was thinking of home. This park reminds me of a place there."

They strolled under a teal-leafed tree. "Do you miss New York?"

"I'm kinda homesick." Leaves fluttered above in the cooling breeze. She ran her hand over the orange bark. "I mean, I'm having a great time here. I've seen so many new and unusual things, and I'm meeting interesting people. I miss my friends and the people at the shelter where I volunteer, but I like being here."

They wandered to a bench in the shade. A nearby pond mirrored the surrounding trees and clouds above. A breeze carrying a jasmine-like scent ruffled Guin's hair.

"What makes Boden tick? To use an Earth expression." She studied Boden's profile as he gazed at the pond.

"Not much of a mystery here, Griffin. What do you want to know?"

"Do you live in the palace?"

"Sometimes. I have a place in the country."

"You do?" She sat forward. "Why did I think you only lived in the palace? What kind of place is it? Do you live alone?"

"Why the sudden interest?"

"We've never had a chance to talk." She leaned her forearms on her knees. "I'm curious to learn more about you."

"I live alone on a ranch, and I don't know why you thought I lived in the palace. Happy?" He smirked down at her.

"Yes. Do you have animals?"

"I raise turatang and breed horses."

"Turatang?"

"They're kind of a cross between a pig and a cow. They taste a little like both."

"Whoa, now that I gotta see. Could we go to your ranch sometime?"

"Why?"

"I want to check out where old Scowly McSmirkyface lives. Maybe then he won't be such an enigma."

He chuckled. "I'm an enigma?"

"Definitely."

"In what way?" He sat back against the bench, the dimples making another rare appearance.

"Let's see, the first time I saw you, you smirked at me, and for the rest of the night, you glowered at everything. The next time I saw you, you were drunk off your butt and kind of funny. The third time I saw you, you hated me. You would have slapped me if you thought you could get away with it."

Boden frowned. "That's not true."

"Yes, it is. You were the only one here who almost made me leave a room in tears. But I don't cry easily. My grandmother would have been very disappointed if I had. Luckily, I had a few ruvins to shore me up, or *I* might've slapped *you*."

"I'm sorry, Griffin." He stared off into the distance. "I never meant for you to believe I hated you."

"Yes, you did." Her voice softened. "You were trying to protect your friend and his people. Your people. I understand. Totally misguided, but I get it." She touched his arm. He tensed. "I don't bite, Boden."

"I didn't hate you. I was worried about Jaxzon. He fell hard, he couldn't concentrate, he talked about you constantly, he was a completely different person after you two met." Boden grinned. "I shouldn't be telling you this."

"It'll be our secret, cross my heart."

He nudged her with his elbow. "So how does that make me an enigma?"

"You're not easy to figure out. You can be so...*exasperating* would be putting it mildly. You're smirking one minute, scowling the next. You never dress properly. You defy Orist. Yet you take the best care of Jaxzon and those around him. You," she said, poking his arm, "are a whole with two completely different halves."

He glanced down at his clothes. "What's wrong with the way I dress?"

She tugged the rolled-up sleeve of his red plaid shirt. "How many of these shirts do you own? I bet you have one suit, that you only wear on special occasions, and even then, I'll bet someone has to beg you to."

"See, I'm not such an enigma—you've got me pegged. And you're wrong." He held up two fingers. "I own two suits."

"With everything I pointed out, your biggest concern is what I thought of your clothes." She shook her head. "You're too funny."

He smiled, squinting at the suns sinking behind the tallest buildings. "We better get you back. We meet Jaxzon after sunsdown."

She linked her arm through his, and he escorted her from the park.

AFTER CHANGING, Guin followed Boden from the Hub. They waited at the curb for Jaxzon's hover. The suns had set. A pinkish-purple glow tinged the sky.

She wore a simple black, form-fitting dress ending mid-thigh, and matching, low-heeled pumps. Fussing with her hair, she checked the hastily made braid she'd whipped it into. She hadn't had a date in six years, not counting Raney's haphazard attempts at matchmaking.

"You look nice." Boden brushed a strand of hair from her face, then dropped his hand and looked away.

When the vehicle arrived, the door opened. Guin slid in beside Jaxzon.

"Are you going ahead to Uetov4?" he asked Boden.

"Yes, the security upgrades should be installed in the castle by the time you arrive tonight. I'll give it a test run to make sure."

"See you there." The door closed. Jaxzon took Guin's hand. "You look beautiful tonight." He kissed her lightly on the lips.

She snuggled into his arms. "I missed you."

"I missed you too."

"Where are we going?"

His eyes sparkled in the dim light. "It's a surprise."

The hover came to a stop before a building bearing a marquee with bold symbols. A group of reporters had wedged themselves and their cameras into the small vestibule outside a grand lobby.

He helped Guin from the hover and guided her past the cameras and through the doors to the entrance of what could only be a movie theater.

"I wanted to keep our date private." He tilted his head toward the journalists.

"Genius. I'm surprised you have movies here."

"One of the great amusements we've borrowed from Earth culture. Cinema has become quite a fad in recent years."

The theater belonged to them. A substantial swath of seats had been removed from the center and in their place, facing the wide screen, sat an intimate table for two. A black and red uniformed server greeted them.

"Right this way Your Highness, Lady Guinevere."

Jaxzon held Guin's chair for her then sat beside her. The enormous screen curved across an entire wall, framed by black velvety curtains. The aroma of savory herbs filled the air.

"What's the movie?" she asked.

He shrugged. "No idea. I told them we wanted their most popular film and to give us complete privacy."

"I love it." She glanced around. "Can I try something?"

"What?"

"This." She removed her loqu. "Will you talk to me? I want you to speak to me in your language."

"*Quid ego dicam*?"

Guin leaned over and kissed him. "That's beautiful. What did you

say?"

"I said, 'what should I say?'"

"You rat." She gave his arm a gentle slap. "What a way to romance a girl."

"Arwon's language is rooted in Latin, and there are many sayings and words from ancient Greek mixed in. Several worlds in this galaxy were visited by ancient beings, Symbyads. They passed along much of their own history and mythology."

Guin widened her eyes. "Really? That's fascinating. I wondered how there could be so many parallels."

"Remind me to tell you more when we have time."

"I will." Placing her elbows on the table she rested her chin on her folded hands. "I want to know everything. How many languages do you speak?"

"I speak many languages from many planets. My favorite from Earth is French. I love the way it flows."

Fluttering her eyelashes, she asked, "What would you say to me in French?"

"*Je t'aime*, in French. *Se agapo*, in Greek. *Te amo*, in Latin. *Bov butan*, in Mikonian. I love you, in any language."

"*Je t'aime aussi*."

He seemed surprised. "You speak French?"

"*Oui, je parle un français parfait*," she purred. "My mother was from Quebec. *C'est au Canada, ils y parlent français*."

"Perfect huh? *Savez-vous ce que je dis maintenant*?"

She laughed. "Yes, I understand what you're saying, and yes, I speak French perfectly. Do you doubt me?"

"I would never doubt you." He brushed a strand of hair from her forehead. "Did you get my message?"

"*Oui*, all three."

"I wanted you to know, I only think of you, no matter who I am with."

Guin kissed his cheek. "You're so sweet. Speaking of other women, how was your kiss with Vertuma?"

His expression soured. "*C'était friktos! Póso tolmá aftí*?"

She laughed. "That bad?"

"Sorry. I said, 'It was awful, how dare she?'" He shook his head. "She took advantage of the cameras. She knew I would never say anything."

"I'm sorry she took advantage of you." She gave him a sidelong look. "I guess I'll need to behave and keep my lips to myself."

"You would not dare."

"How much privacy do we have here?"

"Once the lights go down, we will have complete privacy. They are supposed to bring our drinks. The meal will arrive after the movie starts, then we should be alone until it ends."

"Awesome. I see our drinks coming."

The server brought a bottle to the table and filled each glass with a clear, bubbly liquid. She set the bottle in a hovering bucket of ice before leaving.

Jaxzon raised his glass. "To the most beautiful woman in the galaxy."

"To the handsomest man in the galaxy." She touched her glass to his.

His eyes pierced hers. "*Yosen dai, tofee ven du, soré par na tu.*"

"What did you say?"

"'Until the end of time, you are my love' in Uetovian, my mother's language and the primary language of Uetov4."

"*Yosen dai, tofee ven du, soré par na tu.*" She kissed his cheek.

Smiling he put his arm around her. She replaced her loqu as the lights dimmed.

The most popular movie ended up being an action thriller, complete with explosions, laser fights, and rough language. She laughed five minutes in, and Jaxzon joined her.

Not the most romantic movie for a first date, but she was soon captivated by the plot, and after their dishes were cleared, she enjoyed the movie. Holding hands, she and Jaxzon stole kisses in the dark, laughing at the absurd one-liners made by the glib action hero.

The journalists trained their lenses through the windows when Guin and Jaxzon entered the lobby.

"Excuse me." He went to the auto-concession, returning with his arm behind his back, and a foolish grin lighting his face.

She squinted. "What are you up to?"

He produced a long-stemmed red rose. "For you."

Bringing the flower to her nose and inhaling the sweet fragrance, she laughed.

"Boden filled me in." His grin widened. "I thought we could give them a bit of a show." He indicated the reporters with his chin. "I doubt they'll get the reference. But I wanted you to understand, as publicly as I dared, I'd choose you."

"I want to kiss you so badly."

The dimples in his cheeks deepened. His eyes sparkled. "Would you like to take a stroll? Though Kurrel's night life isn't as exciting as New York's, there is a place we can go for coffee or tea if you'd like?"

"Coffee sounds great." She waved the rose toward the cameras.

"Besides, your fans are dying to see you again."

"My fans? You've made more fans in a few weeks than I've accumulated in a lifetime." He gestured to the reporters. "There are three times more tonight than the last three nights. They want you."

They exited the theater amidst camera flashes then proceeded to the heart of the city. The media shadowed their every move, with commentators speaking into their mics, speculating where they would go next. The small coffee house became cramped as the cameramen attempted to find the best vantage points. Ignoring the bustle behind them, Jaxzon and Guin perused the drink menu.

"I can't read a word," she whispered.

He read the menu, while she attempted to understand the symbols and learn their meanings. They made their choices then decided to take their drinks with them, leaving the reporters scrambling to catch up.

Arm in arm, they meandered through the city talking quietly and window shopping. At the end of their date, her hover appeared. Za'Had exited and stood by as Jaxzon kissed Guin's hand. "Goodnight my lady, and thank you for an enchanting evening."

"Thank you, Your Highness. I had a lovely time."

She slid into the vehicle, followed by Za'Had. The hover floated down the street and around the corner.

Guin waited at the Shift Station for Jaxzon to arrive. His security entourage joined them. They were taken to a dimly lit room. Orist handed her a dislocater. He and four of the security team Shifted first then sent an all-clear. Jaxzon and Guin went through the unseen door.

Everything went black.

CHAPTER TWENTY-FIVE

Guin lurched out of Jaxzon's arms and fell forward, striking her head against the wall. Catching her before she hit the floor, he knelt, cradling her against him.

Her body shook, and she stared blankly.

Jaxzon held her against him as she trembled and moaned. "Orist, bring the attendant."

The attendant rushed into the small room and used a shairgan device to inject a medication into Guin's wrist. "She wasn't supposed to Shift without a dose of trivol. I'm sorry, Your Highness." She ran a scanner over Guin's head then down her body. "She'll be fine, just a slight bump."

Guin's eyelids closed. Her body stilled. Her breathing evened out, and she opened her eyes.

He smoothed the hair from her face. "Guin, can you hear me?"

"Yes." Her eyes focused on his face.

Still worried, he helped her sit. "You had a bad Shift."

"Damn. Has it been thirty days?" She put a hand to her temple. "I completely forgot."

"This has happened before?"

"When I first came with Derek." She rubbed her forehead where a small lump had formed. "Did I fall?"

He winced. "You took us by surprise. Although I caught you before you hit the floor, you struck your head pretty solidly against the wall."

"Did I hurt you?"

He smiled. "No, and the technician said you'll be fine. No concussion."

She put a hand to his cheek. "I didn't mean to frighten you. I feel better now."

Orist cleared his throat. "Your Highness, we're running behind schedule."

Jaxzon narrowed his eyes at the commander, then took Guin's hand. "Can you walk?"

"Yes. I feel like a fool. I'm so sorry."

He helped her to her feet. "You have nothing to apologize for."

They were met by Boden and escorted to a waiting hover. Boden, Orist, Guin, and Jaxzon rode together. Boden reported the castle's upgrades had been completed and security had been doubled.

In the distance an aurora danced across the sky. Swirling shades of blue, green, and violet tinged with gold and silver shimmered brightly on the horizon, only fading when twin moons arose.

She stared, a look of awe on her beautiful face. "How many moons are there?"

"Five. Three small and two larger ones. When they align, they wreak havoc on the tidal systems." Jaxzon pointed to a golden-hued moon. "That one is Minos. Our government has small research colonies and several mining sites there."

They passed through a set of airlocks and entered the immense dome. The winding drive led to the top of a hill upon which sat his mother's grand castle with tall spires, lit by a thousand tiny lights.

"Like a fairy tale," Guin whispered. "I can almost picture Rapunzel sitting in that highest window."

He took her hand, and they exited the hover. "Welcome to Neylain."

"It's the most beautiful thing I've ever seen." She ran a hand over the shiny, lavender masonry that comprised the castle's walls. "Do you come here often?"

"I used to come with my mother. My father built this castle for her when they married. She loved this place and visited whenever she could. I haven't been in months. But I wanted to share it with you before the others arrive tomorrow."

The front door opened. A man's silhouette stood outlined in the doorway. "Your Highness."

Jaxzon recognized the voice. "Ahret!" He rushed forward to embrace his friend. "I had no idea you'd be here. Ahret Aqul, this is Lady Guinevere Griffin."

He kissed Guin's hand. "The Angel of Arwon."

A slight blush colored her cheeks. "Pleased to meet you."

"Your Highness," Orist said. "Excuse me for interrupting your reunion. But with your leave, I would like to dismiss this detail and debrief the rest of my team."

"Of course, Orist. Goodnight and thank you," he told the men, who bowed and filed from the room through the side door. He took Guin's hand and put an arm around Ahret's shoulder. "When did you arrive?"

"Earlier tonight. Your housekeeper said you would be here soon. I told her I wanted to surprise you at the door." He extended his hand to a smiling Boden. "It's wonderful to see you again."

"Good to see you too. You missed the trip to Earth."

"I was on Minos. So many moving parts with this new dome tech we're working on. The mechanics are frustrating, but we'll get it." His gaze fell on Guin. "I heard a few things about the Earth visit; seems they were true."

"You're all old friends?" she asked.

Jaxzon nodded. "Ahret was my sister's fiancé."

Her hand covered her mouth. "Oh. I'm sorry for your loss."

"Thank you," he said with a nod.

Jaxzon escorted them to his mother's library, a richly decorated room with floor-to-ceiling bookcases lining the walls. Boden and Ahret took seats in a grouping of leather, high-backed chairs facing each other.

Guin sat on the matching sofa. "Go talk with your friends. I'll kick back here."

He kissed her hand and joined the others. Ahret had spent the last five years dedicated to developing a new technology in creating an atmosphere on the moon. He regaled Boden and Jaxzon with stories about the new mineral discoveries and informed them that the ichor deposits ran deep and were plentiful. "We'll be completely ichor independent by this time next year."

Jaxzon put a finger to his lips. "Keep that information under wraps for now. Ichor's a very touchy subject when it comes to Mikonia and our treaties."

Ahret laughed. "A very touchy subject indeed."

Jaxzon gazed at Guin who had curled up on the sofa and appeared to be sleeping peacefully. "My father will be glad of the news. He's under a lot of pressure. Maybe this will calm him. But for now, I must make my guest comfortable, she's had a long day."

She opened her eyes when he touched her shoulder.

"You must be exhausted." He smiled down at her. "Would you like me to show you your room?"

They arrived at her room. Eedras bowed from his station in the hall. Not wanting to leave just yet, Jaxzon ushered her through her door. "I'll show you how the shower works. They can be tricky."

The door closed behind them. She burst out laughing. "How the shower works? You couldn't come up with a better excuse?"

"Come here." He extended his arms.

Guin flew to him. Their lips met in a passionate kiss. Her arms went around his neck. His fingers knotted in her dress.

Smiling against his lips, she asked, "You gonna show me how the shower works?"

"My lady, are you trying to seduce me?"

"Your virtue's safe with me, but my shower had better have cold water."

"Guin." He tilted her chin and gazed into her eyes. "You've no idea."

"Jaxzon." She interlaced her fingers through his hair, tugging him down. Her mouth grazed his. "I do." She flicked her tongue across his lips.

A low moan turned growl, rumbled in his chest. He tightened his arms around her waist, then trailed kisses along her jaw. "I have to go."

"Ah." Her head dropped back. "I wish..."

He gazed into her eyes. "Soon, and then..."

"And then?"

"And then we will always be together." He held her close, wishing he could hold her for the rest of their lives.

Resting her head against his chest, she asked, "Jaxzon? What if—"

"No. Let's not talk of what-ifs. There are no what-ifs. Right?"

"Right."

He kissed the top of her head then caught her lips again in a tender kiss. "I love you, my lady."

"I love you too, my prince."

Though he longed to stay, Jaxzon let himself out.

THE NIGHT of the Uetov4 ball, fewer guests attended then previous gatherings. Four ladies remained in the Vekdromic: Vertuma, Uso, Un'Un, and Guin. The small, modern ballroom held an electronic orchestra with instruments playing themselves. Silver light fixtures hung from the ceiling, filling the dance floor with abstract, holographic designs. They floated through the air, vibrating and dancing to the rhythm of the soft background music.

Guin wore a dark red gown. She French-braided her hair, starting at her forehead on the left, and ending over her right shoulder. The loose ends hung over her chest in gentle auburn curls.

After the formal announcements had been made, the orchestra played an ihli. She sought Jaxzon and when their eyes met, he smiled.

Once again, before she could reach him, Vertuma intercepted him, stealing the first dance.

"That was rude," Bree said. "Technically, the prince should dance with Un'Un first. This is her planet."

"'Rude' is Vertuma's middle name," observed Derek.

Guin shrugged. "Foiled again. Do they serve ruvin here?"

"Only one way to find out." Bree linked her arm through Guin's, and they went in search of a server.

"You are more beautiful than ever," Jaxzon told Guin when they danced—thanks to Derek running interference with Vertuma.

"And you're more dashing than ever."

"Were there any problems with your plumbing last night?"

"No. Although I do know for a fact, Your Highness, the cold water works perfectly."

Jaxzon lowered his voice. "During our next trip to Neylain, we will learn together if the hot water works as well."

The heat rose in Guin's cheeks. "Hush, or I'll kiss you right here on the dance floor."

Jaxzon laughed. "I love making you blush.

Guin's heart sang.

Uso waylaid him for the next dance.

Guin went to the bar and took a seat when Boden made his usual late appearance. "Looking sharp tonight, Boden. Someone's trying to make an impression. Who is she?"

Dressed in a fitted gray suit, he wore his hair combed back from his unusually clean-shaven face. He held his hand out. "I don't know what you're talking about, Griffin. May I have this dance?"

She placed her hand on his shoulder. "Mmm, smelling good too? Now I *am* impressed."

"Do I normally smell bad?"

"I didn't say that." She inhaled. "But do me a favor and dance with Bree. She has *got* to get a whiff of this cologne."

"If this is the reaction I'm going to get, I'll never wear it again."

"Ah, come on, Bodey, I'm just messing with ya."

After their dance, they joined Bree and Derek. The orchestra launched into another song, Boden extended his hand to Bree. "Would you like to dance?"

She took his arm. "What's with the cologne?"

CHAPTER
TWENTY-SIX

Back at the Vau'uan's estate a few days later, familiar tapping sounded on Guin's door. She removed her earbud. "Come in Derek."

Her tele-screen displayed electronic flashcards, their meanings and pronunciations translated through her loqu. She'd been attempting to learn to read Arwonese since Delori told her she was to read a speech during the ceremony on Tendraq.

"Delori wants us ready to Shift first thing tomorrow morning." Derek ran a hand across her dresser. "Need help packing?"

"No thanks, I'm all set. Packed last night." She winked. "Keeping one step ahead of your sister is my favorite game."

The next evening, they arrived on Tendraq. Council member Ulzon Domme was to host a day of remembrance for the destruction of the planet, Na'atak the following day. Tonight he received the Vekdromic in his home, welcoming them with a small reception in his garden.

Mauve palm trees, multi-colored flowers, and exotic plants adorned the courtyard. A bright orange and red plant whose flowers were over two feet tall, soared several feet into the air.

"Not like Earth?" Ulzon came to stand beside Guin.

"It's breathtaking. Is this an orchid?"

"Very similar." He stroked his graying beard. "*Iodaid* is the botanical name. The common name for this one is *Qosil's Flame*, after the cultivator."

Guin nodded. "Very apropos. It's as though the petals were on fire. They're much larger than the ones on Earth."

"Tendraq is a tropical paradise filled with mountainous islands surrounded by bountiful oceans. The planet's rotation makes possible temperate climates across every continent, creating an enormous hothouse with rich soil and lush growth." He brushed his hand over the flower. "Everything grows to giant proportions here."

"Fascinating." She took a deep breath and summoned her courage "May I ask you something about the ceremony tomorrow?"

"Of course."

"I'm told I will be reading something?"

They strolled through a grandiose hanging garden. Ink black flowers swayed on a trellis and gave off a gentle mist, cooling the air yet drying instantly wherever it landed.

"Yes, we ask that each lady read one piece of our thank you speech. Is there a problem?" Ulzon asked.

"I can't read your language."

Ulzon laughed. "Of course, you can't. I hadn't considered that. Could you memorize your part?"

"Yes, I'm sure I could. Is my part long?"

"Not at all." He waved a hand. "I'll have the speech interpreted and sent to your room."

Dipping her head she said, "Thank you for understanding."

"We wouldn't want to embarrass our future queen, now, would we?"

Guin laughed. "Where I come from, we'd say that's counting our chickens before they hatch."

"We have a similar saying." He returned her smile. "But I do believe I am speaking with our future Queen."

Guin found Bree chatting with Uso. Bree excused herself. Guin relayed her conversation with Ulzon.

"Guin, that's phenomenal! Ulzon and Heldivar have the most influence over the Council, and you only need two-thirds of the votes to be chosen."

"What happens if no one gets two-thirds?"

"Prince Jaxzon would be given the choice between the women with the most votes. You have this. Everyone loves you. Besides, you have the king on your side. Even if the Council had close to the number of votes for Vertuma, the nobility would never vote against the king. He could make their lives miserable if they did."

Guin's heart palpitated in her ears.

"Are you okay?"

Guin gripped her friend's arm. "Bree, I might actually marry Jaxzon and become queen."

"You *will* be queen," Bree assured her.

After the reception, Guin and Bree sat cross-legged on Guin's bed, memorizing her part of the speech. A rapid tapping sounded on Guin's door.

"Come in, Derek."

He entered, slump shouldered, with none of the usual sparkle in his eyes, and sat beside her.

Guin put an arm around him. "What's wrong?"

"Delori told me the next event is the Mikonian Ball."

"Boden mentioned something about that. Why so gloomy?"

"I hoped we could host the last event. I throw some wicked parties." He put his head on her shoulder.

"Aw, poor Derek." Guin mussed his hair. "You can throw a wicked party after everything is over. That will be my first decree as your new queen." She told him of her conversation with Ulzon.

"Ulzon told you that? Wow! We did it, didn't we?"

"I think so."

"This is the best news ever. I can't wait to tell Delori." He headed for the door.

"Wait, let's not jinx everything. I'm excited too, except I don't want to tempt fate by believing we 'have it in the bag,' as they say." She glanced from Derek to Bree. "Just between us. Okay?"

"You're right," he agreed. "We can keep the news to ourselves for two more weeks."

"It's over in two weeks?" She laid back on her pillows, dazed. "So soon?"

"Only two more weeks, Queen Guinevere."

She grinned. "Cut the queen crap, Derek."

Na'atak Remembrance Day came bright and early. Guin rehearsed her part of the speech—terrified she would freeze and forget the words. Dressed in a somber, dark gray skirt and jacket, with a cream blouse with ruffles around the neck and wrists, she made her hair into a loose French knot then dabbed on a touch of lip gloss. The mirror reflected a confident young woman. *You can do this.*

Thousands of people gathered for the ceremony, filling a massive stadium. A sizable podium, cluttered with microphones, sat upon a wide stage with hundreds of cameras representing news stations from around the galaxy, hovering above. Behind the podium, sat Guin and the three remaining ladies, the Council, and members of the realm's nobility. The chatter of thousands of people filled the stadium.

Uso and Un'Un flanked Guin. Vertuma sat on Uso's right. The three noblewomen appeared cool and collected. Guin's stomach buzzed.

The stadium hushed as Ulzon approached the podium. "We are gathered to mourn the horrific loss of a world and to celebrate those delivered from the destruction. Over three-and-a-half decades ago, the Druthenian government established diplomatic relations with Na'atak—a world at war with itself. When diplomacy failed to bring peace, our government made the decision to transport volunteers from their planet to ensure the continuity of the Na'atak people. Today we, along with the two thousand Na'atak men, women, and children who were saved on that fateful day, mourn their losses while rejoicing in their prosperity."

A cheer arose among the mass of people. He waited for quiet, then announced, "Prince Jaxzon has honored us with his presence and would like to say a few words."

The prince approached the microphones to thunderous applause. "Thirty-five years ago, billions of lives were lost over the short space of a few hours. Please stand for a moment of silent reflection for those lost." He bowed his head.

After several beats, he continued, "Though we honor them, we will not dwell overly long on the losses suffered. Instead, we shall hold them in our hearts and celebrate the lives of those spared, who now live among us as citizens of our realm and throughout the many realms of our galaxy.

"This day coincides with our Vekdromic. We have invited the four remaining ladies to say a few words in your honor. Please give a warm welcome to Princess Vertuma Syndow of Mikonia."

Vertuma strode forward to polite applause, taking her place at center stage.

"Lady Uso Buqan of Uetov4." Lady Uso took her place beside Vertuma.

"Lady Guinevere Griffin of House Vau'uan and New York." The stadium exploded in applause as cheers rang out. Shouts of "Angel" echoed throughout the stadium as Guin came to stand with Uso. Guin curtsied, causing another outburst of applause and shouts.

"And your own, Lady Un'Un Vodis of Tendraq." A new wave of intense cheers arose when Un'Un blew a kiss.

Once the crowd settled, Vertuma read from the screen facing the stage. "We mourn with you today the terrible losses you experienced and offer our condolences for the sorrows suffered thirty-five years ago."

Uso continued, "We thank you for enriching our lives with your generosity and for sharing your unique traditions and cultures with the peoples of our worlds."

The sea of faces focused on Guin. "Let us celebrate our coming together and the joining of our multi-cultured worlds, as we appreciate the peace and prosperity enjoyed by all." A roar of approval echoed throughout the stadium.

Un'Un raised her hands, and the crowd quieted. "The citizens of Druthenia once again welcome you, the people of Na'atak, with open arms and open hearts. Let the celebration of life begin!"

The onlookers broke into raucous applause. Guin and the others returned to their seats. Ulzon Domme thanked everyone for coming. After testimonies from the Na'atak Elders, the stadium took on a fair-like atmosphere. Food and gaming booths lined the outer walkways, filling the air with exotic scents, sounds of laughter, and celebration. Holograms depicting costumed dancers flitted around the stadium and music played overhead.

Bree caught up to Guin when she left the stage. They went into the arena, searching for something to eat. Guin followed her nose in the direction of an enticing aroma when a passing young man asked for a picture. They left the path to lean against a stone wall, smiling for a selfie.

A teenaged girl also asked for a picture, and Guin soon found herself amid a small crowd wanting photographs. She laughed and joked, enjoying her newfound celebrity. Word spread of her presence. The crowd rapidly became a mob. They pressed forward, calling out for the Angel of Arwon.

Guin and Bree were soon surrounded by a massive throng. The wall prevented their escape as the crowd thrust forward, forcing her and Bree against the stonework.

She clutched Bree's hand. "Please move back!"

A blonde child fell at their feet. Guin wrapped the little girl in her arms, turning her back to the crush of bodies. The child clung to Guin as they were crushed against the wall. The girl screamed.

Guin crouched against the wall, curling protectively around the child. Her grip tightened in desperation when strong arms scooped Guin off her feet.

CHAPTER TWENTY-SEVEN

Powerful voices bellowed for the mob of people to disperse. Boden held Guin and the child in his arms. A band of security guards backed the crowd away. Bree gripped his arm with tears welling in her eyes.

Guin yelped in surprise, almost dropping the child. Her blonde hair transformed into dark auburn. Her blue eyes turned green as her face elongated.

Eedras brought forward a frightened woman who took the girl and thanked Guin for keeping her safe. The child's hair paled, returning to its natural blonde as the pair disappeared into the dissipating crowd.

"You can put me down now, Boden." He set her down. She straightened her clothes. "Thank you. Are you okay?" she asked Bree.

"I'm fine, but that was scary."

He escorted them through the milling people. "You shouldn't have gone anywhere without proper security."

"We wanted to try the food," Bree told him.

"Then you're in luck. You're invited to the royal banquet."

Eedras, Za'Had, and several guards accompanied them to an

immense tent at the back of the stadium. When they entered, mouth-watering aromas drew Guin and Bree to a row of tables laden with local delicacies. One dish appeared to have live pink beetles swimming through light blue water. The two women filled their plates with exotic seafoods—avoiding the beetle dish—then found an empty table at the back of the room.

"Did you see that little girl?" Guin asked between bites.

"She was cute and lucky you picked her up. She might have been hurt."

"There wasn't anything unusual about her?" *Did I imagine it?*

"I wasn't paying attention. After Boden picked you up, I hid behind him." Bree's dark complexion reddened. "Our hero."

"Something strange happened. When I first held her, she was blonde, then her hair was auburn, like mine. Her face changed, and her eyes turned green." Guin picked at her food. "I sound crazy."

"Guin, she's Na'atak." She cocked her head to one side. "They're shape-shifters."

Guin's mouth dropped open. "Say what?"

"I'm sorry. I'm not sure why I assumed you knew. They're polymorphs. The people of their planet shape-shift. She was probably changing to look like you."

"Is it some kind of magic?" Guin asked, awestruck and feeling foolish at the same time.

"No. More like a biological function. I heard a lot of people freaked out when Na'ataks first arrived in Druthenia."

"I can understand why."

Jaxzon sat at the head table with King Jaezain, King Nov'Xam, and Princess Vertuma. Un'Un and Uso sat together near the head table, an empty chair beside them.

"I guess I'm supposed to be sitting there. Why didn't Delori tell me about the banquet? She's usually on top of me regarding this stuff."

"I imagine he's why." Bree inclined her head to where Delori sat with Ahret.

"Is she smiling? That's surprising. I wonder what the story is there?"

"I don't know. She looks happy for a change."

Prince Kapre joined them. "May I sit here?"

"Sure, this is a free country." Guin glanced at Bree. "Isn't it?"

She shrugged. "I think so."

Kapre took a seat across from Guin. "Am I interrupting?"

"No, we were talking about New York and the party Derek wants to throw after Guin's chosen. Will you be attending?"

Guin kicked her under the table. Bree gave her a sly smile.

"I wouldn't miss one of Derek's parties for the world," he said. "He always invites the most, shall I say, *interesting* people?"

"This won't be one of his usual parties," Bree told him. "It will be royally sanctioned, not a bimbo bash."

Guin and Kapre burst into laughter.

"Is throwing a bimbo bash a regular occurrence for Derek?" she asked, still chuckling at the notion.

Bree cocked her head. "Well..."

"Yes," said Kapre. "Derek is a renowned cad. He puts me to shame." He winked at Bree.

Guin glanced at Derek, who sat nearby, dining with several young people. "He's always been a gentleman around me."

He grinned. "Of course, he has. You aren't quite his type, are you? He's had to be on his best behavior around you."

"Derek is a real heartbreaker," said Bree. "A real love 'em and leave 'em type. More than a few of my friends have fallen victim to his charms."

"Mine too," chimed in Kapre.

Guin quirked an eyebrow. "My Derek? He's so sweet and kind. I can't picture him purposely hurting anyone."

"Oh, I don't believe he does it on purpose." Bree leaned her chin on her palm and gazed at Derek. "He has this boyish charm many find irresistible. He's not looking for a relationship and most understand how the affair will end. Maybe they imagine they will be the one to change his mind."

"There was a certain lord who Derek almost settled down with, but—"

Bree elbowed Kapre. "That's an old rumor and was never confirmed. Let's just say Derek met his match and leave it at that."

Guin raised an eyebrow.

Bree mouthed, "I'll tell you later."

"So, you admit you're a cad?" Guin asked Kapre.

"That's me, the consummate bachelor." He flashed her a charming smile. "Heartbreakingly handsome, obscenely rich...did I mention I'm a prince?"

"Not impressed, sir," she said, yet laughed when he waggled his eyebrows.

They Shifted back to Arwon the following day. Bree's mother became ill and called her home. Business on Uetov4 had Jaxzon's full attention. Boden left to take care of some problem on his ranch, leaving Za'Had and Eedras to safeguard Guin. Even Derek had left on some family business.

Alone and dreading the trip to Mikonia, Guin grew depressed. The day before the ball, she wandered the solarium in a melancholy mood. Homesickness creeping in.

By midday she lay in bed, nursing a headache, when someone knocked. "Come in."

Delori entered and placed a box on the bed.

"What's this?"

Delori read the card. "'*For my Ethereal Angel, a gift from my newest line, inspired by my fairest Muse. I pray my humble offering will bring you good health and good luck. Forever yours, Valdid.*'" Her brows arched. "It's rare for Valdid to allow his designs to be worn before they're shown. You must have left quite an impression."

Guin lifted the gown from the box. "I can't believe this. It's gorgeous! I'll need to send him a thank you note."

The gift lifted her spirits. She couldn't wait to wear it.

On the morning of the ball Jaxzon messaged Delori to ask what color gown Guin would be wearing.

"Why?" Guin asked.

Delori shrugged. "I think our prince has something up his sleeve, as they say on Earth."

AFTER SHIFTING TO MIKONIA, the Vau'uan's and Guin arrived at the Syndow palace, where to her irritation, she found her room in a different wing from the other guests. She assumed Vertuma had something to do with the arrangement when she learned this wing housed the serving staff.

Boden was given a room nearby, and Za'Had and Eedras were stationed in the hallway, alternating shifts. Cameras throughout the castle grounds recorded everything. Boden warned Guin that she and Jaxzon would need to be discreet. "King Jaezain and Jaxzon will be staying at a hotel in the city. Orist doesn't fully trust Mikonia's security."

The Syndow palace could only be described as colossal, and the most modern palace Guin had seen yet. The metallic walls reflected the lines of bright lights embedded in the ceiling. The floors were made of a shiny material, much like the sidewalks of Kurrel, but gave off no reflection. Moving stairs carried visitors to and from the building's seven floors.

That night, Za'Had escorted Guin to where she joined Derek at the ballroom's entrance. She gazed across the cavernous room. Huge, golden light fixtures illuminated lines of tables filling half the room. A full orchestra and dance floor occupied the rest. Androids delivered drinks and cleared glasses.

After her announcement to the room, she followed Derek to the head table set on a raised dais overlooking the room.

"Royalty and high Council members will sit there. You and the other two ladies will sit at these three tables." He led her to the nearby tables, each set for ten.

"Who am I sitting with?"

Derek checked the placards. "Sarya's across from you. The rest are Council members."

"Just my luck. Vertuma's favorite minion. I hope she doesn't kick me."

"You can always kick back." He indicated her heels. "Those things look lethal."

Guin glanced at her four-inch gold and maroon stilettos and grinned. They matched Valdid's creation perfectly. Golden, braided fabric trimmed the dress's maroon bodice and the single strap over her left shoulder. The maroon skirt flowed around her knees at the front then fell in layers to the floor on the sides and back. Her auburn hair fell loosely over her shoulders and down her back in thick curls.

Prince Jaxzon's name rang out. The room quieted, as guests bowed. He entered wearing a dark, chocolate-brown suit with a maroon waistcoat and tie. A matching kerchief peeked from his breast pocket.

Sitting across from Sarya turned out to be tougher than Guin could have imagined. She soon understood that every Council member within earshot supported Vertuma.

Upon taking her seat, Sarya commented on Guin's gown. "Is it new?"

Guin smiled politely. "Yes, it is."

"Truly?" A cruel gleam flashed in Sarya's golden eyes. "I'm surprised anyone would still carry such an old design. That style has been out for ages."

"That's odd." Guin frowned down at her dress. "When I received the gown yesterday, Valdid's note indicated he'd designed it specifically for me to wear tonight. He'll be so disappointed when he hears his new designs are outdated."

Sarya's cheeks darkened when titters came from the other guests.

At the head table, Vertuma leaned in close to Jaxzon. The princess's gaze met Guin's. She smiled a slow Cheshire-cat smile.

The conversation went on to several diverse issues, and Guin believed Sarya might leave her alone, until Prince Kapre was mentioned.

"It appears as though you've become rather friendly with Prince Kapre, Lady Guin." Sarya raised an eyebrow then glanced at the others. "He never stops talking about her. Vertuma says he's quite smitten." Her eyes glinted. "What is this power you wield over our men? It's almost scandalous. You spend an hour in private with one and he becomes a slave to your whims. Do tell us your secret."

All gazes fixed on Guin, yet before she could respond, her tormentor continued, "It must be difficult juggling a known philanderer, two princes, *and* your personal bodyguard."

"I'm not sure what you mean, Sarya. I spend time with many of my friends." Guin mustered a smile. "But, if you're implying something more, I'm sorry to disappoint you." She drained her glass of water and asked a server for a refill.

"I suppose your gown and Prince Jaxzon's matching accessories weren't planned?" Sarya's faked sweetness slipped into an icy tone.

"Not by me." Guin glanced again at the head table, wishing to see Jaxzon's smile. He appeared preoccupied with whatever Vertuma attempted to feed him from her fork.

"The rumor is," Sarya went on, "she and her bodyguard, Boden, had a fling. And he's Prince Jaxzon's best friend."

"Is it true you and Derek dated on Earth?" asked a young Councilwoman. "I heard they were frantic, and because everyone knows most of his women here, they picked you out of desperation."

The faces around Guin wore the same smug, pretentious expressions as Sarya's. "I'm sorry, I don't listen to rumors or understand why people say such slanderous things, and where I'm from, this is not polite dinner conversation."

A few embarrassed faces looked away. Sarya smirked.

“I hope you have a pleasant meal.” Guin set her folded her napkin on her plate. “But if you will excuse me, I’m finished.”

“Yes, you are,” muttered Sarya.

CHAPTER TWENTY-EIGHT

Guin made her way to the powder room. Her pale reflection stared at her from the vanity mirror. She brushed a strand of hair from her face with a shaky hand. *I'm not cut out for this. I can't compete with Vertuma.*

Taking a deep breath, she closed her eyes. *Vertuma and her minions aren't worth your time or energy, Guinevere. Vertuma is an insignificant blip on the radar. Jaxzon is who's important, concentrate on him. You can do this. You and Jaxzon are meant to be together. Don't let Vertuma's venom poison your dream.*

Opening her eyes, she squared her shoulders, then went back to the ball.

First Vertuma, then Sarya, then Uso hijacked Jaxzon for every dance during the first hour of the ball.

Kapre touched Guin's elbow. "May I have this dance?"

"Of course."

Jaxzon and Vertuma spun past as Kapre and Guin swayed to the music. "Your prince is too polite for his own good. You'll never have a chance at this rate."

"He's too much of a gentleman to tell your sister to bug off."

He threw back his head in laughter. "You're probably right. When this song ends, I'll run interference with my sister. You grab your prince."

"Why would you do that?"

"Just helping a friend," he said with a shrug.

"I didn't know you and Prince Jaxzon were close."

He clutched his chest. "You wound me deeply, my lady. It's not Jaxzon of whom I speak."

Guin smiled. "Maybe I misjudged you."

"You're not the first." Kapre led her closer to Jaxzon and Vertuma, and as the song ended, he turned Guin toward Jaxzon, and took his sister's hand, asking her to dance.

Vertuma managed a brief glare before her brother pulled her away.

"What a happy surprise." Jaxzon bowed to Guin. "May I have this dance, my lady?"

"Always, my prince."

When he took her in his arms, she relaxed for the first time that evening.

He brushed a wayward hair from her eyes. "I missed you."

"I missed you too. I love your new tie. Thank you for being so thoughtful."

"A pleasure, my lady." He leaned in whispering, "Anything for my future queen."

"I wish there was a door we could dance through."

"I've found my first royal decree." His lips grazed her ear. "All ballrooms shall henceforth possess open doors leading to dimly lit gardens."

Guin laughed. They whirled around the floor, while she gazed lovingly into his eyes, oblivious to anything else.

Though she longed to dance with him the whole night, Jaxzon said he didn't wish to insult the Syndows so, they parted after two songs.

Derek danced with Bree, Delori with Ahret, Jaxzon with Vertuma.

Guin sipped a fruity drink and sighed. The princess ran a hand through Jaxzon's hair, and he smiled. A heaviness filled Guin's heart. An urge to cry gripped her.

You don't belong here. You're an intruder.

She frowned. *That isn't true. Jaxzon's eyes don't sparkle when he dances with Vertuma. He only smiled to be polite. They aren't meant to be together. I will surely be chosen.*

Will you?

Boden appeared at her side. "Mind if I sit?"

"Of course. I mean no, please, sit."

"Are you okay?"

She swallowed the lump in her throat. "I guess I'm a little homesick."

"Aw, Griffin." He punched her arm. "Once this is over you can go for a visit. Probably next week."

"Seriously? I haven't really thought much further than the next few days. Everything's closing in on me, like when those people mobbed us. Boden to the rescue, again. Thank you for that."

He gazed across the room. "Jaxzon's got himself trapped again. Always too polite to say no, even to those harpies."

Vertuma and Sarya had the prince backed against a table. The two women blocked any hope of escape.

"Poor Jaxzon."

"Yes, poor Jaxzon." His voice held more than a hint of sarcasm.

"What's that about?"

"Nothing. I guess I'll go rescue our poor prince."

Guin frowned.

"Are you unwell?" Jaxzon asked, after Boden extricated him. "You look tired."

"Does it show? I'm sorry. I feel... Shift-lagged. These different planets and time zones are catching up to me."

"The evening is over soon. You should go to bed, get some rest. You're going to need all you can get for tomorrow."

She nodded, turning her face from his view, fighting to control her emotions. When the song ended, she bade Jaxzon goodnight then hurried to her room.

~

GUIN AWAKENED with a terrible headache and an equally terrible thirst. She crawled from her bed, commencing her usual morning routine. Peering into her closet, she contemplated what to wear when someone knocked on her door.

Out of habit she called, "Come in Derek."

The door opened. A short, blue, cylindrical droid with four arms wheeled in. "Sorry, my lady. I am not Derek."

"Oh! Come in. What can I do for you?"

"I'm here to clean the room."

"What time is it?"

"The thirteenth hour and twelve. Are you leaving for the midday meal?"

"Yes, give me a few minutes please." She changed, then went to the dining room where she found Derek and Bree.

He grinned. "Someone partied too hard last night."

"I didn't drink alcohol last night and went to bed early." Guin rubbed her temples. "I guess I'm having some sort of massive, delayed jet lag." She snagged a piece of toast from a platter and ordered a glass of juice from the serving-bot. "Where's Jaxzon and Her Royal Pain?"

"Jaxzon had to go back to Uetov4 with Ahret. Something huge happening there, all hush-hush." He shrugged. "Not sure where Vertuma is. Don't actually care. Everyone heads back to Arwon tomorrow for the vote. The big announcement's the day after. Are you excited?"

Guin nodded, her headache lessoning with the toast and juice.

The day dragged on. Jaxzon wouldn't arrive until sometime in the evening. Guin's emotions ran the gamut from excited to distressed. By the time they announced the evening meal, she was in a strange state of agitation. She'd asked for and received something for her headache, then managed to put away two pitchers of water, yet her thirst still burned.

She laid in bed when someone knocked. "Come in."

Boden opened the door and stuck his head in. "Jaxzon sent me. Would you like an evening stroll in the garden?"

She threw her legs over the side of the bed. "Definitely!"

He escorted her through the back hallway to a side door. "Remember, the Syndows have security cameras everywhere, so be discreet. You don't want a scandal now."

"Thanks for the warning," she snapped. "You know, because I had planned to jump him right there in the topiary." She took a few steps before realizing he was no longer beside her. She glared back at him.

He blanched. "What's wrong with you?"

Guin put a hand to her forehead. "I'm so sorry, Boden. I'm stressing out. I don't feel right. That's no excuse. Please forgive me?"

Putting an arm around her shoulder, he continued guiding her along the garden path. "I understand. I'm sure it's only nerves."

They found Jaxzon. He offered his arm. "My lady, would you accompany me for a walk?"

"It would be my pleasure, my prince."

"Mind the microphones," Boden reminded them before taking his leave.

She and Jaxzon made small talk, and she reveled in his company. He led her to an ornate fountain. Guin laid her head against his upper arm. Water splashed, overflowing from one tier to the next.

She straightened at the sound of footsteps.

"How dare you be so disrespectful!" King Jaezain's voice shook with rage, his face reddening in anger, his hands balling into fists. "You are in the Syndow's home! Yet you're here, with her. Right under their noses."

"Father, I—"

Jaezain raised his hand. "I won't stand for this! I will do everything in my power to sway the vote for Vertuma." His eyes burned with fury. "I will never allow a common Earthling to seduce my son and my people. You will never be queen!"

He stormed off before Jaxzon or Guin had time to react. They stared after him, then at each other.

"Excuse me." Jaxzon hurried after his father.

Guin's head spun. *What did I do? What's changed?*

"He won't talk to me," Jaxzon said upon his return. "He's gone back to the hotel."

"What does this mean? Why has he changed his mind? What did I do?"

"I don't know. I've never seen him this furious." He took her hand. "I'm sorry for his cruel words, and I'm sorry to leave you now. I must speak with him and discover what's happened."

"I understand." Guin swallowed. A sensation of deep dread washed over her. A tear fell from her eye, but she brushed it away because *'True Griffins don't cry'*. "Go. I'll see you tomorrow?"

"Of course." He kissed her cheek. "Please, try to get some rest."

Guin took a deep, shuddering breath then followed the dimly lit path to the door she'd come through with Boden.

A creeping numbness spread through her limbs. Her body ached. Her mind refused to focus. Fully clothed, she laid on her bed and fell into a dreamless sleep.

A pounding woke Guin late the next morning. She pulled the pillow over her head to block the light. The thumping was more than in her head.

Someone banged on her door.

"Come in," she called then cringed at the sound.

"The door's locked," came Boden's muffled voice.

Guin rolled off the bed, stumbling to the door. It flew open when she turned the lock.

He strode into her room and grabbed her suitcases from the closet. "Get packed, we're leaving. Now."

"What's going on? Is it Jaxzon? Boden, please, tell me! What's happened?"

"King Jaezain," he said in a hoarse whisper. "Guin, he's been murdered."

CHAPTER TWENTY-NINE

Jaxzon stood in the living room of his father's hotel suite.

Mikonia's largest city spread before him through the floor to ceiling window. *Murdered.* Jaxzon still couldn't believe it, even after seeing the body and touching his father's cold, lifeless hand.

Upon leaving Guin the night before, Jaxzon had run into Boden outside the Syndow palace.

"What happened?" Boden asked. "Griffin looked upset."

"I don't have time to talk. I must speak to my father."

His friend followed him to the hover and climbed in with him. "You can tell me on the way."

He'd told Boden what his father said.

His friend frowned. "He called her an Earthling? That doesn't make sense. He's never shown prejudice before. What could she have done to anger him so terribly?"

"She did nothing. That's what I intend to learn. He must change his mind." He met Boden's eyes. "She has to be the one chosen."

Boden's eyebrows went up. "What if she isn't? You know there's always been that possibility."

"I'll leave." Jaxzon had thought about this possibility before but had never put a voice to it. "I'll step down. We'll go somewhere we can live in peace. My father will be forced to take back his rule and figure out who will be his new heir."

Boden shook his head. "But you ca—"

"Yes. I can. And I will. My mind is made up. If they choose anyone other than Guin, I will abdicate."

"But your people!" Boden's eyes darkened, he'd clenched his fists. "How could you do this to them? To us? Would you truly leave us without a king?"

Jaxzon's temper flared. "You have a king! My father is still king and has done this to himself. *He* invoked the Vekdromic. *He* wishes me to enter a loveless marriage. *He* would have me live my life bound to that selfish shrew. You yourself have said it for ages; women only want one thing from me. Guin loves me for who I am. Why can't we be happy?"

They had arrived at the hotel and the door lifted. Before Jaxzon could leave, Boden grabbed his arm. "I can't believe you would do this to your people, Jaxzon. I thought you were more honorable. How can you let a woman come between you and your duty?"

"Duty be damned." Jaxzon had pulled his arm away. "I love her, Boden. Nothing will ever change that."

His guard joined him as he entered the hotel, but not before Boden called after him, "We'll see Jaxzon. You never really know a person's motives."

Orist hadn't allowed Jaxzon to see the king, stating His Majesty had retired and given commands that he was not to be disturbed. On this, Orist wouldn't budge.

Not having slept the night before, Jaxzon waited for a decent hour to confront his father when Orist summoned him to the king's suite.

The King's Guard stood at attention on either side of the suite entrance. Two more stood guard at the door to his father's private room. His father's personal physician joined them in the living area.

"What is it?" Jaxzon asked, puzzled by the physician's presence. "Is the king ill?"

"Your Highness." The physician averted his eyes. "I'm sorry to be the bearer of this terrible news. The king is dead."

Jaxzon went numb, then asked to see his father.

"I'm sorry, Your Highness," said Orist. "I have been ordered by the Mikonian government to not allow anyone to enter the crime scene."

"Crime scene?"

"Yes." Orist cleared his throat. "The king has been murdered."

Images whirled through Jaxzon's mind, his father's face reddened in anger, the day of his mother's and sister's funerals. He was left light-headed and dazed. A hot fist squeezed his heart. But before he could react further, the suite's door opened and Mikonian police poured in, giving orders, separating Jaxzon from the physician and the Commander.

Jaxzon needed advice. He wanted to speak with the king. The burning fist tightened its grip in his chest—he was king now or would be soon. Taking a long, slow breath, he closed his eyes, calming his mind. Duty commanded that sorrow wait.

He contacted Boden, unsure of what to say, but wanting to tell someone. Guin didn't have a telecon and Boden was the only person he could trust with this news. "The king—Father—he's been murdered. I need you to take Guin back to Arwon. Take care of her, I have to stay and make arrangements."

"What? How?"

"I don't know yet. But I want her safe."

"I'm so sorry, Jaxzon." His friend sighed into the speaker. "I-I'll take care of her. Keep me informed."

"Thank you, Boden. I will."

After two hours of answering questions, Jaxzon stood by as his father's body was removed from the bedroom. "May I see him, please?"

The medic halted. "Of course, Your Highness. The scene has been processed." She pulled the cover from the king's face.

Jaxzon glanced away at the sight of his father's dead blue eyes and the blood staining his graying hair. Raising his hand to his father's face, he asked, "May I?"

The medic bowed.

After closing his father's eyes, he gripped his cold hand. Jaxzon touched the knuckles to his forehead and kissed the back before returning it to his father's side. He nodded and the medic covered the king, then guided the hovering stretcher from the suite.

Orist handed Jaxzon the Royal Signet. The ichor-made Eye that had hung around his father's neck since he'd been crowned and around his father's before him. He turned the seal over in his hands, wondering why. *Why would someone do this?*

"Excuse me, Your Highness."

"What now, Orist?" He pocketed the signet, uncomfortable with the thought of wearing it while specks of his father's blood still dried upon the shining metal. *I'll have to have it washed.* He pushed the absurd thought from his mind and glanced at the bald commander. "What is it?"

Orist cleared his throat. "The Mikonian government has restricted Shifts from their planet. King Nov'Xam has issued a statement that no one is to leave until they have been interviewed. It appears that every Council member and noble person is requesting an audience with you. King Nov'Xam sends his condolences and asks that you remain here as well. He apologized that he is unable to speak with you directly at this time, but the palace is in lockdown, and no one is to enter or leave."

Jaxzon frowned. "The murder happened in this hotel. Why would he lock down the palace?"

"I'm unsure. I believe they must have a suspect, and that person or persons may have a connection to the Vekdromic."

To think that his father would be murdered over who Jaxzon was to marry left him bewildered. The only person who might have something to gain considering his father's anger—he shook his head. Guin had nothing to do with this. He was positive. *Then who?*

A knock sounded on the door and Orist went to answer. High Council members, Ulzon Domme and Heldivar Grint were let into the suite.

"Your Highness." Dame Grint bowed. "Allow me to express my deepest condolences."

"And mine as well," said Ulzon. "The Council is stunned and outraged. We have called an emergency meeting to be convened before the vote."

"The vote?" Still in a state of shock, Jaxzon gawked at the Council members, puzzled. "In light of my father's death, wouldn't the vote be postponed?"

"On the contrary," Heldivar said. "It is more important now than ever. The kingdom cannot be left without a king for long. The law states that the king must be wed or betrothed prior to taking the throne. The death of a king in no way changes this sacred law."

Bewildered, Jaxzon nodded. A numbness crept over his limbs. Having lost a night's sleep, along with the shock and realization of what now needed to be done overwhelmed him. He held up a hand. "Please. Give me a moment. I need time to think."

"Of course, Your Highness." Heldivar dipped her head. "The meeting will convene at the thirteenth hour, the vote at the fourteenth. We will arrange for the ballots to be Shifted to a neutral location."

Orist showed the two Council members out. "Is there anything you need from me, Your Highness?"

"No. Thank you. I'll call for you shortly. I want a full briefing on what you know."

Orist bowed and left.

Jaxzon sighed, slumping into the nearest chair. A deep sadness lay over his heart. He yearned for Guin—needing to hold her, to tell her how empty he felt.

The rest of the day went by in a rush. That afternoon, Jaxzon was again questioned by another person, a Detective Quaalnos. The man's demeanor changed when Jaxzon mentioned his father's anger the night before.

"Do you mean to tell me that the king was going to vote against the Angel of Arwon? I figured everyone would be voting for her. I don't follow these things, but my wife tells me all about Lady Guin and how she came from Earth to marry a prince. How long have you known her? Does she have friends here?"

"Only the Vau'uans and a few others that she made since she's been here." He gave the detective Bree's and Boden's names and contact information.

"Are you sure she didn't know anyone prior to her arrival here with Lord Vau'uan?" The man gave Jaxzon a sideways look.

"What are you trying to imply?" His anger flared. "Do you believe she had anything to do with my father's murder? Because if you do, I can assure you that Guin is incapable of hurting anyone, let alone killing."

Quaalnos held up a hand. "Now Your Highness, I meant no disrespect. In my mind everyone is a suspect. I am simply narrowing the suspect pool. It's a very long list at the moment, and I have to ask the hard questions."

Sighing, Jaxzon nodded. "I understand. But you must understand, Guin is everything the media has made her out to be. She's kind and caring. I don't know what my father was told about her to anger him so. I was never given the chance to ask. Before last night, he'd given us his blessing and had told me she was my match, and that she would make an excellent queen."

"Did he now?" Quaalnos scribbled something on his notepad. "And did Lady Guin know about this?"

"Of course. He told her himself."

"Uh-huh, and when would that have been?" Jaxzon gave him the date.

"Thank you, Your Highness. That should be all for now." The

man opened the door to leave, but turned back, a hand in the air. "Just one more thing."

"Yes?"

"I'm very sorry for your loss. Your father was a good man." With that, Quaalnos closed the door before Jaxzon could respond.

CHAPTER THIRTY

"Murdered?" The heat drained from her body. She sank onto her bed.

"Yes, Griffin. Murdered." Boden cleared his throat and glanced away. "We're leaving."

"What about Jaxzon? Where is he? He must be in agony after what happened last night."

He took her by the shoulders. "Don't mention that to anyone."

She flinched at the intensity in his eyes. "What's wrong, Boden? Tell me, please?"

"Pack." He crossed to the wardrobe, yanked her clothes from the hangars, throwing them on the bed.

Guin stuffed clothes into her bags. Boden scooped everything into her toiletry kit. He picked up her luggage then propelled her from the room and through the hall to the front entry.

An armed guard in black and gold blocked the exit. "King Nov'Xam ordered all guests detained until formally interviewed."

"I'm under Prince Jaxzon's orders to take Lady Guin to Arwon immediately."

"Prince Jaxzon doesn't rule here. I'm under orders to detain everyone by the ruler of *this* realm."

Boden spun her away from the door, leading her back to her room.

"Stay here. I'm going to find Derek and Bree. I'll try to contact Jaxzon."

She sat on her bed hugging her knees to her chest. Confusion fogged her mind while thirst clawed her throat. She contemplated asking for a doctor. "What the hell am I thinking? Jaxzon lost his father, and I'm moaning about jet lag? Pull it together Guinevere."

Boden returned with Derek and Bree. Bree ran to Guin, throwing herself into her arms. "He's dead, Guin, our king is dead."

Guin embraced Bree. Derek's red-rimmed eyes caused tears to spill from her own.

Boden's shoulders slumped. He sat at the vanity. "I haven't heard from Jaxzon. The Mikonian government wants everyone to stay until the investigators allow us to leave."

Derek sat on the bed, wrapping an arm around a crying Bree.

Boden's telecon buzzed. "Hello? Yes, I understand. Right. Jaxzon, I'm so sorry... See you then." He glanced at Derek. "Jaxzon wanted to delay the vote until we returned to Arwon. The Council insisted the selection take place as scheduled. The law does not change for the death of the king. His coronation is the day after tomorrow. The realm cannot be left without a king, and he must be married or betrothed before he's crowned."

"Did he sound okay?" Guin asked, aching to see Jaxzon.

"I guess, Griffin. How are you supposed to sound when your father's been murdered?"

She recoiled at his tone before recalling Boden's father had also been murdered. "I'm sorry, Boden, I didn't mean..."

Derek put his arm around Guin, frowning at Boden. "What now?"

"I guess we wait for the investigators to interview us. No one is allowed to Shift from the planet."

Derek and Boden left to find food and check for news.

~

GUIN DOZED until the morning's news crashed into her conscious mind. Bree lay curled beside her. She sat, startling Bree.

"Where is everyone?"

"I don't know." Guin found Za'Had stationed at the end of the hall.

"Where are Derek and the others?"

"In the dining hall."

The room was crowded with guests waiting for news or permission to leave for their own planets. Derek beckoned to Guin and Bree. "Jaxzon is on his way. The vote took place this evening at the Arwon Embassy. They will announce the results at the ceremony tomorrow."

"The investigators will be here in the morning."

Boden took the seat across from Guin. "Hopefully, we can leave shortly after the announcement." His voice dropped to a whisper. "Orist is heading the investigation for our part."

"Why would anyone kill the king?" she asked. "He was planning on stepping down. Who would benefit?"

"That's the question of the day, isn't it?" Boden's eyes bored into hers. "Who would stand to gain if King Jaezain were dead?"

"What about the scanners? Can't they trace where he was and who was with him at the time?" she asked.

He dropped his gaze. "To ensure their safety, Royals don't have tracers. I'm sure they're checking for anyone near him at the time."

"Do you know where he was when he—when it happened?" Bree asked.

"He was in his suite at the hotel, and apparently no one saw anyone enter or leave. His guards are being interrogated by Orist, who's enraged. Can't say I blame him. The king was murdered under his watch."

"This is so depressing." Bree glanced around the quiet hall. "Can we go back to Guin's room?"

The room wasn't much better. Derek and Bree exchanged memories of King Jaezain. Za'Had delivered a pitcher of water. Guin's throat remained dry, her mind fuzzy.

Boden refilled her empty glass. "Can we talk in private?"

"Of course."

She followed him to the bathroom. He closed the door then took her by the shoulders, bending to meet her eyes. "What was the argument between Jaxzon and his father?"

Guin blinked at his intensity. "T-the king told us he was going to persuade the Council to vote against me."

"What did Jaxzon do?"

"Nothing. The king left then Jaxzon went to the hotel to talk to him." Her eyes widened. "No, Jaxzon would never—"

His jaw tightened. He turned his back to her, speaking between clenched teeth. "I know he wouldn't. How could you even think it?"

Her chin quivered. "Why are you angry with me?"

He whirled around, dark hair flying, hazel eyes blazing. "Because none of this would have happened if you hadn't come. There's a good chance Jaxzon is a suspect, and we'll have lost our king and our future." A burning wave of hatred radiated from him. "I wish we'd never met you."

Guin recoiled. His words hit her with the force of a physical blow.

Boden stood between her and the door. She put her back to the wall and braced herself. "I'd like to leave please."

He ran a hand through his hair and came toward her.

"Don't! I know self-defense, and I *will* hurt you." She balled her hands into fists, absurdly trying to remember the Taekwondo lessons she'd taken between the ages of twelve and fourteen.

He groped for the handle and swung the door open.

Derek and Bree stared after Boden as he left the bedroom. Guin trembled with anger, fear, and anxiety.

"What was that about?" Derek asked.

Before she could answer, Jaxzon came through the open door. Derek embraced his friend. "I'm so sorry."

"Thank you. Do you mind if I have a private word with Guin?"

Bree gave Jaxzon's arm a brief squeeze before following Derek from the room.

Guin rushed into Jaxzon's open arms. "I'm so, so sorry."

He crushed her to his chest and drew a shuddering breath. A single tear tracked down his cheek. She kissed it away, then his mouth was on hers.

Caressing Jaxzon's neck, she returned his kiss. His chest heaved. His heartbeat thumped in her ear as she rested her head against him. She held him in a fierce embrace, aching for his pain.

Jaxzon's grip relaxed. She eased him onto the bed, then lay beside him. He rolled to his side, and she curled up next to him, his nose touched hers. "I love you, my lady."

"I love you too, my prince."

He snaked his arm beneath her. "I needed to be with you, to hold you."

"I wish I could ease your pain." She kissed the curve of his neck.

"You have." He drew in a jagged breath. "Being with you brings me peace. I felt so alone." He brushed a strand of hair from her face. "Soon we will always be together."

"Always, my love." She caressed cheek. "Who did this?"

"I haven't a clue. It makes no sense." His eyes squeezed shut, and his voice broke. "His last words to me were in anger."

"Oh, Jaxzon. This wasn't your fault. Please don't."

Hot tears fell into Guin's hair as sorrow shook his body. He cried himself to sleep in her arms.

Guin awoke with a start and bolted upright. Boden stood beside the bed, arms crossed, wearing a scowl.

"Boden? What time is it?" murmured Jaxzon.

"After midnight. Orist has half the guard searching for you. I told him I knew where you'd be, and I was right." He handed Jaxzon his coat. "You shouldn't be here. People will talk."

"People be damned. At this point, I don't care what people do. No matter what they voted today, my decision is made. I'll hear no more."

"I—"

Jaxzon raised a hand. "Not another word Boden. I'm warning you."

"Yes, Your Highness." Boden bowed then left.

Frowning after him, Jaxzon sighed. His shoulders slumped.

"What just happened?" Guin asked.

"Nothing you need to worry over." Putting an arm around her waist he planted a passionate kiss on her partially open lips. She laced her fingers around his neck, deepening the kiss until he broke away. "I have to go. I will see you this afternoon. I love you, my lady."

"I love you, my prince."

He rubbed his nose against hers. "I truly love you, Guinevere Griffin, and don't you ever forget that."

CHAPTER THIRTY-ONE

A tapping sounded on Guin's door. She rolled over, planting her face into the coolness of the pillow, her head pounding, her throat a desert.

"I'm sorry to wake you," said Derek, letting himself in. "I thought you'd rather not miss the announcement."

Guin's eyes flew open. The king had been murdered, the Council had voted, and the results would be announced today. The bees came back, churning in her gut.

Dark half-circles underlined his eyes. He appeared to have slept in his clothes. He set a box on the vanity.

She blinked away the sleepiness. "What's this?"

"It arrived this morning." He handed her a card. "From your greatest admirer."

"Valdid." She recognized the unique signature. "He must have sent another gown. What does the card say?"

"'*Though you will not need it, good luck. Your humble servant, Valdid.*'"

She opened the gift and set aside the paper covering. Lifting the gown by the straps, she held it above her head, admiring the layers of gauzy, pink chiffon pooling at her feet. Intricate, flowery lace overlaid the low-cut bodice and flowed over the hips of the flaring skirt. A pair of matching pink pumps lay in the bottom of the box. "This is absolutely gorgeous."

"Don't just stand there staring. Go try it on."

Guin went into the bathroom. The bodice molded to her shape. The V-neck ended below her breasts, and the back plunged lower. The skirt flowed from hips to floor in layers. A short train floated behind her. Her waist-length hair cascaded down her back in gentle curls.

"Valdid sure has a flair for the dramatic." She showed Derek the back.

He whistled between his teeth. "You're going to knock Jaxzon's socks off."

"Thank you, Derek. I can always count on you for an honest opinion. Help me with these shoes?" She sat on the bed, lifting the skirt's layers to her knees.

Derek knelt and placed the shoes on her feet.

"Now I seriously feel like I'm in a fairytale. I hope I can keep them both on when I run home at midnight."

He frowned. "Why are you going to run home at midnight?"

"Remind me to tell you Cinderella's story someday, but right now you need to get ready too." She rubbed her temples. "Do you have something for a headache?"

~

UNTIL POTENTIAL WITNESSES WERE INTERVIEWED, no one was permitted to leave the planet. Therefore the announcement would be held on Mikonia, and for matters of security, would take place in the Syndow's palace.

Fidgeting with her hair, she paced between the bed and the vanity. Guin straightened then re-straightened the gown. Her personal guard brought pain medication for her headache and a pitcher of water to ease her burning thirst.

She drained the last of the water into the glass when a knock came at the door. “It’s open.”

Za’Had opened the door. “My lady, the investigator is here to see you.”

“Thank you. Please, send him in.”

The guard allowed a short, dark-haired man to enter. “Lady Guin, it’s great to finally meet you. My wife is a big fan. Talks about you nonstop.”

“That’s so sweet. Mr.?”

“Sorry, my lady. The name’s Quaalnos. Detective Quaalnos.”

“Please, just Guin, Detective Quaalnos. Would you like to sit?” She indicated the chair by the vanity.

“No, no, I’m good. Please, take a seat yourself. I’m sure those heels get tiring.” He glanced at the shoes peeking from beneath her skirt.

She sat. “They do. Thank you.”

He strode across the room, his dull black shoes clicking on the floor’s solid surface. His knee-length, beige coat swished against his dark brown pant legs. He gazed into the courtyard below her window. His hair stuck out at angles as though it hadn’t seen a comb today, and judging by the shadow along his jaw, he hadn’t shaved either.

His brown eyes sparkled impishly as he absently patted his clothing. Removing a pad and pen from his inside breast pocket, he tapped them together. “I’ve never been able to take notes on those devices.”

A memory skittered across the back of Guin’s consciousness then scrambled away before she could catch it. This man seemed familiar, but her high-strung mind couldn’t pinpoint why.

He asked her full name, age, date of birth, birthplace, and address on Earth. “And where are you staying on Arwon?”

“I’m staying with the Vau’uan’s. I don’t know the address.”

He waved a hand. "I have it in my notes. When was the last time you saw the king?" She hesitated and he gave her a sharp glance.

"In the garden two nights ago. He was angry with me for some reason. He said some things that weren't kind."

"What did he say, exactly?" Quaalnos observed her closely.

Guin couldn't lie if she wanted to and told him everything she remembered.

"Right. Precisely what we heard on the recording."

"Sir, I would have told you the same if I hadn't known everything was recorded. I'm not a liar. I understand this looks bad for Jaxzon. He didn't do this. He loved his father dearly."

Quaalnos tipped his head to the side and peered at her from the corner of one eye. "More than he loves you?"

She frowned, caught off guard by his question.

"Don't worry about it." He waved dismissively. "The prince had nothing to do with it. He has a solid alibi. His whole security team has vouched for him."

She breathed a sigh of relief. "Do you have a suspect?"

"Yes. A good one, as a matter of fact. We need to interview a few more people. We should be making an arrest soon." He went to the door. "You have a good evening, Lady Guin. My wife is going to be so pleased I actually got to meet the Angel of Arwon." Shaking his head and chuckling, he opened the door then stopped, one finger raised. "Just one more thing."

"Yes?"

"Good luck tonight." He gave her a crooked smile, then left.

Guin went to the door and called, "Thank you."

He waved without turning and ambled down the hallway.

THE TIME for the announcement had come. Derek and Bree accompanied Guin to the ballroom where she made her way through the mixture of reporters, camera operators, and black and gold uniformed palace guards.

Her knees trembled. Her head had a fuzzy haziness she couldn't shake. She had expected to see Boden yet didn't spot him in the crowd.

The five members of the high Council came from behind a curtain of a makeshift stage. Heldivar Grint explained the history of the Vekdromic. She related there needed to be a two-thirds collective vote from the Council and nobility of the realm.

"If a single candidate does not receive at least two-thirds of the votes, the two top candidates would be presented to the prince. He would then be given the choice between those two. On that note," she announced. "We seem to find ourselves in such a situation tonight."

Those in attendance gasped.

She smiled at Guin. "Prince Jaxzon will choose between Princess Vertuma and Lady Guinevere."

Guin gasped, her heart skipping in her chest.

Bree squeezed her hand and squealed in her ear.

A single, "Yeah!" escaped Derek, his grip tightening on her waist.

Cameras clicked. Reporters talked excitedly.

Jaxzon came from behind the curtain. His dazzling smile lit his face upon spotting Guin.

Her heart swelled. Their dreams were coming true. He produced a pink, long-stemmed rose, then approached the podium, bending to speak into the microphones.

Orist appeared from behind the curtain, rushing toward Jaxzon, knocking Council member Jenk Milton to one side in his haste. Orist seized Jaxzon's arm then rushed him from the stage. They disappeared behind the curtain. The five Council members followed.

"What's happening?" Bree asked.

Derek frowned. "I don't know. Maybe they caught the killer?"

Guin's heart thrummed.

After what seemed an eternity, Jaxzon reappeared, stone-faced. The light had left his eyes. The rose gone. Not casting a glance in her direction, he approached the microphones. His voice held no emotion when he said three words before disappearing behind the curtain. "I choose Vertuma."

A cold hand's frozen fingers seized Guin by the throat. Those three words echoed in the sudden emptiness of her breaking heart. Time slowed. A queasy numbness filled her. The atmosphere took on a nightmarish quality. A thunderous thumping reverberated in her skull.

The voices around her muted, becoming muffled as the hall erupted around her. People shouted. Cameras flashed. A clear bubble of silence surrounded her, separating her from the chaos yet amplifying her own movements. Her heartbeats roared deafeningly in her skull. Her gasp reverberated in her ears as her train caught, jerking her backward.

Black gloves hooked her elbows, dragging her away from her friends. Bree and Derek stared after her, their expressions mirroring her own shock and confusion. Derek said something, his words made incoherent by the hammering in her head. Her feeble attempts to pull free rendered useless by the powerful hands.

"Jaxzon!" she called, her voice weak.

He'd left. Unaware of or indifferent to her plight.

The gown's train entangled in her shoes, nearly wrenching her from her feet. Her body twisted sideways. The fabric tore. Her captors spun her around. Two black and gold uniformed Mikonia National Police officers gripped her arms.

Dazed and frightened, she struggled while being propelled to the top of the palace steps. She dug in her heels. Her shoe caught, wrenching her ankle. The shoe slipped from her foot. Terror twisted within her when they forced her down the stairs then into a waiting police hover. Through the crowd of staring people, her pink pump remained upright, stuck at the top of the stairs.

The solitary shoe struck something deep within her. A crippling déjà vu washed over her. The world took on a surreal, dreamlike quality.

Her pulse beat a staccato against her temples. The dryness in her throat threatened to strangle her. "Why are you doing this?" she pleaded, her voice scarcely above a whisper.

"You're under arrest," said the stone-faced officer.

"For what?"

"Regicide."

"*What?*"

"For the murder of King Jaezain."

The air left her lungs. Darkness engulfed her.

CHAPTER THIRTY-TWO

Disoriented, Guin opened her eyes. A shadow hung above her. Through a thick haze, a light shown first in one eye, then the other. The shadow took the shape of a brown-uniformed woman holding a penlight. The woman grunted then left the small gray room.

Guin's back spasmed against the rigid bench she laid on. A chain connected her shackled wrist to a ring set in the floor. Her head spun. She propped herself on her elbows. Valdid's gown hung in tatters. Dirt and scuff marks marred the skirts. The train had been torn off.

Memories overwhelmed her, knocking her back against the bench.

The bright lights above seared into her numbed brain. Her chest tightened. She choked back tears. *True Griffin's don't cry.*

This is all wrong. Someone's made a mistake. The detective knows I didn't kill the king.

The chain would not allow her to step more than a foot from the bench. The cuff bit into her wrist when she stretched for a better view of the hallway. She sat, ready to explain they had the wrong person.

I need to talk to Quaalnos.

A man's familiar voice echoed from the hallway, his words unintelligible. Touching her ear, she encountered only flesh. The loqu was gone.

Detective Quaalnos and a tall, slim man in a green suit with a yellow bowtie entered the room.

Quaalnos cocked his head to one side and smiled. "*Den tu ven silut blende*?"

A wave of relief washed over Guin. "I lost my loqu." She pointed to her ear. "I don't understand you. May I get another?"

The detective chuckled then, shaking his head, he unlocked the cuff.

"Thank you." She rubbed where the cuff had pinched her skin. "May I go now?"

Gripping Guin's elbow he hauled her through a white-tiled hallway.

They entered another gray-walled room and passed a short, uniformed man sitting behind a glass partition. Lieutenant Quaalnos shoved Guin against a wall then motioned to the floor, indicating she stay where she was. After he joined the person behind the glass, a beam of light shot from the ceiling, then fanned out, engulfing her in its glow. The fan of light slid over her body before disappearing.

The man came from behind the glass carrying a gun-shaped device with a large needle at the business end. He gripped her hand, turning it palm up. In one swift movement he thrust the needle into her wrist then pulled the trigger. She screamed as a bolt of burning agony shot from her wrist to her shoulder.

Quaalnos ushered her to another room where a thin, gray-haired woman waited at a desk. He cuffed Guin to another chain on the wall.

"*Bayudavi.*" With a smile and a wave, he left the room.

The woman donned a pair of gloves, sneering at Guin with open hostility. She removed the earring from Guin's right ear then dropped it into a plastic container. She winced when the woman jerked out the other. She unclasped Guin's necklace then ran her fingers through Guin's hair, removed her remaining shoe, placing it with the jewelry.

"*Gen du verinda.*"

"I don't understand what you're saying."

The woman tugged the dress strap. She unlocked Guin's wrist, then crossed her arms and waited.

She understood she was to remove her gown. Turning away she slid the straps from her shoulders. Humiliation heated her face at having to strip in front of this woman who so obviously despised her.

Disrobing, Guin let the gown fall to the floor. The woman yanked the dress from under her feet, further ripping the lace. She rolled the gown into a ball and stuffed it into the container.

The guard tossed a pair of mustard-yellow coveralls to Guin, who put them on, fastening them in front. The rough material chafed against her skin and had the odor of a musty attic.

The woman handed her a small iPad-like tablet and a stylus.

Alien symbols filled the screen. "I can't read this."

The woman snatched the stylus from Guin and placed an exaggerated *O* next to a line. She indicated the box of clothing, then the tablet.

Guin signed her name on the line beside the O, assuming this was the inventory of her belongings, praying she wasn't signing a confession to the king's murder. The woman took the stylus then passed the tablet over a small mechanism attached to the box's lid. The device beeped. The lid closed and locked.

Guin was led from the room by another uniformed guard.

~

GUIN'S CELL contained a metal bed, a toilet, and a small sink.

The guard waved her wrist over a screen on the wall. A silver sheet of light fell from the ceiling. The woman pointed to the silver sheen then wagged her finger at Guin, indicating not to touch the electric wall humming between them.

Guin sat on the edge of the bed. *Would she be allowed a phone call?* Tears slipped from her eyes.. She blinked them away. *This is why Jaxzon chose Vertuma. He believes I killed his father.*

The concept tipped her over a precarious ledge. She fell to her side, sobbing into her blanket. Within her mind an ominous fog gathered, attacking all coherent thought. Beating the grayness back with flailing fists of will, she leaned against the wall, hugging her knees to her chest.

Are they going to leave me to die in misery? A misty haze wrapped itself around her distressed mind. Her head sank to her knees. Consciousness retreated to a dark place.

The screech of metal sliding on metal. The blur of a black uniform on the other side of the electronic wall. The pungent odor of cooked fish assaulting Guin's nostrils, turning her stomach. The sharp taste of bile rose to the back of her throat.

The blur passed a tray under a gap in the sheen. Footfalls echoed through the hall. The whisper of a door closing left her in silence. Before gray clouds came to take her back into herself, some vague part of her remembered her manners.

She mumbled, "Thank you."

Sometime later, the hiss of a door caused her heart to leap. *Is someone coming for me?* A blur appeared and sighed. Metal slid against metal. The blur removed the tray of uneaten food. Footsteps, a hiss, silence.

Her confused mind swam through the gloom. She laid her forehead against her bent knees.

Consciousness returned. *I'm blind.* Part of her understood someone had switched off the lights. The other part didn't care. Guin allowed the ever-deepening haze to fill her, sinking into the comforting depths. Hours or days later, her eyes screwed shut against glaring lights. The inky fog cleared to a light gray.

Her legs had fallen asleep and now tingled painfully. She stretched. The blood rushed into them. She used the toilet then climbed onto the bed, laid on her side, and waited for someone to come and take her home.

Approaching footsteps. The blur of a person, the sound of metal on metal, the repulsive scent of food, retreating steps, a hiss.

Guin lost count of how often food passed beneath the silver curtain then was taken away uneaten. *Seven times? Fourteen?* She waited, swimming through the murky waters of her mind. *Waiting for what? Come on, Guin, concentrate.*

She closed her eyes. *Jaxzon!* His face floated in the gloom. Agony flooded her heart. *Jaxzon believes I killed his father. He chose Vertuma!* A hot poker of misery drove through her shattered soul.

How could anyone believe me of such evil—especially Jaxzon? She willed the shadowy darkness to remove her from these torturous thoughts, sinking blissfully into oblivion.

With night came darkness. Upon closing her eyes Jaxzon's accusing stare filled her mind. She forced her lids to open. The vision cleared. She snuggled back into obscurity. Lying curled on her mattress, lost in the mist, she forgot herself, finding peace in the void.

A bright light shined overhead. Needles stabbed through her brain. Guin curled into a ball, blocking the light with her hands.

The humming ceased. Rough hands jerked her into a sitting position. A woman shouted. Guin's head rocked back from the force of a blow. Stars burst behind her eyelids. A sharp pain spread across her face.

A woman's red face hung inches from Guin's. She yanked Guin from the bed by her arm. Another guard gripped her other arm. They dragged her from her cell.

Maybe they've discovered their mistake? Maybe they will allow me to leave? The further they travelled, the more her hopes grew.

The guards hauled her through a doorway then strapped her to a padded table. Beside the table, shining medical instruments lined a metal tray. The words *lethal injection* ran through her benumbed mind. Terror thrust the shadows aside. She opened her mouth to scream she was innocent. A meek whisper escaped. She fell back, exhausted. Too weak to struggle.

Helpless, friendless, with nothing to live for, Guin gave in to her fate. This could be the easy way out. She wouldn't have to imagine Jaxzon with Vertuma or her friends hating her for something she hadn't done. She closed her eyes, waiting for the pain to be gone forever.

"*Bev tu nee vous lin*?" A beautiful, light cobalt woman smiled down at her.

Guin shook her head.

With a gentle touch, the woman gripped Guin's chin, peering in each ear. Her brow knitted. "Loqu?"

"No."

The woman sighed. She offered a glass of clear liquid to Guin, who turned away.

The woman drank from the cup, then lifted Guin's head and placed the glass to her lips. "Tia."

Guin took a small sip. Water. She drained the cup.

The woman produced a fluid-filled bottle which she hung from a hook in the wall. A tube ran from the bottle to a needle in the woman's hand. Guin flinched, struggling against the straps. The woman lifted the cup and pointed to the bottle. "Tia."

"Tia. Water?" Guin croaked.

The woman nodded then inserted the needle.

Cool liquid entered Guin's vein, spreading through her arm, creeping into her shoulder. She braced herself. When nothing happened, she sighed, relieved as her heart retained a steady beat.

"Loltu," the woman said, touching her own chest. "Loltu."

"Loltu," she whispered, understanding this was the woman's name. "Thank you."

Loltu placed a comforting hand on Guin's shoulder, causing replenished tears to leak from her closed eyes. She soon lost herself to the smoky mist wrapping around her weary mind.

She resurfaced when Loltu withdrew the needle. A beam of light glowed from a telecon-like device being passed over Guin's arm, sealing the hole left by the needle. Loltu wiped away a drop of blood.

A dull mist hung before Guin's eyes; her skull ached. She thrust aside the mist, focusing on Loltu as she loosened Guin's straps. She removed a bottle from a drawer and shook two pills onto Guin's palm, then refilled the water cup. She touched her own forehead, widening her eyes.

She smiled at the mime. "To clear my head?"

Loltu nodded.

She threw back the pills, washing them down with a gulp of water. "Thank you Loltu, you've been very kind."

Retightening the straps, she said, "*Vasilissa,* Guin."

CHAPTER THIRTY-THREE

A stout, jolly guard came into the room talking away, apparently not caring whether Guin understood what she said. She released Guin's straps then gripped her elbow. A gray hallway led to a well-lit garage full of parked hovers. Cuffs once again encircled her wrists. She took a seat in an empty hover. The door slid closed.

The blur of lights flew by. The hover came to a stop, and the door opened. She winced as a guard yanked her from the vehicle, then steered her through another gray building to an enclosed area with a short bench.

Guin leaned against the wall, fussing with the shackles on her wrists. She closed her eyes. Visions of azure eyes tortured her. *How many days can a person stay awake without going insane?* She wished for a pill to make her forget the last few months.

Maybe they'll let me go home. I want to see Raney. I want to see my sisters.

Stop! Balling her fists she pressed them against her eyelids until tiny flares of white sparks danced behind them. Memories of family or Earth were more torturous than those of the people she loved here. She forced herself to concentrate on what might happen next.

A thin man with a dull brown suit and the gaunt face of a cadaver came into the room, taking a seat beside her. He handed her a tablet and a stylus.

"Please, I don't understand what this says. I need a loqu so you can tell me."

He shrugged, gathered the items, then left.

Time passed. The pills wore off. Shadows closed in. Guin slipped into periods of obliviousness, her mind blank until a guard took her by the elbow and steered her through the hall. A set of double doors opened to a wood paneled room with benches set in lines. The room's resemblance to television courtrooms, faintly surprised her. Cameras filled the courtroom. On some level she understood they were here because of her. This bewildered her, until she remembered —regicide.

Floating in bold red, capital letters before her, the word terrified her. She wished she could pull the fog around her ears and snuggle back into oblivion.

A pair of chrome tables faced the judge's bench, two chairs at each. Near the ceiling hovered a black, round device, resembling a shiny, onyx bowling-ball. The ball rotated. A disheveled, auburn-haired woman, dressed in hideous, oversized yellow coveralls stared from the reflection of a camera's lens.

The guard nudged her toward the seat beside the man in the brown suit.

Is he my attorney?

A man wearing a black-and-gold uniform shouted. The man next to her stood, motioning for Guin to do the same. The door behind the judge's bench opened. A red-robed man entered. The man glared at her, radiating a hatred she'd only experienced once before.

A lump rose in her throat. She forced Boden's image aside, focusing on the new hatred emanating from the person in scarlet.

The man beside her elbowed her in the ribs.

"I don't understand. They took my loqu. I don't know what you're saying."

The judge shouted at her. His face grew livid, matching the red hue of his robes. He pointed a finger at her. Spittle flew from his lips as he continued his tirade, banging his fist with each syllable. He redirected his finger at the attorney, his voice shaking with fury.

The attorney waved his tablet and glared at her. The judge turned his wrath back on her.

Guin was first stunned, then bewildered, and finally blank as the fog closed in around her. Wrapped in the soothing embrace, she disregarded the cameras, the lawyer, and the screaming man in the crimson robes.

~

GUIN REGAINED consciousness in the tiny room. She lay on the bench, cuffs encircling her wrist, a dark tiled ceiling above her.

Loltu appeared beside her, a loqu on her palm, a smile on her face.

Taking the tiny device, Guin tilted her head. It slipped into her ear, the filament securing itself.

"Better?"

If not for the cuffs, Guin would have thrown her arms around the petite woman. She gripped Loltu's hand instead. "Thank you, Loltu. This means so much."

"Don't thank me." Loltu kept her voice low. "You still have friends in high places, Lady Guin."

Guin frowned in confusion. "Who?"

Loltu glanced at the uniformed woman and gave a slight shake of her head. "Luck be with you."

The guard unlocked the cuffs, then took Guin back to court, where except for the uniformed man and the bowling ball, the courtroom had emptied.

"Please stand for Lord Dikastis, Gerent of Mikonian justice," the man called, glancing at her.

She clutched the edge of the table for balance. The judge entered, no longer wearing his robes. "Remain standing," he said, then dropped his gaze to a tele-screen on the desk before him.

Guin swayed. Her eyes wouldn't focus. She'd lost the ability to concentrate. She tightened her grip on the table's edge.

The judge glared. "Miss Griffin, you are accused of the heinous crime of regicide. The deliberate killing of a monarch, namely King Jaezain, ruler of Druthenia with the special circumstance that you willfully committed this crime for personal gain. If convicted, you will be put to death. If convicted of the special circumstances alleged in this case, your death will be by *Phax'En*." This last word brought a sadistic smile to his face. "How do you plead to these charges?"

The clouds dissipated somewhat at the word "death." She focused on the word, the rest of what he said forgotten. The men stared at her, waiting for an answer to a question she hadn't understood. "What?"

"Miss Griffin, you apparently have a benefactor high within our government who believes a murderer such as yourself should be treated with respect. I am trying to give you such, but if you don't show the same consideration and answer the questions asked by this court, I will enter a plea for you and put you back in your cell to await sentencing." He leaned forward with a cruel gleam in his eye, enunciating each word as though speaking to a child. "Now, answer my question. How. Do. You. Plead?"

Her legs trembled, Her body shook. But her mind cleared sufficiently to understand. "Not guilty, Your Honor."

"Fine. You will be remanded to the custody of the Mikonian government until your trial in thirty days."

Guin's throat tightened at the prospect of spending thirty days in her cell, knowing she wouldn't live that long. *I should have pleaded guilty and been done with it.*

The bowling ball rotated and dipped. A persistent beeping came from the console before the judge.

Sighing in apparent exasperation, he glanced at the screen. His face reddened. He appeared incensed by what he saw. Dikastis squinted at the screen, then at Guin. "It seems we will be releasing you." His face pinched in disgust. "You have been fitted with a tracer, and to ensure you do not abscond before your trial, I order the implantation of a *guttan*. Is that clear?"

Not at all. "Yes, sir." She understood only that she would be released.

"I order you released under the restriction of the guttan. You are hereby ordered to turn yourself over to the custody of the Mikonian government one day prior to your trial."

Will they truly let me go? She once again warmed the bench in the tiny room. After hours of waiting, her thoughts grew fuzzy. She slipped into a stupor. The gray mists washed in. Darkness consumed her until she came to while being strapped to a gurney. A guard wheeled her to an antiseptic-smelling room, leaving her under an imposing machine with an array of lethal appearing blades and needles attached to each of its many arms.

With a warm smile, Loltu entered. She waved her wrist over the wall. A table slid out beside Guin. The guard returned, observing Loltu while she worked.

Loltu showed Guin a tiny device. "This is a guttan."

It resembled the fuse her father replaced when his classic car's radio died, but shorter and slimmer. "What does it do?"

"Using the *silnieth*." Loltu indicated the evil-looking apparatus above. "I will implant the guttan near your heart. If you fail to return for deactivation, your heart will be stopped, and you'll die."

"That's barbaric," Guin said in a terrified whisper.

"Yet effective. Come back before the ninth hour, Mikonia time, the day before your trial. We will deactivate and remove the guttan at that time. Understand?" Though her tone was one of business, sorrow showed in her eyes.

Guin nodded.

"I'm sorry, Lady Guin," Loltu whispered. "This is going to be painful. They don't allow us to anesthetize prisoners. Please try to remain still."

Baring Guin's chest, she flipped a switch on the silnieth then placed the guttan into a slot. "Once the guttan is programmed, I will use this needle to insert it into your chest." She pointed to a straw-sized needle attached to one of the silnieth's arms.

A rising tide of panic rushed over Guin. She closed her eyes tensing when the arm extended toward her bared chest. The excruciating pain of the needle piercing her skin then driving through her sternum forced her eyes open. She had been holding her breath in anticipation, but now let it out in an agonized cry.

The pain abated with the removal of the needle. Loltu sealed the hole between Guin's breasts. "It is done."

"Thank you for your kindness," Guin whispered.

Loltu smiled.

The guard unfastened the straps.

In a new small gray room, a guard removed Guin's cuffs, pointing to one of two chairs. "Sit."

Held at bay in anticipation of her release, the fog slept. But a new terror awoke at the prospect of leaving the relative safety of jail. She had nowhere to go and knew of no one on Mikonia who might offer their help.

Her mind threatened to withdraw into itself. Visions of padded cells and straitjackets filled her mind. Driving these thoughts away, she tried to concentrate on one thing at a time.

A guard entered carrying the box filled with Guin's belongings. She handed over a stylus and tablet. Her previous signature above a blank line glowed upon the screen. She signed her name. The guard waved the tablet over the box. The lid popped open. She told Guin to change then left.

She shrugged out of the coveralls, then slipped the soiled, tattered gown over her head. A flood of memories threatened to break the dam and release the torrent of tears she held at bay. Her grandmother's mantra floated at the back of her mind. The numbing fog of oblivion drifted through her mind, ebbing and flowing like the ocean's waves.

She tore a piece from her skirt, wrapping her jewelry and undergarments, then tying the ends. Lifting the lone shoe, she recalled its mate, abandoned on the top stair of the Syndow's palace. She dropped the pink pump into the box.

The guard led her to another room where a pale, black-haired woman waited behind a table. The woman slid a tablet and stylus to Guin. "Sign here."

She scribbled her name, not caring what she signed, if by doing so they'd let her go.

The woman led her to a covered, fenced-in courtyard. She ushered Guin through the exit then along a cement path to another door.

"After you go through here, you will be in a small alleyway. The gate at the far end leads to the sidewalk."

"Thank you." Guin entered the alley. The door behind shut with a whoosh. The narrow alleyway lay in shadow, sandwiched between the gray cement jail to her left, and a shining silver building to her right.

Light green sky hung above. She forced her sluggish legs toward the gate. The smooth black walkway chilled her bare feet. She stumbled and clung to the door's handle, her body trembling from the effort of traveling the short distance. Steadying herself, she turned the latch then pulled the gate. She exited to the sidewalk, letting the door close behind her.

CHAPTER
THIRTY-FOUR

Head bowed, too terrified to glance back, Guin staggered forward, not knowing where to go except away. Vaguely aware of how conspicuous she must appear in her bare feet and torn gown, she hid behind the veil her hair created, concentrating on one step at a time.

"Guin!"

Reporters!

She broke into a shaky run only to trip on her skirts. She fell, catching herself on her hands. Curling into a tight ball, she covered her eyes with bleeding palms.

Angry voices hurled questions, some shouting to be heard over one another.

"Guin, why did you do it?"

"Murderess!"

"How does it feel to have fallen so far?"

Someone stepped on her hair. She prepared for the kicks and blows that would surely follow. Guin flailed and scratched with the last of her strength when someone lifted her from the ground.

With the hiss of a hover's door, the shouts grew muted. A familiar face hung above her, framed by the dark interior.

"Boden?"

"Hi, Griffin." His voice held a tenderness she thought him incapable of.

"I thought I'd never see you again," she murmured. "I didn't do it."

He gave her a gentle smile. "Of course, you didn't. I never believed you did."

"Thank you," she whispered.

Boden shook her. "Griffin, wake up."

Guin ignored him.

He shook her again. "Please wake up."

She shrugged his hand away.

"We're going to miss our phase. This is the last to Arwon in this area."

Her eyes flew open. The name brought both hope and anxiety. "Arwon?" She found herself lying across Boden's lap in the center of an empty field lit by the blue glow of the full moon. "Where are we?"

"About eight kihals from the city. We would attract too much attention at a Shift Station." He helped her to her feet. "I've been waiting all night for a phase to take us closer to home. We need to catch this one or we're in for a long walk."

Her knees buckled. She sank toward the ground. He wrapped an arm around her waist then handed her a dislocater. He assisted her in stepping forward. They vanished from Mikonia.

White lights exploded. Spasms racked Guin's body. Her mind dove for the cloudy mists. The faint echoes of agonizing torture faded. A comforting darkness engulfed her.

She awoke in a plush, four poster bed with a blanket pulled to her chin. The pain from the bad Shift gone.

Dark, highly polished wooden walls surrounded her. Bright daylight peeked around the edges of drawn curtains covering two broad windows. A rocking chair rested near the wall across from the bed.

She took the glass of clear liquid from the bedside table. Bandages encased her throbbing palms. Her hands trembled. Sniffing the liquid she took a tentative sip. Water. She gulped down the rest.

Her tattered gown had been replaced with a red plaid shirt. *This must be Boden's home.* Smiling, she snapped the waistband of a pair of silky, purple boxer briefs.

The door opened. Boden poked his head in and smiled. "Hey, you're awake. How do you feel?"

She cleared her throat. "Better, thank you. Is this your house?"

"Yes. Welcome to my humble abode."

Plucking at the sleeve engulfing her arm, she asked, "Is this one of yours?"

"Yeah."

Heat crept up her chest. "Did you dress me?"

He reddened, scratching the scruff on his chin. "I couldn't leave you in those rags. We Shifted into a rainstorm. You jerked from my arms and landed in a puddle of mud. You scared the life out of me, Griffin. I didn't know what was happening. Your whole body shook so badly I nearly dropped you a few times on the way here. I recalled Jaxzon mentioning you having a bad Shift with him. I figured it happened again.

"I got you here and into the shower, cleaned you up, dressed you in one of my shirts, then put you to bed." He crossed the room. "I searched the Circuit for what to do. Rest is best if you can't get medication, so I left you to sleep it off." Sighing, he said, "I didn't look if that's what you're worried about."

She giggled. Her sides ached, yet she couldn't stop.

"It's no more than I saw at the spa."

She sobered and a warmth spread across her face as she recalled that she had taken off her towel and Boden had given her another.

"You're my hero." Guin squeezed his hand. "You've been there every time I needed help."

He placed her hand back on her lap. "What are friends for?"

"I'm glad you still consider me a friend. I thought you hated me. I thought everyone hated me."

Boden sighed. "I know, and I'm sorry. But you need to eat. You're skin and bones."

She smiled. "You would know."

"Seriously, Griffin. When was the last time you ate?"

"The day after the ball, maybe?"

Shock crossed Boden's face, promptly replaced by anger. "Didn't they feed you in that place?"

"I wasn't hungry." Black memories entered her mind. "I wanted to die. It hurt so bad."

"Oh, Guin." He wrapped his arms around her in a gentle embrace.

"It was horrible. I was confused and couldn't think straight. I didn't understand what they were saying." She clung to him, burying her face in his chest. Her breath came in short gasps. "Everyone hated me."

He untangled her hair with his fingers. "Let's talk about this when you're stronger. It's been eight days since you've eaten. You're wasting away."

"That long?" She drew a shuddering breath. "Jaxzon is king now." More tears threatened. She willed the mists to take her away from the misery, but her mind remained clear, leaving only anguish and Boden, the only person she had left. Her fingers, feather-light, touched his cheek.

He jerked back, then carried her to his dining room, depositing her at a table.

Somehow, she'd pictured his ranch as a man cave attached to a barn, and yet this was a home. The chair she sat on—though a plain, wooden chair—had downy cushions and a footrest to keep her bare feet off the cold floor.

He worked at a sizable, roughhewn butcher-block separating the kitchen from the dining area. The kitchen floor was rustically cobbled. The cupboards were made of the same dark timber as the walls. Hardwood floors joined the dining area to a spacious living room, where two over-stuffed chairs and a roomy sofa faced a substantial stone fireplace. A tele-screen hung beside the mantle and brimming bookcases filled the available wall space.

Nodding Guin said, “Your house suits you.”

“It should. I built it.”

“Seriously?”

“I’m full of surprises.” Dimples appeared with his smile. “You only have to get to know me.”

“I guess so.” A door at the end of the hallway stood open. “Is that your room?”

“Yes.” Boden set a bowl of soup on the table. “Sorry it isn’t much, just broth. I read that after a fast you shouldn’t eat anything too heavy.”

Aromatic herbs filled the air. Her stomach rumbled. “This smells heavenly.” She took a spoon from the rack of utensils in the center of the table and blew on the hot liquid, then moaned after the first sip.

“Good?”

“Exquisite.”

“Go slow,” he cautioned.

Guin savored each spoonful. “Who would’ve thought grumpy old Bodey could cook?”

“It’s only soup. Wait ’til I really cook for you.”

“I can’t wait.”

His face flushed. With a cough he left the table, busying himself in the kitchen. When she finished, he cleared her dishes, washed, dried, then put them away.

A furry, blue snakelike appendage slinked through a small door within the front entry. On the end, a pair of nostrils flared, sniffing the air. Her eyes widened. “What’s that?”

“Symon.”

At the mention of his name, Symon bulldozed through the door, snuffling his way to the dining room. Attached to the snake-like nose was a hairy creature—a seeming cross between a medium-sized sheepdog and a tiny elephant. His footlong nose gently probed Guin's gauze-wrapped palms then sniffed her fingers.

Flecks of silver and cobalt adorned his shaggy indigo coat that was as silky as a chinchilla's fur. A blue tongue poked from beneath his trunk and licked her wrist. His body waggled and bounced. Amber eyes peeked from beneath a fringe of fluffy bangs.

"Hi, Symon." She scratched between Symon's floppy, oversized ears. His nose probed her face, his fur tickling her cheek. "What is he?"

"Symon, down." Symon sat, keeping his nose in Guin's hand.

"He's a Bandutcher, a cattle dog of sorts. They come from Bethion. He helps with the turatang and watches over the horses at night."

"Nice to meet you, Symon." She patted his nose then picked at her bandage. The pain radiating from beneath the gauze, a sad reminder of how she came to be here. "Boden, why were you the only one who came for me?"

Dark circles under his eyes and the new lines on his face, proved that he had cared when she'd believed no one had. He sat beside her. "I'm positive someone's framed you, although not everyone believes you're innocent."

"Who doesn't believe?" she whispered, afraid of his answer.

He shook his head. "I haven't seen Jaxzon since that day. He refuses to see me. I'm not sure what he thinks. Derek and Delori are under investigation as accessories."

"What? Why?"

"Don't worry. They're back home and under Jaxzon's protection. Derek told me their attorney advised them to have no contact with me until after your trial. I'm also a suspect."

"Why would you be a suspect? I understand Derek and Delori since they sponsored me. Why you?"

Boden showed her a photograph. He and Guin stood under a tree, engaged in a passionate kiss.

"What? This didn't happen. How can they—I-I don't understand?"

"Someone altered the photograph. There's more."

The video on his telecon showed the hallway outside her door in the Syndow's palace. She entered, dressed in Valdid's maroon gown. Several minutes later Boden entered. The recording's timestamp displayed a passage of over an hour. The door opened. Boden left, his jacket slung over his shoulder.

Her heart sank. "Jaxzon saw this? This is why he chose Vertuma?"

"Dame Grint said Jaxzon was shown these before you were arrested."

"You talked to Heldivar?"

"You still have friends, Griffin. She made sure you were given another loqu then pressured Dikastis to release you."

"How did she know? Was she in court?"

"Every Circuit in the galaxy carried it live. That man shouldn't be a gerent. He obviously had prejudice before stepping foot in the courtroom. Heldivar contacted their government to make sure they followed protocol with your case. She gave me your release time. I was in a hover on the other side of the building and didn't see you until the reporters went after you. I'm sorry."

"Don't be. It wasn't your fault." She put her hand on his arm. "Thank you for everything. I meant it when I said you were my hero."

Boden gave her an uneasy smile. "Let's get you to bed. You need more rest."

CHAPTER THIRTY-FIVE

The media speculated as to where the "young lovers" had run off to. The photographs spread throughout both Druthenia and Mikonia's kingdoms, causing outrage and indignation. Many wondered how King Jaxzon could have been fooled not only by an Earthling, but by his best friend too.

The talking heads from every media outlet featured hour-long talk shows discussing the significance of the fact that Boden's mother was also from Earth.

Guin switched off the tele-screen and rubbed her eyes. "I guess news reporters are the same everywhere."

"I don't understand why you watch this garbage. You should be resting." He took the control, setting it on a shelf.

Boden ran errands, cooked, and cared for his ranch, while she worked at regaining her strength, both physical and mental. Neither mentioned Jaxzon. The betrayal was too painful.

Boden said no to her request to join him on his trip to town, keeping a low profile himself. He bought her a few pairs of pants, some shirts, a pair of shoes, and old-fashioned pajamas with tiny bow-shaped buttons.

"Thank you, but if it's okay, I'll stick with your shirt." She put a shoe beside her foot. Her toes overshot the end. "Sorry Bodey, these won't fit."

"Not my fault you've got huge feet. I'll take them back next trip."

Her moods swung from highs to lows as she struggled to regain her strength. On the third morning, she attempted to detangle the bird's nest of knots from her hair. She threw the brush in frustration.

He retrieved the brush, sat on the bed, and combed through the labyrinth of snarls with gentle strokes.

Guin burst into tears.

He smoothed the hair from her face. "Don't cry, Griffin."

"He hates me, doesn't he?"

"No, Guin. He loves you."

"Would you love me if you believed I was in love with your best friend?"

"Yes." He set the brush aside. "C'mon, food's ready."

The following day, the alluring aroma of whatever Boden prepared wafted under her door.

Guin left her room. "Oh my god, that smells good."

"You're looking better." He held her chair then set a plate in front of her. Red eggs over blue toast, orange hash browns, and crispy meat that appeared and smelled like bacon.

"I am better, thanks to you."

He waved dismissively. "You're a strong woman, Griffin. You needed some nourishment and rest. All I did was cook."

She snagged a fork. "And a great cook you are."

After breakfast, he left to tend his ranch.

She puttered around her room. The closet held dozens of plaid shirts, along with two dress shirts and two gray suits. Pairs of men's shoes and boots stood in a neat line across the back wall. She smiled at the contents of the dresser drawers. Men's clothing in each confirmed her suspicion—Boden had given her his room.

She slipped a clean plaid button-up over her T-shirt, then ventured barefoot outside, squinting against the brilliant sunslight.

A tall, burnt-sienna barked tree with a canopy of bright teal leaves grew in the center of a neatly trimmed, dark aqua lawn stretching between the house and a barn. A thick forest of trees lined the horizon, creating a bluish haze against a fuchsia sky.

Guin rested against the tree. Dark pink flowers loaded the branches, giving off a sweet cherry blossom scent. Symon leapt between the corral pipes, bounding across the grass. He raced in a circle around the tree then flopped on the ground beside her, pressing his snout into her hand. She scratched his ears, and he rolled over for a belly rub.

Four horses followed Boden's every move. They responded to his words with affection, whinnying and nuzzling his neck. He waved to Guin.

She waved back and smiled. *What sweet nothings does he whisper that made the horses react the way they do?*

The sunshine and fresh air had a reviving effect. After Boden left on horseback with Symon to check his fencing, Guin—more alert than she'd been in days—searched the kitchen for the makings of the evening meal. She found ingredients for a salad and a package of what appeared to be steaks in the refrigerator.

Hoping to bake bread, she explored the cupboards for dry goods and discovered an ample supply of ruvin. She poured herself a small glass. The liquid burned its way to her toes then gradually spread warmth throughout her body. She prepared dinner, happily taking an occasional sip.

When he returned from his errands, the table was laden with fresh bread, salad, broiled steaks, and sautéed purple, asparagus-looking vegetables.

He stopped short, staring in surprise from the table to Guin, who leaned against the butcher block, sipping her ruvin.

She raised her glass. "You've been holding out on me."

"Apparently you held out on *me*." He sniffed the air. "Smells good, Griffin."

"I wish I could say the same of you." She wrinkled her nose. "You could use a shower. You smell like a horse."

"What's wrong with that? My horses smell good." He grinned, then headed down the hall to his room.

Sharing the bottle of ruvin and eating, Boden filled her in on the chores he'd finished and other assorted small talk.

She refilled her glass. "What made you build your house way out here?"

"We aren't that far from the palace grounds. It's a short hover ride away."

"Did your mother help? I feel a woman's touch. Tell me everything."

"That's a long and sordid tale, Griffin."

"We seem to have time for long and sordid tales, Bodey old man." She smirked at him over her glass. "Come on, let me in. Show me yours and I'll show you mine."

He squinted. "You've had one ruvin too many."

"Come on Boden. Let me in."

"All right. But you get the condensed version, or we'll be here all night and I won't get to hear yours." He poured another glass, then sat back, staring at the ceiling. "You know about my father's murder."

"Yes, and I'm so sorry."

Boden nodded. "I was sixteen was in training for the king's guard. Jaxzon, Derek, and I attended the same private school. All these nobles always surrounded us. They had their grand manors, palaces, you name it." He took another drink. "My mother returned to Earth to care for her parents. Her father was ill, and her mother couldn't take care of him alone, so she left me here. The rocking chair, the books, and the chair cushions were hers."

He sighed, running a hand through his dark hair. "After Mom left, the palace apartments we'd lived in were given to the interim Commander. The king gave me a room, yet I realized I'd never have a place of my own unless I built one myself. My mother earned a stipend after my father died. Since the government couldn't send anything to Earth, she established a fund for me here. I saved every unit and when this land came up for sale, I bought it. Took me two years, but I own it outright."

He poured himself another drink and topped off Guin's. "The three of us would come here and work on the place in our spare time. Derek's sister had an old barn torn down, and we scavenged the wood for the floors, the walls, and the cupboards. The stone siding, the fireplace, and the kitchen cobbles are from a small part of the palace the king had refurbished. Almost everything you see is secondhand."

He glanced around. "I wanted everything low-tech, no cleaning robots, no scanners, no holograms. The only electronics are the telescreen and data port. I like living simply, keeps things peaceful. By the time we finished, the king made Orist commander, I quit the king's guard, bought some turatang and a few horses, and that's the short of it." He threw back the rest of his ruvin then reached for the bottle.

"Very impressive." Her image of Boden rose a few notches. "That's a pretty short story. What did you leave out?"

He gave her a speculative look then shook his head. "Not tonight. I don't usually talk this much. Maybe someday I'll fill you in on the rest."

"Fair enough. Except, what's up with you and Orist?"

"That story would take a while to tell and I'm not up to it. Besides, it's your turn."

"All right, but just so you know, you would beat him in a scowling contest."

He scowled.

Guin laughed. "Yeah, like that. I'd give that one a nine-point-five."

Boden chuckled. "Come on, Griffin. Let's hear your tale of woe and happy endings."

"More like tales of woe, not so much the happy endings."

"All right then, what brought you to the point of driving four hapless aliens around the big city? There's gotta be a story there."

Guin's heart ached at the memory of that fateful night. "All right, you showed me yours. Mine truly is a tale of woe, so get ready to cry in your ruvin."

He topped off both glasses then raised his, grinning over the rim. "Ready."

"I'll have to go with the condensed version also, because my story begins with my being abandoned and adopted at the ripe old age of two." The amber liquid swirled and dimpled as she rotated her drink. "We skip to me at ten, finding out I was adopted. That was a bit of a shock." She took a pull from her glass.

"Jump ahead to my adoptive parents dying in a car accident a week after my sixteenth birthday." She drew a shuddering breath before continuing, "Grandmother blamed me. She never liked me before, but after, she hated me. She was appointed guardian for me and my sisters. I was removed from private school and sent to a public one. I lost contact with most of my friends. When I turned eighteen, she said I was an adult and had to find a place of my own. For some reason, my parents left everything to my sisters, so all I had was my car—the last birthday present my parents ever gave me." She threw back her drink and gripped the bottle. "And that is how I came to be driving four hapless aliens around the city."

"*Viyet*, Griffin. I had no idea." He reached for her hand.

"Don't, or I'll be a blubbering mess, and true Griffins don't cry."

Boden frowned. "What do you mean?"

Guin sighed. "According to my grandmother, when I was a baby I cried a lot, and the thing with elevators apparently drove my parents nuts. I would convulse and go into hysterics, 'screaming like a banshee.' When my sisters were little, my grandmother would tell them, 'true Griffins don't cry,' using me as an example I guess, since I was not a Griffin, and they were. When I learned I was adopted, I took those words to heart because I *wanted* to be a true Griffin."

"That's messed up."

Guin shrugged. "Sometimes life's messed up. You just have to make the best of it. Besides, since coming here I seem to have had a few breakthroughs in the no crying department. I've cried more in the last few months than in a lifetime back home."

They both took drinks from their glasses. The conversation moved on. Guin had Boden laughing over some troubles she and Raney had gotten themselves into during their high school years.

Boden told a similar story of a prank he and Jaxzon played on Orist, and Guin grew morose. "I'm sorry. Do you want to talk about it?"

"No. Not yet." She stacked their plates.

"You cooked. I'll clear." He took the dishes and headed to the kitchen.

"My mess, my job."

Throwing her a towel he washed, while she dried.

"Has Boden ever been in love?"

He stopped washing for a beat, then continued scrubbing the baking dish. "Yeah, Griffin, a couple of times."

"Seriously?"

"Why so surprised?"

"I don't know. I never took you for the type."

"What's *the type*? Fairy tale endings? Love at first sight?"

"'Who ever loved, that loved not at first sight?'" Guin quoted.

Boden stopped scrubbing and grinned. "'But are you so much in love as your rhymes speak?'"

Her jaw dropped. "'If thou rememberest not the slightest folly that ever love did make thee run into, thou has not loved.'"

"'Neither rhyme nor reason can express how much.'" He finished with a flourish of the dishrag.

"Boden! Quoting Shakespeare? You truly are a romantic." She shook her head. "I never would've guessed."

"Mom brought the whole collection." He inclined his chin to a bookcase in the living room. "When I was a kid she would read to me, and sometimes we would act out the parts."

Guin let out an exaggerated gasp.

He reddened. "Hush, Griffin."

"Missed a spot." She pointed at the pan.

When he bent for a closer look, she splashed water in his face. After registering a brief moment of shock, he splashed her back. Guin popped him with the dishtowel, and he tossed water from the pan over her head.

Soapy water dripped from her hair as she wound the towel for another strike. "Oh, you're so dead."

"Oh yeah?" He seized the towel and tugged.

There ensued a brief tug-of-war. Guin's bare feet slipped and clutching Boden's forearms for support, she dragged him with her. They fell to the floor.

"Ow!" She rubbed the back of her head.

"Are you hurt?" Boden lifted his weight with his elbows.

"No." She giggled. "The floor broke my fall. Are you okay?"

"No." He brushed a strand of hair from her face. Their eyes locked. Sliding his arm beneath her, he drew her to him.

Guin turned her face away. "I can't."

Boden froze. He closed his eyes.

"I'm sorry, Boden. I didn't mean to..."

He helped her to her feet. "I'm the one who's sorry."

"Boden, I-I—" Guin touched his arm. "Please look at me. I'm sorry. I still love him."

"I know. I do too. It won't happen again. Go to bed. I'll finish up in here." Taking a mop from the closet he wet it in the sink.

"Can we talk?"

"Nothing to talk about. Please, go to bed."

"But—"

"Please!" Anger flared in his eyes. "Just drop it. We've both had too much to drink. Go sleep it off."

Guin went to her room, throwing herself across her bed. *What just happened?*

An inner conflict raged within her inebriated mind.

You wanted him to kiss you.

No, I didn't.

Yes. You did.

No.

He could help you forget.

I don't want to forget. She'd locked away so much. The knowledge that Jaxzon and her friends could abandon her so easily was too new, too painful.

Boden gave her hope. He showed her kindness. He'd shown her, what? Affection? Or was it simply compassion for a friend? She didn't want to banish him from her thoughts. Who would she have left? Her affection for him conflicted with the love she had for... She willed herself not to go there; it meant only anguish.

~

HUNGOVER AND GROGGY, Guin squinted against the bright daylight coming through the windows. There were no signs of life in the house. She headed for the kitchen, hoping to surprise Boden with breakfast. His morning dishes sat unwashed in the sink. Her heart sank. He'd been up and gone. *He's probably letting you sleep,* she admonished herself.

The front door opened, and Boden carried his shopping carton, with a bag balanced on top, to the table. Symon bolted through his door then ran through the hall to Boden's room with his trunk wrapped around a red ball.

He placed groceries on the table.

Guin put them away.

"Thanks."

"You're welcome."

He set the empty box aside then removed a pair of shoes from the bag, a sheepish smile on his face.

"Oh, Boden." Throwing her arms around his waist, conflicting emotions tumbled within her as his arms wrapped around her. She laid her head against his chest. His erratic heartbeat pounded in her ear.

Meeting his gaze, she couldn't read his expression. He tilted his head toward the ceiling. When he faced her again, his eyes burned into hers. The telecon buzzed in his breast pocket. He released her, mumbling something under his breath. "Hello?" He handed the telecon to her. "For you."

Her heart raced as she put the device to her ear. "Hello?"

CHAPTER THIRTY-SIX

"My dear, how are you? Calen and I were so concerned."

Boden retreated to his room.

"I'm much better, ma'am, thank you."

"Now Guin, call me Heldivar. You must realize, I and many others, do not believe you are responsible for King Jaezain's death. I am in the process of engaging a Mikonian attorney for you. A rather difficult task, as many of the best are unwilling to risk their reputation defending someone with these charges. Rest assured, we will find one."

"Thank you, Heldivar. I'm truly grateful for your help."

"Those people treated you horrendously. If that man were a gerent in our realm, he would have been removed immediately. We are fortunate that others within our government believe in your innocence. Stay positive, my dear. The truth will prevail."

The call boosted Guin's spirits and raised her hopes. Although, if the top attorneys wouldn't touch her case, what hope did she have? She thrust the thought away, tucking it in a corner where her memory of Jaxzon sat, waiting to incapacitate her at any moment.

She knocked on Boden's door, hoping he wasn't angry.

"What's up?" he called.

"Can we search Mikonian regulations and find out what my rights are? Maybe they'll let us see the evidence against me, or we can get copies." She hadn't watched all those CSI episodes without gaining some legal knowledge. She hoped the laws were similar here.

After a quick Circuit inquiry, Boden found she was entitled to a copy of everything the Mikonian police had against her. He sent a request for the electronic forms.

"Will we get the videos from the palace and the park?" Guin asked.

Boden wouldn't meet her eyes. "I suppose. That's what the regulations say."

"How did they fool the investigators with those? They're obviously faked."

"I've no idea."

Guin laid a hand on his arm, wanting him to understand she still cared for him. "I'm sorry, Boden. I truly am."

He placed his hand over hers. "Nothing to be sorry for. Friends?"

She smiled. "Forever."

BODEN DOWNLOADED THE ELECTRONIC FORMS, then helped Guin fill in signatures and dates. He uploaded the completed documents to the Mikonian courts. They received an immediate response, allowing access to transferable evidence. Certified copies would be sent the following day.

They reviewed the recordings from the park and the hallway, fingerprint and DNA results, and photos of the crime scene on Boden's telescreen.

She covered her mouth at the sight of the king. His throat had been slit. Blood had pooled around his body, soaking into the pillow and bed covers.

One video showed many angles of Guin, Jaxzon, and his father in the Mikonian palace garden. Her heart dropped, and she closed her eyes. They had been so happy that night, so in love, then everything fell apart.

Symon snuggled against her calf, and she scratched his head.

Another recording was of her, leaving her room alone on the night of the murder. "Boden, I never left my room that night. I swear on my life."

"I believe you. The report says three experts confirmed the authenticity of the videos. On the other hand, your guard told investigators you didn't go anywhere."

They sat at the table, studying the death report when there was a sharp thump at the front entrance. Symon rumbled low in his throat, staying near Guin.

Boden jumped to his feet. Someone kicked the door again. The hackles raised on Symon's back.

A muffled, yet familiar voice came from outside. "Open up, it's me."

Boden froze.

Guin sprang from her chair.

Symon bolted toward the entryway, braying like a laryngitic donkey. Boden threw the door open.

"Little help here?" Kapre pushed past Boden. His eyes met Guin's. He shoved several boxes into Boden's arms. He strode forward, sweeping Guin into an embrace.

She hung from his arms in a mild state of shock. Symon snuffled Kapre's feet, his body wagging in a frenzy.

"I hoped I'd find you here." He released her. "The Circuit live-streamed Boden carrying you to his hover, then you two vanished. I had a friend keep watch for anyone asking about your case. When your request came in, I was able to trace it here. Everyone is looking for you. I made sure they deleted your information from the system. You're completely off the grid, aren't you?"

"Down Symon. You're a pathetic excuse for a watch-bandy."

Boden scowled at Kapre. "I like being off grid. Keeps the pests away. What do you want with us?"

"I'm here to help." He gestured to the boxes. "These are copies of everything we have. Delivered to your door as requested, and a day early."

He took Guin's hand. His expression softened. "And I wanted to ask your forgiveness. The way you were treated by my government was disgraceful."

She shook her hand free. "Why would we trust you, and why would you want to help a murderer? Your sister is going to be queen, and your family will control half a galaxy."

"An accused murderer," he corrected. "Not many believe you capable of killing King Jaezain. Even if you and Boden had a fling—"

"That's a lie." Guin glared. "Those videos were faked."

Kapre raised his arms in surrender. "I believe you. I suspect my sister. Who else has anything to gain?"

She blinked in surprise. "You think...but she's your sister. Why would you help us if it means implicating your own sister?"

"Because helping you is the right thing to do. Vertuma is evil. I've seen it firsthand, but she's gone too far this time." He shuffled the cartons around, opening and closing their lids.

Boden exchanged a puzzled glance with Guin.

"With the help of a few loyal friends, I did a little investigating." Kapre produced a small container. "Do you have a digital player?"

The container held a flat, square metallic object, which Boden slid into the side of the tele-screen. The interior of the restaurant where Guin, Bree, and the other women had eaten lunch on Xaitera, appeared onscreen. The server seated the women and took their drink orders. The sound quality was superb as Guin ordered an unsweetened tea.

Bree, Guin, and Nuala left the table for the lady's room. The server returned with their drinks. Vertuma helped distribute the glasses, placing Guin's beside her own.

Kapre raised his hand. "Freeze. Now go forward frame by frame.

Stop. There." He pointed, Vertuma held something in her hand. "Go forward another frame. There." She poured something from a tiny vial into the glass.

A shockwave ran the length of Guin's spine. "She poisoned Nuala."

Boden frowned. "Wasn't that Guin's drink?"

"Hit play."

Guin and the other women returned. Vertuma and Sarya left. Nuala took a sip from her glass then complained. Guin and Nuala traded.

"She put it in the wrong one," Boden said.

Kapre glanced at Guin. "Yes, and we know how that backfired."

She clutched her queasy stomach. "She was trying to poison me."

"The hospital ran tests. She had ingested a drug that induces vomiting, nothing deadly. Although I'm not sure how you would have been affected. No one knew you were from Earth at the time. Vertuma may have only wanted to make you sick."

"What made you go back and get this video?" she asked. "Nobody thought Nuala was drugged. We assumed she had a reaction to her food."

"King Jaxzon asked me to."

"What?" Guin's legs went weak. The room swayed.

Boden rushed forward and put an arm around her, lowering her to the sofa. Symon whimpered and put his head on her lap, nuzzling her neck with his trunk.

"You might have opened with that," Boden said. "Can't you see she's fragile?"

Kapre had appeared startled when Guin swooned. He knelt beside her. "My apologies, lady. I assumed he'd been in contact with you."

"Why?" Boden and Guin asked in unison.

"He contacted me and said he needed information regarding any interactions between you and my sister."

"Has he seen this?" asked Boden.

"Not yet. I haven't heard from him since his coronation. I'm sure he's only being careful. After all, my sister must have accomplices."

"Does he believe I'm innocent?"

"I assume so. Why else would he be trying to find evidence to prove it?"

"Jaxzon would never have believed it," Boden said. "We shouldn't have doubted him."

Kapre raised an eyebrow.

"Do you have anything else?" Guin asked.

"I obtained this from Bree. She sends her love." He played the video from the Xaiteran ball.

The person serving the drinks was not fully in frame. The camera captured a glimpse of curly blond hair, the face obscured along with most of his body. The video showed Guin handing her drink to Bree then leaving with Jaxzon. Bree handed the drink to Maldea.

"These I obtained on my own." They observed surveillance from the spa. There were lengthy blank areas. The same went for the recordings from the day of the fashion show.

Boden interlaced his fingers on top of his head. "They've been corrupted."

"Yes, but there is this." Kapre fast-forwarded through one recording.

A clear picture of Guin appeared, typing at a control panel in a dark room before being lost in a flurry of electronic snow.

"I've never been anywhere like that."

"It's the elevator control room at Benstoke Towers. The video was taken before the fashion show."

"How can that be? I never did those things; we were in the stairway."

"Yeah, with your suspected accomplices," Boden reminded her.

Guin frowned. "This is crazy,"

"This one's from the night of the murder." Kapre put another drive into the player.

A view of a grand hotel appeared. A hover stopped, then a

woman dressed in jeans and a pink sweater exited the vehicle. She entered the hotel.

The view shifted to the lobby. Guin entered facing the camera.

She gasped. "Where is this?"

"The hotel where the murder took place," he said.

"How? I was never there."

Her double waited for the elevator. When she entered, the view changed to the interior. She leaned against the back wall, resting her hands on the railing while the car rose to the fiftieth floor. The view switched again to a hallway. She exited the elevator then knocked on a door.

Guin's heart soared. "Jaxzon knows! He really knows, Boden."

CHAPTER THIRTY-SEVEN

Kapre frowned. "What do you know that I don't? This is their most damning evidence. It's the reason they arrested you."

Boden grinned. "Griffin can't handle elevators."

"I can barely ride one floor before I nearly pass out. Let alone fifty."

"I believe you, but how can that be proven?"

"I don't need to prove anything to Jaxzon. He knows, and he's the only one who matters."

"Fine." Kapre folded his arms across his chest. "Go ahead and tell yourself that when the airlock opens, and you're sucked into space."

"What?"

Boden glared at Kapre. "She wasn't aware of that, you idiot."

"What are you talking about?"

"Dikastis ruled if they find you guilty of regicide with special circumstances..." Boden sighed. "You will receive the highest punishment of their land, *Phax'En*."

"I remember that word, but I didn't understand the meaning." Guin sank into her chair. "What does it mean, Kapre?"

"Phax'En is a barbaric form of execution." His nose wrinkled. "They take the condemned into space, place them in an airlock, then open the door. The convict is sucked into open space, simultaneously suffocating and freezing to death."

"Oh." Guin examined her fingernails then took a deep breath, her dismay becoming resolve. "I'm sure Jaxzon believes I'm innocent. If the impostor mimicked me in the elevator, then he must realize someone imitated us both the other times." She squared her shoulders. "What else do you have, Kapre?"

Later that day, Symon bounced beside Guin, holding her hand in his silky trunk as she paced between the sofa and the dining room table where Boden shuffled through depositions. Kapre kicked back in a recliner, using the remote to rewind and fast forward through videos.

She pointed at the screen. "Whose room did the imposter go into?"

Kapre froze the frame. "King Jaezain's. But no one saw her leave. Unfortunately, the recording from a few hours before and after the murder have damage, and he dismissed his guards shortly beforehand."

Boden's head snapped up from the autopsy report he'd been reading. "What did you say?"

"Which part?"

"His guards. You said he dismissed them?"

"Yes, according to the reports. Why?"

His expression darkened. "Would *your* father dismiss his security team while staying in a hotel on another planet? Especially one that's threatened hostilities in the past?"

The prince's eyes narrowed. "What do you mean threatened? We've never—"

Guin raised her hands. "Stop. Please, this isn't the time. Boden, tell us why this is important."

"King Jaezain would *never* be without security. Not for one minute under those circumstances. Now it makes sense why no one saw you going into his room."

She clenched her teeth. "I didn't go into his room."

"I meant your double." Boden rubbed the back of his neck. "I'm tired. This reading is giving me a headache."

"Let's take a break." She slid off the sofa. "We could use a walk."

She wandered to the barn and fed the horses the sweet, gelatinous cubes Boden kept for treats. Curious, she climbed the ladder to the hayloft. Symon whined when he couldn't follow. "It's okay boy, I'll be back."

The suns rode low in the sky, shining through the loft's window, creating a perfect square of light on the floor near a stack of what appeared to be hay. The bales had a strange purple tint, and the rough texture and the sweet, grassy scent of hay.

She leaned against a bale. A pink and black speckled spider-like creature wove a neon-green web across the open window. In the wooden rafters above, a footlong, magenta caterpillar crawled across a beam. The plump body stilled. The front legs released the beam, and hanging upside down, the critter curled into a J.

She'd often been fascinated with the changes a caterpillar went through to become a butterfly. Guin closed her eyes. She was five, facing the corner, unsure of what crime she had committed to deserve the punishment. Her grandmother told Guin's younger twin sisters how beautiful their golden curls were, likening them to their father's. Standing in that corner, she day-dreamed of spinning a cocoon then waking up with blonde hair and blue eyes. Believing if she could, her grandmother might love her too.

The memory shifted to the girl who'd morphed in Guin's arms, who unlike a caterpillar, had the ability to appear as whomever she wished.

A proverbial light lit in her mind. "Boden! Kapre!" Yelling as she went, she flung herself down the ladder. Symon brayed and bounced as the two men ran into the barn.

Boden gripped her shoulders. “Are you okay? What were you doing up there? You might have fallen.”

“Polymorphs! They’re polymorphs, they’re Na’ataks.” She clutched Boden’s forearms and shook him. “Our doubles in the videos! Don’t you see?”

“That’s it.” Kapre ran a hand through his hair. “Guin, you’re right. They must be.”

“Wait, wait. You’re saying the murderer is Na’atak?” Boden asked.

“Yes. A shapeshifter is the only thing that makes sense. We’re sure they weren’t us, yet three experts say the recordings are legitimate. Who else could they be?”

Kapre rubbed his chin. “Although, the possibility has been considered.”

“What?” She clutched his arm. “What are you saying?”

“Every Na’atak has an implant, except the person in the elevator didn’t. The only people without tracers are royalty and you. I’m sure any Na’ataks have been ruled out by now.”

They crossed the lawn. “Can’t the tracers be removed?”

Boden raised his right arm. “Ours are in our wrists. Na’atak’s tracers are implanted within their torsos and not easily extracted. Someone would need complicated and highly illegal surgery to extract one. Most doctors wouldn’t take the risk of being reported.”

She rubbed her own wrist. “How about some underground surgeon?”

“I guess anything’s possible. There isn’t a big demand for something like that here. The surgeon would face a death sentence if caught. To risk everything wouldn’t make sense. Crime isn’t rampant here like on your world, Griffin. The jails are mostly empty.”

Symon’s trunk wrapped around Guin’s wrist. She tickled his chin.

“When did you learn so much about this, Boden?”

“My training in the King’s Guard. I also know a Na’atak who had his tracer extracted legally.”

"Oh."

He stopped short, a mixture of horror and disbelief on his face.

"What?" She searched the ground where he appeared to be staring.

"Orist is the Na'atak with no tracer." His eyes grew wide, then drew down in a scowl. "When he joined the King's Guard, they removed it for security purposes."

Kapre and Guin exchanged a surprised glance.

Boden's gaze hardened. "Has Orist ever touched you?"

"I don't think so." She shook her head. "No, I'm sure. He's never come close enough to touch me. I think?"

"Unless he touched her when she wasn't looking? My mother used to tell us stories of how she and her friends played tricks on other kids. Pretending to be them by sneaking a touch, like some strange game of tag."

Guin gawked at him. "Your mother was Na'atak?"

"I thought everyone knew."

The hair prickled on the back of her neck. "Do you mean you and Vertuma can change too?"

"No. Only a full Na'atak can shape-shift. It's extremely rare for a half-blood to be a polymorph."

"But not impossible?" Boden asked.

"Not impossible. Yet I'm pretty sure I'd know if my sister could shape-shift."

"What would Orist gain?" Guin asked. "And how is he tied to Vertuma?"

Kapre shook his head. "I'm not sure. I've never met the man."

Boden stared at Kapre. "We'll need more information."

The two men searched for clues in the paperwork, each reading aloud to Guin, who fast forwarded through the videos again.

"There have to be two of them," she mused. "One for me and one or Boden."

"Orist must have ordered the security detail to stand down." Boden shuffled through paperwork. "He could have become the king, ordered his men to leave, changed into Guin, then committed the murder."

"No," Kapre said. "The timelines don't match. He would have given the order at the same time Guin's double was leaving the palace. The times are authenticated."

"Can you get this information to Jaxzon?" Boden asked.

"I'll need to meet him in person to be safe. Although, if Orist is our main suspect, I'm not sure we'd be left alone."

Guin yawned, fighting to stay awake. They'd spent hours searching for a crucial clue that might solve the mystery and save her life.

Boden slapped his hands together. "I'm calling it. You need rest. You're still recovering, and your drinking the other night didn't help matters."

"I'm not sleepy."

"If you don't go to your room, I'll throw you over my shoulder and carry you."

"You wouldn't dare."

Boden bent toward her.

She jumped to her feet and made a beeline for her room. "Okay, bossy Bodey. Goodnight, boys."

CHAPTER THIRTY-EIGHT

Muffled voices raised in anger carried through Guin's bedroom door.

"Guin had nothing to do with it. You yourself believed her yesterday. Besides, what would she gain? Orist has no connection to her, and she couldn't do it alone. And don't you dare implicate me again, or I'll knock you through that door."

"Calm down, Boden. I never said she did anything. I'm simply saying the video of King Jaezain telling her he would turn the nobility against her doesn't bode well for her."

She dressed then joined the men in the dining room. "Good morning." She crossed her arms. "I'm glad you're still on my side, Kapre."

"I never doubted you. I was explaining to Boden what others might perceive and he blew up on me."

"I'm sorry if we woke you. You ready for breakfast?" Boden went to the kitchen.

"Just toast and juice please."

"You should eat more. You're still too thin."

"Yes, Father. You sure are bossy lately." She sat across from Kapre. "What's the plan for today?"

"Jaxzon wants to meet with me this afternoon."

"He's agreed to meet you?" Her mood brightened. "That's the best news we've had in forever. I wish I could see him."

"You can. He's giving a press conference tonight regarding the wedding plans."

Her hopes raised and plummeted in the space of a nanosecond. Her chest tightened.

Boden scowled in Kapre's direction. "I swear you don't have the brain capacity of a *zynah*." His gaze met Guin's. "You don't have to watch if you don't want to."

"I need to."

"Me too." Boden set scrambled eggs, toast, and a glass of juice in front of her.

"Thank you." No longer hungry, yet not wanting to insult his cooking, she picked at the food in a half-attempt to eat. "What's a zynah?"

Kapre's gaze dropped. "A one-celled, brainless worm."

She bit her lips to keep from smiling. The half pout on Kapre's face tipped her over the edge, and she laughed.

The two men regarded her with raised brows. Her laughter evolved into guffaws, tears streaming from her eyes.

"I believe this is what a hysterical woman looks like," said Kapre, glancing at Boden.

"Could be." He sipped his tea. "Never seen one, though I've heard stories."

When she regained control, her sides ached from the exertion. "Oh, I needed that. Thanks, Kapre." She flashed him a smile then finished her breakfast.

Boden and Kapre exchanged a glance. "Women," mouthed Boden.

Kapre smiled.

Guin polished off her juice. "I saw that."

Before Kapre left for his meeting with Jaxzon, the three pored over the rest of the documents. The men took turns reading to Guin. She separated the evidence into piles. The stack against her outweighed anything she could use in her defense.

Kapre promised to be back later in the evening.

She killed time by continuing to teach herself to read Arwonese. Bree had taught some of the letters, helping Guin learn to put a few words and sentences together. But the symbols were more complex and numerous than Chinese or Japanese, with something akin to Egyptian hieroglyphs thrown in for good measure, making the task difficult.

Boden tended to the horses and worked around the house. Symon amused himself by suctioning a pink ball against his nose, huffing it across the room, then chasing after it.

Kapre returned, shaking his head. "He couldn't say anything; Orist never left his side."

"You've been gone for hours. What did you talk about?" Guin asked.

"We talked about the wedding. He asked me to be his *paranymph.*"

"His what?"

"It's like his best man." Boden put a hand on her shoulder. "Jaxzon wants Kapre to stand with him."

"Oh." Her heart sank with the reminder of Jaxzon's impending wedding.

"I believe he wanted to tell me something." He glanced at Guin. "I don't know him well, and yet I felt there was something wrong with him. Like he was half-asleep. He's thin and pale, as if he hasn't eaten or slept in days."

She put a hand to her throat. "Poor Jaxzon."

Boden sat beside her. "Was your sister there?"

"Yes, she's going to be with him at the press conference. They're announcing the date."

"He doesn't deserve this." She paced from the table to the sofa. "They're putting him through hell. We need to figure out the connection between Vertuma and Orist. There has to be something. I feel it. The more I think about the shapeshifting, the more I believe it has to be them." She stopped in front of Kapre. "Is there a way to obtain the surveillance tapes from the night of the ball and the day of the murder?"

"I suppose, but it would take hundreds of hours to go through them all. There are at least two hundred cameras throughout the palace."

"It doesn't matter, I'm not going anywhere. At least not for another twenty-three days." Guin continued pacing. "If we're sure Orist and Vertuma are behind this, we need to know where they were those nights. They must have made mistakes. They couldn't have committed the perfect crime."

"You're right. I'll go home and pull everything."

"Also, I want to know where I was and where Boden was when they were in my room together. And the night of the murder, how did they get in there and steal my clothes? That person left, but I was still in my room." Trying to visualized the Syndow's palace, she shook her head. "I can't remember exactly what I did and when. So much has happened since, and my memory of those nights..."

"Make a timeline." Boden handed her his tablet. "We need the videos from those nights to get the whole picture."

"I'll find what I can while Vertuma's on Arwon. She said she would be returning to Mikonia in two days. That'll give me enough time to get everything we need." Kapre kissed Guin's hand. "Take care of yourself, Guin. You too, Boden. Keep her here. If what we believe is true, she could be in danger."

Boden saw him to the door. "You be careful too."

LATER IN THE EVENING, Boden activated the tele-screen. "Are you sure?"

"Positive."

A podium in the Arwon palace ballroom filled the screen. Journalists yammered non-stop of Guin's disgrace, referring to her as the "Fallen Angel." When Jaxzon and Vertuma appeared, the newscaster quieted.

Vertuma wore a radiant smile. Jaxzon appeared tense, his smile stiff. Not caring to hear about their wedding plans, Guin removed the loqu, wanting only to hear his voice. Dark half-moons lay below his sunken eyes. His tailored suit hung from his shoulders. When he addressed the cameras, her breath caught. The sight of his face and the sound of his voice were both heaven and hell. He didn't speak for long before Vertuma cut in and babbled away in a cheerful voice.

She finished her speech, but before leaving, Jaxzon brushed an imaginary hair from his face and tucked it behind his right ear.

Guin put her face in her hands. "I love you too, Jaxzon. He remembered, Boden."

"I'm happy for you, Guin. But I think you should have left the loqu in."

She replaced the translator. "Why? What'd they say?"

"The date they set for the wedding is the day of your trial."

"What? Why would they do that?"

"I guess this way, if you're acquitted, it won't matter."

"Why not get married tomorrow?"

"By law, he must wait thirty days to marry the one chosen by the Vekdromic."

Guin's shock became determination. "Then we'd better find the killer soon."

CHAPTER THIRTY-NINE

Guin and Boden sat at the table when someone knocked. The door opened.

"Jaxzon!" Guin ran to him, throwing her arms around his neck.

He lifted her and carried her to the bedroom. He lay back on the bed, bringing her with him. "I want you, now."

She straddled his legs and unbuttoned his shirt, running a hand down his chest. Where she touched, a trail of ghastly, purple bruises appeared.

Guin gasped.

His pupils expanded, consuming the azure irises. Pitch-black orbs bugged from his skull. The skin beneath her hand rippled and expanded. His body twisted and warped. His jet hair turned white, falling out in bloody clumps. His chest swelled and stretched. The flesh covering his skull pulsated and boiled. Hatred radiated from onyx eyes. His mouth drew down into an impossible scowl.

The face bloated, mutating into a hideous, yet familiar shape—a gruesome representation of Orist. Smiling a ghastly, black-toothed grin, he thrust a scabby, deformed fist through her chest, seizing her heart and crushing it in a steely grip...

A high-pitched screeching filled her ears. She bolted awake. "Boden!" The name brought a stab of pain to Guin's throat as she screamed again. "Boden!"

The door crashed open. The light came on. Boden, after a quick search of the room, sat next to her. She clutched at him. He gathered her in his arms. Guin's breath came in ragged gasps. She clung to him, his bare chest warm against her cheek.

"What happened?"

"Jaxzon." Guin trembled. "He morphed into Orist. Except he was a monster. He tried to kill me."

"Shh, you're safe. It was only a dream." He tightened his arms around her.

"I'm sorry I woke you."

"You didn't wake me, although you may have raised the dead with the sound you made. I thought a ship crash-landed."

"That was me?"

"I hope so, otherwise there's a banshee loose around here."

"Oh Boden, it was so horrible." Her voice broke.

Cradling her against him, he rocked her in a gentle side to side motion.

"Please don't leave me. Everyone else is gone. You're the only one left."

"I'm not going anywhere." He laid her back on the pillow then stood.

Guin seized his hand. "Don't leave."

"I'm going to shut off the light. I'll come right back." The light went out at his touch. He went around the bed. "Go to sleep." Sitting next to her, he leaned against the headboard.

Guin gripped his hand and rolled to her side.

~

THE SUNS PEEKED over the horizon, causing a slight glow around the edges of the drawn curtains. Boden snored quietly, his head resting beside hers. She held his arm against her at what seemed an uncomfortable angle. Releasing his arm, she inched her way off the bed. Boden stirred.

"Sorry, I didn't mean to wake you," Guin said.

"You've got quite a grip, Griffin." He sat up, flexing his fingers. "I'm not sure I'll ever have the full use of this arm again. You okay?"

"I'm a little confused. Why are you here, and why was I holding your arm in a death grip?"

"You don't remember?"

"Not at all."

"You had a nightmare. You asked me to stay. I stayed." He headed to the kitchen.

She dressed, brushed her teeth, braided her hair, and joined Boden. "Did I tell you what I dreamed of?"

"Nope. I was in here getting water when you hollered for me. You fell back to sleep pretty fast, but I couldn't pry my arm from your grasp. I guess I fell asleep waiting on you to let loose."

Guin chuckled. "Sorry. Thank you for staying."

He waved a hand and finished making breakfast.

They played the video from the night of the ball, checking the times and racking her brain to remember everything from that night. Guin recalled sitting at the table with Sarya and her snide remarks.

She noted the approximate time. "I went to the lady's room, then talked with Derek and Delori. I watched Jaxzon dance with Vertuma until Kapre helped me rescue him. Then you and I talked. You were angry about something. What was it?"

Boden shook his head. "I-I don't remember."

"Then you ran interference, and I danced with Jaxzon. What did you do after you left?"

"Hmm." Boden stared at the ceiling. "I found a server to get a drink. I'd only had some non-alcoholic, fruity stuff. I needed something stronger."

"I remember being so tired. I felt jet-lagged and went to bed. I remember waking up and feeling awful, like I'd been drinking all night." Her brow creased. "Are you sure those fruity cocktails didn't have alcohol?"

"I don't think they did, didn't taste like it anyway. The server said they didn't, so I ordered a ruvin."

"Right, what did you do next?"

"I don't remember." His brow furrowed in concentration. "I must have gone to bed, at least I woke up there."

"That must've been one strong drink." She tapped her stylus against her lip. "What were you wearing in the morning?"

"Boxers. I remember because I never sleep in boxers. I always change into my pajama bottoms."

"That's interesting."

"Why is what I sleep in interesting? You've seen me in them several times."

"Elementary, my dear Watson. Whoever posed as you, dressed in the same clothes you wore to the ball, and unless Na'ataks can morph their clothing, someone must have stolen yours." She pretended to light a pipe then blew an imaginary puff of smoke into the air. "Therefore, I put it to you, sir—you were drugged, stripped, and put to bed in your boxer shorts."

"You say some crazy things, but I believe you're on to something." He smiled. "So, in your little detective fantasy, I'm the sidekick to your Sherlock?"

"You know Sherlock Holmes?"

"Required reading in my house. Tellurian mother, remember?"

"I remember. Do you ever visit her?"

"I want to hear more from Sherlock."

"What's next?" She scrolled through her notes. "Oh. Was your suit back the next day, and how did you feel in the morning?" Bringing the pipe to her lips, she took a drag and blew imaginary smoke rings, poking her finger through the last one.

"Yes, the suit was lying across the bottom of my bed. I have no clue how I felt that morning. I didn't wake up until late midday. Drugged?"

"Yes, my dear Watson, drugged." She made a note. "I was obviously drugged too because I didn't wake until one of those maid-bots came to clean the room around midday. How do you think we received the drugs? Didn't everyone drink those fruity things?"

"Possibly in our food?"

"I didn't eat. Sarya and her friends were giving me a hard time. I only had one bite and left." She shook her head. "No, the drugs had to be in the drinks. I remember being so thirsty and drinking tons of water."

"We need to wait for Kapre to bring the videos. Maybe we'll be able to see who served us, or if someone put something in our drinks during the ball."

"On the day of the murder, I went to the dining room for breakfast," she recalled. "I wasn't hungry and only had toast and a glass of juice." She laid back against the sofa's cushions. "Jaxzon had gone. Bree tried to teach me to read. I couldn't concentrate, like I was hungover."

"I talked to Jaxzon when he returned from Uetov4. He was excited about what they'd found, but we couldn't talk freely. He asked me to have you join him in the garden."

"Right, then King Jaezain yelled at us." She put the time in her notes and hung her head. "He called me an Earthling."

"I heard."

"That really hurt coming from him."

"That wasn't the king." Boden put a hand on her shoulder. "I can't see him speaking to anyone in that manner, especially you."

"True," she said, comforted by his words. "For all we know he was already dead at that point."

"You could be right. I wonder if that could be proven?" Boden dug through the pile of evidence and found the autopsy. He pored over the report again. Guin went back to her timeline.

She noted on her tablet that after Jaxzon left she had gone to bed depressed and feeling ill.

CHAPTER
FORTY

The days passed at a sloth's pace. Boden read reports to Guin. They analyzed the recordings until their eyes ached. Guin's timeline was complete for now, and they waited for Kapre.

To help relieve the tedium, Boden taught Guin to ride. In the afternoons they went on short jaunts, exploring the ranch and surrounding woods. Symon ran ahead, clearing the trail of three-tailed, squirrel-sized critters with light violet fur, who chittered from the trees when the horses passed.

Upon Kapre's return, he begged their forgiveness. "I'm sorry I didn't contact you before. I didn't want to risk giving your location away. My government, along with every reporter in the galaxy, is searching for you both. Rumor is you're attempting to find a surgeon to remove the guttan. Every Shift station and phase to Earth are being monitored." He took a thumb drive from his pocket. "Unfortunately, there are thousands of hours of video."

"Let's start with the time of each incident and backtrack," Guin said. "Maybe we'll get lucky."

They first reviewed the night of the murder. The video showed her entering her room, then the imposter emerged wearing different clothing. She went through the palace then into the garage where she entered a hover.

"Where were my guards? Eedras told them he never saw me leave my room, yet there I am, waltzing down the hall."

They reviewed Eedras's interview. He'd told the investigator Guin hadn't left her room. However, he admitted to taking a restroom break and may have been away at the time in question.

She rubbed her eyes. "That's a big help."

The video showed Eedras leaving the hallway, then shortly after, Guin's double left her room.

"Convenient. Almost seems orchestrated." She made a note.

By afternoon they needed a break. Guin and Boden headed to the barn to saddle the horses.

"Can I join you?" Kapre asked.

Boden's eyes narrowed. "Can you ride?"

"Ten years playing Dhustars." Kapre grinned. "Our palace has extensive stables."

Boden stopped in his tracks. "You played Dhustars? Which team?"

"What's Dhustars?" Guin asked.

"It's kind of like polo," explained Boden. "Except the ball can evade."

After their ride, they skimmed through another day's worth of recordings. Hundreds of cameras covered the palace grounds, making their progress slow and tedious.

They soon settled into a daily routine, breakfast, review videos, lunch, more videos, afternoon ride, videos.

They ate the evening meal and examined videos into the night. Kapre spotted the waiter who served their fruit drinks.

Guin recognized him as the man who'd served the ruvin on Xaitera. "That's him! That's the guy who gave Bree and I our drinks."

Boden took a close look at the man. He froze the frame then

enlarged it, then printed a screenshot. "He looks familiar for some reason. But I don't know from where."

She put the photo with her evidence. Afterwards they kept watch for the man.

One afternoon during their daily ride, Kapre rode into the woods alone, returning long after Guin and Boden. Each afternoon Kapre set out alone, returning later than the day before.

"Where did you go?" she asked one night.

"I've been exploring the other side of the woods. There are interesting plants and wildlife on this planet."

"Never took you for a nature freak."

"There's a lot you don't know about me, Guin."

Uneasiness gnawed at her. "I guess."

The next evening, Boden and Guin were removing the saddles from their horses when Kapre rode to the fence. Instead of riding through the gate as usual, he dismounted then tied his horse to the railing. The hood of his jacket was pulled forward, hiding his face. Symon bristled, sniffing the air.

Guin froze. "Boden, that's not Kapre."

Boden dropped his saddle and stepped in front of Guin. Symon growled a low rumble.

The man's pace increased. He dropped his hood.

Boden stiffened.

"Jaxzon!" Dropping the reins, she broke into a run.

Jaxzon's sunken, purple-rimmed eyes gleamed. Sunlight flashed in his hair.

An icy fist gripped her heart. She skidded to a stop and whirled around, flying back to Boden. "It's not him! He's not Jaxzon!" She clutched Boden's arm, attempting to drag him away.

The two men froze.

Guin threw her arms around Boden, burying her face in his chest. "Orist!" she shrieked. "He's here to kill us. He's not Jaxzon. His hair, his hair!"

Symon had run with Guin and now whined. His hair bristled. His nose probed the air in the man's direction.

"Symon, heel." Symon sat at Boden's feet. "Who are you? What do you want with us?"

"Boden, it's me. Jaxzon." He spread his arms and took a step. "Guin, what's wrong?"

Boden raised a hand. "Stay where you are!"

The man halted, a confused frown on his face.

She shuddered. Infuriated with the deception, she turned to face him, fists clenched at her sides. "Leave us alone. We know what you are."

"How can I prove I'm me?" Sunken, azure eyes searched hers.

Her anger became confusion, and she took a step forward.

Boden gripped her shoulder. "Ask him something only Jaxzon would know."

"Where did we go in New York?"

"Coney Island." The man grinned, showing his dimples. "You took me racing."

Her heart leapt. *Could it be?*

Boden held her back. "We all knew that."

"What was the name of the man at the track?" Guin asked.

"Tony."

She was out of Boden's grasp and into Jaxzon's arms faster than either man could react, almost knocking Jaxzon to the ground in the process. "It is you, oh my god, Jaxzon!" She buried her face in his neck, breathing him in. "I was afraid I'd never see you again."

"Go inside," said Boden. "I'll put the horses away. Symon, come."

Guin led Jaxzon into the house.

"I'm so sorry." He brushed a stray hair from her face, tucking it behind her ear. "I wish I could change everything."

"Shh. You did what you had to do." She gripped his lapels, drawing him down into a passionate kiss.

Jaxzon swept her into his arms. She reveled in his touch, his scent, his warmth.

The door opened, and Boden cleared his throat. They broke apart.

"Excuse me." He walked between them into the house, followed by Symon, who stopped to waggle while snuffling Jaxzon's feet.

He scratched the bandy's head. "Hey, Symon."

Boden washed up in the kitchen. "Where's Kapre?"

"Avoiding my guards, I hope. We switched horses. When he visited the palace, I mentioned I rode most afternoons. Two days ago, I found him on the edge of the woods between here and the palace grounds. He told me his plan. We met this afternoon, switched coats and horses, and I rode here. Why did you think I was Orist?"

Boden dried his hands. "Kapre didn't fill you in?"

"We didn't talk long. I'm still under heavy guard. He said Guin was here, told me to wear a hooded coat, and meet him in the clearing today."

"Orist is Na'atak, he can shape-shift," said Boden.

"Okay, but why would you believe he'd changed into me?"

"We're pretty sure he and Vertuma killed your father and framed Griffin."

Jaxzon's eyes widened. "What? You think Orist had something to do with this? Why?"

She shrugged. "It's the only logical explanation. Those weren't us in those videos."

"And if the recordings were officially authenticated, they had to be people who were identical to Griffin and me," Boden added.

"So, they had to be Na'atak," she finished.

Jaxzon blinked in surprise. "Vertuma's Na'atak? Are you sure?"

"Kapre told us," Guin said. "He didn't know if she could shape-shift, but we suspect that's how they did it."

"But why Orist?" Jaxzon ran a shaky hand through his hair. "He's been in my father's service for years."

"Because he's had his tracer removed." Boden placed a hand on his friend's shoulder. "He had knowledge of where everyone would be at any given time. Orist was the first to access the videos and could easily destroy them without being detected. He's also the only one who could get to your father without interference. We believe he was with you and Griffin in the garden the night of the murder."

"What would he gain?" Jaxzon sank into a kitchen chair.

"We haven't figured that out yet," Boden said. "Are you aware of a connection between him and Vertuma?"

Jaxzon's brow creased. "I'm not sure they'd met until recently, since we've been together." He glanced at Guin. "I'm so sorry. I owe you two an apology. I doubted you both when I was shown the video. Please forgive me."

"We don't blame you," said Boden. "I almost believed it myself."

"I told you. No need to apologize." Guin squeezed Jaxzon's hand. "I know this comes as a shock to you, but we need to learn how they did this and find the evidence to prove my innocence. We're still going through everything." She indicated the small pile of boxes. "But it's taking forever. The Syndow palace has thousands of hours of video to go through, and we're not sure we can find any hard evidence before my time's up."

"Right." Jaxzon stood. "How can I help?"

"Can you get us everything your government has on Orist?" Guin asked. "Personal stuff, who his friends are, where he came from, something in his background that might lead to this."

"I should have access to everything."

"I would hope so." A grin spread across Boden's face. "King Jaxzon."

Guin smoothed Jaxzon's hair from his forehead. "I'm sorry I missed your coronation."

"You have no reason to be sorry. After everything, I'm surprised you didn't run screaming the moment you laid eyes on me. Oh wait." He kissed her nose. "You did."

Guin frowned. "I'm not sure what came over me."

"Your nightmare. I didn't say anything the next day because I didn't want to upset you all over again." Boden gave her a sheepish look. "But in your dream, Jaxzon became Orist."

"What?" she asked in surprise. "The night you slept with me?"

Jaxzon raised his eyebrows. "You slept together?"

"She was frightened and asked me not to leave, nothing more."

She grinned. "Don't you dare be jealous. Boden's been the best friend anyone could ask for."

"I'm sorry, I should have known better. When I saw the footage from Guin's release, I trusted you'd take care of her." Jaxzon tightened his arms around her. "I must leave soon. I'm not sure how long Kapre can fool my guard. I usually ride far afield, but they observe me from a distance."

"Don't trust any of them," Boden warned.

"And don't drink or eat anything Vertuma or Orist try to give you," Guin said. "We think they made those videos. They drugged us and assumed our forms. You saw the recording from the elevator?"

"That clinched it for me. I knew she wasn't you."

Guin's heart sank. "Did you believe that was me before?"

"No, I was certain you didn't kill my father, but when Orist showed me the video and photograph, in that moment..." He glanced from Boden to Guin, his expression pained. "Ulzon advised me that in light of the recording, Vertuma was the only choice. Afterward, I learned you'd been arrested. Their government wouldn't let me see you, and after my coronation the Council voted to take temporary rule of the realm and set the date for the wedding."

Guin frowned. "How can they take over like that?"

"There is an obscure law allowing the Council forty-five days of temporary rule during a transition between rulers. I'm in protective custody." He rubbed his eyes. "I wanted to see you both, but until Kapre came up with his plan, I had no way of contacting you."

"I wondered why you blocked my calls," said Boden.

"All my calls are monitored. My security has been doubled. The Council has called off any further investigation into my father's murder and have declared you both suspects. I'm obligated to go along with their directives until this temporary rule ends. Kapre came to me before my coronation and confided that he didn't trust his sister. I asked him to do some investigating. After the Council took over, I had no way of communicating with him without being overheard. I never truly trusted Kapre, and yet he's proving to be an invaluable ally."

They showed Jaxzon what small evidence they had gathered.

He promised to help from his end. "There are a few people in my service I trust implicitly. One will bring whatever I can find on Orist. But I should go now. I'm worried about Kapre. Before I leave, you should know—my father was dying."

"What?" Boden and Guin asked.

"He had Kroten's disease. A form of what they call cancer on Earth, untreatable and incurable. He didn't have long."

Boden frowned. "Wouldn't that be mentioned in his autopsy?"

"It should be there." He took Guin's hand, and they followed Boden to the horse.

"Did he tell you before?" Boden asked.

"No. Not a word. His private journal explained everything. His illness forced him to order the Vekdromic."

"If something happens to me—" Guin raised a hand, stopping his protest. "If we can't solve this before...before my trial, you have to do everything in your power—once you have it back—to stop them even if you have to marry that witch and prove her guilt afterward."

"I would rather die than marry her."

"Jaxzon, she's evil. Your father deserves justice. Don't let me die for nothing. Promise?"

He brushed the stray strand of hair from her forehead. "I promise. Although it will never come to that. I will do everything in my power, and with Kapre's help we will prove your innocence. I only wish I could do more." He touched his lips to hers.

Boden cleared his throat then busied himself with a loose strap on the saddle.

Jaxzon held her close. "There is so much more I need to say."

"We'll tell one another everything after this is over. I love you, no matter what. Please believe I will always love you."

"I love you too." Their foreheads touched. "Always. I only chose her because—"

"Shh." Her mouth covered his in a sweet kiss.

"Thank you for taking care of her." He embraced Boden. "You've always been like a brother to me."

Boden returned the hug then clapped him on the back before Jaxzon swung into the saddle.

She put a hand on his knee. "I love you, my king."

"I love you, my lady." He rode away, waving one last time before the trees swallowed him.

CHAPTER FORTY-ONE

Boden skimmed through the coroner's report. "It isn't here."

Guin peered over his shoulder. "What isn't there?"

"I would assume an autopsy would reflect a deadly disease." He shuffled the documents. "This doesn't mention Kroten's."

"Are pages missing?"

Boden flipped through the forms. "They're all here."

"What does this mean?"

"I think King Jaezain invoked the Vekdromic under the false assumption that he was dying. This may be more premeditated than we thought."

Kapre burst through the door, out of breath and wearing a grin. Guin punched his arm. "Why didn't you tell us what you were up to?"

"I couldn't be sure it would work. I didn't want to raise your hopes for nothing."

She kissed his cheek. "Thank you."

"My pleasure." He took a seat at the table. "I was almost caught. They may have become suspicious of my riding in and out of the woods every so often. Jaxzon came back in time, although I'm not sure we should try again."

"You shouldn't." Boden checked the roast in the oven. "If Orist finds out, you could both be in danger."

Guin joined Boden in the kitchen. "I agree. Jaxzon knows what's going on now, we can't risk his safety."

Boden filled Kapre in on the autopsy and what they'd learned from Jaxzon.

"Could the king's doctor have made a mistake in the diagnosis?" asked Kapre.

"Possibly. Can we check into that?" asked Boden.

"I'll see what I can find. I want to go to the jail and obtain Guin's toxicology tests. They might show you were incapacitated the night of the murder. If we obtain enough circumstantial evidence, we might be able to sway the gerents."

Guin took a bowl from the cupboard. "Gerents?"

"Five gerents will hear your case, including Dikastis."

"Do we only need to convince three of them?" She tore a head of pink lettuce into pieces, dropping them into the bowl.

"No, we have to convince all five."

Guin's eyes widened. "I'm dead."

Boden frowned. "Don't say that."

A heaviness filled Guin's chest. "Talk to Loltu. She was kind to me. She might be a doctor. She did my implant." Guin touched the spot on her sternum where the guttan had been implanted. "Kapre, what does *vasilissa* mean?"

"Royal, or queen. Why?"

Guin smiled. "Never mind."

The following morning, Kapre left for Mikonia. Guin and Boden went back to their routine, reviewing videos, searching for anything unusual.

Later in the week, they had a visitor. Guin hid in her room with Symon, keeping the door opened a crack. Boden answered and conversed briefly with a member of the king's guard. The woman left and Guin joined Boden who held an envelope with the king's seal. Inside were Orist's records from when he'd arrived from Na'atak, along with his recruitment paperwork and pictures. The recruitment pictures showed a young man with blond, curly hair.

Guin's eyes widened. "He's the man who served our drinks."

"He is."

"Why is he so different now? Didn't you know him when he was younger?"

"I'm twelve years younger." Boden scanned through the documents. "He's been balding since I met him. But his face, he's changed, and I don't believe it's from age."

"Why would he become his younger self to do these things? Wouldn't that be risky?"

He lifted his shoulder in a half shrug. "Who knows? Orist has always been more than a bit cocky."

"What's next?" She settled into a chair, put her feet up, and wrapped her arms around her knees. "We have proof Orist is involved, now who do we take this to?"

"We should wait for Kapre. He could tell us who to trust on Mikonia."

"Has Heldivar made any headway with finding an attorney?"

"I'll message her. She should have had some luck by now."

Guin's anxiety doubled after Jaxzon left. Now that they had absolute proof of Orist's involvement, her fears for Jaxzon's safety multiplied. "I'm running out of time, and I hate not being able to do anything. I hope the evidence will be enough to sway the gerents."

Boden messaged Heldivar, giving her an update on what they'd found.

The boxes of evidence against her outnumbered the small carton in her defense by a ratio of fifty to one. The trial would take place in seven days and her evidence was at best, circumstantial.

The following day Kapre sent the blood test results from the prison. He included a list of side effects of the drugs found in her system.

Boden interpreted the report. "They found four separate drugs normally prescribed to insomniacs. 'A combination of sleep aids, if taken with alcohol or in abundance, can cause paranoia, depression, suicidal ideation, hallucinations, dehydration, and mild to severe catalepsy.' The effects can last up to two weeks after discontinuing."

"What's the last one, catalepsy?"

Boden checked his telecon. "A physical condition usually associated with catatonic schizophrenia, characterized by the suspension of sensation, muscular rigidity, fixity of posture, and often by loss of contact with the environment."

"That explains so much—why I couldn't concentrate, my blackouts, why I was so thirsty, and why we both slept through everything. Is this enough to postpone the trial?"

"I don't know. I'll contact Heldivar with this latest. When Kapre returns, we can go from there."

She filed the test results with the other evidence and brought the box to her room. She changed into her red plaid and a pair of Boden's boxers then went over the evidence, cataloging everything on her tablet in order of importance.

A LOUD NOISE woke Guin from a deep sleep. She waited for the sound to repeat. A piece of paper crumpled beneath her. She clicked the button for her bedside lamp, but nothing happened. Gathering the paperwork and photos in the dark, she tucked them into the carton then set it beside the bed.

A strange hissing came from beyond her door. She put her ear to the door only to be knocked back when an explosion rocked the house. Smoke billowed into her room. The kitchen burst into flames.

"Boden!" She sprinted for his room but was sent flying when her foot caught on something solid. Hitting her head on Boden's doorjamb. She landed in a heap. Rousing herself, she crawled back to his prone form.

"Boden." Running her hand along his body, she checked for a pulse. Relief washed over her when his chest rose and his heart beat against her palm. Gripping his arms, she tried dragging him to the living room. She strained against his weight, but he didn't budge.

Groping her way to his room she removed his bedspread. Crawling beneath the smoke, she spread the cloth on the floor beside him. In desperation, she braced her back against the wall. Planting her feet against his body, she rolled him onto the blanket. Stooping below the smoke, she grasped the edges and dragged him across the smooth floor. Her eyes watered and her throat burned as thick smoke filled the house.

Guin hauled Boden through the door and down three stone steps to the pathway between the house and barn. She coughed and gagged, doubling over, her hands on her knees. Her lungs burned. She couldn't get enough fresh air.

The evidence!

Taking a deep breath, she ran back into the house, racing through the intense heat to her room. The raging fire had spread throughout the kitchen. The butcher's block exploded in flames. She slammed the bedroom door behind her.

Ducking beneath the smoke, she found the container. She fumbled along the window's ledge, searching for the lock. She flipped the latch, threw open the window, then punched through the screen. Black smoke billowed around her into the night sky. Dropping the box over the sill, she fell into the bushes behind it.

Illuminated by the flames of the burning house, she set the carton beside Boden's prone figure.

CHAPTER FORTY-TWO

"Boden." She caressed his pale cheek. "Can you hear me?"

A trickle of blood oozed from a gash on his temple. Tearing strips from the blanket, she pressed one against the wound. She wrapped another around his head, tying the ends. A low whimper came from somewhere near the barn.

"Symon?" Guin followed the sound to the barn's door. He lay on his side, air hissing through his nose, his tongue lolling in the dirt. "Oh, Symon." Guin ran her hands over his body, searching for injuries. Finding none, she carried him to Boden. Symon's nose snuffled across his master's face then lay still.

Boden's eyes fluttered open. He attempted to sit up.

She put a hand on his chest. "Shh. Stay still."

"What happened?" Pain clouded his eyes.

"I don't know, there was a noise and... Oh, Boden, your beautiful house..."

"Are you hurt?"

She rubbed the lump on her forehead. "I'm fine, but you hit your head, and something's wrong with Symon."

He stroked Symon's fur and was rewarded with a sniff and a

hushed bray. "Good boy. You'll be okay." She helped Boden sit. He leaned forward, resting his arms on his knees. "I heard something. When I went to check, someone clobbered me. They must have got Symon too. We need to get the horses out. This could spread to the barn."

Smoke drifted into the stable through the open windows. Guin wrapped an arm around Boden, guiding him to the barn. The animals stamped and snorted. She left him leaning on the gate then released the horses from their stalls. They went to him, nuzzling his neck and shying from the blood-soaked cloth.

Bathed in the glow of the burning house, Symon lay beside Boden, his trunk resting on his hand. Closing her eyes, she leaned her head on Boden's shoulder, saddened and in shock.

Dawn broke. The stone fireplace remained standing, silhouetted against the brightening sky as the suns peeked over the horizon. Twists of smoke rose into the air above the rubble.

Boden heaved a sigh. "I guess that's it."

"I'm so sorry." She smoothed the hair from his forehead. "Who would do this?"

"I can only think of one person."

"But how did he find us? Could Jaxzon's guard have betrayed him?"

"Someone did. We were lucky this time. Next time they want us dead, we will be."

A shiver ran down her spine. "What do we do now? I didn't have time to search for your telecon. I was barely able to save the evidence."

He patted his pocket. "I grabbed it when I left my room. The power was out, and I didn't have a chance to activate my light before I was hit."

"Can you contact Heldivar? Maybe she can help us Shift to Mikonia before this thing kills me."

Boden messaged Heldivar and received an immediate response. "She's sending a hover and coordinates to her estate on Tendraq."

"Can you ask her for some trivol? I don't want to go through another Shift without a dose."

He sent the request.

"What about Symon? Can we take him?"

"No, he can't Shift. I'll have my caretaker come for him and the horses."

Heldivar sent the phase information and arranged for transportation. When the hover arrived, they found a dose of trivol inside next to two dislocaters. The vehicle dropped them off several miles from the ranch.

They each held a dislocater. At the scheduled time, she gripped his hand. They went forward into the phase.

A single streetlight illuminated a low dark vehicle parked on an abandoned road. He peered inside. "This must be Heldivar's."

A short underground tunnel took them to a lighted garage. The hover's door opened. A smiling Heldivar greeted them. "So good to see you. Come, you both need a wash and a change of clothes." She inspected Boden's wound. "Someone will take care of this when you're done."

They followed her to a bedroom with an adjoining bath. Clothes had been left on the bed. A dress for Guin, pants and a shirt for Boden, and undergarments for both.

"I hope you don't mind sharing the room. This is a small estate. Message when you're ready." Heldivar closed the door behind her.

He sat on the bed. "You go first."

"Not gonna argue." She gathered the clothes, closing the door behind her. Hot water washed away the shock and bone-weary exhaustion. After, she rummaged through her carton, sorting the evidence.

He exited the bathroom holding a washcloth to his head.

Guin lifted the cloth. A sizable lump lay beneath a jagged gash. "You'll probably need stitches."

Calen came to fetch them to a study after receiving Boden's text. He offered each a cup of hot tea, then ran an instrument over

Boden's wound, healing the gash without a scar, though the lump remained.

He wiped the last bit of blood from Boden's scalp. "You might experience a headache for a few days. These things only work on the outer soft tissues."

"Thanks. It feels better already."

Heldivar sat behind her desk as Guin went through the box, explaining each piece of evidence.

"Superb," Heldivar said. "I believe an attorney may win a postponement with this information."

Guin replaced the items in the box. "When can we talk to one?"

"We meet him in the morning." Heldivar checked the time. "In nine hours. Until then, you two need rest. Come." She led them to their room, then bid them goodnight.

Their pajamas had been laundered and lay folded at the foot of the bed. Guin took hers to the bathroom and changed. When she exited, Boden was lying on the bed in his sweatpants.

She took a pillow. "You're hurt, you take the bed."

"Come on Griffin. I think we can sleep in the same bed after all we've been through. We've done it before and survived."

They crawled under the blankets. He hit the switch on the bedside lamp.

The light of a full moon shone through the window casting purple shadows throughout the room. She rolled to face him. "Do you think the gerents will believe us?"

"It's the truth. Once they realize it, a real investigation will be conducted, and you'll be freed." He brushed the strand of hair from her face. "Stop worrying. How could anyone believe you would murder someone?"

"I'm terrified they're going to get away with this, and I'm going to end up..." She trailed off, fearing to speak the words for the reality they invoked.

"Listen, nothing is going to happen to you. You didn't do anything wrong, and we'll prove it. Okay?"

"Okay. So long as you're there to rescue me."

"We're about even on the rescuing. I would be a well-done steak if you hadn't dragged me out of my house. Besides, what are friends for, right?"

"Right." She pecked his cheek. "Goodnight, Boden."

"Goodnight, Guin." He kissed her forehead and laid back on his pillow.

The following morning, someone knocked. Guin found Kapre in the hallway, a grin lighting his face.

"Kapre." She threw her arms around him. "We were so worried about you. How did you know we were here?"

"Heldivar contacted me. Sorry about your house, Boden. How's your head?"

"I'll live, thanks."

"The attorney from Mikonia should be here soon. I'll take you down."

Heldivar and a short, balding man, whom she introduced as Boliad Ancun, met them in the study. After the pleasantries, Boliad went through the box of evidence, asking questions regarding each piece. He viewed the videos while listening to their suspicions.

When they'd finished, he sat back in Heldivar's chair then steepled his fingers. "I believe a case can be argued for your innocence. Though I would not wait to take this to the gerent's panel. I would take this directly to His Majesty, King Nov'Xam." Leaning forward, he tapped a ringed finger upon the desk. "You may not be able to persuade the panel to postpone your trial on this evidence. But, the king might grant an extension, and would be more easily convinced than five gerents. This evidence needs vetting, and because the crime took place in his kingdom, he would be the one to order further investigation. In the public's mind, you have already been found guilty. Going to the king may be the only way to receive a fair trial."

"Will your father hear us?" Guin asked at Kapre.

"I believe he will."

Boden appeared skeptical. "Even if his daughter is implicated?"

"This evidence only implicates Orist," said Boliad, "not Princess Vertuma. We need only prove your innocence, not that anyone else is guilty. For now, this should suffice."

Kapre shook the attorney's hand. "I'll arrange for the Shift tomorrow, and a meeting the following day."

"Excellent." Boliad shook Guin's hand. "If you manage an extension, I will be available to handle your case."

The next morning Guin checked Boden's telecon. She had two Mikonian days before the guttan needed to be deactivated. *At least I'm going to the right planet.* Snagging her change of clothes, she headed to the bathroom. When Boden awoke, they ate the morning meal in the study.

Heldivar joined them. "Kapre contacted me this morning. King Nov'Xam will be unavailable until tomorrow. I will accompany you to Mikonia. I wish the king to understand you have a powerful ally."

"Thank you, Heldivar."

"That's cutting things pretty close, isn't it?" asked Boden.

"We must be content that the king will see us at all," said Heldivar.

~

MIKONIA'S SETTING sun cast its last rays on the spires of a small stone tower with barred windows. Four Mikonian guards met Heldivar, Boden, and Guin, then escorted them across a small courtyard toward the building.

A sign hung below a stone skyway, casting a shadow across their path. Passing beneath the sign, Boden wrapped an arm around Guin. He whispered, "Something's not right."

Shivering, she hoped he was wrong.

A tall female guard in Mikonia's black-and-gold opened the door. She grinned from behind her visor as they entered the sparsely furnished, stone-built room.

King Nov'Xam sat on one of two chairs. Two men guarded the door while the woman and another guard took positions on either side of their king. Heldivar bowed to the king then sat beside him.

Boden and Guin bowed.

"Is Prince Kapre joining us?" she asked, darting her eyes around the room.

"He should be here shortly," Nov'Xam answered.

A distant bell rang sixteen times, marking the evening hour.

A guard opened the door for Kapre. The prince set Guin's evidence at his father's feet then came to stand with her and Boden. "Tell him what we've found, Guin."

She explained the evidence. "Would you like to watch the videos? You might understand better if you see them for yourself."

King Nov'Xam stroked his graying beard. "What would Orist gain from this?"

"Father, we believe Vertuma is working with him. We haven't made the connection yet, but we believe if you postpone the trial for another thirty days, we might be able to prove it."

"But by then, your sister will be Queen." His gaze flicked to Guin. "And you will be dead."

The warmth drained from Guin's limbs, leaving her cold and numb. Her heart dropped. Her stomach twisted into a queasy knot.

"But Father, you can stop both from happening. Guin didn't do this."

"Enough!" King Nov'Xam bellowed.

Kapre stiffened as the king stood, flanked by his guards. Heldivar smiled.

"Do you truly believe I would implicate your sister to help an Earthling?" Nov'Xam held his son in a cold stare. "You've always had more looks than intelligence."

Kapre flinched.

"When you lost our chance to rule by failing to win the hand of Princess Jalain, who took care of it?" His stony glare lit on Boden. A cruel smile curled his lips. "Orist."

Boden drew a sharp breath. His jaw clenched. His hands balled into fists.

The prince held him back, placing a hand on his arm. "You had them killed? But, why?"

The king flipped his hand. "Power, control, wealth." Nov'Xam relaxed into his chair, crossing his ankle over his knee. "You are a foolish boy. Do you understand nothing? Must I spell everything out for you?"

Kapre squared his jaw.

"Fine. I'll make this simple, so you'll understand. After your failed courtship of Princess Jalain, we eliminated her, the queen, and Orist's greatest hindrance." His merciless gaze flicked to Boden. "Commander Darcyd. At the time, Prince Jaxzon was too young to marry, and later his father wouldn't agree to a betrothal. Therefore, we devised another plan— force the Vekdromic.

"Luckily for us, poor King Jaezain's cheaply bought physician diagnosed him with a rare and deadly form of Kroten's. Guiding His Majesty in the right direction was surprisingly simple from there. The Vekdromic would commence, and thanks to our woman on the inside, Vertuma would be chosen."

Heldivar winked. Guin burned with rage. Boden put his arm around her.

"Then, this Earthling appeared." Nov'Xam's eyes narrowed. "We attempted to eliminate you. When that failed, and you gained and held the people's attention, we decided to use you. Cause a split in the vote, eliminate the king, and implicate you. Ridding ourselves of Jaezain had always been the weakest part of our plan. We thank you for solving the problem and providing the evidence of our mistakes." He toed the box.

"You'll never get away with this," Kapre said. "I'll never go along with murder."

"Of course, you won't. In some ways, I almost regret what I must now do." The king raised his hand. The female guard smiled and placed a weapon on his palm. Nov'Xam pointed the weapon at Kapre and fired. A bolt of blue light hit him in the chest.

Guin screamed.

Kapre flew back several feet, landing in a heap. Smoke rose from his chest.

Boden shielded Guin's body with his own as Nov'Xam pointed the weapon in their direction.

"No need for that." Nov'Xam handed the weapon to the guard. "You won't die today. Your guttan will take care of you." He turned his attention to Boden. "And you will die trying to help her escape her fate. Always the hero. Although now, you will be remembered as the traitor who attempted to help a murderous Earthling deactivate her guttan and flee justice. Jaezain's good doctor will unfortunately be caught in the crossfire attempting to help. We will save the taxpayers trials and executions, and will have, what is your saying?" He glanced at Guin. A sly smile spread across his face. "Killed two birds with one throw? Then there's poor King Jaxzon."

Guin shoved away from Boden to face the king.

Nov'Xam chuckled. "It truly is too bad you and your king couldn't go on to live happily ever after. You are a sweet couple." His dark eyes glimmered. "But alas, once your king and Vertuma have conceived an heir, we will have no further use of him."

"Vertuma is a vile witch." Guin took a step toward the king. "Jaxzon would *never*—"

"A vile what?" The woman guard glared. Her face lengthened and rippled, transforming into a sneering Vertuma. She strode forward and backhanded Guin.

The blow rocked her head back as stars exploded across her vision. Boden lurched forward, but she held him back as three weapons trained on him.

"He may *never* with Vertuma," the king said as his daughter returned to his side. "Although what Jaxzon doesn't know... show them, dear."

Vertuma's face contorted, her hair and body morphed until

another Guin, draped in the guard's oversized black uniform appeared before them.

"With a few strategically placed hallucinogens, your good King Jaxzon won't know the difference. And once an heir is on the way, Orist will take Jaxzon's place, and the king's body will never be found."

"All this for power?" Guin fought the urge to slap the smug grin from the man's face. "Doesn't a king have enough?"

"Never."

She glared at Heldivar. "What's in this for you?"

"Wealth." Her smile widened. "More than one can imagine."

A wicked smile played on Vertuma's lips as she morphed into herself. "Dear Heldivar is heavily invested in our little ichor mining operations. You do remember ichor?" Her cruel eyes glinted. "When we control the realm, we control the ichor. That idiot Jaxzon believes he can keep Minos a secret from us? He never suspected we had a Council member on our payroll."

Guin's arms tightened around Boden. "I thought half Na'atak's couldn't shape-shift."

"Although rare, it has been known to happen," Heldivar said. "Her mother kept her skills secret, not wishing her daughter to be saddled with the stigma of being polymorph. When we planted Orist in the king's guard, we counted on his trace being extracted, and as a Na'atak, he made a perfect spy. At the time we had no idea he would become Commander and make our plans so much simpler." She gazed at Vertuma. "When he and the princess became lovers, our plan was complete."

Vertuma batted her lashes.

"Is there anything else you'd like to know?" King Nov'Xam stood. "No? Then we will leave you two alone. I'm sure you have much to talk about." He motioned to the guards. "Take his telecon, and dispose of that." The king indicated Kapre's body. "Now, if you'll excuse us, I've a wedding to prepare for, and a bride to give away."

The two guards followed, dragging Kapre's body from the room.

CHAPTER FORTY-THREE

The scrape of the electronic deadbolt sliding home echoed in Guin's ears. "What the hell just happened?" She choked back a sob. "He killed Kapre."

Boden's arms tightened around her. She laid her head against his chest, swallowing the lump in her throat as shock transitioned to anger. Fear for Jaxzon replaced both. "We can't let them do this. We need to get out of here and expose their murderous conspiracy. There has to be a way out." She twisted out of his arms and searched the room.

There wasn't much to search—a twenty-by-twenty room with only a small, doorless room for toilet use and a heavy, steel door on the back wall. The furniture consisted of two chairs and a wide metal cot. High, barred windows allowed in slivers of dying daylight. Darkened light fixtures hung from the ceiling. She ran her hands along the beige stone walls, searching for weaknesses in the mortar. They both tried the door. The hinges were on the outside.

He rammed his shoulder against the door, discovering the steel to be completely solid.

Guin dropped into a chair. "How could he murder his own son so callously?"

Rubbing his shoulder, he shook his head.

The light faded and the air grew frigid. A chilling rain fell, and a freezing dampness permeated the room as the distant bell chimed twenty times. Guin hugged herself. The thin dress she wore offered little protection from the sinking temperature.

Boden set his chair beside hers and put an arm around her shoulders. She huddled against him, clenching her jaw against chattering teeth. "There has to be a way out of here."

"We won't find it tonight. Maybe in the morning. For now, we need to get you warm. C'mon."

They laid on the cot. His body enveloped hers, sheltering her from the cold.

"Thank you." She nestled into the warmth of his arms. "You truly are my hero."

"And you're mine." His breath warmed her neck. "If it weren't for you, I would've died tonight with my hands around Vertuma's throat."

"I would have loved that. Not the you dying part, just the choking part."

"I can't sit by tomorrow while you—" His voice became a hoarse whisper.

"I don't want to think about it, or of what they're going to do to you and Jaxzon." She squeezed her eyes shut. "I hope there's something after this life and I'll see you both there."

"Shh. Let's talk about something else."

She settled her head in the crook of his arm. The darkness was so complete, she couldn't see his face, only inches from her own. "Tell me about when you first met Jaxzon."

"Guin, I—"

"Please, Boden. I need a distraction. I need—" A sob caught in her throat.

"Shh." His arm tightened around her. "We were only seven at the time. My father had recently become Commander, and we'd moved into the palace. I was playing swords with two older boys whose fathers were also in the Guard. One became angry with me for something I don't recall. He took a swing at me behind my back. We hadn't known it, but Jaxzon had been watching us play. He yelled at the boy, calling him a coward and ordered him to apologize."

She smiled, trying to picture them. "Awe, little Jaxzon was your hero."

"My hero? I didn't think so. I told him I was old enough to defend myself and to mind his own business. I threw down my plastic sword and challenged him to a fight. The other boys ran off. Jaxzon removed his jacket, folded it neatly, then proceeded to kick my ass. We've been friends ever since."

"Even after your fight?"

"Yeah. Jaxzon came looking for me the next day. He said I was the only person who'd ever treated him like an ordinary kid. I kind of felt sorry for him. I noticed how people behaved around him, and worse, how they acted toward me when we were together."

"What do you mean?"

"After we became friends, the other kids treated me different. They were too *nice*. I never had a decent fight again. Later, with women...things got worse. Being friends with Jaxzon changed everything for me."

"But you're still friends." She squeezed the arm lying across her chest.

"Yes, we're still friends."

"Tell me more. I want to hear everything about little Jaxzon and Boden and the trouble they caused."

He talked into the night, telling stories of how they played pranks on the guards, and how Queen Neyris and Boden's father would defend them to the king. Both believed a prince needed to be a regular boy sometimes.

"I wish I'd known you both then."

"What was little Guin like?"

She laughed. "Boring in comparison."

"Come on, talking will warm you up."

"Okay but be prepared to be put to sleep."

She talked about growing up in Manhattan and how she and her best friend, Charlie, had kidnapped a rabbit and kept it in Guin's closet for a week before her mother found out. She explained how Raney had kept the nomination for prom queen a secret, and how DeShawn and others had campaigned behind her back. "I was so naïve. I never realized how many friends I truly had until prom night."

He chuckled. "Queen Guinevere."

"Yeah, queen for a day." She blinked; sunlight shone against the ceiling. Morning had arrived. In the distance, the bells rang six times.

"He was going to abdicate for you."

"What?"

"Jaxzon told me the night of the murder. We argued and that's why I was angry with you. I'm so sorry I said those things to you. I never meant them." He cleared his throat. "He loves you more than anything."

"I would never have asked him to. His people mean too much to him."

"And he is everything to his people."

The sun's light shone through the high windows, dispelling shadows as daylight grew.

"Boden, have you ever been in love?"

"Didn't we have this conversation?"

"Kind of, although you never told me with whom." She rolled onto her elbow to face him. The faint light outlined his profile. "Can you talk about it?"

He didn't say anything at first, then nodded. "She was only with me for one reason. She wanted to live in the palace and be surrounded by royalty. She wanted everything I didn't." His voice held an emotion Guin couldn't place.

"I'm sorry. If it's too painful, you don't have to tell me."

"No, not painful. She was one of those harpies always hanging around Jaxzon. She used me. After we married, she didn't want to live in my home. She expected to live in the palace and be part of the royal court. She—"

"You were married?"

He ran a hand through his hair. "Yes."

"What happened?"

"She left five years ago. I went on with my life."

"There's never been anyone else?"

"Only one." He met her eyes. "Guin, I—only you. I love you. I wanted to tell you before—" He took a deep breath and swallowed. "I needed you to know."

Guin leaned forward, touching her lips to his. He drew a sharp breath. His arms went around her, crushing her against him, returning the kiss.

"I'm sorry." She drew away, swinging her legs over the side of the cot. "I shouldn't have done that. I love you too Boden, but it's not the same. We've been through so much and you'll always be my hero. But Jaxzon..."

"I know." He put a trembling arm around her shoulder. "I only wish I could save you now."

The room grew lighter.

"Did they say when—what time?" he asked.

"Loltu told me I had to be back by the ninth hour today, Mikonia time." Her heart weighed heavily in her chest. She couldn't bring herself to look at him. "I don't want you to see."

"I love you, Guin." He lifted her chin. His eyes held hers. "I won't let you face this alone."

She hugged him then slipped off the cot. Going to the cubicle she splashed her face with water, trying to force her exhausted, stressed brain to concentrate.

When she returned, she found Boden checking the strength of the back door, which appeared as formidable as the one in front.

He shrugged. "Worth a try."

"I'm not giving up. We need to figure something out. How long would it take to deactivate this thing?"

He shook his head. "I have no experience with guttans."

"Let's take a closer look at this door."

They searched their cage again. What they believed to be a back door, instead led to another room. A low hum came from inside, increasing in volume as the morning wore on. He boosted her on his shoulders. The bars were too high, the light fixtures out of reach.

"It's hopeless." She leaned a shoulder against the wall.

He sat on the cot, staring at the floor, hands dangling between his knees.

Eight bells rang in the distance.

"My last hour." She said, sitting beside him. "Could you hold me?"

He put an arm around her. They lay, her body spooned within his.

"After I—" She squeezed her eyes shut. "When they come for you, hide in the bathroom and fight them. Try to disarm one of the guards and get away. Maybe you can save Jaxzon." She cleared her throat. "Promise?"

"I promise." His arms tightened around her. "I'll do my best. Anything's possible, right?"

"Thank you, Boden. You've been a good friend."

"I love you, Guin. You're the kindest, sweetest, bravest person I've ever known." His voice broke. He held her, burying his face in the crook of her neck.

CHAPTER FORTY-FOUR

The bells chimed nineteen times. The air held a sharp chill.

Footsteps approached. Boden put their plan into action. His fingertips slid across her hand, then he proceeded to the bathroom.

The hurried footfalls drew closer, then halted outside the cell door. The bolt slid in the lock and a light shone, darting around the room, shining on Guin's face. Closing her eyes, she held her breath.

The light moved away. She peeked from one open eye. The silhouette of a man stalked toward the bathroom.

She rose, tiptoeing behind him, raising the chair over her head, then swinging it down with a thud.

The man shouted then crumpled to the floor. Boden rounded the corner swinging his chair. He struck the prone man across the back, eliciting a "*whoof*" as the air left his lungs.

Bending over the black-uniformed guard, she took his weapon, training it on his back. Boden snatched the lamp from the man's helmet, pointing the beam back at him.

"Guin, don't shoot!" The man rolled to his back, his hands in the air.

"Kapre?" Handing the rifle to Boden, she dropped to her knees. "You're alive!"

"Barely. I thought you were asleep."

Her heart raced as she laughed with relief. "I thought you were dead."

Boden chuckled. "I can't believe your plan worked, Griffin. But, then again, it's only Kapre. Wasn't much of a challenge to begin with."

"Hush, Boden." She helped Kapre to his feet. "I'm so sorry. I didn't know it was you."

Boden handed him the rifle. "How are you still alive?"

"I'll explain while you change." Leaving the room, he returned with a bundle. "Uniforms. Put them on."

Guin lifted her dress over her head. Boden turned his back then punched Kapre, forcing him to turn around.

"What's the story?" He kicked out of his clothes and dressed in the uniform, while she struggled into the body armor behind them.

"I wore a deflector vest under my clothes and recorded everything. The men who removed me from the room are loyal to me."

"Genius," said Guin.

"Thanks. They plan to announce my death after the wedding. For now, I'm officially missing. They will paint me as a traitor who died trying to help you escape. Guin is assumed dead. Boden is armed and dangerous, your whereabouts unknown. Eventually they will find you, tragically dead by your own hand out of grief for the loss of your lover."

Boden snorted while buckling the armor over his chest. "What happened to their original plan? Wasn't I was supposed to be caught with the surgeon in some gun battle?"

"Said doctor has conveniently disappeared, thanks to a few strategic telecon messages. He probably won't reappear until the trial."

Boden tightened his deflector's straps. "What's the plan from here?"

"We're going to Arwon. I have a meeting with a journalist who will broadcast the recordings over every air wave and live-streaming Circuit in the galaxy. The audio is excellent, though the video is blurry after he shot me. I wanted to be sure you two were safe, or I would have made it public earlier."

"When did you realize your father was a part of this?" Guin asked.

"I researched one Boliad Ancun, and he doesn't exist. Boliad was most likely my sister. I knew she couldn't come up with this alone. When it became evident that they wanted you both here, I played along. I really hoped I was wrong, but I went in wired just in case."

She fumbled with her armor's shoulder harness. "What if he'd shot you in the head?"

"I guess we wouldn't be here." He handed Boden a sidearm. "I would have contacted you earlier, but we had to wait for the king to leave. His last security team departed shortly before sundown. I contacted Loltu last night to see if we could deactivate your guttan remotely. She confessed she never activated it."

"What?" Guin asked.

"That would have been nice to know," Boden grumbled. "When I woke up this afternoon, I thought I was lying next to a corpse. Scared the viyet out of me when she yawned."

"You were pretty funny." She winked at Kapre. "He screamed like a little girl."

"Funny for you, maybe." Tightening the straps on her deflector, Boden smirked, showing his dimples.

Kapre thrust open the door to reveal four, black-uniformed guards. "Let's go stop a wedding."

A female guard gave Guin a weapon. They fell into formation with the others. Kapre led them from their prison to a garage where three armored hovers waited. Fifteen armed security guards joined them.

An hour later they surfaced on the dark streets of a large city. On the way to the Shift Station, Kapre explained the plan, the first part being that their Shift would take them near the Vau'uan's estate, where Derek expected them.

Dawn broke on Arwon when they Shifted into a vineyard. In the distance, a lone figure approached through the gloom.

"Derek!" Guin broke into a run. She threw herself into his open arms, gripping him in a ferocious hug.

He caught her, lifting her off the ground as her momentum knocked him back a step.

"I didn't think I'd ever see you again," she whispered against his neck.

"Me too," he said, his voice hoarse.

Boden slapped him on the back. "For once I can honestly say I'm happy to see you."

Derek slung an arm around Boden, who allowed himself to be drawn in for a group hug. The three continued arm in arm the rest of the way to the manor's door, where Delori embraced Guin.

"We believed we'd lost you. When Kapre told us you were coming today, it was truly one of the happiest days of my life."

She returned the hug. "Thank you, Delori."

Kapre conversed in hushed tones on his telecon with the reporter, finalizing plans for their meeting.

Inside, they took seats at the dining room table. "Has anyone talked to Jaxzon?" Guin asked.

Derek shook his head. "Kapre thinks it's too risky."

"Then he thinks I'm dead?"

"Yes."

Her heart sunk. "Poor Jaxzon."

Boden put a hand on her shoulder. "What's the agenda, Derek?"

"Delori and I will be attending the wedding in the old amphitheater. I'm the new paranymph. I'm going to try to warn Jaxzon. He's under heavy guard and Orist never leaves his side. His calls and messages are screened."

"My men have intercepted and replaced my father's guard," said Kapre. "The plan is to release the recording before the vows, in the most public way possible, while they're all in the same place."

Raising her eyebrows in surprise, Guin asked, "Isn't that slightly dramatic?"

"Maybe, but this is the best way to ensure no one escapes."

"What about us?" Muscles aching from sleeping on the hard cot, she stretched, ready to take on the world to save Jaxzon.

"You'll stay here," Derek said. "Kapre is leaving two of his men to make sure you're both safe."

The weariness disappeared. She shook her head. "No way. I'm going."

Boden jumped to his feet. "I'm not staying here, not knowing what's happening."

"We're already dressed." She patted the helmet she'd set on the table. "With our face shields, no one will recognize us."

"Sounds good to me." He gripped the gun on his belt. "I'd like some payback."

"No Boden." She laid a hand on his arm. "No more killing. We want Jaxzon safe and justice for both your families."

He removed his hand from the gun. "When's the wedding?"

"In three hours. I have to dress." Derek gave Guin another hug before leaving.

~

JAXZON TOOK A STAGGERING STEP BACKWARD. He sat in the chair at the head of the conference table. "They're dead?" he asked in disbelief.

The Commander gave a curt nod. "Yes, Sire. King Nov'Xam sent word this morning. Prince Kapre was caught helping them escape, he was killed in an exchange of fire. Sir Boden escaped and they are searching for him now. Miss Griffin is suspected to have succumbed to the guttan. Her body has not been recovered as of the last report."

Regaining his composure, Jaxzon stood. "Where? When?"

"On Mikonia. After the fire at Sir Boden's home, which we

suspect as arson to destroy evidence, it appears they had gone in search of a surgeon to remove the guttan and their tracers. According to our intelligence, they found one. Your father's physician."

"Dr. Servin?"

"He Shifted to Mikonia last night and has not been found. Under intense interrogation, his wife confessed that he had been commissioned to do the illegal surgery. He and his family had plans to move to Anciex after."

Wondering how much of what he was being told was true, Jaxzon paced under the portrait of his parents. He glanced at his mother's eyes, then at Orist. The man was lying. Today was the day for Guin's trial, and if she didn't show...

"Please leave me."

"But Sire, the wedding."

"I said leave me. I need a moment."

The door closed and Jaxzon's world fell apart. A shadow fell over him, casting his thoughts into grayness. *She can't be dead. She just can't be.* But he had known this day might come. *Why would they run? They had enough evidence to at least postpone the trial. Didn't they?* "What am I going to do?" he asked the portrait. He closed his eyes, remembering how it had felt to hold her. The fresh clean scent of her hair. The sweet taste of her lips. Tears squeezed from under his eyelids and rolled down his cheeks. Their last moments together, her last words to him, his last promise.

Revenge. He opened his eyes as his rage built. He whispered his to dead father's portrait, "I will avenge them. I will prove their innocence. I will find your killers and they will be brought to justice. I swear on the love I have for you, Boden, and most of all for Guin. I will keep my promise."

Later, in his room, an attendant helped him dress. The wedding clothes hung on him, but he didn't care, he'd ignored any requests to have them refitted. The thought of marrying Vertuma had seemed an impossibility, a thought his mind couldn't wrap itself around.

He stared at the haggard man in his mirror. The dark purple

under his eyes. The paler than usual complexion. *How did I get here?* A dark cloud of deep depression settled over him. Life would never hold joy for him again.

Jaxzon took a deep breath then straightened, resolve filling out his suit for a brief moment. "I'm ready," he told the attendant, or maybe he was talking to himself.

On the hover ride to the amphitheater, he went over in his mind the plan to uncover Vertuma's and Orist's plot. First, when his rule was returned to him, he would relieve Orist of his duties and appoint another Commander. Someone he could trust. He would demand another investigation into his father's death.

Though, the Mikonian King might not agree to it. He needed a confidant. *You had one, but he's dead.* Kapre had truly been a great ally. He wished he'd known him better.

~

Two hours and one Shift later, Guin, Boden, and Kapre ascended the stone stairs of an ancient domed building. Kapre's head officer, Captain Basul, led his men inside where they assumed their stations near Arwon's guards.

"Set for stun only," Basul had ordered. "Every royal in the galaxy is in there. We don't want any accidents."

Boden set Guin's weapon. They followed Kapre to the entrance then took positions overlooking the vast expanse of the coliseum-like structure.

Rows upon rows of seats, going back hundreds of feet to the top of the dome, faced a raised dais in the center. Intricate carvings decorated the curved, white stone ceiling. Winged cherubs, gargoyles, and dozens of strange, wondrous creatures danced overhead. The double-suns' light shone through the designs, casting complex shadows on the bright banners and the people below.

The last few guests were being ushered to their seats when Kapre's telecon buzzed. He went outside to meet the reporter.

A nest of murder hornets hatched and flew about, pummeling Guin's insides.

Kapre returned. "Be ready."

Jaxzon entered the dome opposite the main entrance then proceeded down the aisle, accompanied by Derek, Ahret, and two men Guin didn't recognize. They came to stand on the dais, facing the aisle to Guin's right.

Boden rested his hand on his gun. "Those are Orist's men."

Dark circles and new lines showed on Jaxzon's pale face. His purple-and-gold suit hung on him. His normally dignified demeanor was replaced by one of weariness and defeat.

Guin's heart sank. Derek hadn't been able to warn him.

Women in royal blue, ruffly, puffy-sleeved gowns followed the men. Sarya trailed behind, dressed in a sleek, dark-violet gown. She took her position opposite Derek.

The assembly rose. King Nov'Xam and Vertuma commenced their silent march toward Jaxzon.

Resisting the urge to run forward and tackle the murderous blonde in white, Guin stared daggers through her visor.

A man in a turquoise robe came forward and placed a hand over the bride and groom's bowed heads, then gazed out over the congregation, opening his mouth to speak.

"Enough!" the voice of King Nov'Xam bellowed from overhead speakers. A jolt of movement rippled across the amphitheater. Murmurs arose among the guests.

The king's voice continued through the loudspeakers, explaining how they'd framed Guin and killed Princess Jalain, Queen Neyris, and King Jaezain.

King Nov'Xam summoned his guards. Heldivar and Calen joined him, only to stare in surprise when Kapre's men drew their weapons, detaining them.

Vertuma stiffened. Orist appeared with Eedras and Za'Had. They rushed toward the dais. Kapre sped down the aisle, followed by Boden.

Ahret and Derek grasped Jaxzon's arms, hurrying him toward the exit and Guin.

"Get him away from here." Boden shouted.

Orist tossed a weapon to Vertuma then aimed his own at Jaxzon.

Guin's world stopped. Boden drew his weapon and fired. The bolt caught Orist in the chest, causing his shot to go wide, knocking him off his feet.

Screams erupted. Guests scattered, diving for cover or stampeding for the exits.

At the sound of Boden's voice, Jaxzon halted, jerking his arms free from Derek and Ahret. He spun around, taking after Boden.

The recording played in a loop, echoing throughout the amphitheater. Smoke billowed as flying bolts of light blasted walls and seats. An acrid odor permeated the air. Guests ducked in confused terror as the small-scale battle raged around them.

Derek and Ahret pursued Jaxzon, who chased after Boden. Orist's men fought against Kapre's. Guin raced after the men. Vertuma raised her weapon.

Through the surrounding turmoil of laser blasts and shouting, Guin screamed, "Jaxzon!"

He skidded to a stop, spinning toward her. Vertuma fired as Guin threw herself into him, knocking him off his feet. She came to a rest on top of Jaxzon, protecting his body with hers.

A streak of blue light left Orist's pistol, striking Boden, sending him flying into the seats.

Jaxzon withdrew Guin's pistol from her holster and took aim as Vertuma raised hers. The bolt connected, hitting Vertuma's shoulder, knocking the weapon from her grasp. She gripped her arm and glared. Murder showed in her icy gaze.

Fury exploded within Guin. With a surge of adrenaline, she leaped to her feet. Engulfed in pure rage, she charged the would-be bride.

Vertuma waited for her, a grim smile on her face. Her swing went wide. Guin drove her body into the blonde's midsection, slamming her to the ground. Gripping Guin by the arms, Vertuma used their momentum to toss her over her head.

Rolling to her feet, Guin squared off. “You’ve lost, Princess. Everyone knows you’re nothing more than a cold-blooded murderer.”

“I haven’t lost yet, and I can still wreck that pretty little face.” Vertuma swung at Guin’s head.

Guin ducked and countered with a punch to the throat. Her opponent staggered back, clutching her neck and sputtering.

Dredging up her training from so long ago, and with every bit of strength she had left, Guin followed with a spin-kick to Vertuma’s face.

Before the woman’s limp body struck the tiles, Guin was running to Boden. Smoke rose from where Orist’s shot had caught him in the side.

A bolt flashed, hitting the seat in front of Guin, blowing her backward. Orist, flanked by Za’Had and Eedras, stalked toward her. She lay paralyzed, her ears ringing.

Orist aimed his weapon.

She flinched at the flash then gasped as the blast struck her.

CHAPTER FORTY-FIVE

"Guin?" Jaxzon's voice echoed from a dark corridor. A jackhammer battered the base of her skull, distracting her from the buzzing numbness encompassing her body. Disembodied voices called her name.

Overwhelmed with pain, she sank into the billowy darkness.

A voice murmured from the abyss, "She's stable. There's no swelling, and she's out of danger. We've decreased the medications and she should regain consciousness soon."

The throbbing subsided, leaving a dull thrum in its wake. A wave of dizziness washed her into oblivion.

Boden's deep voice reverberated in her head.

I must be dead too. The realization floated away. A curtain of velvety blackness enveloped her.

A dull light shone on ceiling tiles. An aching thumping pulsated in Guin's temples. A hand gripped hers. Jaxzon, still dressed for his wedding, slept against her bed with his head resting on his arm, his fingers entwined with hers.

Guin combed her fingertips through his hair, smiling at the familiar texture.

His grip tightened and he stirred. Concern filled his azure eyes.

"Jaxzon?" she whispered.

His chair scraped beneath him. His lips brushed her cheek. "How do you feel?"

"Thirsty."

He put a straw to her lips. "Only a little. They said when you wake, only sips."

Guin took a small sip and held it, moistening her mouth before swallowing. "Thank you."

Jaxzon set the glass aside. He kissed her forehead while depressing a button on the wall. "They will want to check on you, you've been out since yesterday."

A woman in a light pink, form-fitting uniform came bustling into the room. Her face lit in a cheery smile. "Well, look who's awake. Our Angel is back among us." She took Guin's wrist and checked her pulse, then checked the wires and tubes connecting her to various machines. "Do you need something for pain?"

"No, thank you." The woman left. Guin took Jaxzon's hand. "Is Boden...?" She couldn't say the word.

"He's fine, just a nasty bruise where the bolt hit his armor. He came to visit earlier."

"Oh, thank goodness." Guin laid back on the pillow and closed her eyes.

When she awoke, Jaxzon's smile greeted her. "There's someone here to see you."

"Hey Griffin." Boden took her outstretched hand and kissed her cheek. "It's good to see you back in the land of the living."

She hugged him. "I thought you were dead," she whispered.

He grinned. "Orist was always a terrible shot."

"What happened? He didn't get away, did he?"

"No. Jaxzon took care of him. When I was hit, I couldn't breathe. I had a front row seat to you obliterating Vertuma." Dimples appeared in his cheeks. "I seriously believe you *could* kick my ass, Griffin. For a little thing, you've got one heck of a kick. When Orist shot you,

Jaxzon's returning fire mangled the traitor's leg. Kapre's guards were able to subdue him. Nov'Xam, Heldivar, and her kid went down without a fight."

"Orist shot me?"

"The bolt struck your helmet," said Jaxzon.

"He's lucky Jaxzon only aimed for his legs. I thought he was going to rip his head off."

"I would have if Kapre hadn't stopped me."

"The bolt glanced off you and sparked a fire in the drapery. Jaxzon blasted Orist, then went to finish him off. Kapre stopped him and had him take you to safety before the fire spread. His men helped me. Kapre took custody of Orist and your guards."

"I thought you were dead until you moaned." Jaxzon brushed the hair from her forehead. "That was the most beautiful sound I've ever heard. I took you to medics, and we came here."

"And he's been here since." A blonde-haired doctor entered and asked the men to leave. She examined Guin then removed the tubes and wires. "You have a concussion. Bed rest for another day or two, and no strenuous activities for at least a week."

"She released me," Guin told the men when they were allowed in. She dangled her legs over the side of the bed and plucked at the lavender hospital gown. "Do I have anything to wear?"

"I'll go find something," Boden said.

"Thank you, Boden." Jaxzon wrapped his arms around Guin's waist. "I can't tell you how sorry I am for what you went through."

"Jaxzon—"

He put a finger to her lips. "There are so many things I wish I could change. You almost died twice because of me. I would rather have died myself than put you through what you endured. I promise to spend the rest of my life making it up to you."

"Jaxzon, I love you, no matter what. Those people did this to us. You couldn't have guessed what would happen." She gripped his lapels, drawing him into a tender kiss, sinking into the sweetness of his lips and the warmth of his body. Her heart raced at his touch. She combed her fingers through his hair. Her legs wound around his, drawing him closer. She smiled against his mouth. Nothing had changed, they still wanted each other.

Boden cleared his throat from the door. "A nurse offered her extra change of clothes. She said she would be honored if you kept them." He held a pair of yellow pants and a blue flowered blouse.

Guin climbed off the bed and took the clothes. "Thank you, Boden, for everything." She pecked his cheek before heading to the adjoining bathroom.

JAXZON INSISTED on Guin staying at the palace. Although she maintained that she felt fine, he and their friends overrode her protests, making her stay in bed for the next two days, while taking turns keeping her company.

Bree read her news regarding the arrests and how some tabloids labeled her the Ultimate Wedding Crasher.

Derek taught her to play his virtual reality war game.

He placed the headset on her temples. "All you have to do is imagine which weapon you want to use, and it will appear in your avatar's hands."

In the middle of a battle, Guin's avatar leaned against a wall and took a bite from a sandwich.

"What are you doing? They're killing us!"

"I'm hungry." Guin's avatar received a direct hit. Tiny red fragments of what was left of her holographic character rained onto the bedroom floor.

Delori delivered Guin's lunch and shooed Derek away.

Kapre called via video. He'd been coronated after his father abdicated in disgrace. He apologized for not being able to come in person, but sent an array of exotic flowering plants.

An inpouring of cards, letters, flowers, and gifts arrived from admirers throughout the galaxy. Derek devoted the ballroom at their estate to hold them all.

Boden hadn't visited since accompanying them from the hospital.

Sitting on her bed Jaxzon gathered her in his arms. "He's gone to his ranch. He wants to rebuild before the weather changes."

Reveling in Jaxzon's closeness she listened to the steady, calming beat of his heart.

He kissed the top of her head. "I'm calling a press conference. The people want to understand what happened. They want to know how you're doing. Would you join me and say a few words?"

"What should I say?"

"Whatever you wish. I'm sure they'd love to hear from their future queen."

Heat crept into her face. She tipped her chin and smiled.

"I love it when you blush." He captured her lips with his.

In the early evening, Jaxzon delivered a box to her room.

"What's this?"

"I don't know. It's for you."

She lifted the lid. A note lay upon a dress. Opening the card she recognized Valdid's signature. Jaxzon read the note aloud.

"'For the queen of our hearts. Our Angel of Arwon. My Muse. Wear my humble offering in good health. With the fire of your mind, the magnitude of your courage, and the beauty of your spirit, you have proven; a Griffin—like a Phoenix—will always rise from the ashes. Eternally, your humble servant, Valdid.'"

She lifted the blood-red garment from the box by the bodice. The design was identical to the one she'd worn the night of her arrest. Though in place of flowers, lacy orange-and-yellow embroidered flames flowed over the skirt and appeared to flicker and flare in the sunslight streaming through her window.

Jaxzon set the note aside. "Wow."

"Yeah, 'wow.' Valdid's a genius. This is the most beautiful thing I've ever seen."

"Not half as beautiful as the one who will wear it." He encircled her in his arms, tucking her against him, he nuzzled the crook of her neck.

She rested her head against his chest, allowing better access as he planted a trail of kisses along her shoulder.

Her eyes fluttered shut. "Mmm." The dress fell to the bed. He spun her around. Her fingers threaded through his silky hair as she devoured his mouth.

~

Jaxzon finished his prepared statements regarding the arrests and the official breaking of his engagement to Vertuma to the Journalists assembled in the ballroom. He stated he was not at liberty to answer inquiries regarding the ongoing investigation.

Hidden from view behind a set of curtains, Guin waited for him to finish. Derek, Delori, and Bree, stood along the wall behind the reporters.

Jaxzon held his hand out. "There is someone who wants to say a few words."

Guin came from behind the curtain and clasped his hand amid gasps and applause from those in attendance.

"I believe everyone knows my guest, Lady Guinevere Griffin of House Vau'uan and New York."

The heat rose in Guin's cheeks. She waited for applause to end and the reporters to take their seats. "Thank you, King Jaxzon. I didn't prepare a speech, and I can't speak about what happened on Mikonia. Just know that those who attempted to hurt my friends and

I, will pay for their actions. I wanted to say that I am truly grateful to those who stood by me through the worst time of my life. My dear friends and sponsors, Delori and Derek Vau'uan, my best friend, Bree Zestari, and of course, King Jaxzon." She nodded to each. "I owe my life to King Kapre, who risked his to save mine. This is for you, Kapre." She blew a kiss to the cameras.

"Most of all, I wish to thank my dearest friend, Boden Darcyd. If not for Boden, I would most probably have perished fighting for my sanity on the streets of Mikonia. Boden took me from dark despair and gave me a reason to live. He was there for me when no one else could be. Boden lent me strength and courage when mine were gone. He offered me a home when I felt abandoned, and he granted me kindness when I needed it most. Boden saved my life more times than I can count. Thank you, Boden, from the bottom of my heart. You will always be my hero."

Jaxzon took her hand. "Any questions?"

"Zulla Thul'o, *Arwon Crown*. Lady Guin, when is the wedding?"

Laughing, Guin said, "No one's asked me to marry them."

His eyes never leaving Guin's face, Jaxzon said, "I have to make sure she'll say yes first. Although now I'm a little worried about competition from Boden."

The reporters laughed, then proceeded to ask Guin about several subjects, from her scintillating attire to her health, and if she had plans to go back to Earth any time soon. She answered until Jaxzon reminded them that she was still recovering. He thanked them for coming and led a grateful Guin from the podium.

That evening, they dined with their friends, sitting side by side, celebrating into the night. Her only sorrow was Boden hadn't joined them. He should share in the victory as their friends toasted him, Kapre, and Guin, proclaiming them heroes.

She retired for the evening and was about to unfasten her gown, when a knock came at her door. "Come in, Derek."

Derek let himself in. "How do you always know it's me?"

"I've learned to discern your knock from everyone else's." Guin grinned. "Besides, I assume it's you and say, "Come in, Derek" every time. I figure I gotta fifty-fifty shot. What's up?"

"I've been sent to ask if you'd accompany our king for a moonlit stroll in the garden?"

She took his arm. "To misquote Shakespeare, lead on Macduff."

Derek departed after delivering her to Jaxzon, who waited outside the ballroom's closed doors which they had danced through an eternity ago.

He kissed her hand. "My lady."

Even now, after everything, Guin's heartbeat increased. The familiar heat crept into her cheeks. His azure eyes held her spellbound as ever. "My king."

Music floated in the air, coming from behind the doors, faintly at first then swelling—a familiar song. Jaxzon bowed. "May I have this dance?"

"Forever."

He spun her away from the doors, leading her further from the palace. Guin laughed, recognizing the music as the same ihli the orchestra played during their first dance. They circled, moving deeper into the darkened garden. He stopped dancing took her by the hand, then retraced their steps from the night of the ball.

A thousand tiny lights twinkled and danced in the surrounding shrubbery. The full, lavender moon illuminated the area, giving the space an ethereal glow. Sitting her on the bench, Jaxzon placed a finger to his lips, then knelt beside her, his smile dazzling her as always.

Guin's heart stopped then galloped. *Is he proposing?*

He took her shaking hands. "Derek told me a story. Apparently, a beautiful woman went to a ball and met a prince and they fell in love. For some inexplicable reason, she had to leave in a hurry, and when she ran from her prince, she lost something."

He removed two pink pumps from beneath the bench—the one lost at the top of the steps, and its mate from jail. "Evidently, the prince returned the beautiful woman's shoe, and she was so grateful she agreed to marry him, and they went on to live happily ever after."

She grinned. "I believe Derek got a few of the story's details wrong. Although he essentially has the gist."

"Luckily, I never rely too much on Derek for anything having to do with romance, so I did some research. I learned in America, when a man loves a woman and wants to spend the rest of his life loving her, he gives her a token." He withdrew a small, green box from one of the shoes. Inside lay a ring of ichor with a sizable, green gemstone set in the center of a dozen smaller, ruby-red ones. The gems sparkled as Jaxzon removed the ring from the box.

Love-lit eyes gazed into Guin's. "When I first met you in New York, I knew there was something special about you. Something extraordinary, and from the moment we parted, I missed you. For days the thought of never seeing you again tortured me. Then seemingly by some miracle, you were here, so close, so enticing. That first night changed me forever, I only wanted to be with you, to hold you in my arms, to feel your heart beating with mine. We've endured many challenges, and I wish to never again be parted from you. My love for you is stronger than anything else in this life, and I hope that now, beyond my wildest dreams, you will agree to become my wife and my queen. Guinevere Griffin, will you marry me?"

Guin's heart swelled. "Yes!"

Jaxzon slipped the ring on her finger then swept her into his arms capturing her lips in a passionate kiss. "You've made me the happiest man in the universe."

"I love you so much Jaxzon." She laid her head against his warm chest. His heartbeat thundered in her ear. She wished to never let him go.

He tilted back his head and shouted, "She said yes!"

"Yeah!" came Derek's yell, then he, Bree, Delori, and Ahret joined them among the twinkling lights. A staff member carried a tray with six glasses, serving one to each.

Derek raised his glass. "To our king and his future queen, and to Guin never telling anyone to 'cut the queen crap' again."

"I'll drink to that." Guin touched her glass to Jaxzon's. "What if I'd said no?"

He tucked a strand of hair behind her ear. "The thought never crossed my mind."

"When's the wedding?" Derek asked.

"As soon as possible," Guin and Jaxzon said in unison.

ACKNOWLEDGMENTS

A great big thank you to my critique partners, Cindy Lou and Willis. If not for you two crazy kids, this tale would still be 156,000 words long.

Also, a big thank you to my critique group, *Write On!* you were all positive and wonderful to work with. Thank you, Sandy, for the free editing and encouraging words.

And thank you to all who alpha and beta read for me. I can't name everyone, but you all know who you are, and I am eternally grateful.

A special thanks to my brother Glenn for the name. Wink wink.

ABOUT THE AUTHOR

Carde began reading at the age of four and hasn't stopped since. At any time, she might be found with up to twelve books on her nightstand and one or two in her office or car in various stages of being read.

Carde began writing poetry in the sixth grade then moved on to fantasy when she was a young adult. Life happened, then after several years a young woman named Guinevere Griffin began whispering in her ear telling Carde her story. Guin persisted in dreams, waking Carde up at all hours, forcing her to take notes.

Finally, in mid-2019, Carde took the hint, her notes, and began writing Guin's story.

Carde lives with her husband and biggest cheerleader, Ray in Hawai'i.

Carde loves to hear from her readers. You can find and connect with her at the link below.

Facebook: https://www.facebook.com/profile.php?id=100071465731929

I hope you enjoyed *Once Upon a Griffin*. If you did, please write a review and tell your friends.

Love Once Upon a Griffin? Then take a peek into *A Griffin No More* the second book in the Griffin trilogy:

Qarin parted the tattered backstage curtains. The mass of concertgoers undulated to a recording of *Monkey Wrench* by Earth's *Foo Fighters* blasting over the sound system. Shouts and whistles mingled with the crowd's muffled roar. A knot tightened in her midsection. These people would soon scrutinize, judge, and possibly hate her. She took a deep breath then regretted it as the commingled odors of sweat and vape mists crowded her lungs.

The recorded music faded. Zeyeff, the concert's promoter, strode to the microphone amid shouts and catcalls. He thrust two fingers in the air then flipped his hand, showing the back. "Let the revolution begin!"

A hand landed on her shoulder. Dharzun, her band's keyboardist, sidled up, hunched down, and shouted in her ear. "Jel wants to go over the set. How you doin'?"

She raked a hand through her dark blue hair. "Great. If feeling like you're going to hurl can be counted as great."

Dharzun lifted his chin toward the audience. "Once you're on stage doing your thing, you won't even notice them."

"If you say so."

They headed for the dressing room.

"Qarin," Dharzu singsonged. "We're going to make history. Think about it, when Queen Lotundi outlawed Earth music, she never dreamed we'd take over Old Uldrur. Once the word spreads, it'll be anarchy. People will flock to our concerts. They'll protest in the streets. She'll have to repeal her ludicrous decrees. We're gonna win this revolution."

Qarin didn't care about his anarchy or his revolution. She wanted to play the songs she used to sing with her father. If fulfilling her dream meant becoming an outlaw, fine by her.

Backstage, Jelkan finished going over their song choices, he put an arm around Qarin's shoulders. "Everyone knows you've got this.

Besides me, you're the best singer we've got." He showed his uneven, vape-stained teeth. "Have fun and don't get flustered. We're behind you."

The band leader's confidence did little to ease Qarin's queasiness, but she offered a thin smile. "Thanks, Jel."

A stagehand poked his head around the filthy curtain serving as a dressing room door. "You're on."

Slinging the bass strap over her shoulder, she armed herself with her microphone, then followed the rest of the band to the stage. While keeping her head down to avoid the sea of faces, she plugged into the amplifier. Replacing the house mic with her own, she waited for the red light to blink blue as it paired with the speakers.

The band completed their last sound checks as Zeyeff announced, "Let's hear it for Dillinger!"

The crowd cheered.

I hope you're watching, Dad.

Earth music created a special bond with her father. He taught her to play bass when she was six, and she became obsessed with the thought of performing. *Now here you are.* She closed her eyes. *It's gonna be great. This is your dream. They're gonna love you.*

Their drummer, Steviun, tapped his sticks together. Anticipating her first note, she positioned her fingers on the frets. Before her left hand hit the strings, a commotion of shouts and running feet arose backstage, spilling into the band's midst. Techs and members from other bands flooded the stage followed by red and gray-uniformed officers pouring around the curtains.

The audience tsunamied toward the exits.

"Crikey!" Unplugging, Qarin jumped from the stage in a panic, cradling her bass and joining the torrent of retreating bodies.

She didn't get far before someone spun her around. A familiar voice hissed in her ear. "Not so fast."

She jerked her arm. "Let go, Steviun!"

"You're not going anywhere." He held her in a solid grip. "I'm collecting that reward."

What reward? In desperation, she brought her knee up, viciously striking her target. Steviun folded, crashing to the cement floor with a grunt.

Qarin rushed forward with the stream of people flowing through the front exit. The bass strap tightened against her chest, bringing her to an abrupt halt.

Steviun knelt on the floor, one hand holding his injured pride, the other gripping the strap. She wrestled the bass over her head. A uniformed woman approached. With a soft whimper, Qarin abandoned the precious instrument into the hands of the hated traitor, and twisted away in time to avoid the woman's grasp.

The rush of bodies forced the officer in the opposite direction as Qarin was swept toward the dam of people clogging the doorway. She fought against the tide, squirming through the flow of concertgoers cascading back toward the stage.

"Blue hair! Blue hair!" Steviun shouted, pointing in her direction.

She lifted the collar of her Pink Floyd T-shirt over her head to hide the bright cobalt as the crowd ebbed and flowed around her.

A murmur rippled through the crowd. The words, *blue hair* being repeated.

"Take this," a voice shouted in her ear. Several hands held a hooded sweatshirt as a grateful Qarin thrust her arms into the sleeves. Someone tugged the hood over her head.

Screeching in protest, a wide, roll-up door at the end of the building rose in fits and starts. Caught in the current of surging humans, Qarin rushed toward the raising door and the promise of freedom beyond. Concertgoers poured from the building's side exits and leaked under the partially open roll-up. They spilled into the parking lot and broke against rows of parked hovers.

She sprinted for the abandoned buildings plaguing the area, dashing between their rows. Broken glass crunched beneath her boots. Flying along the darkened streets, she skidded around a corner and escaped into the deserted city of Old Uldrur.

Did mom's husband offer a reward for my return? She choked back a scream of rage. *Why were adults such jerks? Why did mom have to marry Veezou?*

Qarin slowed. Her breath came in gasps as a sharp pain formed in her side. The initial adrenaline rush faded, leaving her breathless. She rounded a corner and hurried through the dim, debris-strewn street. Swinging right, she jogged between lines of vacant warehouses.

Pursuing footsteps echoed behind her. Qarin sought shelter within the dilapidated buildings, testing door handles until one opened. She scurried into the foyer. Sweat trickled down her temple. She rolled up her sleeves and dropped the hood. Moonlight shone through the glassless panes above her.

Muffled voices grew closer. She opened the interior door and slipped inside. Hopping over chunks of the caved-in ceiling, she made her way toward a dark mass in the center of the room.

Qarin's vision grew accustomed to the gloom. Her eyes widened. She swore under her breath. "Viyet! What's a starship doing in here?"

Xalea 62 glowed in stark white across the ship's tail. Below the numbers flew a silver Pegasus. The ship's short wing spanned above her head, blotting out the stars.

Fumbling through the dark, she smashed her shins on a set of stairs. Cursing again, she squinted into the ship's black interior.

Backing away, she shuffled her feet in the debris, searching for a way around the steps, and hopefully to the building's rear exit.

Voices echoed in the entryway. Qarin froze. Her heartbeat reverberated in her ears. The voices grew louder, breaking her paralysis. She stumbled her way to the steps, then scrambled into the ship's body.

Fumbling her hands across the wall, she searched for a lever or switch to raise the craft's stairs. A panel lit at her touch, bathing the interior in its dim, green glow. An image of a set of stairs appeared on the screen. She jammed her finger against it. The stairs retracted and the hatch lowered.

The ship sealed with a quiet release of air pressure.

Yes! Her heart pounded. Sliding to the floor she leaned her head against her knees. The dull glow of the panel faded then died, plunging her into complete darkness.

She touched the face of the panel, hoping to find a light control. Her finger passed over the screen. The hatch began to raise.

Crikey! She jabbed the stair image. The door reversed.

Outside a man swore. "Viyet! What's wrong with this thing?"

The ship's overhead lights glared. The hatch began to open once again.

She jogged through the narrow passageway to her left, traversing the length of the ship. The smell of oil and grease led her to what she hoped was the engine room. She hit a button. A door opened. She slipped through.

Qarin headed for the back wall, making her way around the shining machinery. In the farthest corner, two broad chrome cylinders rose from floor to ceiling. She squeezed between them, wedging herself behind the cylinder on the left.

Veezou. If I have to go back to his house . . . and Steviun! If I ever get my hands on that nothus, I'll kick more than his limp–

The swoosh of a door silenced her thoughts of revenge. Several footfalls sounded on the metal floor, mingled with the murmur of men's voices.

"I don't care if your heat detectors led you here," one man said over the others. "There's no one on this ship. My sensors would have read her tracer. We would have found her by now. She probably backtracked and escaped while you were wasting time harassing me."

Qarin scrunched herself as far into the corner as she could manage, but if someone thought to poke their head between the cylinders, they would see her for sure. She glanced up. *Maybe . . .*

Careful not to make a sound, she placed her feet and hands against the hull and the cylinder. She shimmied to the top, then hung from the ceiling, hidden from sight behind a supporting I-bar.

"What size is this person you're looking for?" the same man asked. "'Cause I don't think she's in that drawer."

The drawer slammed. The footsteps drew closer. Qarin held her breath.

A man's voice, dangerously close to the cylinders asked, "What's behind these things?"

"Probably a few dust bandies. I haven't cleaned here in a while."

A helmet thrust head between the cylinders then pulled back. "She's not in the engine room. Let's check the cargo hold."

The footsteps receded. Qarin breathed a quiet sigh of relief. A blond man's head appeared below. He swiveled left, right, then looked up.